THE MANY FACES OF

Van Helsing

THE MANY FACES OF

Van Helsing

Edited by

Jeanne Cavelos

ACE BOOKS, NEW YORK

An Ace Book
Published by The Berkley Publishing Group
A division of Penguin Group (USA) Inc.
375 Hudson Street
New York, New York 10014

This is an original publication of The Berkley Publishing Group.

First edition: April 2004

Library of Congress Cataloging-in-Publication Data

The many faces of Van Helsing / edited by Jeanne Cavelos.— 1st ed.
    p. cm.
  ISBN 0-441-01170-5
   1. Vampires—Fiction.   2. Van Helsing, Abraham (Fictitious character)—Fiction.
3. Dracula, Count (Fictitious character)—Fiction.   4. Horror tales, American.
5. Horror tales, English.   I. Cavelos, Jeanne.

PS648.V35M36 2004
813'.0873808351—dc22   2004040999

PRINTED IN THE UNITED STATES OF AMERICA

10 9 8 7 6 5 4 3 2 1

To George and Eloise Flint

ACKNOWLEDGMENTS

Thanks to Elizabeth Miller, George Stade, Thomas Seay, and Michael Samerdyke for sharing their amazing knowledge of *Dracula*. Thanks also to Ellen Datlow, Leigh Grossman, Steve and Melanie Tem, and Tom Monteleone for their advice; and to Bob Cutchin, Elaine Isaak, and Jim Isaak for their help. Thanks to Lori Perkins, my agent, for making this book happen, and to John Morgan, my editor, for his enthusiasm and endless support. Thanks to my husband, for his superhuman patience during my obsessive preoccupation with this project, and thanks to Igmoe, my iguana, for cutting me a break during mating season. Thank you to the hundreds and hundreds of authors who submitted stories for this anthology, giving me a wealth of wonderful material to choose from. I wish I could have included more of your stories. And thank you, of course, to Bram Stoker. Your story lives on.

Contents

INTRODUCTION

Van Helsing would, I know, do anything for me for a personal reason, so no matter on what ground he comes, we must accept his wishes. He is a seemingly arbitrary man, but this is because he knows what he is talking about better than any one else. He is a philosopher and a metaphysician, and one of the most advanced scientists of his day; and he has, I believe, an absolutely open mind. This, with an iron nerve, a temper of the ice-brook, an indomitable resolution, self-command, and toleration exalted from virtues to blessings, and the kindliest and truest heart that beats—these form his equipment for the noble work that he is doing for mankind—work both in theory and practice, for his views are as wide as his all-embracing sympathy. I tell you these facts that you may know why I have such confidence in him.

—FROM DR. JOHN SEWARD'S LETTER
TO ARTHUR HOLMWOOD, *DRACULA*

B RAM STOKER'S *DRACULA* has become one of the most famous novels in history. In it, the vampire Dracula faces off against his nemesis, Abraham Van Helsing. Both Dracula and Van Helsing have become icons: the vampire and the vampire hunter. Yet while the character of Dracula has been endlessly examined, Van Helsing is arguably one of the most well-known yet least explored characters in literature. When we think of Van Helsing, we picture, perhaps, an elderly man with bushy eyebrows, holding up a cross and exhorting evil to retreat. But this is little more than a stereotype. What is Van Helsing really like? Stoker provides some intriguing facts.

A doctor, lawyer, scientist, and philosopher, Van Helsing seems the ultimate man of logic and reason. He holds many degrees and is well-versed in the latest discoveries. He uses logic and the scientific method to uncover clues and solve mysteries. Yet there is another side to Van Helsing. He is fascinated with myth, folklore, and the occult—forces that defy logic and science. He suffers from bouts of melancholia and hysteria. His son has died; his wife is insane.

On every front, Van Helsing is engaged in a war between rationality and chaos: in himself, in his marriage, and in the world. This may be the chaos of emotions out of control, of sexual desire unchecked, of unadulterated evil. Armed with garlic, sacred wafer, and stake, Van Helsing is determined to repress, restrain, and contain this chaos, which reaches its fullest embodiment in Dracula. Van Helsing's character resonates because of his powerful opposition to the villain, which echoes some of the most compelling relationships in literature. *Dracula* scholar George Stade describes it perfectly: As Victor Frankenstein is to his monster, as Jekyll is to Hyde, as Holmes is to Moriarty, as ego is to id, Van Helsing is to Dracula.

While Stoker provides us with a fascinating character outline, neither Stoker nor any of the authors who have built upon his work have filled in that outline. Yet this very lack of detail and depth provides the ideal conditions for myth to grow, and over the years it has, turning Dracula and Van Helsing into powerful archetypes that can take on an endless number of specific faces.

Stoker's novel has been adapted into many different forms, and in each we see a slightly different Van Helsing. He may be selfless, ruthless, brilliant, foolish, fanatical, vulnerable, or neurotic. He may be an intellectual or a man of action; a loner or the leader of a team. In film, he has been portrayed by Academy Award winners Laurence Olivier and Anthony Hopkins, by leading man Hugh Jackman, and by top character actors such as Nehemiah Persoff, Nigel Davenport, Peter Cushing, Frank Finlay, and Richard Benjamin. Some films and TV shows have expanded Van Helsing's fight to include his sons and daughters, grandsons and granddaughters. Others have transplanted the core of Van Helsing's character into a variety of vampire hunters, most recently the infamous Buffy.

Through countless novels and over 127 feature films, TV movies, TV series, and video games, we have glimpsed some of the many possible faces of Van Helsing, as Stoker's original story has been expanded into an epic struggle ranging across the planet and through all time periods.

But Stoker's character has not only been interpreted in many ways; it has contributed to the rise of many related archetypes. Van Helsing was one of the first supernatural detectives, gathering clues, researching folktales and legends, and tracking down the guilty parties. *Kolchak: The Night Stalker* followed proudly in his footsteps, and in *The X-Files*, Van Helsing was split into two characters: Scully, the doctor and scientist, and Mulder, the expert on the occult. Van Helsing is part holy man, part mad scientist, part prophet of doom.

His character, in all its many incarnations, continues to fascinate. Yet so many questions remain unanswered. How did he become the man we meet in *Dracula*, with "the temper of the ice-brook"? How did he gain the secret knowledge of vampires? When did he first face evil? What experiences led him to the belief that "All men are mad in some way"? How does he reconcile the rational and the irrational within him? What truly drives this archetypal vampire hunter? And what is his fate?

The exciting opportunity of exploring Van Helsing's mysterious and undefined depths remains for this anthology. Within this volume, you'll find many different views of Van Helsing, and many different answers to the questions he embodies. Each author brings his own unique vision and sensibility to this fascinating character. And that is how it must be, for how we view Van Helsing depends in part on how we view ourselves and our world.

Do we live in a world filled with darkness, in which horrors—whether arising from supernatural sources or from frighteningly mundane ones—constantly occur? If so, then Van Helsing is a tragic figure who struggles endlessly with this parade of horrors, against which there can be no ultimate triumph. In "Poison in the Darkness," Rita Oakes shows how horror can strike randomly and destroy a family. Thomas Tessier and Kathe Koja reveal the loneliness of Van Helsing's fight, in which he's surrounded by people who often turn away or actively work against him. Van Helsing's struggle may continue even beyond death, as in J. A. Konrath's "The Screaming" and Christopher Golden's disturbing "Venus and Mars."

Or do we believe our world is one in which good can defeat evil? In that case, Van Helsing becomes a heroic figure, his suffering over his wife and son a path to the wisdom and goodness that allow him to defeat these dark forces. In "The Power of Waking," Nina Kiriki Hoffman shows us the hero's first exposure to the supernatural. William D. Carl and C. Dean Andersson reveal the horrible trials the hero must undergo to face his mission; Chris Roberson and Thomas F. Monteleone show us the hero in action; and in "Hero Dust," Kristine Kathryn Rusch explores what happens when a hero discovers he can no longer do what he has always done.

What if supernatural evil does not exist, though? What if there is only human frailty—selfishness, anger, fear, lust. In such a world, what role is left for the crusader against evil? He may be as subject to negative urges as those he fights, or even more so. Tanith Lee writes a fascinating story of justification and rationalization. Kris Dikeman and Lois Tilton show us the dark underbelly of Van Helsing's "old-fashioned" attitude toward women, while Sarah Kelderman and Joe Hill question the humanity of Van Helsing's scientific method.

Whether the evil is real or imagined, though, Van Helsing is a man who has suffered many defeats along with the triumphs. He lives in a world of fear and doubt, fallibility and failure. And what can one feel, whether tragic figure, hero, or villain, at these defeats, but regret? Kim Antieau and Brian Hodge explore the haunting questions, *Did I do all I could have done? Could I have done any more?* In "Empty Morning," Steve Rasnic Tem and Melanie Tem follow an elderly Van Helsing who has lost so much that he has nearly lost himself. Adam-Troy Castro reveals a Van Helsing longing for death. And in "Origin of Species," A. M. Dellamonica shows us that even from oblivion, one may return and gain new hope.

These stories will take you through different time periods, different countries, and different genres, for this iconic figure has grown far beyond his roots. We should never forget, though, that Bram Stoker is the one who started it all. You don't need to read *Dracula* to enjoy the stories here, but if you've never read that gothic masterpiece, or if you haven't read it recently, I hope you'll take this opportunity to read one of the most popular and exciting novels of all time. It is a joy to read, and the echoes of Stoker's tale still resound through our culture.

Of the twenty-one stories in this book, two offer alternate versions of particular events that occur in *Dracula*. Kathe Koja's "Anna Lee" revisits the night when Lucy Westenra receives her last, fatal visit from Count Dracula, offering a new theory on how he may have gotten past Van Helsing's defenses, including four maids. Lois Tilton's "My Dear Madame Mina" focuses on the burn on Mina Harker's forehead, accidentally inflicted upon her when Van Helsing holds a communion wafer to her forehead. A sign that she is unclean, the burn disappears when Dracula dies in the novel, but in Lois's story, Mina is not so fortunate.

The power of Van Helsing's character is reflected in the stunning power of the stories herein. The authors—ranging from best sellers and award-winners to complete newcomers—have been inspired to extraordinary, exhilarating, moving work. With an amazing variety in style and content, they show that this man of many faces is endlessly compelling. They shine a light into the dark places where this timeless, mysterious character walks, bearing his cross and his convictions, and what you see in that darkness, you will keep with you forever.

—Jeanne Cavelos
Mont Vernon, New Hampshire
October 31, 2003

The Screaming

J. A. KONRATH

"THREE STINKING QUID?"

Colin wanted to reach over the counter and throttle the old bugger. The radio he'd brought in was brand new and worth at least twenty pounds.

Of course, it was also hot. Delaney's was the only pawnbroker in Liverpool that didn't ask questions. Colin dealt with them frequently because of this. But each and every time, he left the shop feeling ripped off.

"Look, this is state of the art. The latest model. You could at least go six."

As expected, the old wank didn't budge. Colin took the three coins and left, muttering curses under his breath.

Where the hell was he going to get more money?

Colin rubbed his hand, fingers trailing over dirty scabs. His eyes itched. His throat felt like he'd been swallowing gravel. His stomach was a tight fist that he couldn't unclench.

If he didn't score soon, the shakes would start.

Colin tried to work up enough saliva to spit, and only half managed. The radio had been an easy snatch; stupid bird had left it on the window ledge of her flat, plugged in and wailing a new Beatles tune. Gifts like that didn't come around that often.

He used to do okay robbing houses, but the last job he pulled left him with three broken ribs and a mashed nose when the owner came home early. And Colin'd been in pretty good shape back then. Now—frail and wasted and brittle as he was—a good beating would kill him.

Not that Colin was afraid to die. He just wanted to score first. And three pounds wouldn't even buy him a taste.

Colin hunkered down on the walk, pulled up the collar on his wool coat. The coat had been nice once, bought when Colin was a straighty, making a good wage. He'd almost sold it many times, but always held out. English winters bit at a man's bones. There was already a winter-warning chill in the air, even though autumn had barely started.

Still, if he could have gotten five pounds for it, he'd have shucked it in an instant. But with the rips, the stains, the piss smell, he'd be lucky to get fifty p.

"'Ello, Colin."

Colin didn't bother looking up. He recognized the sound of Butts's raspy drone and couldn't bear to tolerate him right now.

"I said, 'ello, Colin."

"I heard you, Butts."

"No need to be rude, then."

Butts plopped next to him without an invite, smelling like a loo set ablaze. His small eyes darted this way and that along the sidewalk, searching for half-spent fags. That's how he'd earned his nickname.

"Oh, lucky day!" Butts grinned and reached into the street, plucking up something with filthy fingers. There was a lipstick stain on the filter, and it had been stamped flat. "Good for a puff or two, eh?"

"I'm in no mood today, Butts."

"Strung out again, are we?"

Butts lit the butt with some pub matches, drew hard.

"I need a few more quid for a nickle bag."

"You could pull a job."

"Look at me, Butts. I weigh ten stone, and half that is the coat. A small child could beat my arse."

"Just make sure there's no one home, mate."

Easier said, Colin thought.

"You know"—Butts closed his eyes, smoke curling from his nostrils—"I'm short on scratch myself right now. Maybe we could team up for something. You go in, I could be lookout, we split the take."

Colin almost laughed. He didn't trust Butts as far as he could chuck him.

"How about I be the lookout?"

"Sorry, mate. You'll run at the first sign of trouble."

"And you wouldn't?"

Butts shrugged. His fag went out. He made two more attempts at lighting it, and then flicked it back into the street. "Sod it, then. Let's do a job where we don't need no lookout."

"Such as?"

Butts scratched his beard, removed a twig. "There's this house, see? In Heysham, near where I grew up. Been abandoned for a long time. Loaded with bounty, I bet. That antiquey stuff fetches quite a lot in the district."

"It's probably all been jacked a long time ago."

"I don't think so. When I was a pup, the road leading up to it was practically invisible. All growed over by woods, you see. Only the kids knew about it. And we all stayed far away."

"Why?"

"Stories. Supposed to have goblins. Bollocks like that. I went up to it once, on a dare. Got within ten yards. Then I heard the screaming."

Colin rolled his eyes. He needed to quit wasting time with Butts and think of some way to get money. It would be dark soon.

"You think I'm joshing? I swear on the head of my lovely, sainted mother. I got within a stone's throw, and a god-fearful scream comes out of the house. Sounded like the devil his self was torturing some poor soul. Wet my kecks, I did."

"It was probably one of your stupid mates, Butts. Having a giggle at your expense."

"Wasn't a mate, Colin. I'm telling you, no kid in town went near that house. Nobody did. And I've been thinking about it a lot, lately. I bet there's some fine stuff to nick in there."

"Why haven't you gone back then, eh? If this place is full of stealables, why haven't you made a run?"

Butts's roving eyes locked onto another prize. He lit up, inhaled. "It's about fifteen miles from here. Every so often I save up the rail money, but I always seem to spend the dough on something else. Hey, you said you have a few quid, right? Maybe we can take the train and—"

"No way, Butts."

Colin got up, his thin bones creaking. He could feel the onset of tremors in his hands, and jammed them into his pockets.

"Heysham Port is only a two-hour ride. Then only a wee walk to the house."

"I don't want to spend my loot on train tics, and I don't want to spend the night in bloody Heysham. Pissant little town."

Colin looked left, then right, realizing it didn't matter what direction he went. He began walking, Butts nipping at his heels.

"I got old buds in Heysham. They'll put us up. Plus I got a contact there. He could set us up with some smack, right off. Wouldn't even need quid; we can barter with the pretties we nick."

"No."

Butts put his dirty hand on Colin's shoulder, squeezed. His fingernails resembled a coal miner's.

"Come on, mate. We could be hooked up in three hours. Maybe less. You got something better to do? Find a hole somewhere, curl up until the puking stops? You recall how long it takes to stop, Colin?"

Colin paused. He hadn't eaten in a few days, so there was nothing to throw up but his own stomach lining. He'd done that, once. Hurt something terrible, all bloody and foul.

But Heysham? Colin didn't believe there was anything valuable in that armpit of a town. Let alone some treasure-filled house Butts'd seen thirty years back.

Colin rubbed his temple. It throbbed, in a familiar way. As the night dragged on, the throbbing would get worse.

He could take his quid, buy a tin of aspirin and some seltzer, and hope the withdrawal wouldn't be too bad this time.

But he knew the truth.

As far as bad decisions went, Colin was king. One more wouldn't make a dif.

"Fine, Butts. We'll go to Heysham. But if there's nothing there, you owe me. Big."

Butts smiled. The three teeth he had left were as brown as his shoes.

"You got it, mate! And you'll see! Old Butts has got a feeling about this one. We're going to score, and score big. You'll see."

By the time the rail spit them out at Heysham Port, Colin was well into the vomiting.

He'd spent most of the ride in the loo, retching his guts out. With each purge, he forced himself to drink water, so as not to do any permanent damage to his gullet.

It didn't help. When the water came back up, it was tinged pink.

"Hang in there, Colin. It isn't far."

Bollocks it wasn't far. They walked for over three hours. The night air was a meat locker, and the ground was all slope and hill. Wooded country, overgrown with trees and high grass, dotted with freezing bogs. Colin noticed the full moon, through a sliver in the canopy. Then the forest swallowed it up.

They walked by torchlight; Butts had swaddled an old undershirt around a stick. Colin stopped vomiting, but the shivering got so bad he fell several times. It didn't help that Butts kept getting his reference points mixed up and changed directions constantly.

"Don't got much left, Butts."

"Stay strong, mate. Almost there. See? We're on the road."

Colin looked down, saw only weeds and rocks. "Road?"

"Cobblestone. You can still see bits of curbing."

Colin's hopes fell. If the road was in such disrepair, the house was probably worse off.

Stinking Heysham. Stinking Butts.

"There it is, mate! What did I tell you?"

Colin stared ahead. Nothing but trees. Slowly, gradually, he made out the house shape. The place was entirely obscured, the land so overgrown it appeared to be swallowing the frame.

"Seems like the house is part of the trees," Colin said.

"Was like that years ago, too. Worse now, of course. And lookit that. Windows still intact. No one's been inside here in fifty years, I bet."

Colin straightened up. Butts was right. As rundown as it was, the house looked untouched by humans since the turn of the century.

"We don't have to take everything at once. Just find something small and pricey to nick now, and then we can come back and—"

The scream paralyzed Colin. It was a force, high-pitched thunder, ripping through him like needles. Unmistakably human, yet unlike any human voice Colin had ever heard.

And it was coming from the house.

Butts gripped him with both hands, the color fleeing his ruddy face.

"Jesus Christ! Did you hear that? Just like when I was a kid! What do we do, Colin?"

A spasm shook Colin's guts, and he dry-heaved onto some scrub brush. He wiped his mouth on his coat sleeve. "We go in."

"Go in? I just pissed myself."

"What are you afraid of, Butts? Dying? Look at yourself. Death would be a blessing."

"My life isn't a good one, Colin, but it's the only one I've got."

Colin pushed past. The scream was chilling, yes. But there was nothing in that house worse than what Colin had seen on the street. Plus, he needed to get fixed up, bad. He'd crawl inside the devil's arse to get some cash.

"Hold up for me!" Butts attached himself to Colin's arm. They crept towards the front door.

Another scream rattled the night, even louder than the first. It vibrated through Colin's body, making every nerve jangle.

"I just pissed myself again!"

"Quiet, Butts! Did you catch that?"

"Catch what?"

"It wasn't just a scream. I think it was a word."

Colin held his breath, waiting for the horrible sound to come again. The woods stayed silent around them, the wind and animals still.

The scream cut him to the marrow.

"There! Sounded like *hell*."

Butts's eyes widened, the yellows showing. "Let's leave, Colin. My trousers can't hold any more."

Colin shook off Butts and continued creeping towards the house.

Though naive about architecture, Colin had grown up viewing enough castles and manors to recognize this building was very old. The masonry was concealed by climbing vines, but the wrought iron adorning the windows was magnificent. Even decades of rust couldn't obscure the intricate, flowing curves and swirls.

As they neared, the house seemed to become larger, jutting dormers threatening to drop down on their heads, heavy walls stretching off and blending into the trees. Colin stopped at the door, nearly nine feet high, hinges big as a man's arm.

"Butts! The torch!"

Butts slunk over, waving the flame at the door.

The knob was antique, solid brass, and glinted in the torchlight. At chest level hung a grimy knocker. Colin licked his thumb and rubbed away the patina. "Silver."

"Silver? That's great, Colin! Let's yank it and get out of here."

But Colin wouldn't budge. If just the door knocker was worth this much, what treasures lay inside?

He put his hand on the cold knob. Turned.

It opened.

As a youth, Colin often spent time with his grandparents, who owned a dairy farm in Shincliffe. That's how the inside of this house smelled; like the musk and manure of wild beasts. A feral smell, his grandmum had often called it.

Taking the torch from Butts, he stepped into the foyer, eyes scanning for booty. Decades of dust had settled on the furnishings, motes swirling into a thick fog wherever the duo stepped. Beneath the grime, Colin could recognize the quality of the furniture, the value of the wall hangings.

They'd hit it big.

It was way beyond a simple, quick score. If they did this right, went through the proper channels, he and Butts could get rich off of this.

Another scream shook the house.

Butts jumped back, his sudden movement sending clouds of dust into the air. Colin coughed, trying to wave the filth out of his face.

"It came from down there!" Butts pointed at the floor, his quivering hand casting erratic shadows in the torchlight. "It's a ghost, I tell you! Come to take us to hell!"

Colin's heart was a hummingbird in his chest, trying to find a way out. He was scared, but even more than that, he was concerned.

"Not *hell*, Butts. It sounded more like *help*."

Colin stepped back, out of the dust cloud. He thrust the torch at the floor, looking for a way down.

"'Ello! Anyone down there?"

He tapped at the wood slats with the torch, listening for a hollow sound.

"'Ello!"

The voice exploded up through the floorboards, cracking like thunder. *"PRAISE GOD, HELP ME!"*

Butts grabbed Colin's shoulders, his foul breath assaulting Colin's ear. "Christ, Colin! There's a wraith down there!"

"Don't be stupid, Butts. It's a man. Would a ghost be praising God?"

Colin bent down, peered at the floor.

"What's a man doing under the house, Colin?"

"Bugger if I know. But we have to find him."

Butts nodded, eager. "Right! If we rescue the poor sap, maybe we'll get a reward, eh?"

Colin grabbed Butts by the collar, pulled him close. "This place is a gold mine. We can't let anyone else know it exists."

Butts gazed at him stupidly.

"We have to snuff him," Colin said.

"Snuff him? Colin, I don't think—"

Colin clamped his hand over Butts's mouth. "I'll do it, when the time comes. Just shut up and follow my lead, got it?"

Butts nodded. Colin released him and went back to searching the floor. "'Ello! How'd you get down there!"

"There is a trapdoor, in the kitchen!"

Colin located the kitchen off to the right. An ancient wood-burning stove stood vigil in one corner, and there was an icebox by the window. On the kitchen table, coated with dust, lay a table setting for one. Colin wondered, fleetingly, what price the antique china and crystal would fetch, and then he turned his attention to the floor.

"Where?"

"The corner! Next to the stove!"

Colin looked around for something to sweep away the dust. He reached for the curtains, figured they might be worth something, and then found a closet on the other side of the room. There was a broom inside.

He gave Butts the torch and swept slowly, trying not to stir up the motes. After a minute, he could make out a seam in the floorboards. The seam extended into a man-sized square, complete with a recessed iron latch.

When Colin pulled up on the handle, he was bathed in a foul odor a hundred times worse than anything on his grandparents' farm.

This was the source of the feral smell. And it was horrible.

Mixed in with the scent of beasts was decay; rotting, stinking, flesh. Colin knelt down, gagging. It took several minutes for the contractions to stop.

"There's a ladder." Butts thrust the torch into the hole. His free hand covered his nose and mouth.

"How far down?" Colin managed.

"Not very. I can make out the bottom."

"Hey! You still down there!"

"Yes. But before you come down, you must prepare yourselves, gentlemen."

"Prepare ourselves? What for?"

"I am afraid my appearance may pose a bit of a shock. However, you must not be afraid. I promise I shall not hurt you."

Butts eyed Colin, intense. "I'm getting seriously freaked out. Let's just nick the silver knocker and—"

"Give me the torch."

Butts handed it over. Colin dropped the burning stick through the opening, illuminating the floor.

A moan, sharp and strong, welled up from the hole.

"You okay down there, mate?"

"The light is painful. I have not born witness to light for a considerable amount of time."

Butts dug a finger into his ear, scratching. "Bloke sure talks fancy."

"He won't for long." Colin sat on the floor, found the rungs with his feet, and began to descend.

The smell doubled with every step down; a viscous odor that had heat and weight and sat on Colin's tongue like a dead cat. In the flickering flame, Colin could make out the shape of the room. It was a root cellar, cold and foul. The dirt walls were rounded, and when Colin touched ground he sent plumes of dust into the air. He picked up the torch to locate the source of the voice. In the corner, standing against the wall, was . . .

"Sweet Lord Jesus Christ!"

"I must not be much to look at."

That was the understatement of the century. The man, if he could be called that, was excruciatingly thin. His bare chest resembled a skeleton with a thin sheet of white skin wrapped tight around, and his waist was so reduced it had the breadth of Colin's thigh.

A pair of tattered trousers hung loosely on the unfortunate man's pelvis, and remnants of shoes clung to his feet, several filthy toes protruding through the leather.

And the face, *the face!* A hideous skull topped with limp, white hair, thin features stretched across cheekbones, eyes sunken deep into bulging sockets.

"Please, do not flee."

The old man held up a bony arm, the elbow knobby and ball-shaped. Around his wrist coiled a heavy, rusted chain, leading to a massive steel ball on the ground.

Colin squinted, then gasped. The chain wasn't going around this unfortunate's wrist; it went *through* the wrist, a thick link penetrating the flesh between the radius and ulna.

"Colin! You okay?"

Butts's voice made Colin jump.

"Come on down, Butts! I think I need you!"

"There is no need to be afraid. I will not bite. Even if I desired to do so." The old man stretched his mouth open, exposing sticky, gray gums. Both the upper and lower teeth were gone. *"I knocked them out quite some time ago. I could not bear to be a threat to anyone. May I ask whom I am addressing?"*

"Eh?"

"What is your name, dear sir?"

Colin started to lie, then realized there was no point. He was going to snuff this poor sod anyway.

"Colin. Colin Willoughby."

"The pleasure is mine, Mr. Willoughby. My name is Dr. Abraham Van Helsing, professor emeritus at Oxford University. Will you allow me one more question?"

Colin nodded. It was eerie, watching this man talk. His body was ravaged to the point of disbelief, but his manner was polite and even affable.

"What year of our Lord is this, Mr. Willoughby?"

"The year? It's nineteen sixty-five."

Van Helsing's lips quivered. His sad, sunken eyes went glassy. *"I have been down here longer than I had imagined. Tell me, pray do, the nosferatu; were they wiped out in the war?"*

"What war? And what is a *nosfer-whatever* you said?"

"The war must have been many years ago. There were horrible, deafening explosions that shook the ground. I believe it went on for many months. I assumed it was a battle with the undead."

Was this crackpot talking about the bombing from World War II? He couldn't have been down here for that long. There was no food, no water. . . .

"Mary, mother of God!"

Butts stepped off the ladder and crouched behind Colin. He held another torch, this one made from the broom they'd used to sweep the kitchen floor.

"Whom am I addressing now, good sir?"

"He's asking your name, Butts."

"Oh. It's Butts."

"Good evening to you, Mr. Butts. Now if I may get an answer to my previous inquiry, Mr. Willoughby?"

"If you mean World War Two, the war was with Germany."

"I take it, because you both are speaking in our mother tongue, that Germany was defeated?"

"We kicked the krauts' arses," Butts said from behind Colin's shoulder.

"Very good, then. You also related that you do not recognize the term nosferatu?"

"Never heard of it."

"How about the term vampire?"

Butts nodded, nudging Colin in the ribs with his elbow. "Yeah, we know about vampires, don't we Colin? They been in some great flickers."

"Flickers?"

"You know. Movie shows."

Van Helsing knitted his brow. His skin was so tight it made the corners of his mouth draw upwards. *"So the nosferatu attend these movie shows?"*

"Attend? Blimey, no. They're in the movies. Vampires are fake, old man. Everyone knows that. Dracula don't really exist."

"Dracula!" Van Helsing took a step forward, the chain tugging cruelly against his arm. *"You know the name of the monster!"*

"Everyone knows Dracula. Been in a million books and movies."

Van Helsing seemed lost for a moment, confused. Then a light flashed behind his black eyes.

"My memorandum," he whispered. *"Someone must have published it."*

"Eh?"

"These vampires . . . you say they do not exist?"

"They're imaginary, old man. Like faeries and dragons."

Van Helsing slumped against the wall. His arm jutted out to the side, chain stretched and jangling in protest. He gummed his lower lip, staring into the dirt floor.

"Then I must be the last one."

COLIN was getting anxious. He needed some smack, and this old relic was wasting precious time. In Colin's pocket rested a boning knife he kept for protection. Colin'd never killed anybody before, but he figured he could manage. A quick poke-poke, and then they'd be on their way.

"I thought vampires had fangs." Butts approached Van Helsing, his head cocked to the side like a curious dog.

"I threw them in the dirt, about where you are presently standing. Knocked them out by ramming my mouth rather forcefully into this iron weight I am chained to."

"So you're really a vampire?"

Colin almost told Butts to shut the hell up, but decided it was smarter to keep the old man talking. He fingered the knife handle and took a casual step forward.

"Unfortunately, I am. After Seward and Morris destroyed the Monster, we thought there were no more. Foolish."

Van Helsing's eyes looked beyond Colin and Butts.

"Morris passed on. Jonathan and Mina named their son after him. Quincey. He was destined to be a great man of science; that was the sort of mind the boy had. Logical and quick to question. But on his sixth birthday, they came."

"Who came?" Butts asked.

Keep him talking, Colin thought. He took another step forward, the knife clutched tight.

"The vampiri. Unholy children of the fiend, Dracula. They found us. My wife, Dr. Seward, Jonathan, Mina . . . all slaughtered. But poor, dear Quincey, his fate proved even worse. They turned him."

"You mean, they bit him on the neck and made him a vampire?"

"Indeed they did, Mr. Butts. I should have ended his torment, but he was so small. An innocent lamb. I decided that perhaps, with a combination of religion and science, I might be able to cure him."

Butts squatted on his haunches, less than a yard from the old man. "I'll wager he's the one that got you, isn't he?"

Van Helsing nodded glumly.

"I kept him down here. Performed my experiments during the day, while he slept. But one afternoon, distracted by a chemistry problem, I stayed too late, and he awoke from his undead slumber and administered the venom into my hand."

"Keep talking, old man," Colin whispered under his breath. He pulled the knife from his pocket and held it at his side, hidden up the sleeve of his coat.

"I developed the sickness. While drifting in and out of consciousness, I realized I was being tended to. Quincey, dear, innocent Quincey, had brought others of his kind back to my house."

"They the ones that chained you to the wall?"

"Indeed they did, Mr. Butts. This is the ultimate punishment for one of their kind. Existing with this terrible, gnawing hunger, with no way to relieve the ache. The pain has been quite excruciating throughout the years. Starvation combined with a sickening craving. Like narcotic withdrawal."

"We know what that's like," Butts offered.

"I tried drinking my own blood, but it is sour and offers no relief. Occasionally, a small insect or rodent wanders into the cellar, and much as I try to resist it, the hunger forces me to commit horrible acts." Van Helsing shook his head. *"Renfield would have been amused."*

"So you been living on bugs and vermin all this time? You can't survive on that."

"That is my problem, Mr. Butts. I do survive. As I am already dead, I shall exist forever unless extraordinary means are applied."

Butts laughed, giving his knees a smack. "It's a bloody wicked tale, old man. But we both know there ain't no such things as vampires."

"Do either of you have a mirror? Or a crucifix, perhaps? I believe there is one in the jewelry box, on the nightstand in the upstairs bedroom. I suggest you bring it here."

Now they were getting somewhere. Jewelry was easy to carry, and easier to pawn. Colin's veins twitched in anticipation. "Go get it, Butts. Bring the whole box down."

Butts nodded, quickly disappearing up the ladder.

Colin studied Van Helsing, puzzling about the best way to end him. The old man was so frail, one quick jab in the chest and he should be done with it.

"That small knife you clutch in your hand, that may not be enough, Mr. Willoughby."

Colin was surprised that Van Helsing had noticed, but it didn't matter at this point. He held the boning knife out before him.

"I think it'll do just fine."

"I have tried to end my own life many times. On many nights, I would pound my head against this steel block until bones cracked. When I still had teeth, I tried gnawing off my own arm to escape into the sunlight. Yet every time the sun set again, I awoke fully healed."

Colin hesitated. The knife handle was sweaty, uncomfortable. He wondered where Butts was.

"My death must come from a wooden stake through my heart, or in lieu of that, you must sever my head and separate it from my shoulders." Van Helsing wiped away a long line of drool that leaked down his chin. *"Do not be afraid. I am hungry, yes, but I am still strong enough to fight the urge. I will not resist."*

The old man knelt, lifting his chin. Colin brought the blade to his throat. Van Helsing's neck was thin, dry, like rice paper. One good slice would do it.

"I want to die, Mr. Willoughby. Please."

Hand trembling, Colin set his jaw and sucked in air through his teeth. But he couldn't do it. "Sorry, mate. I—"

"Then I shall!"

Van Helsing sprang to his feet, tearing the knife away from Colin. With animal ferocity he began to hack at his own neck, slashing through tissue and artery, blood pumping down his translucent chest in pulsing waterfalls.

Colin took a step back, his gorge rising.

Van Helsing screamed, an inhuman cry that made Colin go rigid with fear. The old man's head cocked at a funny angle, tilting to the side. His eyes rolled up in their sockets, exposing the whites. But still he continued, slashing away at the neck vertebrae, buried deep within his bleeding flesh like a white peach pit.

Colin vomited, unable to pull his eyes away.

He's going to make it, Colin thought, incredulous. *He's going to cut off his own head.*

But it wasn't to be. Just as the knife plunged into the bone of his spine, Van Helsing went limp, sprawling face first onto the dirt.

Colin stared, amazed. The horror, the violence of what he'd just witnessed, pressed down upon him like a great weight. After a few minutes, his breathing slowed to normal, and he found his mind again.

Colin reached tentatively for the knife, still clutched in Van Helsing's hand. The gore gave him pause.

"Go ahead and keep it," Colin decided. "I'll buy another one when—"

Alarm jolted through Colin. He realized, all at once, that Butts hadn't returned. Had the bugger run off with the jewelry box?

Colin sped up the ladder, panicked. "Butts!"

No answer.

Using the torch, he followed Butts's tracks in the dust, into the bedroom, and then back out the front door. Colin swung it open.

"Butts! Butts, you son of a whore!"

No reply.

Colin sprinted into the night. He ran fast as he could, hoping that his direction was true, screaming and cursing Butts between labored breaths.

His foot caught on a protruding root and he went sprawling forward, skidding on his chin, his torch flying off into the woods and sizzling out in a bog.

Blackness.

The dark was complete, penetrating. Not even the moon and stars were visible.

It felt like being in the grave.

Colin, wracked by claustrophobia, once again called out for Butts.

The forest swallowed up his voice.

Fear set in. Without a torch, Colin would never find his way back to Heysham. Wandering around the woods without fire or shelter, he could easily die of exposure.

Colin got back on his feet, but walking was impossible. On the rough terrain, in the dark, he had no sense of direction. He tried to head back to the house, but couldn't manage a straight line.

After falling twice more, Colin gave up. Exhausted, frightened, and wracked with the pain of withdrawal, he curled up at the base of a large tree and let sleep overtake him.

"THIS better be it, Butts."

"We're almost there. I swear on it."

Colin opened his crusty eyes, attempted to find his bearings.

He was surrounded by high grass, next to a giant elm. The sun peeked through the canopy at an angle; it was either early morning or late afternoon.

"You've been saying that for three hours, you little wank. You need a little more encouragement to find this place?"

"I'm not holding out on you, Willie. Don't hit me again."

Colin squinted in the direction of the voices. Butts and two others. They weren't street people, either. Both wore clean clothes, good shoes. The smaller one, Willie, had a bowler hat and a matching black vest. The larger sported a beard, along with a chest big as a whiskey barrel.

Butts had taken on some partners.

Colin tried to stand, but he felt weak and dizzy. He knelt for a moment, trying to clear his head. When the cobwebs dissipated, he began to trail the trio.

"Tell us again, Butts, how much loot there is in this place."

"It's crammed full, Jake. All that old, antiquey stuff. I'm telling you, that jewelry box was just a taste."

"Better be, Butts, or you'll be wearing your yarbles around your filthy neck."

"I swear, Willie. You'll see. We're almost there."

Colin stayed ten yards back, keeping low, moving quiet. Several times he lost sight of them, but they were a loud bunch and easy to track. His rage grew with each step.

This house was his big break, his shot at a better life. He didn't want to share it with anybody. He may have choked when trying to off Van Helsing, but once they arrived at the house, Colin vowed to kill them all.

"Hey, Willie. Some bloke is following us."

"Eh?"

"In the woods. There."

Colin froze. The man named Jake stared, pointing through the brush.

"Who's there, then? Don't make me run you down."

"That's Colin. He came here with me."

Damned Butts.

"He knows about this place? Jake, go get the little bleeder!"

Colin ran, but Jake was fast. Within moments the bigger man caught Colin's arm and threw him to the ground.

"Trying to run from me, eh?"

A swift kick caught Colin in the ribs, searing pain stealing his breath.
"I hate running. Hate it."

Another kick. Colin groaned. Bright spots swirled in his vision.

"Get up, wanker. Let's go talk to Willie."

Jake grabbed Colin by the ear and tugged him along, dumping him at
Willie's feet.

"Why didn't you tell us about your mate, Butts?"

"I thought he'd gone. I swear it."

Jake let loose with another kick. Colin curled up fetal, began to cry.

"Should we kill him, Willie?"

"Not yet. We might need an extra body, help take back some of the
loot. You hear me, you drug-addled bastard? We're going to keep you
around for awhile, as long as you're helpful."

Butts knelt next to Colin and smiled, brown teeth flashing. "Get up,
Colin. They're not going to kill you." He helped Colin gain his footing,
keeping a steady arm around his shoulders until they arrived at the
house.

In the daylight, the house's aristocratic appearance was overtaken by
the many apparent flaws: peeling paint, cracked foundation, sunken roof.
Even the stately ironwork covering the windows looked drab and shabby.

"This place is a dump." Willie placed a finger on one nostril and blew
the contents of his nose onto a patch of clover.

"It's better on the inside," encouraged Butts. "You'll see."

Unfortunately, the inside was even less impressive. The dust-covered
furniture Colin had pegged as antique was damaged and rotting.

"You call this treasure?" Willie punched Butts square in the nose.

Butts dropped to the floor, bleeding and hysterical. "This is good stuff,
Willie! It'll clean up nice! Worth a couple thousand quid, I swear!"

Willie and Jake walked away from Butts, and he crawled behind them,
babbling.

A moment later, Colin was alone.

The pain in his ribs sharpened with every intake of breath. If he made
a run for it, they'd catch him easily. But if he did nothing, he was a dead
man.

He needed a weapon.

Colin crept into the kitchen, mindful of the creaking floorboards. Perhaps the drawers contained a weapon of some kind.

"What you doing in here, eh? Nicking silver?" Jake slapped him across the face.

Colin staggered back, his feet becoming rubber. Then the floor simply ceased to be there. He dropped, straight down, landing on his arse at the bottom of the root cellar.

Everything went fuzzy, and then black.

COLIN awoke in darkness.

He felt around, noticed his leg bent at a funny angle. The touch made him cry out.

Broken. Badly, from the size of the swelling.

Colin peeled his eyes wide, tried to see. There was no light at all. The trap door, leading to the kitchen, was closed. Not that it mattered; he couldn't have climbed up the ladder anyway.

He sat up, tears erupting onto his cheeks. There was a creaking sound above him, and then a sudden burst of light.

"I see you're still alive, eh?"

Colin squinted through the glare, made out the bowler hat.

"No worries, mate. We won't let you starve to death down there. We're not barbarians. Willie will be down shortly to finish you off. Promise it'll be quick. Right, Willie?"

Willie's laugh was an evil thing.

"See you in a bit."

The trap door closed.

Fear rippled through Colin, but it was overwhelmed by something greater.

Anger.

Colin had ever been the victim. From his boyhood days being beaten by his alcoholic father, up to his nagging ex-wife suing him into the recesses of poverty.

Well, if his miserable life was going to end here, in a foul-smelling dirt cellar, then so be it.

But he wasn't going without a fight.

Colin pulled himself along the cold ground, dragging his wounded leg. He wanted the boning knife, the one he'd left curled in Van Helsing's hand.

When Jake came down to finish him off, the fat bastard was going to get a nice surprise.

Colin's hand touched moisture, blood or some other type of grue, so he knew he was close. He reached into the inky blackness, finding Van Helsing's body, trailing down over his shoulder. . . .

"What in the hell?"

Colin brought his other hand over, groped around.

It made no sense.

Van Helsing's head, which had been practically severed from his shoulders, had reattached itself. The neck was completely intact. No gaping wound, no deep cut.

"Can't be him."

Perhaps another body had been dumped down there, possibly Butts. Colin touched the face.

No beard.

Colin grazed the mouth with his fingers, winced, and stuck a digit past the clammy lips.

It was cold and slimy inside the mouth. Revolting. But Colin probed around for almost an entire minute, searching for teeth that weren't there.

This was Van Helsing. And he had completely healed.

Which was impossible. Unless—

"Jesus Christ." Colin recoiled, scooting away from the body.

He was trapped in the dark with a vampire.

When would Van Helsing awake? Damn good thing the bloke was chained down. Who knows what horrors he could commit if he were free?

Colin repeated that thought, and grinned.

Perhaps if he helped the poor sod escape, Van Helsing would be so grateful he'd take care of the goons upstairs.

The idea vanished when Colin remembered Van Helsing's words. All the poor sod wanted was to die. He didn't want to kill anyone.

"Bloody hell. If *I* were a vampire, I'd do things—"

Colin halted mid-sentence. His works were in a sardine can, inside his breast pocket. He reached for them, took out the hypo.

It just might work.

Crawling back to Van Helsing, Colin probed until he found the bony neck. He pushed the needle in, then eased back the plunger, drawing out blood.

Vampire blood.

Tying off his own arm and finding his vein in the dark wasn't a problem; he'd done it many times before.

Teeth clenched, eyes shut, he gave himself the shot.

But there was no rush.

Only pain.

The pain seared up his arm, as if someone was yanking out his veins with pliers.

Colin cried out. When the tainted blood reached his heart, the muscle stopped cold, killing him instantly.

COLIN opened his eyes.

He was still in the cellar, but he could see perfectly well. He wondered where the light could be coming from, but a quick look around found no source.

Colin stood, realizing with a start that the pain in his leg had vanished.

So, in fact, had all of his other pain. He lifted his shirt, expecting to see bruised ribs, but there wasn't a mark on them.

Even the withdrawal symptoms had vanished.

The hypodermic was still in his hand. Colin stared at it, remembering.

"It worked. It bloody well worked."

Van Helsing still lay sprawled out on the floor, facedown.

Colin looked at him, and he began to drool. Hunger surged through him, an urge so completely overwhelming it dwarfed his addiction to heroin.

Without resisting the impulse, he fell to the ground and bit into the old man's neck. His new teeth tore through the skin easily, but when his tongue touched blood, Colin jerked away.

Rancid. Like spoiled milk.

A sound, from above. Colin listened, amused at how acute his hearing had become.

"All right, then. Jake, you go downstairs and mercy-kill the junkie, and then we'll be off."

Mercy kill, indeed.

Colin forced himself to be patient, standing stock-still as the trapdoor opened and a figure descended.

"Well well well, look who's up and about. Be brave, I'll try to make it painless."

Jake moved forward. Colin almost grinned. Big, sweating, dirty Jake smelled delicious.

"You got some fight left in you, eh?"

Colin lunged.

His speed was unnatural; he was on Jake in an instant. Even more astounding was his strength. Using almost no effort at all, he pulled the larger man to the ground and pinned down his arms.

"What the hell?"

"I'll try to make it painless," Colin said.

But from the sound of Jake's screams, it wasn't painless at all.

This blood wasn't rancid. This blood was ecstasy.

Every cell in Colin's body shuddered with pleasure, an overwhelming rush that dwarfed the feeling of heroin, a full-body orgasm so intense he couldn't control the moan escaping his throat.

He sucked until Jake stopped moving. Until his stomach distended, the warm liquid sloshing around inside him like a full-term fetus.

But he remained hungry.

He raced up the ladder, practically floating on his newfound power. Butts stood at the table, piling dishes into a wooden crate.

"Colin?"

Butts proved delicious, too. In a slightly different way. Not as sweet; sort of a Bordeaux to Jake's Cabernet. Colin's tongue was a wild thing. He lapped up the blood like a mad dog at a water dish, ravenous.

"What the hell are you doing?"

Colin let Butts drop, whirling to face Willie.

"Good God!" Willie reached into his vest, removed a small derringer. He fired twice, both shots tearing into Colin's chest.

There was pain.

But more than pain, there was hunger.

Willie turned to run, but Colin caught him easily.

"I wonder what you'll taste like," he whispered in the screaming man's ear.

Honey mead. The best of the three.

Colin suckled, gulping down the nectar as it pulsed from Willie's carotid. He gorged himself until one more swallow would have caused him to burst.

Then, in an orgiastic stupor, he stumbled from the house and into the glorious night.

No longer dark and silent and scary, the air now hummed with a bright glow, and animal sounds from miles away were clear and lovely.

Bats chasing insects. A wolf baying the moon. A tree toad, calling out to its mate.

Such sweet, wonderful music.

The feeling overwhelmed Colin, and he shuddered and wept. This was what he'd been searching for his entire life. This was euphoria. This was power. This was a fresh start.

"I see you have been busy."

Colin spun around.

Van Helsing stood at the entrance to the house. His right hand still gripped Colin's boning knife. His left hand was gone, severed above the wrist where the chain had bound him. The stump dripped gore, jagged white bone poking out.

Colin studied Van Helsing's face. Still sunken, still anguished. But there was something new in the eyes. A spark.

"Happy, old man? You finally have your freedom."

"Freedom is not what I seek. I desire only the redemption that comes with death."

Colin grinned, baring the sharp tips of his new fangs. "I'll be happy to kill you, if you want."

Van Helsing frowned.

"The lineage of nosferatu ends now, Mr. Willoughby. No more may be allowed to live. I have severed the heads of the ones inside the house. Only you and I remain."

Colin laughed, blood dripping from his lips. "You mean to kill me? With that tiny knife? Don't you sense my power, old man? Don't you see what I have become?" Colin spread out his arms, reaching up into the night. "I have been reborn!"

Colin opened wide, fangs bared to tear flesh. But something in Van Helsing's face, some awful fusion of hate and determination, made Colin hesitate.

Van Helsing closed the distance between them with supernatural speed, plunging the knife deep into Colin's heart.

Colin fell, gasping. The agony was exquisite. He tried to speak, and blood—his own rancid blood—bubbled up sour in his throat.

"Not . . . not . . . wood."

"No, Mr. Willoughby, this is not a wooden stake. It will not kill you. But the damage should be substantial enough to keep you here for an hour or so."

Van Helsing drove the knife further, puncturing the back of Colin's rib cage, pinning him to the ground.

"I have been waiting sixty years to end this nightmare, and I am tired. So very tired. With our destruction, my wait shall finally be over. May God have mercy on our souls."

Colin tried to rise, but the pain brought tears.

Van Helsing rolled off and sat, cross-legged, on the old cobblestone road. He closed his eyes, his thin, colorless lips forming a serene smile. *"I have not seen a sunrise in sixty years, Mr. Willoughby. I remember them to be very beautiful. This should be the most magnificent of them all."*

Colin began to scream.

WHEN sunrise came, it cleansed like fire.

Poison in the Darkness

Rita Oakes

✝

· I ·
1846

THE ROOM WAS SMALL, the furnishings spare: a dressing table with mirror, a straight-backed chair, a narrow, rumpled bed devoid of bedcurtains, a faded rug that might have been pretty once. The single window was shuttered, closed against the damp night air. The oil lamps, shaded with beaded glass, gave off a pink-gold light that should have lent an air of mystery to the chamber, but instead only depressed him.

The young Abraham Van Helsing studied the light to avoid looking at the woman.

"You're shy," she said. "That's all right. I like shy young men."

She was paid to like men, shy or not.

"And handsome," she said. "The young sir is very handsome."

This was not true. He was too gangly, for one thing. Recently his knees and elbows had developed a life of their own, leaving him graceless and a hazard to his mother's Dresden porcelain. A ridiculous fuzz had begun to sprout upon his cheeks. His skin, flawless a mere six months ago, had erupted with acne. No, he was anything but handsome. And he dearly wished he could be elsewhere. Standing a round of beer for his friends, perhaps. Or back home with his nose in a book.

"My—my father sent me," he said, wincing at the stammer and the naked fear in his voice.

She nodded, brushed his cheek with one finger. "Many are nervous the first time," she said, "but I can tell that you and I are going to be great friends."

She was clad in corset and petticoat. The corset pushed her breasts high. The tops peeked in grapefruit-sized mounds above a sheer bodice.

She took his hand, studied the ragged fingernails a moment, the narrow sliver of dried blood upon his thumb where, under the falsely genial gaze of his father in the coach, he had worried at a cuticle. "A gentleman of quality should take better care of his hands," she said.

"I know." His face grew warm. "I can't help it."

"Never mind." She placed his hand upon her breast. Soft. Smooth. Like perfectly kneaded bread dough. Warm, too. Pleasant. Perhaps he would get through this without embarrassing himself too badly. Then he could go home. Back to his studies.

She pulled away, and he let his hand fall to his side. She drew the chair back from her dressing table, placed a foot upon it, jutting out bosom and one hip. "Will you help me with my stockings?"

She lifted her petticoat slowly, past ankle and knee. Van Helsing swallowed, forced himself forward.

Her stockings were wrinkled, spotted a little with mud. Under her guidance, he reached his hand under the petticoat, began to roll down the coarsely knit stocking. She shifted position, and he removed that one as well. She had dimpled knees. The lamplight showed a sprinkling of dark hair upon her calves. Van Helsing caught an odor from under her clothing, something heavier and less sweet than the cloying perfume she wore, something of sweat and brine and musk and mystery. He wasn't sure he liked it. Yet he felt a stirring within his breeches, a quickening of his breath. She smiled at him.

"Thank you," she said. She unfastened his coat, helped him shrug out of it. She passed her hand over his groin lightly, teasingly, before she unbuttoned and dropped the front of his breeches, fishing the blind snake within free with practiced fingers. She spat upon her palm and coaxed his member to reluctant life.

She drew him to the bed and hoisted her petticoats.

He stared. He'd never seen a woman's privates before. There was hair between her thighs. The Greek and Roman statues he'd seen in museums did not have hair. Not there. Perhaps this woman was aberrant. His erection wilted.

She sighed softly, reached for him again. "Come, my young sir, I'll not bite."

He closed his eyes.

She stroked him back to stiffness, guided him inside the coarse thatch between her legs. She pressed his face to her breast.

He spent himself quickly. She released him. He dressed as swiftly as trembling hands would permit. He wanted to be rid of her, be rid of the sour, vaguely animal odor that rose from her skin, be rid of the stickiness that had come from her, or from himself, or from their commingling, be rid of the lingering sense of suffocation and shame. This was what it meant to be a man? If so, he found little to recommend it. Upon her dressing table he left the coin his father had given him.

· II ·

1855

VAN HELSING ENTERED the vast study, which looked out on the botanical gardens of the University of Leyden. Lined on three sides with bookshelves from floor to ceiling, the room housed ancient herbals, early studies of anatomy, treatises on fungi, pharmacology, bee keeping. Van Helsing had a particular love for this room, its vaguely musty odor of old parchment, oiled leather, centuries of accumulated knowledge. He'd always been bookish, and there were tomes enough here, ancient and modern, to keep him in contented study for centuries.

But it was not the room alone he loved.

Miss Marieke Boerhaave sat at a long, dark table near the window, where dust motes danced in a slant of late afternoon light. He admired the graceful curve of her neck as she bent, a little nearsightedly, over her task, delicately pinning a butterfly to a mounting board.

Like her distinguished ancestor, Hermann Boerhaave, Marieke possessed a keen mind. Unlike him, she devoted her studies not to medicine or botany, but to entomology. Lepidoptera. Butterflies.

People said Marieke had the mind of a man. Van Helsing imagined her as a gravely solemn child, curious but always apart, as he had so often felt apart.

As a young woman, she remained grave, but not humorless. Van Helsing had managed to coax a smile from her more than once, and that smile warmed better than the aged and potent *jenever* he sometimes sipped when the evenings grew damp and chill.

Something inside his stomach fluttered, as if her butterflies had magically materialized inside him. Or perhaps the eels he had dined on earlier disagreed with him.

He studied her a moment longer in silence, his throat tight. He had no wish to disturb her until she finished her task. The stark white of her pinafore contrasted pleasantly with her gown of sober gray silk. She took up a pen, dipped it into the inkwell, wrote a label for the specimen in a neat hand.

"The purple emperor," he said. More blue than purple, the butterfly possessed a startling iridescence when illumined by a shaft of sunlight from the window. Splotches of white like careless drips of paint countered dusky brown at the edges of the wings. "Beautiful," he said.

She glanced at him, nodded. "*Apatura iris*. A fine specimen of *Nymphalidae*."

"Some say the butterfly carries messages from Heaven. Others that it represents the soul in flight after death."

"You are the repository of a great deal of fanciful information, Doctor Van Helsing," she said.

So much was true. He was indiscriminate in his tastes, devouring myth as much as mathematics, literature as much as law, religion as much as science. He filed all away in his voracious mind, great truths and trivia, until such time as he might need them. "Is that a condemnation?" he asked. The fluttering in his stomach grew worse. He could not bear it if she should think him a fool.

She considered a long moment before she answered. "No."

"Will you take a turn with me through the gardens?"

He expected her to refuse. And then his carefully rehearsed speech would go unsaid, his hopes no more to fly than the dead butterfly mounted upon the table before her.

"Yes," she said. "I should enjoy a walk."

Spring in the Low Countries, and tulips—red, yellow, pink, white splashed with red, red flamed with yellow—nodded their heads in a breeze scented with distant rain. Hyacinth and narcissus held somewhat lesser stature. The grass, deeply green, looked as if it had been trimmed with scissors, and met the stone path neatly.

They walked side by side in silence. The wind brought a pleasing flush to Marieke's cheek, toyed with the gray silk ribbon of her bonnet. She paused a moment, observing a small orange, black, and cream-colored butterfly at rest upon a hyacinth. "*Aglais urticae,*" she said. The tortoise-shell butterfly flitted away. Van Helsing thought it more pleasant to watch the insects in flight than to see them killed, dried, and pinned, but would not risk her scorn by saying so.

"I have been offered a position in Amsterdam," he said. "I will be able to continue my research there."

"Congratulations."

"The salary will not make me rich, but with sufficient frugality, will permit the maintenance of a comfortable household."

"Then you are indeed fortunate."

Fortunate? Yes. Or rather, he might be. He studied the spiked petals of the brilliant red and yellow Duc van Tol tulip. A very ancient hybrid. Nearby nodded a patch of Rembrandts in white and red. Like blood splashed on snow, he thought. What if she should refuse him? What then? The news of his leaving certainly seemed to cause her no distress. But then, it wouldn't. She was not the sort to succumb to a fit of vapors. He would not find himself so drawn to her if she were.

"Miss Boerhaave—?"

"Yes?"

"I should esteem it a very great honor if you were to consent to become my wife."

She fixed him with a look as sharp as the pins she used to transfix her specimens. He held his breath. His fingers twitched a little, the old longing to gnaw upon his fingernails very strong, though he had broken himself of the habit long ago. After all, who would trust a physician with ragged nails and torn cuticles?

"Very well," she said.

· III ·

1869

I DID LOVE *him once. Alone of all men, he did not treat me as a brainless ninny whose only concern should be a new frock or a filled dance card. He did not look at me as if I'd sprouted two heads when I spoke of matters scientific. He was a good man, a kindly man, though given sometimes to flights of fanciful thinking, despite the rigors of both medicine and law. Brilliant, in his way, but as fascinated by superstition as by science. Sometimes his logic abandoned him altogether.*

When he asked me to marry him, I said yes. My suitors had been few enough, and I neared that age when I began to fear I should be a spinster forever.

It was not so much I desired a home and family of my own, but I had grown weary of the pitying glances and shaking heads of my relatives, which constrained me as fully as the stays of my corset.

He did not mind my somewhat cool nature, my readings of Linnaeus or Darwin, my long hours observing the minute world of insects. My speciality was Lepidoptera, and I suppose that a genteel enough hobby, even for the fair sex.

We were happy. For a time. I came to the marriage bed with more curiosity than fear. He was awkward, unpracticed, I think, and touchingly apologetic for making me submit to embraces he thought I must find distasteful.

I did not find them so, though I will confess disappointment that so momentous an experience proved dull and somewhat silly. Surely, I thought, there was more to the union of flesh and soul than this? What of the breathless passion of the poets?

Poets lie, I decided. No matter. I still had Lepidoptera.

Had I been a man, I should have traveled to Sumatra or Madagascar to collect the largest, most colorful specimens of Saturniidae. As it was, I contented myself with journals and correspondence. I collected the exotics captured by others' nets.

The years passed. I conceived a son and brought him to term without undue difficulty. Jeröen was a joy to us both, sunny-natured and affectionate. Tender of heart, perhaps excessively so, for he always wept when I put my butterflies into the killing jar, or when I later pinned them through the thorax upon the mounting board for display.

I had many specimens—large, iridescent reds and greens shipped to me from the tropics, as well as the smaller species more commonly seen in our Dutch gardens. Framed, they made a beautiful display lining the stairwell and in the room where I studied. Van had one upon the desk in his downstairs study, the common apatura iris, *the purple emperor, which I had been mounting the day he proposed to me.*

We were happy, as I said. Van proved a generous husband, liberal to me with gifts of flowers, books, and chocolates. He was an attentive, loving father and missed Jeröen terribly when the boy went away to school. Truthfully, he missed the boy more than I, for Jeröen had a horror of the things I found most fascinating. Never think I did not love my son, for I did. But I rarely knew what to say to him.

One Thursday afternoon, returning from errands, a sudden rain shower forced me into a bookshop. The sun had long set before the rain slowed to the merest drizzle and I turned my steps homeward.

She stood beneath the gaslight, pale, utterly drenched, quite wretched-looking. Her clothes were of good quality, or I would not have paused. I asked if she was ill. She looked faint, and I took her hand. Quite chill, it was.

"Come," I said, "my husband is a physician. You shall have a glass of sherry and a warm fire, and he shall put you to rights."

"You are very kind," she said. Her Dutch had a charming accent. Italian, I thought. My heart swelled with pity for one so far from home and alone.

The servants were away. I always gave them Thursday evenings free. I quite liked the quiet of an empty house. Jeröen was at school until the next holiday. Van had not yet returned from his rounds at the hospital.

"You must get out of those wet things," I said, and brought her towels and a dressing gown. I poured sherry for her, but she left the glass untouched.

She was beautiful, full of form, pale as marble. Aphrodite, I fancied, and dismissed the notion as something Van would have thought. But in truth, my husband was far from my mind. I felt a sudden weakness in the knees and a rush of pleasure such as sometimes had happened when Jeröen was an infant and suckled at my breast.

She took the dressing gown, but draped it over a chair. She toweled her hair dry. Blond, though dark with dampness. Dark honey shining with points of firelight. My throat felt tight. "Will you not dress?" I said. "My husband—"

"Does not please you."

Stung, I said, "Of course he pleases me. He is a brilliant man. He—"

Lips brushed mine, light as a butterfly wing. I stepped back, startled, though not as appalled as I might have been.

"He lacks passion," she said, and kissed me again, more firmly. My heart drummed beneath the prison of my corset. So loud, I thought surely she must hear. My head felt light, as if I'd taken too much wine. I broke away from her, my face hot with shame.

No. Not shame. Desire.

I thought myself long immune to passion. I had science, after all. Study. My insects, coldly gassed, pinned, displayed. I had never been prone to frivolity, hysteria. I liked things measured, labeled, analyzed. I—

I wanted her. I abandoned sweet reason for this utterly new sensation of melting delight. I trembled, for my flesh could not contain this wanting. I sank to the floor, hid my face. I did not know what to do or say.

She held me, pressed my face to her bosom, stroked the nape of my neck with fingers still chilled from the storm. I had heat for us both. I kissed her, shyly, and then more boldly when she did not pull away. She loosed my hair from its severe chignon, unlaced my gown, my corset.

I felt an ache in my lower back. It had annoyed me all day, presaging the onset of my menses. My insides seemed to dissolve and I felt the curse of Eve between my thighs. Too early. I thought I would die of shame.

I pushed her away. "I am unclean," I said.

Her nostrils flared, and she smiled. "Not to me. There is no shame in blood." She kissed me again, and caressed me with great tenderness. The ache vanished. Pleasure only remained.

She left before Van returned home, pledging to return to me on Thursday next. I drew on the dressing gown, drank the untouched sherry.

Van was worried at my preoccupation that evening, my disordered hair, my flushed skin. Doctor that he was, he bled me, far more painfully than she had done, and put me to bed. It was only when he climbed carefully into the bed beside me that the thought came to me I was an adulteress. I began to weep, I who never wept, and alarmed him further. He held me, and stroked my hair, and asked if I had pain. He had laudanum below, in his apothecary cabinet, but I shook my head and clung to him, clung to this good man, whom I had betrayed.

I abandoned Lepidoptera. Caterina was far more exotic. I felt shattered by my passions, and yet curiously freed by them. Caterina visited me weekly, when servants and husband were away. How precious our time together, how tender.

She was more than a woman—I had forgotten to mention that, I think. Centuries older than I, but forever young, and unfettered by convention. There is, I am sure, a scientific explanation for creatures such as her, but Caterina refused to submit to microscopic analysis. "I am not one of your specimens," she would say and then kiss me.

Yes, she drank blood. She killed sometimes. That is the nature of a predator. But to me, she remained unfailingly tender, taught me to take as much pleasure in the flesh as I had always taken in the mind. I realized I had been only half alive before she came to me.

My only regret was my continued deception of that good man, my husband. It was almost a relief to me when he returned home earlier than expected and discovered us in flagrante delicto.

Such a cry of grief he made, I feared for his reason.

Caterina sprang upon him. He struggled, but could not free himself of her unnatural strength. Her eyes had gone that strange red that told of hunger or rage. She could break him like a dry stick.

"You must not hurt him," I said, drawing on a dressing gown in haste. I, his wife, had hurt him deeply enough.

"Why ever not?" As I said, she could be cruel.

"Because I ask it."

She called me a fool. She drank from him, deeply until he swooned, but for my

sake, she let him live. And a little blood-letting is good for you, is it not? She car-
ried him to his study and deposited him in a chair by the fire. She kissed me then,
and I could taste his blood lingering upon her tongue.

"I must leave here," she said. "It will not be safe for me with him alive, fool
though he is. Come with me."

I wanted to go. The enormity of life without her—I scarce could imagine going
back to my dull, passionless existence. But I could not abandon a husband of
fourteen years so abruptly. And there was Jeröen to consider. Twelve years old, he
was. How could I leave before I saw him grow to manhood? "I cannot."

Her eyes flashed red again. Hurt, as much as anger, I think. But she did not try
to persuade me further. "When he wakes," she said, "ask your so saintly husband
what special ingredient laces those chocolates he brings you so regularly."

"What do you mean?"

"Ask him."

No final embrace. She passed out of my life as swiftly as she had entered.

Van was rousing, so I put aside my grief, placed my hand over his broad one,
with its dusting of freckles and hair like fine copper wires. For the first time, I no-
ticed the strands of gray in his reddish hair, the lines deepening about his eyes. So
vulnerable he looked, and I felt a terrible fondness for him.

He pulled his hand from mine. His shoulders shook with the violence of his
weeping.

Never had I seen a man so broken. I had done this to him, with my hedonist
ways. So Adam must have wept when Eve gave him the forbidden fruit. Oh, but
I was a weak, vile, creature.

Yet I pretended sternness. "Van," I said, "it is not the end of the world."

"It is the end of my world." He fumbled for his handkerchief. "How could you
submit to the embrace of that—that—creature?" He looked at me with sudden,
pitiable hope. "She coerced you, did she not? You were powerless against her. She
is not human. She—"

"I love her." Better, perhaps, if I had lied, given him a sop to his pride, but I
could not. "The chocolates, Van," I said. "What is their special ingredient?"

He blinked through his tears. "Chocolates?"

"Yes, the ones you so kindly bring me every week. They are different from other
confections, yes? I'd like to know how."

A simple question, to focus his scattered wits, but why did he look so startled, so guilty? Had he not felt so undone, I'm sure he would never have told me the truth.

"Mercury," he said.

"Mercury?" I knew enough of his work to know mercury came from cinnabar, and that it was commonly used for disorders of the skin, and for centuries had been the preferred treatment for—for—

Though never prone to megrims, vapors, or any other form of weakness commonly experienced by my sex, I confess I sat down rather abruptly.

Mercury was the preferred treatment for pox.

I should not know such things, but Van had never denied me his books, and I read voraciously on matters medical as well as insectile. Pox. Morbus Gallicus. The French Disease. Or, if you were in France, the English Complaint. Also blamed upon the Spanish, Italians, Germans, and the New World. Syphilis.

Dear God.

If I were tainted—would not my son be also, the disease carried through my milk to his innocent lips? The blood left my face. "Jeröen."

"Jeröen is healthy."

I closed my eyes. "Thank God."

"Yes. Thank God."

I might have railed, screamed, wept, but to what avail? I allowed Reason to reassert itself. Quite calmly I said, "So you have been visiting whores while I thought you were working?"

He turned red to the roots of his hair. "I have not," he said, mustering indignation from the depths of his shock and grief.

"Then you knew you were ill when you married me?" This seemed the greater crime, and my voice trembled with the enormity of it, in spite of my resolve.

He reached out his hand to me, thought better of it. "No. You must not think that. I would never—Marieke, I was ill, yes, but I knew not the cause. The disease mimics many other lesser illnesses. Symptoms can remain hidden for years, decades. When I knew the truth, it was too late."

"You might have told me."

"It is not a subject one speaks of to one's wife."

I pitied him, for the burden he had carried so long alone. He was as much a prisoner of circumstance as I. Yet his deception was years in duration, and has

*killed me. Has killed us both. Not so swiftly as a knife, but with all the tenderness
of the conjugal bed.*

· **IV** ·

JERÖEN CAME HOME from school on spring holiday. Van Helsing loved
his son, a round-faced, laughter-filled, child of twelve. He had inherited his mother's fine intellect but none of her seriousness. Indeed, Van
Helsing frequently wondered where this happy stranger had come from.
He had a generous, affectionate nature totally at odds with Marieke's cool
reserve and his father's own awkward amiability.

"Papa!" Jeröen burst into the study without knocking.

The boy, three inches taller than when last Van Helsing had seen him,
gave him a tight hug and kiss on both cheeks. Van Helsing returned the
embrace firmly, then put both hands upon the boy's shoulders and studied him as intently as he would study a book. Too thin, Van Helsing
thought. The boy was growing too fast. Indeed, he needed new clothes,
for bony wrists jutted from his sleeves. One cuff bore a splatter of ink.
"How is school?" Van Helsing asked.

"I'm doing well in Latin," Jeröen said, rearranging the items on the
desk restlessly. "But Papa, don't you think Julius Caesar was a pompous
bore? I told my professor I thought so, and he went all purple. I thought
he would have an apoplexy right there and then. I told him he must come
to Amsterdam and see you, since you are the finest doctor in all the city,
the finest doctor in all the Low Countries."

Van Helsing laughed. He could not remember the last time he had felt
like laughing. He ruffled Jeröen's blond hair. "How many guilders do you
think to cozen out of me for that piece of flattery?"

Jeröen looked puzzled. "Not flattery, Papa. It's true. Everyone says so.
Do you mind if I don't become a doctor, Papa? I'll never be as good as
you, and to see people suffer—it quite makes me want to weep."

"A doctor's duty is to lessen suffering," Van Helsing said. "Still, you
needn't study medicine. There's always law."

Jeröen's face fell. Van Helsing laughed again. Compared to law, Caesar's *Commentaries* must seem the height of drama. Van Helsing squeezed

his son's shoulder. "Relax, my boy. You need not choose a suitable career this very instant. Go greet your mother and let me return to my work."

"But I have chosen a career, Papa. I should like to be an actor. We saw a production of *Hamlet* last month. It was terribly exciting."

Van Helsing concealed a smile. No father would permit his son to choose so disreputable a career, but within the month or week, he knew Jeröen would light on some other passion, as Marieke's butterflies flitted from blossom to blossom. Art might be next, or astronomy, or soldiering. "*Hamlet*, eh?" he said. "And the sufferings of the wretches in that sad play did not make you weep?"

"Oh, I wept bitterly at the end. But it was only pretend. Will you come and see me in a play when I am an actor?"

"I should be honored," Van Helsing said. "Now, go say hello to your mother. I think she's in the garden."

"One more question, Papa?"

"Just one?"

"How do you know when you are in love?" Jeröen's fair face had flushed a deep red, but his eyes, blue, wide-set, earnest, held a rare seriousness.

Van Helsing felt his own face stiffen into a blankly pleasant mask. "We can talk about that later," he said.

Jeröen quit the study with a quick grin. His son, Van Helsing reflected, had the effect of the sun bursting through a pall of clouds. And when the great orb disappeared into cloud again, all seemed darker and colder than before. "Love," Van Helsing said softly to himself.

Jeröen found me in my garden, trying to recapture the pleasures I had once known with my studies of Lepidoptera. My thoughts turned ever toward Caterina. I should have gone with her when she asked. Jeröen was old enough to get by without me. Van would always have his work.

Jeröen had sought out his father first. He always did. This pained me now, when it never had before. Had I not toiled in agony for hours to bring Jeröen into this world? And he goes first to the Great Deceiver?

"Papa says I may become an actor," he said, kissing my cheek.

I was sure Van had said nothing of the sort. "We are all of us actors," I said.

"Only the stage is lacking." I tapped his wrist, frowning. "You've stained your cuff."

"Yes, Mama. I'm sorry. I was careless."

He shifted from foot to foot. The boy could never keep from fidgeting, no matter how much he tried. I always forgot how exhausting he could be. "Be still," I said, more sharply than I intended. "You will startle the butterflies."

He tried. But soon his fingers plucked at his jacket, or drummed against my chair. "Why do you kill them?" he asked. "Aren't they prettier out here in the sun?"

"You sound like your father."

"Is he well? Papa seemed—I don't know—sad, somehow."

I admit to a total, irrational feeling of rage at this. Jeröen had no concern for my sadness. Weeks ago, I had a woman I loved and a husband I respected. Now I lacked both. Van and I existed in cold silence, each outcast from the other's affection and trust.

The bees droned, sucking nectar from the trailing vines of wisteria and honeysuckle. They did not worry me. I'd always found that if you remained still and did not annoy them, the bees would reciprocate.

"Mama?"

One bee buzzed close by, and Jeröen batted at it nervously.

"Will you not be still?" I shouted.

The bee darted at Jeröen, stung him where pale throat met starched collar. Jeröen slapped at his neck, frantic, and gave a howl of pain. Uncharitably, I wished my son were made of sterner stuff. I did not realize the seriousness of the matter.

Jeröen collapsed, still clawing at his throat. The sting had made a great welt, and his face was swelling horribly. He gasped, seemed unable to catch his breath. I screamed to the servants to send my husband to me at once, knelt to loosen Jeröen's collar. I scraped the stinger away with my fingernail, held my boy's head upon my lap. His eyes were wide and terrified. "Shhh," I told him, brushing the hair back from his brow. "Your father is coming."

Van arrived quickly. The color left his face as he saw Jeröen's state. He swept the boy into his arms and carried him to his study. I hurried after.

He lay Jeröen upon the settee, took his pulse. Jeröen fought for every breath. His skin grew clammy beneath my anxious fingers. "Do something," I said. Why was the oh-so-famous Doctor Van Helsing dithering while his son lay dying? The great hands trembled. The brilliant eyes held uncertainty and panic. He did not know what to do.

Months have passed, and I believe now there was nothing he could have done. God took our boy to punish us both. But I hated my husband then, a hate that solidified with every tortured gasp Jeröen took.

Those gasps ceased. Five minutes only had lapsed between the sting and my son's death. Some form of shock, it was. A rare intolerance to the bee's venom. And I saw in Van's eyes that he blamed me as much as I blamed him. My garden, my insects, after all.

Van grieved as much as I. He threw himself into his work, closeted himself in his study. We became living ghosts, and neither of us sought to comfort the other.

I thought Caterina would return and take me away from this hell of grief and guilt, but she did not. So I brooded, and imagined the syphilis biting into my bones, my heart, my brain, like a caterpillar devouring a cabbage leaf. The flesh fell from my bones like water. My eyes hated the light. My hands, claws now, trembled with weakness. My handwriting, once fine, firm, became nearly illegible.

When Van finally noticed how spectral I had become, he ordered me forcibly fed. The servants bound me and ran a tube down my throat, poured broth into me through a funnel. I struggled and gagged and wept, but the disgusting violation was repeated daily. I grew convinced that Van meant to poison me in this fashion. After all, how far a stretch is it from mercury in sweets to arsenic in broth? Of course, I realize now that if he really wanted to murder me, he need have done nothing but leave me to my slow starvation.

· V ·

1870

A DAMP, DRIZZLY DAY. A busy day, weather notwithstanding. Van Helsing had spent the morning seeing patients at the almshouse, the afternoon performing a dissection for the medical students, revealing for their edification advanced disease of the aorta, undoubtedly the result of tertiary syphilis. He had a touch of catarrh, which the weather did not improve. The lecture left him hoarse.

He could have hired a cab to take him home from the operating theater, but the gloom suited him and he decided to walk. He moved slowly, for rain made the cobblestones slippery. He bowed his head against the cold drizzle and against a grief that had continued undiminished since Jeröen's death a year ago this day.

The boy would have been thirteen now. At least Jeröen had gone to God an innocent, uncorrupted by carnality.

A bee sting. God, the irony. That such a small, beneficent creature, pollinator of flowers, maker of healthful honey and beeswax, a creature whose very name had become synonymous with useful industry, that such an insect should be the instrument of death to his only son—it was almost too much to be borne. And he, Van Helsing, physician of some note, though not as renowned as Jeröen had believed, had been as helpless as any other father to ease the swelling of the tortured throat, the wheezing of the labored lungs.

Nor could he forget Marieke's expression, no matter how much he tried. Without words she seemed to say, "Well, I knew you were not much of a man, but I thought you were at least a great doctor. Now I know you are neither."

Van Helsing lifted the latch of the iron gate, stepped into the cemetery. The grass squelched beneath his feet. He had no difficulty finding the grave. He visited often.

He traced his fingers over the carved letters, the cold of the stone penetrating deep in spite of his gloves. *Jeröen Ambrosius Van Helsing, 1857–1869, Beloved Son.*

Van Helsing took off his hat, the excess water cascading from the brim. "Hello, Jeröen," he said. "Your mother would visit, if she could. She— she—" He drew a ragged breath, fighting tears. He plucked a handkerchief from within his coat. He coughed into the square of fabric, studied the mucus with a critical eye, wiped his nose, wadded the handkerchief, and stuffed it into his pocket. Water dripped inside his collar. He shivered. "She is getting better." That was not quite a lie. She had *seemed* better. Pliant blankness was an improvement over naked hate, was it not? And they took very good care of her at the asylum.

"I've been invited to London. To teach at the Royal Academy of Surgeons. A great honor, but I've not yet accepted. I—I don't like the thought of leaving Amsterdam, leaving you, leaving your mother.

"I never answered your question that last day, did I? I thought we would have so much time, you see. I'm sorry. How do you know when you love someone? For me, it came like a sickness. When I would be near your mother, I felt as though dozens of her damned butterflies had flown into my stomach. I never knew if I was going to laugh or retch. And then one day the butterflies stopped. It hurts, my boy. It hurts so very much."

He put his sodden hat upon his head. "It grows late. We will talk again." Van Helsing turned away, tears blinding him as much as the worsening rain. He felt a sensation in his right hand, as if someone had placed a hand in his and squeezed it once. Ah, he was tired and unwell. The mind played tricks.

He arrived home thoroughly soaked and chilled. He took no supper, in spite of his housekeeper's remonstrance. The servants knew what day it was, and had grown accustomed to his eccentricities. He did accept a towel and dry dressing gown from his valet. In spite of the generous blaze of the fire, more *jenever* than was perhaps good for him, and an extra shawl draped about his shoulders as he bent over his desk, he could not seem to banish the chill. He stared at the notes for the monograph he was writing on the evolution of brain matter. He was in no mood for it tonight.

A pain had begun behind his eyes. His chest felt tight. His throat, uncomfortably raw all day, now felt constricted, inflamed.

He should just seek his bed. Rest was a better medicine than any tonic, bolus, or salve in his cabinet. His eye fell upon the letter from the Royal Academy. He should write, decline their kind offer. After all, what use could he be to them, he who could not even cure himself of the catarrh? He thrust the letter into the pocket of his dressing gown.

He rose, fought a momentary dizziness, no doubt the result of too much *jenever* on an empty stomach. He banked the fire, turned down the lamps, all but one. This he carried into the tiny adjoining room that still served him for bedchamber.

He'd reduced the household to three servants. He had no need of so large a dwelling. For one man—it was extravagant. He should sell, move to more modest quarters near the hospital.

Or take that post in England. Fly from this house with its attendant memories and grief. Longingly, he fingered the letter in his pocket. Let

England ease the weight of a mad wife, a dead child, the bitterness of all his failures.

Yet how could he leave the house where he and Marieke had been so happy, even if that happiness had proven illusion only? How could he abandon the walls that had witnessed the birth and death of his son?

For the rooms rang with Jeröen's absent footfalls, fragments of re-membered chatter, echoes of laughter. The boy seemed as much a part of the house as brick, tile, or plaster.

Van Helsing put the lamp upon a narrow table, removed his spectacles, climbed beneath the cool, crisp sheets with a sigh.

He woke sometime past midnight. He had heard a strange noise. He lay quite still, holding the wheeze of his breath a moment, the better to tell if the noise came again.

So slight a sound, he might have dreamed it. A sort of scrape or hollow knock. He rose, fumbled for his spectacles.

His pillow was soaked with sweat, and his nightclothes clung damply to him. He shivered as the night air, so great a contrast from his over-heated bed, plucked at him. The smell of his sweat reminded him of fried potatoes. He was thirsty, but his throat felt so hot and painful, he did not think he would be able to swallow. Indeed, his own spittle conspired to choke him.

A warm salt-water gargle would help, perhaps. Once he had investi-gated the mysterious sound.

He lit the wick of the lamp, turned the flame high in spite of the stab-bing pain the brightness brought his eyes. He placed the globe back over the wick, lifted the lamp, and crossed to his study.

A thud of something falling to the rug, and a softer sound, a wordless rhythmic whispering, unlike anything he had ever heard before. Halluci-nation, he thought. A product of fever.

For no one was in the room. All looked mostly as he had left it. Oh, the framed purple emperor butterfly Marieke had given him as a wedding gift had tumbled inexplicably from the corner of his desk, but that was all.

He stooped, curled his fingers around the dark wooden frame, the cool oval of convex glass. He was dismayed to note the glass had cracked. The specimen itself remained undamaged, very secure upon its pin.

The wings moved.

Van Helsing nearly dropped the frame in startlement. Wings fluttered slowly and then with increased agitation, brushing against the glass. Whispering.

Impossible. The thing was dead. Had been dead for at least fifteen years, for this was the same *apatura iris* Marieke had been mounting the day he had proposed to her. Dead things did not live again.

Seizing a letter opener from his desk drawer, he pried the back from the frame, lifted off the ruined glass. The wings fluttered even more madly now. Van Helsing seized the pin, pulled it free of the board, free of the thorax of the impossibly reanimated butterfly. The purple emperor lifted in flight, circled the glow of the lamp, disappeared into the shadows of dark beams overhead.

Van Helsing seized the lamp, opened the door of his study, climbed the narrow, curving stairs, his hand damp upon the polished balustrade. More frames, more brightly painted wings in airless struggle. The frames, ornate as any housing a Rembrandt or Hals, banged against floral wallpaper, tilted on their hooks. Wings. Small, large, bright, dull, European native or tropical exotic shipped from Brazil, Sumatra, the Congo. Azure, green, gold, spotted, streaked, splotched, delicately veined swallowtail, muddy-colored wood nymph. Wings battered against glass and screamed. Screamed.

Van Helsing broke the glass, plucked the pins away, felt blood ooze in sticky red from his fingers, but did not care. He barely registered the glass slicing into fingertips, palms, the backs of his hands. He grasped each pin, pulled it free. Wings lifted, fluttered about him, lit upon his nightshirt, his hair, walked upon exposed skin with a strange, light suction, like a hundred kisses.

He raced up the stairs in the dark, lamp forgotten. He knew the way, knew he must free them all, the thousands of souls Marieke had collected for so long. He smashed the cases in her study. A cloud of butterflies surrounded him. Wings cooled his fevered flesh, whispered, whispered.

He spun about the room, heedless of the glass beneath his bare feet. Dark. Dark. He could not see. He fumbled for the window catch, swung the mullioned glass inward, threw open the wooden shutters. The rain had stopped. A cold moonlight spilled on him.

He danced with Marieke's butterflies, felt their soft caress against his swollen throat, his lips, his eyelids, the thinly fleshed bones of his ankles. He whirled with them, laughed in euphoric delight. He could fly with them. Fly.

Dizzy, fighting now for breath, he stumbled. Prisoned by his bulk once more, he sank to his knees. Alas, to remain earthbound, trapped in coarse clay. The butterflies streamed over him before winging away into the cool night. So many. *Death had undone so many. More things in heaven and earth*. Marieke would be angry.

He rolled onto his back, watched the butterflies flutter out the open window. A last one, the purple emperor, paused, flitted about his head, as it had earlier circled the lamp's light. "Jeröen," Van Helsing said, his voice little more than a whisper from his sore throat. Nonsense. The butterfly was older than Jeröen had been at death. Yet it pleased him to imagine his son's soul a tangible thing, and free; pleased him, too, that this one above all others seemed reluctant to leave him, kept hovering protectively, as if it forgave him all his follies. "Go," he said. "You mustn't worry about me."

· VI ·

*I*T'S A YEAR *now since Jeröen's death. I think. It is difficult to keep time in an asylum.*

It's not so dreadful here, except they won't let me have any books. The learned doctors believe it was books drove me mad. The feminine mind should not be over-stimulated. Rubbish. I will ask Van to make them reconsider.

He visits me every Sunday after Church. After Mass, I should say. Van converted recently. The Church gives him comfort. He even wears a cross about his neck. The idolatry of it offends me. But Dutch Reformed or Papist, it matters not. I have no use for a God that will murder a child to punish the parent.

There is a certain liberation in madness. One can say what one thinks. I have even learned to swear.

But I have been good of late. Quiet. They believe I am vastly improved.

Not that they would say so to me. Learned men do not converse with mad-

women. Learned men do not converse with women, mad or not. At least Van was different in that regard.

On his last visit, he told me my butterflies were gone. He said he wanted to prepare me, so I would not be unduly upset when I came home. It was the first time he had spoken of my coming home.

"Gone?" I asked.

"I set them free." He spoke very softly and took my hand. Scabs marred his palms and the backs of his hands, felt rough upon my skin. How they must have bled.

"It was wrong to imprison them," he said. "You do see that?"

I frowned, puzzled. "Are you talking about the butterflies in the garden?"

"No, Marieke. The ones upon the wall. They've all flown away."

"Husband," I said, "those butterflies are dead. The dead do not fly." How is it, I wondered, that I am in an asylum and my husband is not?

"It was a miracle," he said. "I think perhaps Jeröen's spirit had something to do with it."

I pulled my hand away. The syphilis had begun to eat his brain, I decided. It hurt to hear my son's name upon his lips.

I remembered Caterina's final kiss, remembered the taste of blood. I imagined Van's blood flowing into my mouth, filling me, all heat and salt and copper. The thought made me smile.

Van smiled back and I had to suppress a laugh. Poor fool.

"I will not be able to visit you for a little while, but I will write you from London." He kissed me, very sweetly, upon my brow.

I knew what I must do. I had been foolish to think Caterina would return for me. I must prove myself worthy, free myself from my prison. I will drink the blood of evil men.

Van I will spare, for Jeröen's memory, for remembrance of love. In spite of his deception, his disease, his ineptitude, his chocolates, he is a kindly man. But there are others. Like the new orderly who forces himself upon the charity cases. He is a brute. I will have no difficulty seducing him. He will not live long enough to know the gnawing of the syphilitic caterpillar. I will take his seed into my womb, and his blood into my mouth. My skin will run with blue flame. I will burst from the constricting chrysalis of this despised female form a fearsome avenger. I will glut myself on the red nectar. True, I have not Caterina's fangs, not yet. After I drink, perhaps. Or after I die. And then they will fear me.

The Infestation at Ralls

Thomas Tessier

After the unpleasant incident in Regensburg, Van Helsing returned to his home in Amsterdam but stayed only two nights before journeying on to London. He was still angry and shaken, and he felt an urgent need to escape the European mainland, at least for a little while. He believed that a dose of England and his dear English friends would soon restore his spirits and his will—as indeed it did. Within a matter of a few days his nerves settled down and his better humor was in evidence once again.

Late the following week Van Helsing traveled to Margate to spend a few days with his former colleague and longtime friend, Dr. Matthew Pollard. They had not seen each other in nearly three years. Pollard had moved from London and gone into semiretirement, more out of personal inclination than in any bow to the exigencies of age—he was still a healthy, vigorous man. Pollard had a curious, open outlook and a lively intelligence. He was quite familiar with Van Helsing's unique perspective on life and the struggles of this world, and he was sympathetic to it in the main.

Beyond Herne Bay, just a couple of miles from Margate itself, the train stopped at a tiny, unmanned station. The windows were broken, slate tiles had been torn from the roof, and the grounds were strewn with clumps of litter, green leaves, small branches and countless twigs. All of this, no doubt, was the result of the unusually fierce thunderstorm that had blasted through the immediate area two days earlier. The storm had skirted clear of London, but Van Helsing saw a brief report in one of the papers about the swath of wind and flood damage it had caused in the southeast.

The platform was deserted, with no one waiting to board the train or to greet an arriving passenger. Nor did anyone step off at this battered destination. The name on the sign was Ralls, which Van Helsing thought he had heard before, although he could not summon any precise recollection to mind. The train idled there for a minute or two and then continued on to Margate. Pollard was at the station to greet Van Helsing. They dined at a very agreeable chophouse in town that evening, and they continued talking well past midnight in the warm comfort of Pollard's book-lined sitting room.

In the morning, after a fine breakfast prepared by Pollard's housekeeper, the two men were about to set off on a stroll about the town, including a visit to a dealer in rare books and private manuscripts, when a breathless lad appeared at the door. Pollard clearly knew him, and sighed.

"What is it, Harry?"

"Mr. Wingrove, sir. Asks you to come right away. Urgent, he said to tell you. Sent me in the carriage to bring you."

"I cleared the day, and now this," Pollard said to Van Helsing. He picked up his medical bag. "I'm afraid I must attend to it. Do you want to potter about on your own and we'll meet here later, or accompany me on this errand?"

"Of course I'll come with you," Van Helsing replied. "Then we may carry on as we had planned, all going well."

As they rode away from the center of Margate, Pollard explained that his medical duties, though now reduced in time and number of patients, included treating any illnesses or injuries that occurred among the resident staff and pupils at the Ralls School for Young Ladies. Ah yes, Van Helsing thought. No doubt Pollard had mentioned Ralls to him sometime in the past, and that was why the name seemed familiar to him at the train stop.

Situated in the former country home of a wealthy family that had died out years before, the Ralls School accepted a small, select group of girls each year and taught them how to be interesting. The emphasis was on a *useful* knowledge of the arts, history, world events and social behavior—especially the latter, which included the art of conversation and how to be just witty and vivacious enough. The young ladies were the daughters of nobility and privilege, diplomats and statesmen, occasionally of mere politicians or captains of industry. They were supposed to win and marry sons of the same, and the Ralls School was meant to increase their over-all attractiveness.

"They tend to be highly strung. Too much expectation."

Van Helsing nodded, smiling. "From within and without."

"Exactly."

"But you do enjoy this work?"

It was as much a challenge as a question, and Pollard recognized that. He didn't answer for a moment. "Bram, sometimes, often, I think everything is both interesting and uninteresting in more or less equal measure."

Van Helsing didn't respond, and the rest of the journey elapsed in silence. Soon the carriage passed through open gates in a high stone wall. Minutes later, the Ralls estate appeared ahead of them. The main house was a familiar model of the English country home, a long two-storey rectangle, two wings attached to the central, communal rooms. There were a few outbuildings, one of which caught Van Helsing's attention—a church. It was small, no doubt originally the family's chapel, but its exterior had been built as a precise replica of a Gothic cathedral. The detail was impressive. Those who have wealth often indulge in such follies. Van Helsing found it not without a certain endearing quality, the orphan of a lost idea. It appeared that a corner of the roof had collapsed, and three workmen were struggling with pieces of broken stone to repair it.

A round man with a round head, Dean Wingrove greeted them anxiously at the bottom of the front steps. Van Helsing wasn't sure if Dean was the man's first name or his title. He had wispy white hair, and he dabbed a cloth at the perspiration on his brow. He quickly led them inside to his office. He accepted Van Helsing's presence as easily as if Van Helsing were not there at all, ignoring him. Wingrove settled himself behind his desk. He tried to speak calmly, but it soon turned into an anxious torrent of words.

"Charles, one of our young ladies, Miss Emily Barber, confided in a friend of hers, another of our young ladies, that she was carnally assaulted two or three nights ago. In her room, in her bed. The friend saw certain signs, blood on the bedclothes, bruises and scratches on Miss Barber's limbs, some swelling in her face, and a change in her usual manner. The past two days, Miss Barber kept to herself in her room, attributing it to her time of the month. Earlier this morning, Matron and some of the young ladies who live in the adjoining rooms heard Miss Barber moaning and crying. Matron investigated. Something is wrong, seriously wrong. Miss Barber is now showing."

Pollard was momentarily confused. "Showing what?"

"*Showing*," Wingrove answered in a stifled screech.

"That's impossible," Pollard said with sudden impatience. "She may be showing, but it's not from any assault that occurred the night before last. It could only be from some previous—event."

"And I tell you," Wingrove went on, "that a few days ago Miss Barber's physique was perfectly trim, even sylphlike. Her build is naturally slender as it is. There was no suggestion of roundness in her—in that region. Everyone here will tell you that, including Matron and the other students. The ladies each have their own room, but living in the same part of the house together, they inevitably see one another in states of partial dress at times."

"How much is she showing?" Pollard asked.

Wingrove swallowed hard. "Matron says it is as if Miss Barber were in her sixth or seventh month."

"Good Lord—that much in just a few days?" Pollard shook his head. "It may be that her imagination has run riot. Certain people do imagine attacks or other experiences with such vivid immediacy that, unknowingly, they produce the very signs of it on their own person. And certain women do become so convinced they are with child that their bodies act as if they were, though they are not."

"Doctor, I pray you are correct in that."

"Or it could be," Van Helsing now suggested in a grave tone, "that some other terrible but genuine affliction has befallen Miss Barber. Please, my dear sir, take us to her immediately."

They went to the upper floor of the wing opposite the one that housed the students. Miss Barber was isolated in a room there. Wingrove summoned Matron, who was sitting watch at the girl's bedside. A stout, middle-aged woman with a worried expression, she stepped into the corridor.

"Any change?" Wingrove asked anxiously.

"Yes, sir. She's bigger."

"God help us."

"She sleeps fitfully, wakes for a while, then drifts off again."

"Matron, the doctor must examine Miss Barber now. I will need you back here again in forty-five minutes."

As the Matron left, the three men entered the room and closed the door. Miss Barber's eyes widened when she saw them. She was on a narrow bed, reclining on a bank of thick pillows at the headboard. Her legs were splayed out beneath a sheet and a thin blanket. She was indeed quite petite, but for her belly, which was alarmingly evident.

"Miss Emily, how are you feeling now?"

"Big," she replied with a laughing groan, like a child who has eaten too much. "Very, very big."

"Yes, well," Wingrove continued, "that's why we're here. This is Doctor Pollard, our school physician, and his associate, Doctor Hazelton."

"Van Helsing," Pollard corrected.

"Van Helsing. I do apologize, sir. Now, Miss Emily, the good doctors are going to ask you a few questions and examine you. Please cooperate and answer them as fully as you can, so that they may prescribe the best treatment to relieve you of this—condition."

She stared at him in disbelief for a few seconds and then began to laugh. Pollard ushered Wingrove out of the room. When the girl stopped laughing, she regarded Pollard and Van Helsing with wary interest. Pollard placed the back of his hand to her forehead and then to her cheeks.

"Normal, low-normal."

While Pollard checked the girl's eyes and throat, Van Helsing pulled a small wooden chair around to the other side of the bed and sat down on it. He leaned closer. Pollard had his stethoscope out and was about to listen to Miss Emily's heartbeat.

"Matthew, open the top of her nightdress."

Pollard did so and then listened intently.

"Strong, regular. Racing a bit."

"But what do you see?" Van Helsing asked.

Pollard was surprised, then puzzled. "What do I see?"

"Matthew, expose her breasts."

Miss Emily observed this with a look of detached curiosity on her face, as if it were all happening to someone else. Pollard undid more buttons and pulled the upper part of Miss Emily's white garment wide open. The girl's breasts were small but perfectly formed, with flat, pale pink nipples.

"Aha, no lactation," Pollard said. "No engorgement."

Van Helsing nodded approvingly. "So we see."

Now Pollard pulled up the lower portion of the nightdress and moved his stethoscope from one spot to another on her abdomen, listening carefully. Miss Emily's navel was almost completely flattened out by the bulging of her flesh. A minute later, Van Helsing took the instrument and listened.

"Nothing, right?"

"Agreed," Van Helsing answered. "Nothing at all."

"You're both wrong!" Miss Emily's loud outburst startled both men, and she laughed. "There's three of them, and you'll meet them soon enough. Sooner than you may think. Why don't you do your job properly, Doctor, and see if I'm telling you a lie or not?"

"I was about to do so, Miss," Pollard replied sharply.

The girl laughed again. "Be careful! They bite!"

Pollard removed a pouch of antiseptic cloths from his bag and washed his hands with one of them. He reached between Miss Emily's open legs. Several seconds later, he cleaned his hands again and led Van Helsing out of the room. Wingrove approached, but Pollard waved him away, taking Van Helsing down to the far end of the corridor.

"It's not a matter of months or days, it's a matter of hours. Tonight, or in the early hours of the morning, I should say."

"Ah, remarkable," Van Helsing said in a low voice.

"But what is it? Not a foetus, not even a dead one. How could she grow so large, as if with child, in a matter of a few days?"

"Perhaps an unnatural growth in the uterus."

"What, a cyst?" Pollard asked in disbelief. "That large?"

"Or something similar to a cyst," Van Helsing said. "A fibrous body, an errant growth, some malformation of tissue that reached a certain point, a certain degree of mass, and thereby caused this rapid and inordinate swelling in reaction, as her body prepares to expel it."

"Then she should be removed to hospital," Pollard said.

Van Helsing shook his head doubtfully. "But we don't know for certain. If this guess proves to be incorrect, a hospital might only make matters worse, far worse. Here, you maintain complete control, without any risk of interference on the part of others. You must also consider whether the rigors of a journey might exacerbate her condition or even precipitate disaster." Pollard nodded. "Do you have a nurse you can rely on in service?"

"Yes. Miss Feeney. In the town."

"Perhaps you should instruct Mr. Dean Wingrove to send the boy Harry in the carriage to find Miss Feeney and bring her here. Also to give him a list of any supplies you may want her to bring. We have some time yet, if you decide Miss Emily must be moved, but you should prepare to act here."

"Yes, I quite agree. Wingrove needs a bracing, too."

"While you are attending to these matters, I wish to speak again with Miss Emily. Perhaps I can learn something more that will help us."

Pollard nodded once and went off to deal with Wingrove. Van Helsing found that Miss Emily was now drifting in and out of consciousness. But when she noticed his presence, her eyes brightened and she came awake.

"Miss Emily," he said, smiling at her.

"Are you the Jew?"

Van Helsing was hit by an unexpected wave of emotion—surprise, anger and disappointment—but his features remained impassive.

"No, my dear. I am a Christian man," he said. "But please tell me, what made you ask such a question?"

She gave a slight shrug. "Someone."

"Someone? Who?"

"I can't remember. I heard someone say it."

"Say what? That I'm a Jew?"

"Well, no. Not necessarily you."

"My dear Miss Emily," Van Helsing said, allowing an indulgent smile to show at the corners of his mouth, "I am an old man. Please explain and clarify for me, so I understand exactly."

"Oh, you're not so old," Emily responded. "You are *older*, I will say that. But you don't look old. Your friend looks old. His hair is white, yours still has a strong color about it. A manly color."

Van Helsing laughed gently. "Lined with silver."

"It makes you look distinguished, sir." She changed her voice for the last sentence, so that she suddenly sounded like an adoring and compliant schoolgirl of fourteen who was infatuated with her poetry tutor.

"Miss Emily, please. I insist you answer my question."

"Yes, sir," she said immediately, continuing in the same affected girlish voice. "Someone said that a Jew was coming here to Ralls on a mission of great and terrible importance."

"What would that be?"

"To kill us."

"To kill you. Dear God. You say *us*. You and who else?"

"Us, sir. All of us."

"Why would someone kill you—any of you?"

"Because."

"Because is not a reason."

"Yes it is, sir. Because. *Be cause*."

He gazed evenly at Miss Emily but said nothing more for a moment. In the matter of conversing with young ladies, Van Helsing's patience was vast, but the present situation allowed no time for the game of pleasant dawdling.

"Please tell me what happened to you."

He expected a show of reluctance, but Miss Emily surprised him again. She pulled herself up a little more on the bed, eagerness flaring in her eyes. Her nightdress still hung partly open. Van Helsing regarded her keenly.

"I can tell you because we are alone," she said, "and I can see in your eyes that your interest is in *me*."

"You see well, and correctly."

"The storm passed early in the evening," she continued. "It was fearsome and beautiful in equal measure. So much lightning, such brilliant displays, purple or bluish-white daggers stabbing the air. It even blasted away part of our church. The thunder was deafening at times, the windows hummed and we thought they would explode! The rain sounded like thousands of tiny pebbles hurled at the glass again and again, one volley after another. From the front entrance we could see it spattering up gobs of muddy gravel on the drive."

Miss Emily paused a second to catch her breath, and then went on. "The air was so sweet and clean afterward, a delicious taste. The temperature was cool but not unpleasant, so I left my window open when I retired for the night. In the darkness, some hours later, My Lord came to me through that window. He scaled the wall and possessed me. I could not resist, nor did I wish to do so."

The expression on her face was proud and defiant.

"Who is he?" Van Helsing asked.

"I could see little of his features, but he was *beautiful*. His skin was like leather, his body far stronger than a man's. His tongue was long and thin, but wonderful in the sensations it awoke within me. His male part was as large as I could bear, and it was as smooth and hard as polished stone. Doctor, I adore him. And I bear the fruit of his seed."

"I ask you again. Who is he?"

"One of those blind to God's light. Set free!"

"Miss Emily—"

"Look, Jew!"

She pulled the blanket and sheet aside, tugged the hem of her nightdress up until the round expanse of her belly was visible. Van Helsing stared at her and he saw the movement in her flesh, like a strong ripple in placid water. He put his hand on it and felt its kick, its strength. Miss Emily smiled boldly at him, but her eyes closed almost at once and her head fell back on the pillows. After a moment in which Van Helsing sat still, watching as she breathed quickly, her body tossing restlessly, he put her clothing back in place, covered her again with the sheet and blanket, and left the room.

In the corridor, Matron approached. Van Helsing told her to resume her bedside vigil. He also asked her how he could find Miss Emily's room. It was on the same floor, but in the opposite wing. Van Helsing made his way there and let himself in. It was not large, but comfortable, by no means spartan. After a quick look around, he went to the window. A simple latch to open it, a spiked arm to hold it in place. He leaned out and looked down. Two floors below, the ground fell away sharply from the house, providing insufficient angle and hold for a long ladder. The construction of the exterior wall was such that any man would find it exceedingly difficult, if not impossible, to climb. Van Helsing looked closer at the stonework immediately beneath the window. He saw separate rows of thin but clear and sharply incised lines at certain intervals. He turned and leaned out of the window so that he could look upward. He saw the same scattered marks on the stone above, shallow but unmistakable.

Finally, Van Helsing took in the general view from Miss Emily's window. The rolling, parklike grounds, the long gravel drive, the reflecting pond, and the church. For a moment, he watched the workmen in the distance. They stared at pieces of broken stone on the grass, stared once again at the damaged corner of the church roof, and then conferred among themselves.

It seemed likely that Wingrove and Pollard could be found in Wingrove's office, but Van Helsing was in no mood to join them yet. He made his way down the stairs, out of the building, onto the grounds, and he walked toward the church. He sat down on a flat, protruding rock near a clump of birches and lit a cigarette. His hand shook. He watched the workmen beside the church.

In Regensburg he had encountered evil masquerading as reason and enlightenment. Van Helsing had been invited to address the philosophy faculty. He had nearly reached the midpoint of his discourse on the many guises of evil in the present time when some of the students—and teachers, he recalled bitterly—began to chant and shout at him, accusing him of promoting old superstitions and "Jewish thought." He was "a Jew" or "a Jew-lover," who wanted to drag Europe back into the Dark Ages. Van

Helsing's heart felt crushed to hear such things in a Faculty of Philosophy. His attempts to answer them were lost in the growing derisive clamor. They were blind to their own ignorance and unreason. Finally, he abandoned his futile efforts to communicate with them and walked out of the lecture hall.

Evil came in many shapes and guises, sometimes human and sometimes other than human. Christians and Jews were allies in the struggle against evil, but the ancient division between them was the devil's own playground. Evil nurtured the growth of ignorance, fear and suspicion, the better to spread hatred across the face of the land and turn the day itself into unending night.

Was it a coincidence that Miss Emily asked him if he was a Jew, so soon after his bitter experience at Regensburg? Or was the demon who possessed her speaking through her, taking the measure of Van Helsing and trying to stir up a turmoil of emotions within him, thereby distracting him and diffusing the precise focus of his attention? He could not allow it.

Van Helsing stood up and crossed the lawn to the church. He gazed down at the scattered pieces of broken stone. He slowly walked around the church from one side to the other and back to his starting point, studying it closely. He was again quite impressed by the fineness of all the Gothic detail incorporated in the outer structure. There was no need to look inside.

"There you are!" Pollard approached. "What are you doing? I looked for you throughout the building. I'm concerned—"

"Matthew, look here," Van Helsing interrupted, pointing to the damaged area of the church. "In the storm, a lightning bolt struck there, and it shattered a stone gargoyle similar to the ones positioned at the other three corners. As you know, in times gone by there were fervent and devoted members of the faithful who believed that using such stonework served to trap and imprison local demons as firmly as if they were in the grip of God Himself."

Pollard stared, thinking for a moment. "You're not suggesting—"

"I am stating it to you. Evil can take many different forms. It hides now because the light of day blinds it. But it will emerge again, soon, and its spawn is what grows within poor Miss Emily."

Pollard struggled visibly within himself. "My instinct is to reject what you say, but I know better than to doubt you. If you're wrong, it won't matter, as we would treat Miss Emily to the utmost of our abilities in any event. If you're right, what action must we take?"

"First, we shall hunt down and destroy the beast. We have time yet, but we must hurry and do it. He cannot flee into daylight."

"But, where?"

Van Helsing pointed to the main house. "You can see one small window there, and another there, just below the line of the roof. An attic."

In Wingrove's office they learned that there was indeed an attic floor at the top of the house. Wingrove did not accept that "an intruder," as Van Helsing put it, could be hiding there, because only one door provided access, it was kept locked, and Wingrove had the only key. Nonetheless, he agreed to let them conduct a search. He reluctantly complied with Van Helsing's further request for the help of the three workmen outside and the provision of whatever weapons might be at hand on the estate. Within the hour the group was assembled. Two of the men had pitchforks, the third a shotgun. Van Helsing and Pollard took hatchets. Each of the five also carried an oil lamp, burning at its brightest.

The staff had already been directed to take the students to a garden that was set away from the house. They were to remain there until Wingrove sent for them. The only other people left in the house were Matron and Miss Emily, who were locked in the same room. Van Helsing instructed Wingrove to lock the attic door behind them and to open it only if he was certain he recognized the voice on the other side.

"Are there many windows in all?" Van Helsing asked.

"One or two on each side," Wingrove replied. "I can't remember, since we never use the space. The basement is adequate for our storage needs, and it's much easier to take things in and out of."

"You mean there is nothing in the attic?"

"Hardly anything, as I recall. The family whose home this was used it to store their mementoes and extra possessions, but all of that was removed before the school was established."

"Excellent," Van Helsing said. "This part will soon be done."

He led the party up the inner stairs and heard Wingrove dutifully lock the door below. They were in the central area between the two wings of the building. Empty, the attic seemed vast. It ran the entire length of the house, and the few low windows in it provided pockets of light that extended only a short distance inside. Most of the attic was cast in a murky grayness.

"Gentlemen, we should stay within a few paces of each other so that we can focus the strength of our lamps," Van Helsing told them. "We want to drive him into a corner. The light will blind him and allow us to complete our work. I caution you, the one we seek may not appear as any ordinary man, but you must not falter or turn away. Use your weapon well."

Van Helsing led the way and the group advanced slowly into the portion of the attic that was above the students' rooms. They had not gone very far when they heard a noise ahead of them, a vague scuffling. They immediately steered toward the area it seemed to come from, fanning out a little more but keeping the rays of their lamps in a tight focus. They heard a noise as of something running, off to the side and away from them.

"Quickly," Van Helsing shouted. "Cut him off!"

The men broke into a trot. A shape appeared at the edge of the light and then veered nimbly, circling back into the dark. Then the sound gained speed in a sharp burst, the sound of heavy leatherish feet loudly smacking bare floorboards. The men turned and tried to recover, but their quarry raced past them, beyond the reach of their light.

"He's going into the area above the other wing," Van Helsing said. "We must make better use of our lamps. The light blinds him, he fears it. Spread out more. When you hear him again, run toward him, but try to stay in front of the sound so as not to let him get past us again. If we can force him to run through us, not around us, then we have a chance to converge and spear him or trip him up with the forks."

They moved ahead steadily, their lamps now sweeping the entire area in front of them. They moved farther apart, forming a longer, looser line across the width of the attic. They passed the opening to the stairs again and a few moments later Van Helsing calculated that they were into the other wing. There was a rank odor in the air, like the stench of rotting animal flesh.

"Be ready," Van Helsing told them. "He must be close now."

Then they heard the sound. It came from a place directly ahead of them. It wasn't moving. It was a harsh breathing noise that conveyed a clear warning. It was softer and deeper than a hiss, similar to the throaty sound that certain Asian and African snakes are able to produce, but much stronger.

The demon leapt out of the darkness, charging them in a bounding motion, like a tiger. The shotgun blast did nothing to slow it, the pellets lodging in the surface of the thick hide. But the men with pitchforks set down their lamps and seized it, one by the upper leg and groin, the other by the shoulder and neck. They struggled to hold it as the creature lashed at them with arms that were long and surprisingly thin but tightly muscled.

Van Helsing jumped in and swung the hatchet at the gargoyle's skull, but it turned and the blade slashed less effectively along its prominent jaw. It was about the size of a small man, and it thrashed violently, at the same time letting out a hideous sound, a shrill high skirling wail. The man with the shotgun leaned in and fired again, this time the muzzle just inches from the demon's face, and the blast gouged a much deeper, circular wound. Dark liquid oozed out; the creature shrieked even more and continued to struggle. Van Helsing struck again and again with the hatchet, now aiming at the throat. He chopped through the tough outer skin, which was a mottled black and gray in coloration and beady in texture. He hacked at tendons as resistant as braided wire cables, through muscle layered in plates. Pollard dropped his hand ax to the floor and held his lamp close to the grotesque creature's face. The light revealed a pair of eyes like unmarked stone, full of wild nothingness. The demon's body did not stop moving until several minutes after Van Helsing had cut its head away completely.

"Observe the claws in its hands and feet," he said. "So strong and sharp it could scale a smooth stone wall as easily as a dog runs across a field." He set the head down beside the body, now still and lifeless. "You will find that one of the windows here is in need of repair."

"A fiend from Hell," one of the men gasped.

"Truly it is," another said in awe.

Van Helsing nodded. "And we have sent it back to Hell. You must wrap it in some cloth, remove it from here and burn it. Burn it until the last ember dies and then crush any pieces of bone that remain. Shovel up all the ashes into a pail and dump them into a river or stream—it must be running water. Tell no one of what you have seen and done here today. They would only believe you have lost your reason. God bless you, men."

Pollard stood nearby, gazing in fascination at the remains of the gargoyle. "And this beast was hiding here for three whole days since the storm, in the same building as Miss Emily—and the other young ladies." He turned anxiously to Van Helsing. "You don't think . . . ?"

"Let us hope not," Van Helsing said grimly. "Come along now, Matthew. Pick up your ax. The worst part of our work here remains to be done."

Downstairs, he spoke to Wingrove. "It would be better if you ask us no questions at this time. You must allow the workmen to finish what they are doing now, and do not interfere. When they leave, you may have the students and staff return and go about their normal business. Now please, dear sir, direct the lad Harry to bring some boards to the room where Miss Emily is; also a hammer and nails. If Harry has not returned with the nurse yet, bring those things yourself, as we need them without delay. Ah, and some rope and a knife as well, thank you. No, *please*. I will not discuss this now. For the sake of everybody, and for your school itself, you must do as I say."

Wingrove glanced down once more at the hatchet in Van Helsing's hand. The blade was wet with blackish gore and bits of gristle. He looked at Pollard, who simply nodded once. Wingrove hurried away.

The doctors found that Miss Emily's time was very near. Matron was asked to leave as soon as Nurse Feeney arrived. Pollard took her aside to let her know what to expect—she turned quite pale, but then nodded firmly. It was dark outside when Van Helsing finished boarding up the only window in the small room. He checked the lock on the door and found it adequate. Miss Emily was now in a state of restless delirium, her body twisting and shuddering. She cried and moaned in an unnerving high-pitched voice. Van Helsing cut two pieces of the rope and tied her wrists to the bedposts on the headboard to ensure that she would not be able to attack them.

"Keep your wits and remember this," he said quietly to Pollard and Nurse Feeney. "Whatever is born here tonight must not leave this room alive." Then he sat on the wooden chair beside the bed and watched the girl in silence.

Shortly after eight, Miss Emily's water broke—a sickly grayish fluid that gave off a foul smell. Layers of towels absorbed most of it. The girl shrieked and struggled against the ropes, kicking wildly. Pollard and the nurse each took hold of a leg and used their bodies to pin them back.

A black-speckled gray hand reached out of Miss Emily, dug its tiny claws into her flesh, drawing blood, and pulled itself from her body. The vile creature emerged quickly, about the size of a small dog, but with the grotesque look of a willfully deformed human. Van Helsing seized it before it was completely free of its host-mother and smashed it on the floor. Holding it down with his shoe, he cut it in half with one blow of the hatchet.

He turned back to the bed in time to see the second one leap at Pollard's face. The doctor fell away, screaming. Miss Emily began to kick her free leg at Nurse Feeney. Van Helsing stepped around the bed and snatched the gargoyle from Pollard's face—his cheek was torn and blood flowed from the ragged wounds. The second demon squirmed, bit and clawed savagely at Van Helsing's hand, but he despatched it as he had the first.

Then he swung the hatchet and hit Miss Emily in the head with the flat side of the blade, rendering her unconscious for the moment. The third beast was not yet free, emerging feet first. Van Helsing used a hand towel to grasp it and pull it out. He was horrified to see a mortal rush of blood pour out with the ugly creature, splashing into the air and onto the floor. The claws of both the demon's hands had clutched and dragged a portion of Miss Emily's entrails with it in its birth. Van Helsing hammered it several times, then turned the hatchet around and chopped it in two.

For a few moments the three of them stood as if stunned and paralyzed by what they had just seen and done, and by the ghastly remains around them. Whether it sprang out of the darkness to prey on the weak and innocent, as here at Ralls, or coiled its tendrils from within to shrivel and corrode the hearts of ordinary men, as at Regensburg, evil was the same—unforgiving, savage and utterly relentless in the pursuit of its own fulfillment. And what is that ultimate impulse of evil, Van Helsing thought, if not a profound, incalculable hatred of life itself? The days will dawn, the sun will still shine, but the invisible darkness will slowly leak through and gather strength, until it shows itself again.

He looked around. Nurse Feeney had been kicked several times but was not seriously injured. Pollard might bear scars, but he was not in danger. Van Helsing went to the bed and checked Miss Emily, though he already knew it was pointless; her heart had stopped beating.

Anna Lee

Kathe Koja

My name is Anna Harrington. I am sixteen years old, I will be seventeen next All Souls' Eve. I have lived in Whitby all my life. No, my father is dead. My mother—my mother, sir, is married to the verger of St. Mary's.

I have been in the employ of Mrs. Westenra for eight months, since I left employ with the Misses Foster, when— Why, I do not work in the kitchens, sir, peel spuds and empty slops, no. Pippa does that. I am lady's maid to Miss Lucy. I keep—kept—her things tidy, assisted in her *toilette;* I lay out her clothes—such pretty frocks, sir, you never saw, silk and lawn and brushed bombazine, throat lace as fine as cobwebs, all bedewed. She and I are of a size. Her dresses would have just fit me. You would not think so, to look at us? *Do* you look at a lady's maid, sir?

I am sorry. Pertness, yes. It was why I left the Misses Foster. They said I— Miss Lucy, yes, and her friend Miss Murray, who was stopping with the family. The night of the shipwreck storm, sir, I brought them both a tisane, a sweet tea drink, to soothe their fright. The waves were so loud, they sounded like boulders rumbling through the dark, the clouds like torn rags white against the black sky. We could not see the stars that night. Ellen—she is the parlormaid, sir, you spoke to her just before me—Ellen said they looked like unwaked souls, the souls of the damned rushing pell-mell off to doom. Ellen was that frightened, she begged me not to go up the hill. . . . To the churchyard, sir. I go when I can, for the view of it. From up there you can see the whole harbor, all the way to where Kettleness stretches out to the sea. I watch the boats, and think of where they might be sailing, far away from here. . . . Yes sir. Miss Lucy and Miss Murray shared a room, until Miss Murray left to join her fiancé. Both of them were to be married, Miss Murray and Miss Lucy. . . . I do not know, sir. She left us on the twentieth. I remember Miss Lucy saying that Miss Murray's fellow was ill with some sort of fever. I know Miss Murray was in a headlong rush to be gone.

Miss Lucy looked poorly after that, I thought. Missing her friend, maybe, but still— That pale she was, a haggard kind of look in the mornings, as if she'd tossed and turned all night. Pippa—the scullery girl— Pippa said she had heard noises, funny noises in the garden, but Ellen and I, we heard nothing. Nothing at all.

That was when Dr. Seward came. Such a lovely gentleman, and so handsome. And very clever—a doctor, yes, at the lunatic asylum. Fancy spending all your days with mad people! . . . Then *he* came, too. The foreign gentleman, Dr. Van Helsing, yes. Like him? No sir. I mean, he was a gentleman, sir, he— No, sir, I did not like him. His queer talk, his way of looking at you, staring with those heavy frowning brows—expecting you to drop whatever you were doing and rush off, find this, fetch that, kitchen shears and boiled water, snips of garden wire; and those awful flowers. White garlic is all they were, nothing special about that, even if they did come all the way from Amsterdam.

And then he must needs fix them to the windows, and rub them on the doors, and wind them like a horse necklace for Miss Lucy. Faugh! the smell! Worse than slops. It got in my hair, in my clothing, it clung like— No sir. Never. *Never* did I touch them; why should I? It was none of my affair. —But that was Mrs. Westenra, sir, at her orders! She ordered me and Ellen both to take them off the windows—the smell, she said, was making Miss Lucy worse. As well it might!

I did *not*, sir, and it's wicked to say so. I only wanted what was best for Miss Lucy. Ask Ellen if you don't believe me. We two begged Dr. Seward to speak with the foreign gentleman, that we might sit and watch through the night with her. But Dr. Van Helsing sent us away. As if *we*, who knew her, could not take better care of her than he. See what his care did for her in the end! And poor Mrs. Westenra, too, found like she was with those flowers in her hands, all wild-like with death—I screamed when I saw her, I couldn't help it. All night the dogs howling, and Pippa sniveling, and then Mrs. Westenra— We did for her what we could, we closed her eyes and covered her decent. Then Miss Lucy sent us for the sherry, to brace us up— Drink, sir? Oh no, sir. May be a drop of cider once or twice, but never sherry. Does a *verger's* house keep spirits to serve their guests? Or do they drink plain water, and weak tea, as befits a temperate churchman? . . . Once my father made us a punch for Christmas, boiled oranges, cinnamon, and wine, he even let me have a drop. And afterwards he and my mother danced, oh, you would have clapped your hands to see it. But now—it's why I took service, sir, God be my witness. Because it was like living in a coffin there, him with his weak tea and sweep the church and never you mind, missy, what's over the ocean, never you mind what's afoot in the dark! Just sweep and pray and keep the world turning. . . . The world! As if he'd ever seen it! My *father* was a sailor, sir, he was a mate on a cargo ship: the *Anna Lee*, it's what I'm named for. Anna Lee, like a girl in a fairy story, a princess in lace and silk. He used to take me to the churchyard and show me the sea. Mother says I was too small to remember, but I do. The water like black glass in the moonlight, the wind in the trees moving like fingers, beckoning— I *remember*. And my father saying, low in my ear, *Don't be afraid of the dark, Anna Lee. Never be afraid of the dark.*

And I am not, sir. And neither am I lying when I say that I would have sat up all night with Miss Lucy no matter what Pippa said, her bogeys and ghosts and midnight knockings, I am not afraid of— No, sir! *Anyone* could have drugged that drink! May be Dr. Van Helsing did it himself. I wouldn't put it past him. May be he wanted us out of the way, we the servants who loved Miss Lucy, may be he was the one who frightened Mrs. Westenra to death—oh, sir, if you had seen him! Shouting at us when we cried, why should we not cry for Mrs. Westenra? and we in our bedgowns still dazed and stumbling from the dreadful night, and the drugged drink, doing our best to get the fire going, and the water heated, with Pippa still snoring on the chaise where Dr. Seward set her down—was she asleep? or winking, so to get out of work? She's a liar, Pippa, don't believe a word she tells you. Even Ellen, steady as she is, might misremember—

I am *trying*, sir, I'm telling it all as best I can. The next thing I recall is Dr. Van Helsing standing over me, stabbing his finger in my face: *Who haff removed my flowers? Who haff broken the window, and so let the night inside?* Red-faced and roaring, like the verger, as if the night is anything to fear! I tried to tell him, to explain that we were sleeping, that none of us heard anything amiss until—the dogs, yes, but dogs will howl at anything, a stray cat, anything, and the rest was only Pippa's fancies. Until the window broke—and we had a time sifting the glass out of the carpet, I can tell you—we slept.

I? I sleep in the servants' quarters, same as Ellen. Pippa bunks in the kitchen, by the fire; or should. That night she was in with us. When I woke I found her snoring on the carpet, she— When the window broke, I said. We woke when the window— Oh. But seeing Pippa was just a blink, one eye open and closed again; I didn't stir. And it was that quiet, all shut up like a tomb, the windows and doors double-latched as if we were under siege or— The dogs? Sir, I don't know, all I know is that they were howling, they were— I meant quiet *inside*, sir. The house was quiet inside.

Mr. Morris? It was Ellen who let him in—I was busy boiling water, doing Pippa's job—I didn't see but a peep of him until later, when I brought him some wine and biscuits. Quite a gentleman, even if he is American. And handsome, too, though he was pale, from the, the giving of blood— the transfusion, yes. I heard them talking, down in the dining room— how could I not? Dr. Van Helsing was near-shouting: *We must haff another transfusion, but I fear to trust these women*—that's us, he meant, fear to trust *us*, who were that devoted to Miss Lucy. But Mr. Morris was there, so they took it from him instead. So much blood . . . And Dr. Van Helsing hunched over the bed, his fingers on her wrist, scowling at me from underneath those brows: *We need you not here. Go down!* Like an old gore-crow, like the verger, all in black and hissing to Dr. Seward: *Open the veins!* Blood on the sheets, dark spots on the white lawn pillowslip . . .

I'm sure I don't know, sir. It was the doctors' affair, not mine. . . . Pippa! Pippa is not to be trusted, she says anything that comes into her head, any wild story, *a nightwalker, a vampire! That's what they think is after Miss Lucy!* And Ellen crying and wringing her hands: *I'll not stay another night in this house, I'll go over my sister's in Kent*— Me, sir? Do I believe in such things? in hell and heaven, and the spirits who walk between? But how could I not believe in God, living so long with the verger? And if there is God, there is the devil. The verger taught me that, too. And I know from my own lost father that there is power in the darkness.

The little golden crucifix? Yes, I took it. Why should I not? She was— was gone by then, she had no more need of jewelry. And she had promised me a trinket, she had seen me so often admiring her things, turning over her pins and rings and ear-bobs and *Would you like one, Anna?* she had said. *When I am wed, I shall tell Mamma to give you something nice.* She had a bounty, why should she not share? Rich girl with all her jewels and silks, a rich fiancé too, Lord Godalming if you please, riding in a coach-and-four . . . And me left with nothing, *nothing,* no more position, even, with her dead and Mrs. Westenra dead, and me, what? out in the streets? Or back to the verger's? I would rather die.

What are you asking? Did I alter the sherry, remove the stinking garlic, let him in? Am I the one? Now, did you deduce all that yourself, sir, or did you have it straight from Dr. Van Helsing? Shaking that little cross in my face, calling me names: *worthless wretch, robber of the dead and the living* and *You wish he haff come for you, no? You want to be the devil's bride, and not Miss Lucy!* The "bride?" Who marries a servant girl but another servant? and live in Whitby forever, always the same streets, same church, same everlasting round of toil and slops and prayers and—

Did I see him? the nightwalker, the vampire? Yes. I saw him smile. . . . Does that shock you, sir? I saw that smile in the dark and I thought, *Yes.* Like standing in the midnight churchyard, above the black-glass water, all the dark alive around you: yes. You might go anywhere in such darkness, do anything you like, and no one would hinder you, no one would see— Handsome, sir? Oh handsome is as handsome does, that's what the verger taught me! So when I let him in, I must have been beautiful, don't you think! Because he smiled on me, sir, he smiled like my father, because like him I love the dark. . . .

Troubled? Oh, no, sir, not a particle. I could shout my story from the rooftops, and no one would believe me, just as no one will believe *you*. You may drag me to the magistrate, for the taking of the little golden cross; he may put me in gaol. Do I care? Doors open, and windows are only glass. . . . Oh, save your lamentations for the verger. If Almighty God were truly my father, my own father would never have died and left me so.

As it is, the dark comes every night, sir. And I am ready.

Venus and Mars

CHRISTOPHER GOLDEN

UNDER THE STREETLIGHTS, the building was flamingo pink. Had it been on the main drag leading down to the Santa Monica pier it might have seemed proudly Californian, a nod and a wink to the tourist trade. But a mile from the ocean, tucked away in a forgotten corner of a maze of one-way, badly paved roads, it was a sad and faded reminder of more hopeful days for this neighborhood. The L.A. area was littered with blocks like this, smeared with gang tags and bordered with chain-link fence that was not a part of the original design. But here, even the gang tags were faded.

Even the 'bangers don't bother with this corner of the city anymore, Gray thought. *Miracle the streetlights even work.*

His throat was so very dry. He wore a long jacket that he knew would be conspicuous if anybody was suspicious enough to give a shit about such things. His arm pits were damp and he pressed his hands to them, allowing the fabric of his shirt to absorb any moisture there, any stink.

Not that Gray smelled badly. He never did.

He had parked his Buick farther down the block. It was a green dinosaur that had seen its best days around the same era that someone had thought painting this building pink was a terrific idea. But it ran, and the radio worked, and with L.A. traffic those were the only things that mattered.

Oh, and the windows were darkly tinted. That helped.

Gray gazed at the pink building. He flexed his fingers without even being aware of it. His throat was still dry; he was thirsty. Hell, come to that, he was hungry, too. He bounced on his toes and brought one hand up to his lips, biting the thumbnail.

Just go, he thought. *Just do it. How long are you going to wait?* A tremor went through him. One corner of his mouth turned up in a smile, but he dragged the back of his hand across his lips, and the smile disappeared.

Gray started down the street, keeping away from the pools of jaundiced illumination cast by the streetlights. Other than the one that was his destination, the buildings he passed were as plain and unremarkable as the women who took his money at the supermarket. Between them ran Dumpsters and chain link. He peered deeply into the shadows behind those Dumpsters, and he narrowed his gaze and studied those plain stucco building faces, wondering if anyone observed his approach.

It would not do for him to be seen approaching the flamingo building.

Though he was no stranger to the unpleasant underside of the world, to ugliness and depravity, Gray had never dug this deeply into the filth before. Never been so low. He could not escape the paranoia, the feeling of accusing eyes upon him, the vulnerable sensation that fluttered in his stomach. There were those who would judge him for just being here tonight. Those who would judge him harshly. Even violently. To hell with them. They could never understand the things that drove him here. They were still operating in the daylight world, where stories had happy endings.

Gray's world was the night. The dark.

One last time he surveyed the area for witnesses. Then he darted across the street through a splash of streetlight, hurrying into the shadows in the inset doorway of that faded pink structure. He allowed himself a single glance backward, but there was no more hesitation in him. Gray knocked softly but insistently on the door, waited a moment, and then knocked again. There was a spy hole in the door. Though he was tempted to look at it, to see if he could see someone looking back at him, he averted his eyes.

The lock slid back and the door opened. Framed in the doorway was a thin but powerful-looking man with olive skin and a hideous burn scar on the left side of his face. He was tall enough that he had to stoop a bit, there in the door. When he smiled in greeting, his lips only moved at the corners, like a teenager loathe to display his braces.

"Can I help you?"

"My name is Gray. I spoke to Kellie on Instant Messenger. I have an appointment."

The tall man studied him for a moment, then ducked his head out the door and glanced up and down the street. Only then did he retreat into the building and step aside to allow Gray to enter.

"Come, Mr. Gray. Let's get you inside."

Gray trembled slightly as he stepped over the threshold. On the other side of the door was a tiled foyer. The muffled thump of bubblegum pop music emanated from behind the walls. A curving staircase led to the second floor, but the landing at the top of the steps was lost in shadows and silence.

The tall man locked the door behind Gray. There were no windows off of the foyer, but from the outside he had noted their location.

"I am Taki," the tall man said. "Follow me."

As he turned, Gray caught a closer view of the burn scar on his face. The damaged tissue had an opalescent quality in the light. Just looking at it nauseated Gray. He wondered how the man had come by that burn, but did not dare ask.

Taki led him across the foyer to a door and opened it. The bubblegum pop blared out of tinny speakers. In the midst of the music there came a burst of giggling.

Three girls played Twister in the middle of the room. The nearest to him was a thin redhead in a short charcoal skirt, a white button-down shirt, and socks with ruffles around the ankles. Her hair was in pigtails. She was bent across a Latina girl dressed tough in a belly tee and low-rider jeans. She had a navel ring that flashed in the light as she tried to keep her balance. The third girl, who had one arm beneath the others but was otherwise stretched out to reach almost impossible places on the Twister mat, was a blonde who wore only a flannel pajama top, and nothing else.

The Latina was probably the oldest, and she couldn't have been more than fourteen.

"Come on, Aja, spin it!" the blonde called.

For the first time, Gray noticed a fourth girl. The spectacle of the Twister game had drawn so much of his attention that he had not really taken in the rest of the room. The walls were the same pink as the exterior and covered with posters of pop stars. There was a table in the far corner piled with stuffed animals. A trio of sofas made a kind of U against one wall. On one of those sofas sat a girl with elegant features and skin so black it seemed to have a tint of blue.

This must have been Aja. She wore a bottle-green summer dress with a pattern of darker green flowers on it. If he had to guess, Gray would have placed her at thirteen. On her lap was the cardboard color chart with the spinning arrow that controlled where the Twister players would have to put their hands or feet next. When she saw Gray noticing her, Aja smiled.

"Aja!" the blonde called again.

But it was too late. One of them lost her balance and the girls collapsed in a pile of smooth limbs and giddy laughter.

"Say hello to Mr. Gray, girls," Taki instructed.

One by one they extricated themselves from the tangle and propped themselves up to look at him. The blonde and the redhead gave him shy hellos. The Latina girl just stared at him from under thick lashes and raised one eyebrow. On the sofa, Aja gave him a little wave.

"Hello," Gray said to them. "On the . . . on the website, it said you had six girls."

Once more Taki gave him that not-quite smile. Gray had discovered them on a website that trumpeted its L.A. Lolitas. Beautiful young girls, the site had promised. And he had been corresponding for more than a week with Kellie, one of the girls. She had told him they would have to run his credit card to check him out, to make sure he wasn't a cop. Gray had done his homework. He had known the risks involved. It was possible Kellie was a cop herself and that he would be throwing himself into the lion's den by coming here, by providing them with that information.

But the girls were for real. The L.A. Lolitas were right in front of him. He might even have overestimated how old they were. Makeup and attitude could do that. He trembled, his throat dry again.

"Sasha's upstairs with a guest," Taki explained. "And Lolly . . . she left us, unfortunately."

Gray nodded, swallowing hard, surveying the girls in front of him. "Which . . . which one of you is Kellie?"

The redhead smiled coyly and raised her hand as though she was in a classroom and he was the teacher. "I'm Kellie. Nice to meet you in the flesh."

A soft chuckle came up from Gray's throat. "Yes. In the flesh."

Taki put a hand on his shoulder, and Gray felt the strength in his grip. "Would you like to spend some private time with Kellie?"

Gray nodded. His long coat hung heavily on him, but he lightened it a little by reaching into his pocket and removing a thick envelope. When he handed it to Taki, he could still smell the crisp new-money scent from within. Taki opened the envelope and quickly danced his fingers over the cash inside, counting silently. Then he smiled and glanced up.

"Please," Taki said, gesturing toward innocent-faced Kellie in her school uniform. "Enjoy yourself."

Kellie leaped up from the floor as though she had something to celebrate. With a grin she took Gray by the hand and led him back out into the foyer. He took a last glance into that room, at Taki and the other girls, and then Kellie was leading him up the stairs and he did not hesitate.

This was what he had come for.

As he followed Kellie up to the second floor he watched the way she moved, how light she was on her feet. His gaze returned again and again to those ruffled socks. They were white with a fringe of pink on the ruffle. In his mind, Gray played back hundreds of images he had discovered on the Internet, a trail of websites, of girls, of promises.

His fingers twitched as he followed Kellie down the left branch of a shadowy corridor that went off in both directions from the top of the stairs. His palms were wet and he wiped them on his coat. In the gloomy hall her pale legs seemed almost ghostly. She entered the last room on the corridor.

Gray paused in the doorway, and as she turned and saw him standing there, something flashed across her eyes, as though for a moment her mask had slipped. It might have been alarm or sadness or hopelessness, but whatever it was it was colored by hatred. She hated him, this girl, though she had lured him here.

He understood. He could live with that.

"Well. Aren't you going to join me?"

Something thrummed deep within him, a rhythm in his blood, a heat and a pulse. But he no longer trembled.

Gray followed her into the room and Kellie closed the door behind him. There was a four-poster bed. More stuffed animals on the floral-print spread. Makeup on the bureau. When she faced him, any glimpse beneath the mask was impossible. Her smile was playful, innocent, and she tilted her head, pigtails bouncing, and gazed at him with wide, heart-breaking eyes. Kellie giggled and approached him, reaching for his coat.

"You . . . you first," Gray said, voice cracking.

Kellie pirouetted, socks sliding on the wood floor. Her skirt flew up and he caught a glimpse of lace. She stopped only inches from the bed, the backs of her legs nearly at the mattress, and began to unbutton her shirt. Her eyes were wide, her lips pursed. She slid the shirt down over her shoulders. Her bra was the same white lace. Kellie reached up to unsnap it.

"Wait," Gray whispered.

She gave him a knowing look and dropped her hands. She shifted her weight, jutted out one hip, and let him inspect her. Gray moved toward her, unbuttoning his coat. She took his left hand and placed it on her chest and he left it there a moment, just staring at her.

Her smile broadened. Her white teeth were perfect. Sharp.

Gray moved his left hand up, his strong fingers clamped around her throat, and he drove her down onto the bed, scattering teddy bears and a plush elephant onto the floor. Kellie tried to scream, but the sounds were no different than others that might be expected to come from this room.

She fought him, legs flailing, and another man—one less prepared—might have been thrown off. But not Gray.

From a sheath sewn into the inside of his jacket he withdrew a long dagger with an ivory handle and a silver blade. The handle had been etched with symbols that its maker insisted were magical. Gray was not a believer in magic, but he figured it couldn't hurt.

Kellie screamed when she saw the dagger, the light glinting off its silver edge. He choked off as much of the sound as he could. She clawed at his arm but the jacket was thick and so was the shirt beneath it. Her fingers hooked into cruel talons, and she slashed at his face. Gray darted his head back, but one of her nails caught his chin and cut him.

His lips curled back and he snarled at her, baring his teeth.

She did the same.

Her rear incisors had thrust up from the ducts in her upper and lower palates, and she hissed at him. Her eyes had been a gentle blue-green before. Now they were yellow, predator's eyes.

Gray plunged the dagger into her chest, throwing his arm across her throat, his weight on top of her. She bucked beneath him, twitching.

And then she crumbled, her entire body collapsing like the ash tapped off of the tip of a cigarette.

"Rest now," Gray whispered, biting his lip. His throat was dry again, yet moisture gathered in his eyes. He shuddered as he rose up from the bed, from the charcoal skirt and the other clothes that lay amidst a pile of ash upon that demure, floral bedspread.

For a moment he stood in the center of that room. He steeled himself, opened his coat further and reached into another interior pocket. Gray withdrew a large crucifix on a chain and hung it around his neck. Then he took a deep breath, flexed his grip on the dagger, and went to the door. He pulled it open and glanced into the hall.

No one.

Gray slipped into the corridor, as swiftly and silently as one of his prey. He opened the first door but found the room empty. At the second he paused. An unsettling sense of menace radiated from within. Over the years he had learned to trust his instincts, to trust what he felt in the air.

Gently he turned the knob, praying it was not locked. When he pushed, the door opened and he heard a sucking sound.

The hinges gave a single small squeak.

The girl did not turn from her task. In the near darkness of the room, her pale skin was luminescent. She was younger than any of the others, a small slip of a girl with short black hair. She crouched atop her guest, mouth fastened lamprey-fashion upon his throat.

As Gray moved toward her he saw that her eyes were closed and fluttering. She was lost in the blood, in her hunger. Gray felt a chill move through him, turning his flesh as cold as that of his prey. At the very last moment she sensed him, her eyes snapping open, and she hissed, her mouth still against the dead man's throat, an animal protecting its fresh kill.

He grabbed a fistful of her hair, hauled her upward, and drove the silver blade through her back. Punching it between bone and through muscle took both strength and skill. Gray had spent years developing both. When he pierced her heart, she sighed as though she had waited for this moment her entire life.

A shower of ash fell on top of the corpse on the bed. Gray paused, tilted his head, and studied the dead man a moment. The fucker had died with a smile on his face.

Gray flinched. Scowling, he dredged something up from his throat and spit on the corpse.

He left the room, moving more quickly than he had before. He passed the top of the stairs and continued on down the other end of the corridor. There were four more doors. The first was wide open, an empty bedroom. The other three were closed. He went silently to the far end of the hall and moved backward toward the stairs from there. The two doors at the end of the corridor were empty bedrooms. That left only one room he had not explored, midway along that branch of the hall. It turned out to be a bathroom. He was inside the bathroom when he heard whispers. Peeking out through the open door he saw two of the remaining girls—the Latina and the little blonde—cresting the stairs.

"—don't know why I have to dress," the blonde said, glancing angrily back down the stairs. "The customers know what they're here for. Or they think they do," she added slyly.

"To keep them off guard," the Latina said with a shrug. "I don't know. Aja's running the show. It's working."

"Oh, fine," the blonde huffed.

She started down the hall, passing that first empty bedroom. Gray ducked back into the bathroom. She was going to walk right past him.

"Psst," he said as she went by.

When she turned and saw him, her eyes narrowed with confusion. That expression was still on her face when he buried the silver dagger hilt-deep in her chest. Her pajama top seemed almost to float in the air a moment as the ash rained down to the floor. Then it fell with a whisper of cotton.

"Emma?" the other girl said.

Gray exploded into the hallway. Stealth was secondary now. Priority one was destroying this creature before he had to face the others as well. One at a time was dangerous enough. In groups . . .

"Aja!" screamed the beautiful, caramel-skinned girl. "Taki!"

Fuck. Gray ran at her, but he was too far away. She turned back the way she'd come, seeming almost to glide down the stairs with an impossible agility, her feet touching only every second or third step. One outstretched hand touched the banister with each stride, steadying her. She would be out of his reach in a moment.

Gray jumped.

He collided with her about halfway down the stairs, drove her down under his weight. His left arm wrapped around her throat and he stabbed her deeply with the dagger, not going for the kill, just trying to keep the blade away from his own flesh as they fell together. They rolled over one another for the last half dozen steps. Gray's head banged against the wall and pain shot through his skull. Black stars blossomed behind his eyes and for a moment his mind was dull and slow.

The girl was on him.

"*Maricon!* I'll fucking kill you!"

He tried to bring the dagger up but she slammed his arm to the ground and knelt on his wrist. In her fury she struck his face once, twice, a third time, before she even bared her fangs. She hissed, eyes turning that feral yellow he knew so intimately.

But she was a little slip of a thing. A monster, yes, but a child. Her weight was on his right wrist, but he thrust his left hand inside his coat and brought out the silver dagger's twin. His coat made a hushing sound—or perhaps that was the blade—as he bucked against her. She tried to hold him down, but he pushed his left hand up toward her face and swept the dagger to the left, slicing her throat.

Her eyes went wide. She blinked several times, releasing her grip on him. She tried to look down, to see the place where he had cut her, but she could not. Her hands reached for the long gash on her throat where the edges of the cut pulsed like some hideous second mouth. It would not have killed her, but she had been human once, and she was horrified at such a wound.

Gray impaled her.

As he stood, the ash that had been that beautiful, deadly creature spilled off of his coat to the floor. But it was in his eyes now, and in his mouth, and in his hair. He spit on the floor, trying to get rid of the taste of her.

The door at the rear of the foyer swung open and Taki appeared. The cries, the thumping on the stairs—of course he had heard. His smile stretched the burn scar on his face as he stepped out, wary. He slammed the door closed.

"Well, well. To think I had you pegged as just another sweaty freak."

Gray crouched slightly, a silver-and-ivory dagger in either hand, waiting for the man to attack. The etchings in the dagger handles pressed into the flesh of his palms as he tracked Taki, anticipating the man's attack. This was better. With the girls, he had felt a hesitation, a reluctance. He had destroyed dozens of monsters, but only rarely had they been children. He felt as though he ought to have his eyes scoured from their orbits. It didn't matter what their true ages might have been. He could only think of the fragile things they had been before death, before soulless resurrection. It hurt him.

Taki, though. Taki was just a leech.

The leech hissed. His fangs extruded, longer than any Gray had ever seen. A clear fluid dripped from them, not venom but a natural sedative. With a laugh, he sprang.

Gray tried to get under him, ducking and driving both blades upward. But Taki was agile. He turned in the air, his lunge twisting into a kick. His boot took Gray in the side of the head, and the hunter went down. Gray let the momentum carry him over into a backward somersault, but Taki was on him quickly. The tall man kicked his left hand, and Gray could not hold on to the dagger. It skittered away across the tiled floor of the foyer.

Waving the other blade in front of him, Gray leaped to his feet. The silver was poison to the creature, but Taki only smiled and came on. He dodged and swayed, looking for an opening. Gray stepped in nearer, tried to block with his left arm so that he could bring the blade down, even just to wound.

Taki slapped his arm away, backhanded him across the face. Gray's jaws clamped down hard on the tip of his tongue, drawing blood. Before he could react, Taki struck his right wrist, and Gray dropped the second dagger.

Taki smiled. "Just another Van Helsing neverbe. When will you assholes learn?"

Gray's heart pumped wildly in his chest. His blood drooled down his chin. He let his hatred and fear show on his face, even as he jammed his hand into the outside pocket of his coat. His fingers wrapped around the gun and he tugged it out. Taki saw what he was doing and was about to attack again when he narrowed his eyes at the pink plastic gun in amazement.

"Take a lesson," Gray said.

He squirted holy water into Taki's eyes.

The monster screamed, his voice a pitch impossible for a human being. Like the torture of angels.

Taki had his hands over his eyes. Smoke rose up from them and vitreous fluid ran down his cheeks. The flesh around his eyes blistered and popped.

Gray dropped the pistol and reached into the other pocket. Taki was blind, but already he had begun to heal. He crouched, listening for Gray, trying to gauge where the attack would come from. Swift and silent, Gray moved around behind him, extended the garrote he had retrieved from his pocket—a thin strand of razor-thin wire with small wooden handles at either end—and slipped it around Taki's neck.

The leech continued to scream until his windpipe was severed. Only the spinal column gave Gray any trouble. But just a little. The head turned to ash even before it hit the floor, and the body followed suit a moment later. Delayed reaction in decapitation. He had never understood that.

Gray spun and stared at the rear door. There were no others and he knew that there must be more rooms beyond it aside from the one he had seen earlier. The last of them, the girl Aja, was back there somewhere. She was the one in charge of it all. She would have heard. She would be hiding, but he doubted she would have hidden in fear. She would be waiting for him.

Quickly, shooting glances at that door, he gathered his weapons again. When he went to the door he had only one dagger out. It was best to keep one hand free.

The door was unlocked.

Gray pushed it open.

He would not have to hunt for Aja. She was still in her place on the sofa, but now she was not alone. Aja had a guest, a client who must have come in after Gray. There was no way they could have failed to hear the skirmish with Taki in the corridor, but Aja must have shushed her client, must have assured him that Taki would take care of things.

But Taki was dust now.

The client was on top of Aja, moving over her, there on the couch. Beads of sweat stood out on his face and he wrapped his fingers in her hair, his weight on her, pushing her into the plush cushions.

"You've been a bad girl," he grunted, tugging on her hair. "Now you be a good girl for me."

"Yes, Daddy," Aja said.

Her eyes were as dead as her heart. Bored, she let her head loll to one side and she caught Gray in her gaze. He felt trapped by her eyes, frozen there, more violence in his soul than he had ever felt there before.

Aja only smiled.

Then the client noticed her distraction and turned as well. He ceased his rhythm and just remained poised there, above her, looking ridiculous now. He muttered something, some curse, and shifted his weight to climb off of her, off of this little girl.

With one swift hand she wrapped her fingers around his throat, nails cutting tiny crescent wounds into the flesh of his neck. He gurgled like a baby and tried to pull away, but her nails cut him deeper as she clutched onto him more tightly. Little rivulets of blood ran down his naked flesh from his throat. She was far too strong for him.

"What's the matter, Daddy?" she asked, the words hideous in her mouth. "Don't you want to play with your bad girl anymore?"

"Jesus," the man hissed, eyes shifting from Aja to Gray and back again. There was terror in his face, but it was not at all clear if it was terror of Aja, or of discovery. "Please?" he whispered.

"Oh, no," Aja said. "You don't stop now. Don't you want me to be your girl anymore? Show me how much Daddy loves me."

The man tried to shake his head.

"Show me!" Aja snarled. Her free hand dug into his back and she forced him to resume his motion, to move atop her, to continue the abominable intrusion Gray had interrupted.

The man began to weep, tears rolling down to mingle with the trails of blood on his throat.

Aja turned her gaze upon Gray once more, but her smile was as hollow as her gaze.

Throughout the entire exchange, which had taken long seconds, Gray had remained frozen. The sight hurt Gray, cut him deeply. He winced as though the wound were physical and averted his eyes, just for a second. She was a child. Just a little girl. It was an abomination.

But there was more than one kind of abomination here. For she was not *just* a little girl. She was both more and less.

He had devoted himself to the pursuit of her kind, to their destruction. Gray followed the news and searched the Internet, poring over tales of unusual murder and bodies found in shallow graves. He studied reports of missing persons and tracked surges in those statistics. The years had made him a special sort of detective, an expert in locating a very specific brand of killer. Only recently he had discovered a strange trend in the L.A. area, a series of disappearances of known pedophiles and the makers of child pornography, and a number of instances in which men had gone missing, only for the investigating detectives to turn up disturbing material while searching their homes.

More than one of them returned later, but they weren't human anymore. Gray could not decide which of their incarnations was more monstrous.

The trail had led him, both in the physical world and in the ethereal realm of the Internet, to this place, this garish little corner of hell. In all the years he had been hunting the hunters, he had been terrified many times, but only rarely had he mourned his victims.

Aja stared at him, yellow eyes burning in the shadows. Around them the pink walls pulsed like the inner chamber of a heart. He shook his head and squinted to drive away a moist heat that had snuck into the corners of his eyes.

"Hypocrite," she said as she forced the man to continue, her voice a tormented whisper. "How can you do this? How can you not see?"

Gray held the dagger steady as he advanced toward her. Aja's nails dug more deeply into the guest's throat and back. The man whimpered, turning to Gray, eyes silently urging him not to come any closer. Gray stopped, just at the edge of the Twister mat that still lay at the center of the room.

Aja shook her head. Her yellow eyes were limned now with blood, and crimson tears formed there, but when they fell they were lost against the darkness of her skin.

"So you're a hunter. Big man," she said, voice growing stronger now. "Don't you think about what you're doing? I'm a hunter, too. I haven't killed a single innocent. Not one. You don't have to look in the shadows for the monsters, Mr. Gray. I've got one right here."

She gripped the man's throat even more tightly and he began to whine like a puppy.

"You call this human? This *thing*?" Aja demanded. "Men like him took me, Mr. Gray. They took me, and they used me and they made me their thing, and then they sold me. Did they know the buyer wasn't human, that he was a blood-drinking animal? Maybe. It didn't matter. At least he only used me the once, took what he wanted, and then threw me away. Threw me away, Mr. Gray. He tossed me in a fucking Dumpster."

Gray shuddered as Aja went on.

"When I realized what had happened, when I knew what I'd turned into . . . I had nowhere to go. I wanted blood, but more than that, I wanted to hurt them back. Not just the ones who did it to me, but all of them. So I gathered up other girls like me, and I found Taki, and he understood. The monsters I'm after aren't any less terrible, any less soul-crushing, than the ones you hunt."

Gray's chest rose and fell with shortened breath. He ran his tongue over his lips, wetting them. His mind was awhirl with her words, with her logic. Aja stared at him, waiting for some kind of response.

"I agree," he said at length.

For just a moment she seemed to relax. Then Gray took another step forward and Aja tensed again, eyes widening, head tilted to one side.

"What are you doing? Look, just leave me. You want to protect people from . . . from things like me, that's fine. I don't hunt ordinary people." Aja's feral eyes narrowed now. "I *will* kill him, y'know?"

Gray nodded. He felt his upper lip curl back in disgust. "Fine. I told you, I agree."

He switched the dagger to his left hand, reached around under his coat to the rear waistband of his pants, and unclipped the gun that he had holstered there. This one was not plastic. It did not have water in it. This one was just in case. Just in case.

Gray raised the gun and took aim.

"You idiot," Aja said, snarling, showing her fangs, letting her true face show. "That won't kill me."

Gray shot her victim through the head. Aja screamed as blood and brain spattered onto her face. She pushed him off of her. The corpse of the freak, the child-fucker, the monster, slipped to the floor with a wet smack.

Aja whirled on him, madness in her eyes. Gray thought they must have reflected his own.

"What are you doing?" she snarled.

"Expanding my horizons. Your kind are vermin," Gray said, nodding to himself. He gestured at the corpse with the barrel of the gun. "So are his. I can't leave you alive. But I'll carry the weight of what was done to you. And to so many others. I've spent most of my life hunting in the dark. The only difference is that now I'll be hunting two kinds of monsters."

Gray started for Aja, trembling with his hatred of what she was, and with the weight of the grief he felt for her. She would fight him, of course. But not for long.

His throat was dryer than ever. He felt so thirsty. So drained. He felt the burden of her crusade upon his shoulders, now. He had given his life over to his own mission, his purpose, and now he would embrace hers as well. Until the day it killed him.

Aja began to move, gaze darting about as she gauged her chance at escape. Now that she was away from the sofa, the light was brighter and he could clearly see the bloody tears on her face. Gray felt warmth upon his cheeks and tasted salt upon his lips and he realized that he was also weeping.

Vermin, he thought. *No exceptions.*

The Power of Waking

Nina Kiriki Hoffman

Before they went I asked Dr. Seward to give me a little opiate of some kind, as I had not slept well the night before. He very kindly made me up a sleeping draught, which he gave to me, telling me that it would do me no harm, as it was very mild. . . . I have taken it, and am waiting for sleep, which still keeps aloof. I hope I have not done wrong, for as sleep begins to flirt with me, a new fear comes: that I may have been foolish in thus depriving myself of the power of waking. . . .
—Mina Harker's Journal, 1 October, *Dracula*

AFTER SPENDING THE DAY in the Antiquities Department of the British Museum, studying artifacts from many now-buried cultures in the process of being unearthed, the boy wondered if he was ready for the evening's entertainment.

His father had bought tickets to front-row seats at London's Royal College of Surgeons Lecture Theatre, where they would watch an Egyptian mummy unrolling performed by the famous physician Thomas Pettigrew, who, seventeen years earlier in 1834, had published the first scientific treatise on the mummification process practiced by the ancient Egyptians.

Abraham was not sure how he felt about the coming spectacle. This trip from Amsterdam to London with his father was a way for them to leave behind their house, made sad and weary by the long, wasting death of Abraham's mother. They had spent the previous day at the Crystal Palace in Hyde Park, walking through the fabulous Great Exhibition of the Works of Industry of All Nations. Abraham's initial fascination had worn down during the long day, but he had slept well that night for the first time in ages, pleasantly exhausted by thinking about things other than his grief.

The thought of the mummy unrolling invited his mother back into his mind. During the course of his mother's illness, Abraham had found in booksellers' shops texts full of mysteries alchemical and scientific that lit fires in his brain. His mother was the one who had given him the gift of reading, of questioning, of studying; she had been a botanist before she turned ill.

As his mother's illness progressed, the boy had studied old and new texts with feverish intensity, hoping the ancients could supply him a means of curing her. Some of the tomes he brought home to his mother; they studied texts and illustrations together in those brief moments when she regained a spark of her previous fortitude.

Abraham had borrowed from a sympathetic bookseller a copy of Giovanni Belzoni's memoir of exploration and excavations in Egypt, published thirty years earlier. Abraham's mother had studied the watercolors of tomb inscriptions and monuments. In other books, they had examined reproductions of Egyptian funerary art. The boy's mother laid her fingers on images of human-headed, winged figures. "It was such a different, dark, and primitive world," she had whispered, "and yet, here are the winged ones, in the land beyond death."

Abraham had read about the medical theories of an earlier age, when physicians prescribed powder of ground-up mummy for their ailing patients in the belief that the resin in the mummy wrappings held curative powers. Such ideas had been discarded, and the thought of them made Abraham ill. He searched for other cures that made more scientific sense. He carefully followed antique recipes whenever he discovered something that struck him as having merit.

His mother drank the potions and took the powders he concocted without complaint, but nothing slowed the wasting of her flesh, and very little eased the pain in her abdomen.

By the time she said farewell, she had turned into a flattened sketch of the gentle, loving mother he had known. It had hurt him to look at her, and though he would not let himself think such thoughts, the smell of her sickness repulsed him. Her hand, as he clutched it before her last breath and the death rattle that followed, felt cool and frail, sticks wrapped in stretched hide. It hurt him that her luminous spirit had had to be housed in such a frail receptacle, and he felt a shameful relief when she was gone.

Abraham and his father stepped down into the street from the confines of the hansom cab. They had not been able to get close to the entrance of the Royal College; the approach was clogged with other cabs and carriages. Gas lamps lit the street. The London air was fetid with the odors of coal smoke and sewage and the Thames, that artery running through the heart of the city that received much of the city's offal.

A crowd of well-dressed men and women out for an evening's entertainment caused a crush in the doorway, where the ticket collector stood.

"What do you suppose he'll uncover tonight?" one man asked another.

"I went to an unrolling last year, and there were several amulets, some of stone, with strange inscriptions on them. The mummy's fingernails, toenails, and eyelids were gilded. The nails were fastened to the fingers and toes with wires. The corpse looked frightful, so dried and twisted. Is this truly their vision of immortality? Strange people, those Egyptians."

"I went to an unrolling where there was a peculiar sort of varnish over the inner bandages, and Dr. Pettigrew could not break through it, though he employed all sorts of tools. All the mummy's secrets were left undisclosed; he had to dismiss us without completing the task. The entire audience was disappointed."

"Papa," Abraham murmured.

"My son?" His father put a hand on his shoulder.

"My stomach . . ." His stomach had been sour for some time—since before his mother's death. His appetite had been poor: no food stirred his desires. When he ate, he ate only because he knew he must. Everything tasted of ashes.

"Have a peppermint." His father fetched a peppermint drop from a small sack he kept in his waistcoat pocket for just such complaints, and handed it to Abraham, who put it in his mouth.

Abraham's father handed the tickets to the collector, and they went inside to their reserved seats in the front row.

The linen-wrapped mummy lay on a table under hissing gas lamps. Abraham settled in his seat and stared at the crisscross of narrow, time-browned bandages that bound the body.

A dead person lies before me. Someone who died thousands of years ago. What if it were Mother being unwrapped here, in front of the eyes of strangers, when she has no way of maintaining her dignity? How would I feel? How would she feel? Despite the peppermint, his stomach churned. Abraham closed his eyes. The scent of damp felt, wet wool, heavy perfumes, pipe smoke, and sweat sickened him.

"Abraham." Papa's hand gripped his shoulder.

Abraham drew strength from that firm clasp. He swallowed bile and opened his eyes. They were here to watch science, to learn the secrets of an ancient civilization, to participate in one of the wonders of an enlightened age. He must be awake to opportunities.

"You would bring a child to such an event?" asked a low, pleasant woman's voice from Papa's other side. She sounded cultured and faintly amused.

"Madam?" said Papa. Abraham could tell he was shocked that a stranger and a woman would speak to him without an introduction.

"How old is the boy?"

"Eleven and a half."

"Surely this is a spectacle for mature minds, not for children. Do you wish to give him nightmares?"

"My son is wise beyond his years."

The woman leaned forward and peered past Papa into Abraham's eyes. Her eyes were dark and bold, unpleasantly intrusive. "You are accustomed to such events?" she asked.

"I have never been to an unrolling before," he said in careful English, "but Papa has me brought to other marvelous things. Always I look forward to a chance to expand my knowledge."

She smiled, shook her head. "Ah, well." She leaned back, and Abraham lost sight of her.

A bearded man in a speckled suit, attended by two younger men with shaven chins, high collars, and side whiskers, came into the room from a door on the other side of the mummy. The murmurs of the crowd quieted.

"Good evening," said the bearded man. "I'm Dr. Pettigrew, professor of anatomy at Charing Cross Hospital. These are my associates, Mr. Willis, a clerk, and Mr. Cruikshank, an illustrator. They will make notes of everything we discover tonight. Welcome to another in my series of explorations into the funerary customs of the ancient Egyptians. They were a people who spent all their lives preparing for their afterlives. Their knowledge of anatomy and the science of embalming was in some ways superior to our own. We have much to learn from them."

Abraham thought of his mother's wasted face the last time he had seen her, at rest in her coffin. The terrible tension had eased from her cheeks, leaving her face empty, unfamiliar, without character. Clearly she had left her earthly body behind. Had her spirit gone on?

He had not been able to bear looking at what lay in the coffin, his soul was so alive with the fierce longing to turn back the clock and rescue her before the disease could devour her.

"Tonight's mummy is from a collection of Egyptian antiquities that just came on the market last week. It has been in private hands since the early days of exploration in Egypt. Its provenance is uncertain; hence, we will have to look to clues in the wrapping and mummification to determine in which dynasty this mummy was made, if such identification is even possible. From the style of the wrappings I would venture to guess that this is a middle- or late-period mummy, but we shall learn more as we proceed. Gentlemen. Let us commence with the unrolling." Pettigrew turned to his two accomplices, who came forward and took up seats beside the mummy, took out portable desks with paper on them, set opened bottles of ink in their ink wells, and dipped their pens.

Pettigrew turned to a surgical tray of implements beside the table and lifted a scalpel. "We begin with the bandages of the head." He carefully sliced through one of the strips of linen binding the head, and then, rolling the bandage as he unwrapped it from the corpse, he worked his way around the head, speaking all the while of how recent microscope studies had determined that all mummy bandages were indeed linen, not cotton as had previously been believed. He talked about the study of insects that had hatched within bandages after mummies had been interred, and then he discoursed on what people had surmised from studying texts on the insides and outsides of the nested mummiform coffins, often two or three deep, in which the mummies of rulers, priests, and the wealthy were buried.

"George, note this as Bandage One," Dr. Pettigrew said to one of his assistants, who made a note on a small square of paper and pinned it to the first bandage. Dr. Pettigrew tugged at a different piece, removed another layer of linen from the figure's head and neck.

Abraham listened with only half his mind. The other part of his brain was concerned with thoughts of his mother's coffin, buried in consecrated ground in Holland, the service said over her before they had cast ritual handfuls of dirt into her grave, a visible and tactile farewell. Would unknown people hundreds of years hence dig up his mother's grave, study her poor, decaying corpse? Display her for the idle rich, discuss her habits? Did she still cling to her remains?

"Ah," said Dr. Pettigrew. "Here at the throat, three layers into the wrappings, we find our first amulet."

A gasp came from everyone in the audience as Dr. Pettigrew held up a red object. "This shape is what we call a buckle. We believe this amulet is sacred to the Goddess Isis, a plea for her to protect the mummy with the powers of her magic and blood. I will set these objects on a table, here"—he turned and placed the amulet on a cloth-covered wheeled table behind him—"where Mr. Cruikshank can sketch them and make notes about their placement on the body. After I complete the unrolling, those interested may come up for a closer look. I will donate all these objects to the British Museum following the exercise, with complete notes as to their placement."

It's a treasure hunt, Abraham realized. He glanced around at the people in the audience. They leaned forward, their eyes hungry, mouths slightly open as though to feast on the strange spectacle.

"Many different lengths and widths of bandages were used in wrapping the mummy," Dr. Pettigrew said. He held up a bandage he had just removed from the chest. "This one has fringes, and is hemmed in a different color. Look here." He showed them a central part of the bandage, where faded ink scrawled indecipherable outlines. "This may be a prayer, or the name of the deceased. I'll give these materials to the scholars."

Abraham raised his hand. "For what was the writing, Doctor?"

"A spell, a protection, or just to commemorate the person. It may be the person's name. Names were important to them; they left their names everywhere. These Egyptians were a superstitious lot. They had spells for everything. Perhaps the writings were supposed to protect them from tomb robbers."

Manifestly, the spell hadn't worked in this case.

What was he thinking? Heathen magic flew in the face of logic and science. Not only that, but it blasphemed against the true faith. This was just an exercise in observation and information collecting, a study of the quaint customs of a vanished people whose belief systems had been fatally flawed.

The doctor unrolled more bandages, lecturing as he went. Abraham leaned forward like everyone else, anxious, now, ready to have the bandages gone. He had seen mummies in the British Museum that afternoon, but they were still swaddled in linen. Did a perfectly preserved body lie inside the wrappings? When the bandages parted over the face, would it look as fresh as the day it was prepared, three or four thousand years earlier?

Was there a chance of resurrection? Of life after death, even after a sleep of a thousand years?

"Ah," said the doctor, "here's the heart scarab." He held up a green lump the size of a child's fist, and there came a collective gasp from the room again. "A particularly fine specimen. The Egyptians believed that the heart was the source of knowledge and intelligence. To them, it was the most important organ in the body. The inscription on the bottom of the heart scarab instructs the gods of the afterlife not to weigh the mummy's heart too heavily in the scales of justice. As we do in our faith,

the Egyptians believed that evil deeds could condemn them. Good
deeds and the right intercessions by the gods could elevate them to a
land of eternal bliss. Bad deeds made their hearts weigh heavier than the
Feather of Truth, and the Devourer of the Dead waited beside the scales
during the weighing. If judgment went against the deceased, the Devourer ate the heart, and the dead person's self was lost forever."

Abraham shivered. In his darkest hours, he had reached for hope that
he would someday meet his mother in the realms of the blessed, restored
to her true self, and happy. What if she had done something wrong in her
life? What if she had gone to the other place?

What if he used his life badly, and never reached that reunion?

The doctor went back to work, meticulously unrolling, speaking all
the while. Then he gasped. Everyone in the room drew in a breath and
leaned forward. The doctor had not been surprised by his previous finds,
only pleased. What had he discovered now?

"What a lovely thing." He held up a silvery amulet. It had the body of
a bird, with wings outstretched, and the head of a woman. "This represents the *ba*, the part of the soul that wanders. The ancient Egyptians believed that there were several parts to the soul. This was the part that
could leave the body and explore the world, so long as it returned to the
body afterward."

The wings glinted in the gas flames. *The part of the soul that wanders,*
Abraham thought, and remembered thin fingertips brushing lightly over
images of winged beings. *Mother: does a part of your blessed soul wander?
Does it linger here on Earth? Are you waiting for me to discover how to see and
speak with you?* He rose and walked toward the doctor and the amulet.

"Abraham!" cried his father.

"Son?" said the doctor. He glanced around. Men who had been standing in shadow against the back wall converged.

Abraham's hand lifted, hovered near the winged image. *Do you wander
still, ancient one? Can you speak to others like yourself?*

Can you be a conduit between one who yet lives and one who has gone beyond?

Oh, but this was foolish. It defied rationality, and it was one of the
temptations away from the true faith.

He thought, *I believe in the remission of sins, the resurrection of the flesh, the life everlasting. This poor soul, or part of a soul, is not saved—*

"Please. Return to your seat. You may examine the finds after the lecture is concluded," said the doctor, taking a step back.

Abraham touched the silver amulet with his fingertips. At first, it was cool and smooth to the touch. Then fierce heat gathered. A glow surrounded the amulet. Light flowed from the amulet to envelope his hand, stinging like nettles. Shock radiated through him, and he stumbled back. Heat raced like rivers of molten metal through his body. He cried out.

Something was present. Something had survived.

"Abraham!" Papa leaned over him, a shadow against the light. He lifted his head and faced Dr. Pettigrew. "Doctor, I am so sorry! He is in general the best-behaved boy in the world. I don't know what possessed him. Please forgive us."

Papa knelt, lifted him, carried him out of the hall.

He struggled, tried to see past Papa's chest and arms to the body that still lay on the table. *My body,* whispered a soft, mournful voice, perhaps female. Abraham was too tired to fight his father's grip.

The evening air was cool and damp and filthy. His father carried him toward the corner. Gas lamps made glowing halos in the mist. The clopping of horses' hooves, the ring of wheels against the cobbles, echoed between buildings.

"Son, you have disgraced me," Papa said. He quickened his stride, hailed a passing cab. Abraham felt a twinge of shame, then an overwhelming weariness.

The driver pulled his horse to a stop and released the door. "Where to?"

"Morley's Hotel on Trafalgar Square." Papa set Abraham on the seat and settled beside him in the darkness of the cab's interior. The door closed, and the cab swayed as it set off.

"What into you has gotten?" Papa asked.

Abraham could not answer. He didn't yet know what this was, this molten spill that had burned into his bones and etched itself onto his organs.

A voice spoke from his chest, though not aloud. *Where am I?*

Abraham pressed his hand to the heat that had gathered under his breastbone. *What are you?* he thought.

Don't you know my name?

No.

I caused it to be written on my wrappings. It was on the walls of my tomb. It was inscribed on my heart. What is my name?

Abraham's breath was hot as it rushed out over his tongue, cool as he drew it in. His breathing was so loud he couldn't hear anything else.

My name, the part of my soul that lives forever so long as one person remembers. What is my name?

"Abraham!" said Papa.

Abraham. That wasn't my name before.

Abraham is my name, not yours.

Abraham, said the voice.

"Son? Are you weeping?" Papa touched the tears on his cheek.

Abraham could not explain: not any of it. The amulet had called to him—how? Why? What had wakened after a sleep of thousands of years? Who was now resident inside him, remembering the scent of spices and unguents from ancient times, the taste of honey on the tongue, the heat of a blazing, dusty midday and the fretted shadows of palm fronds across pale stone?

What remnant of personality was it that, defying science, had lasted millennia to live again, even in such a tattered form?

Death was not final. If one soul could survive death, might not another? Suppose his mother had left a piece of herself in something at home, something he had not touched since her death—

He lay back against the seat, his gaze fixed on the roof of the cab as though he could see through it, past the mists and smokes of the London sky to the stars above, and beyond.

The sky cracked open and the possibility of wonders rained down.

The Life Imprisoned

WILLIAM D. CARL

A FTER MY RETURN from London, where I had studied medicine and philosophy among some of the greatest surgeons in that estimable land, I found myself on the staff of the Valdaker Asylum, a hospital for the insane, run by my good friend Henrik Vanderpool. It was a modest establishment, located just outside Haarlem, and its reputation had always been impeccable. I found it quite a relief to be back among my fellow Dutch, speaking my native language once again. For all of its beautiful confusion, the English language remained elusive to me, and I always felt as though my fellow schoolmates were judging me because of my poor syntax. "Poor Van Helsing," I could imagine them whispering behind my back. Now, speaking Dutch, my views and ideas retained their original meanings, and I was accredited with the intelligence I knew I possessed. My theories were taken seriously, even some of my more outlandish ones.

I had set up house with my young wife, Mathilde, a few blocks away from the hospital. In the two years that we had been man and wife, she had epitomized the ideal of a perfect spouse: humble, but with opinions, intelligent, witty, and quite lovely in my estimation. Her golden hair and ice blue eyes brought about comparisons to the great Nordic goddesses of long ago.

My adoration of her became complete when tragedy struck her family in the guise of a carriage accident that took the life of her sister and brother-in-law. They had left behind a son, age six, whom they had named Kris. Without a second thought, my wife and I adopted the lad, and I consider him my son as though Mathilde had borne him herself. My throat can still catch when he calls me "Pappa."

Soon after we took him into our home, it was discovered that his lungs were terribly weak and he had trouble with simple breathing. I can remember distinctly the way that Mathilde held our son in her arms on his seventh birthday, during one of his more violent attacks, and her words: "If he can not breathe for himself, then I shall breathe for him." She covered his mouth with hers and blew several long puffs of air into his tiny body, and he did seem to recover for a time.

The poor child could not understand why he was not allowed to run and play with the other moppets in the neighborhood, resulting in fits of sobbing despair that would reduce my wife and me to similar tears. Often, my good friend and colleague Vanderpool would create a concoction of the herbs he grew in his greenhouse to help stimulate the tissues of the boy's lungs, but they never provided more than a temporary relief.

While Mathilde was comfortable with the child, I often found my own words clumsy and awkward when dealing with him, my hands large and ungainly. Although I loved the boy, I had trouble speaking with him. Once, during an especially terrible episode, Kris looked up at me from the corner of his room, where he sat gasping and ashen, and released a tortured, scraping whisper. "Pappa. Pappa."

He wanted me to go to him, to say something, make it better. But I could not. I knew not the words to say. I could offer no treatment, no hope. What use was a father such as me?

His gaze fixed on me, Kris wrapped his arms around his knees and rocked back and forth. Gradually, his heaving gasps smoothed, calmed. The movement seemed to ease his attack.

Possessing some rudimentary carpentry skills, I took the day and built my son a little rocking chair, and I purchased a silver cross on a chain, a duplicate of the one Mathilde had given me on our first wedding anniversary. Kris often toyed with mine when I bent to kiss him goodnight.

That evening, I presented Kris with his gifts. He immediately began rocking in the little chair, and he hung the cross around his neck.

"As long as you wear that cross," I said, "God will be with you."

"Oh, Pappa, now I shall never be afraid, not even of dying. Now I know that if I should die while wearing my cross, I shall be with God. I'll never take it off. Just like you!"

"Well," I said, smiling, pleased with his delight, "I'm glad you like your presents."

He threw his arms around me, crying, "You *do* love me, Pappa. I always knew you did. Somehow, I always knew."

I moved my rigid arms around him, returning the hug in my own clumsy manner. The right words refused to come; what an unfit father was I, that my son had no evidence of my love but these poor gifts.

Mathilde and I tried to enjoy the precious moments that remained 'til he rejoined his true mother in Heaven. Still, it was very difficult for me, and I knew it was doubly problematic for my beloved wife. She had to confront Kris's sickness every hour of every day, until there was little left in her life except this diminishing child. At least I had my work as a portal of escape. When I was at the hospital, I could forget that Kris was dying. I began to work longer hours, taking refuge from my anxieties, thankfully forgetting all about the child for hours on end.

I admit that I was neglecting my family and my home, immersing myself in the daily machinations of the insane. My assigned tasks at Valdaker Asylum were fairly simple. I performed many of the routine surgeries alongside the more experienced staff, but on more advanced procedures I was relegated to the role of observer. Despite my limited duties, I was entranced by the mysteries of the human body. I had a theory, one I was determined to prove, that any small bit of tissue from a man contains every piece of that person, that tissue acts as a blueprint to all the features one exhibits. If a man has red hair and freckles, the determination for these attributes lies somewhere within the flesh on a cellular level.

I once voiced my theory to my friend, Vanderpool, and his eyes sparked with interest. He claimed that he had a volume, one of many in his home, entitled the Egyptian Book of the Dead, an ancient text on religious and magical ceremonies. Vanderpool claimed that in this book were statements similar to mine, that the antediluvian rantings of a group of pagans coincided with my own ideas. His excitement increased as the connections he made between my theory and this heathen text grew more tenuous. Shrugging my shoulders with indifference, I told him that his concepts were ill-formed, if not downright silly. I was not dealing with some supernatural ideal, but a scientific theory based upon known facts, a theory that could one day be proved with the aid of the Scientific Method. Lowering his eyes, he withdrew a bit from me, and the subject was never broached again.

Then, the great and terrible news came from that amazing new contraption, the telegraph. On August 27th, 1883, the volcanic island of Krakatoa, just west of the Dutch colony Java, exploded, causing the deaths of untold thousands of people. Reading the newspapers frantically, we scanned for any new items that would inform us of this catastrophe and the terrible tsunamis that followed. It became a national obsession, especially since several thousand Dutch citizens lived on Java and the nearby islands, farming exotic spices and trading with the Chinese. There was a haunted look to the eyes of many of the citizens of Haarlem, each worrying about friends or relatives who had sailed for those distant shores, unaware of the dangers that lurked underground.

The names of the deceased began trickling in from Java, along with the astonishing stories of destruction that now dominated the newspaper headlines. Within a few weeks, some of the human remains that could be identified were shipped back to Amsterdam. People swarmed the docks in search of their loved ones. Of course, most of the dead were buried by the terrible, flowing lava, the explosions of rock, or the massive tidal waves created by the volcano's eruption.

The scientific community went wild, and I admit that I was as anxious as the rest. The Royal Society of England formed a Krakatoa Committee to study what remained of the island, and many other countries joined in their efforts. I would have gladly joined them, but I was forced to remain in Holland with my sickly child and wife, neither of which could have borne the ocean voyage. Science marched forward, and I lingered in Europe with my family, my ignoble job, and my cockeyed theories about the flesh.

I hate to admit that I felt this way, that my desire to study a dead island was greater than my familial bonds. As a husband and now a father, I began to believe that I was terribly lacking in affection. I was sure to hide my disappointment deep within my false smiles and joviality that I displayed around the hearth. Still, I suspect that Mathilde, at least, gleaned my true desires, and she withdrew from me a bit. Since the discovery of Kris's illness, she had removed herself from the connubial bed, preferring to expend her energies upon her son while he lived. I had tried not to resent this abstinence, but now I could feel her watching me with a mild contempt. I was a scientist, damn it! Could the woman not understand?

In direct relation to her coldness towards me, I removed myself as much as I could from her view. She had always been a sweet girl, and I missed that sweetness almost as much as I cherished my little son. One day, I hoped, she would get over her anger at my neglect, and she would once again become that angel I had loved when I had met her in Amsterdam. It was during this time that I first noticed myself making a bizarre hissing noise, a nervous tic that would follow me throughout my life, appearing every time I was mentally disturbed. It sounded as though my anger and frustration were leaking out from between my lips, like air hissing from a balloon.

Four weeks later, Henrik floated into my office, a telegram in his tiny hand, a delighted look on his face. "Abraham," he said, "I have news, such wonderful news."

He slammed the papers down on my desk in front of me, and I found myself grinning as well. According to the telegrams, several bodies were being shipped to various hospitals so that they could be examined closely by the best medical minds in Holland. Two bodies were to arrive within the week at Valdaker Asylum.

We were to take the bodies, dissect them as carefully as possible, and report our findings back to Amsterdam, where the reports would be gathered into a volume, *On the Trauma Inflicted Upon the Human Body by Vol-*

canic Disturbance. Our little hospital was to be a part of this important scientific study, and my spirits immediately lifted. My friend informed me that he wanted me to serve as his assistant in this experiment.

Rushing home that night, I grasped my wife by the waist and spun her around the dining room to peals of laughter from little Kris. After a brief moment of happiness, she glanced at the boy, and her mood soured again. That night, as usual, she rebuffed my attempts at pleasant conversation, and I grew even more frustrated.

We prepared as much as we could at the hospital. Tables were equipped for the poor souls who had died so violently, and I made ready the terrible instruments of our trade. Laid out beside the tables, they gleamed in the candlelight of the examining room. There were no windows in this chamber, the better to decrease the chance of contamination from anything outside its walls.

When the corpses arrived, they came in large coffinlike crates. Prying them open, we saw that there was one male and one female. The male was in worse condition than his cotraveler, the body burnt brown and black, the skin shriveled like the skin of a fig. Its eye sockets were open, but the eyes had melted down the sides of its face, the mouth pulled back in a grimace of resignation. The corpse was reclined upon its back, arms and legs straight along its sides, as though the man had been caught unaware by the volcano while sleeping. Only one foot appeared to be untouched by either fire or burning lava, the pink flesh startling in contrast to the blackened skin of its leg, as though there were still some life left in it, imprisoned at the end of the extremity. Oddly, the decay and putrefaction, which were omnipresent upon the female corpse, had not seemed to touch the body of the male.

The woman's body, in contrast, was twisted and gnarled, the black, burnt limbs contorted as though caught in the act of running, legs akimbo, arms reaching out for some unattainable goal. The broiled skin clung to her bones, chipping away in places. Little of her humanity remained in her face, a skull haphazardly covered with flakes of crisp, Stygian derma.

We operated upon the woman first, taking skin samples, then making a long incision. Her internal organs were charred to a point where recognition became almost impossible. When we breached her skull, we were astonished to find that many of the brain's normal wrinkles had disappeared; the gray matter looked smooth and ironed-out, boiled within her cranium. The procedure was long and tedious, so we decided to wait until morning to perform the vivisection upon the dead man. We finished our notes, then I returned home.

Mathilde seemed even more aloof that evening, sitting silently by the fire, refusing to converse with me about the corpses. Indeed, she informed me that the subject repulsed her. My faithful Kris, however, stayed at my side, absorbing all my stories of volcanoes. Rocking in his little chair, his eyes remained rapt with wonder at his father's tales. His breathing was more labored, and I wondered again how long my son had left to live. I believe I held him closer than ever that evening, the air between us was cold when he left my arms to skip off to bed.

The next morning, I arrived at the hospital before Vanderpool, and I took the chance to examine the male corpse closely before we began the autopsy. The pale flesh of the untouched foot seemed brighter than it had the previous day, nearly luminescent in the light of the oil lamps. Scratching my head, I peered closer at this foot; the healthy skin was past the ankle. I hissed, consulting my notes. Yesterday, I had written that the healthy, pink flesh ended just at the ankle, yet this morning it reached at least two inches above that spot. Was this man's body healing itself?

Vanderpool was also at a loss, agreeing with my notations that it did appear as if the burnt skin was repairing itself, starting at the man's toes and working its way up towards his knee. He decided to wait on the operation in order to see what would happen in the following days. To ensure accuracy, we took copious notes and measurements. I also removed skin samples from the charred flesh around the man's chest and head, as well as several samples from the healthy-looking foot.

The next morning confirmed our suspicions. Now, the corpse's leg appeared healthy, if a bit pale, up to his knee. In addition, his other foot seemed to be healing itself, three of his toes rosy and fit. We continued to check for any sign of life from the man, but there was no pulse, and his skin was cold and clammy. His clenched lips, frozen in a rictus of a smile, emitted no breath. The eyeless sockets stared blankly at the ceiling.

We came to the mutual decision that we should remain with the body, in case it further healed itself. Being a bachelor, the doctor could stay at the hospital any time he desired, but I had to send a note to my wife that I would not be returning home for a few days. I knew that she would be angry with me, but I hoped that she would eventually understand.

Vanderpool returned later that day with a bottle of wine, and we drank, watching the corpse. The second foot was now nearly whole again.

"My dear Abraham," the good doctor said, raising his glass, "I don't pretend to understand what we are seeing here. It most certainly appears to be of a supernatural bearing. I would like for you to remain with the body and measure the healing progress hourly. I want to consult several books in my library at home."

It was the first he had spoken of the supernatural since our conversation about the Egyptian Book of the Dead. Although I was concerned about his unscientific beliefs, I knew that something was happening that I couldn't explain. Perhaps somewhere in his musty books he could discover the answer to the healing corpse.

I agreed that I would stay, although it gave me pause for a moment. Remaining with this thing through the night would be terrifying, no matter how scientifically significant. Vanderpool thanked me and left.

The healing progressed through the night hours, as I noted in my journal. Each hour, the burnt carrion knitted itself into healthy tissue, slowly, inch by terrible inch. I was getting extremely tired when I checked the man's breath. I was shocked to see a tiny, grape-like object nestled within each eye socket. The beastly thing's eyes were beginning to grow back!

This demonic regeneration was not the work of our God in Heaven. In my heart, I knew that when this being completed its transformation, it might resemble a man, but it would be something far more devilish and cruel. Evil was growing in this dark room. I turned up the oil lamps more than once during those long hours.

Alone, I was left to confront my inner thoughts. If this beast was able to reconstruct its heat-ravaged body, what else could it rejuvenate? Was the power locked within its very tissues? Was this an ability that it could share with others . . . such as little Kris? Could it repair my son's tortured, weak lungs?

By the time Vanderpool returned to the room in the early morning, I was exhausted, and the thing on the table had recreated its body to mid-thigh on the one leg and to its calf on the other. The process seemed to be quickening. Fear and fascination had kept me awake through the night, but I jumped at Henrik's suggestion that we sleep for a few hours before beginning again. Neither of us could bring ourselves to sleep in the same room as the thing, so we locked it securely within the examining room and retreated, myself to my home, and the good doctor to his office.

I could not help myself. Before I left for a few hours of sleep, I appropriated several bits of the thing's healing tissue. The only help for my son seemed to lie within the skin of this corpse.

Taking the boy aside, I forced him to swallow the ghastly tidbits, a terrible Communion, making sure he drank several glasses of water. He rocked in the chair I had made for him, gulping the water and touching the cross he never removed from his body, his attempt to emulate his father.

"Pappa," he said, and my heart melted, "I'm glad you are home."

As I removed my clothing, I sent a prayer to Heaven that the curative powers of the beast could help my young son's lungs heal themselves. Then I lay down, and I was asleep before I could count to ten. I dozed soundly, the long hours of work finally catching up to me.

At the designated time, my wife awakened me. I could tell from her stern look that she disapproved of my return to the hospital and the abandonment of my family. I wondered if I should explain the importance of what we were doing, tell her of the meal I had fed Kris, but I decided to give it some time. Her temper would eventually cool, and if the flesh worked its magic upon the boy's lungs, then she would be pleasantly surprised.

When I reached my office, I found an excited Henrik waiting for me. "I believe I have uncovered the identity of our stranger downstairs," he said, leaning back in his chair. "You once called my interest in the supernatural silly, but I believe that the answer lies within that realm. I've never told you, nor anyone, that I have a rather large selection of volumes dealing with the occult and the supernatural. My interest began as research into the various herbs and plants I grow in my greenhouse, then it seemed to take on a life of its own. I became fascinated with all that was unearthly. Last night, I peered through my library, and in one of my volumes, I discovered details of a creature called a Nosferatu."

"I've never heard of such a beast."

"Few have, but in my studies, I found several mentions of Nosferatu, mostly in areas where there had been caverns in the earth or deep fissures. Who knows what strange waters or gases leak from these dank spots, such as Krakatoa? These demons are alive only at night, preferring the darkness, for the light of the sun burns them, although it will not kill them. They are already dead. They are, literally, the dead who walk the earth, searching for human blood to satisfy their beastly cravings. They sleep and heal during the daylight hours. After they feed upon their human prey, many of the victims are converted to their accursed state. It seems it works in the blood somehow, and the humans die and rise with the night to become Nosferatu themselves."

Kris had tasted none of the beast's blood. If it did carry some disease of the blood, then he would not be affected, would he? My heart pounded against the cage of my ribs. "These folktales seem incredible. True or not, though, the beast is surely evil. Yet what are we to do? *Mein Gott*, if molten lava will not kill it, what will?"

"According to the texts, a wooden spear must penetrate its heart, and its head must be severed from its body, the mouth and skull filled with cloves of garlic. They also have severe aversions to religious iconography—crosses, crucifixes, saints medals—as well as sunlight." He hesitated. "Still, I am not sure if we should take the incentive to murder this beast. I propose we take a few more days to observe the Nosferatu, if that is what it truly is."

"Are you mad?" I shouted. "This is an unholy thing, a blasphemy vomited up from Hell. If it can pass its curse on to others— Of course we should kill it, and I propose we do so now."

His face became rigid. "Perhaps. Let us go check on the patient."

The beast's healing had progressed to its waist, its pale genitals hanging loosely between its muscular legs. Striations of pink skin seemed to have infected its necrotic torso, and tufts of blonde hair emerged in small gardens across its blackened scalp. The eyes were much larger now, nearly filling the sockets, but the eyelids were still missing. As we watched, the bright blue eyes moved, scanning the room. Its lips parted slightly, dislodging bits of dead skin, which fell into its mouth. I could see the sharp, all-too-white fangs that were hidden by the thing's smile. It was truly ghastly to witness, a blight upon God and the world.

Henrik became distressed, and he touched my shoulder. "My friend, you were right. We can not allow this demon to leave this examining room. The teeth . . . dear God, its teeth . . ."

"I think it still too weak to put up much of a battle," I stated. "We must find something we can use as a weapon."

On the grounds, we found a rather large branch from a dogwood, the wood of Christ's cross, and Henrik whittled it down with his pocket knife until it had a sharpened edge. I removed an ax from the gardener's shed. We absconded with several cloves of ripe garlic from the kitchen. Each of us made sure that we were wearing crosses around our necks for protection against the beast. The sun had nearly set when we made our way back into the examining room.

I held the ax in my hands, while Vanderpool clasped his wooden stake and a mallet. Never were two men so intent upon their purpose! We set our lamps on the table by the door and took a few steps into the room. The door slammed behind us.

Turning, I saw the darkness behind Vanderpool shift. The movement began to take form, solidifying, and I recognized the healthy flesh of the legs and waist that carried the lifeless upper torso.

"Look out!" I shouted, pushing him out of the way. The creature lunged at him, snarling with rage, baring canine teeth that were far too large for its ragged mouth. The lidless eyes gaped in a perpetual look of surprise. It thrust out black, claw-like hands, and I noticed for the first time that sharp fingernails had started growing back on its fingers.

It fell upon Vanderpool and pinned him to the floor. I recoiled in terror, the ax clasped tightly to my chest. Vanderpool struggled to free himself from the creature's grasp, but the Nosferatu's half-living, half-dead body proved too strong for him. It began to lower its chasmal mouth to the front of his throat, drool like sap hanging from its slavering lips.

"For God's sake, Van Helsing," Vanderpool cried out, "do something! Use your ax!"

Blinking, I rushed forward, emerging from my state of shock. With a mighty swing of the blade, I struck the beast's neck. Pale liquid spattered across my face. Its head hung from its neck by some skin and a few strands of muscle, but its gaze was just as fierce when it released Vanderpool and turned its attentions to me. The thing walked a few staggering steps towards me, its head lolling on its shoulders. Screaming in revulsion, I swung the ax again, and the monster's head flew across the room, landing sideways on the examining table. There was a silence that stretched out to a full thirty seconds before the body collapsed upon itself, caught in the throes of violent tremors.

In a flash, Henrik was crouched above the headless, shuddering bulk, hammering the sharp piece of wood through its heart. Across the room, dreadful howls came from the monster's head, a single yowl for every *clink* of the mallet striking the stake. With one final blow, the monster lay still beneath Vanderpool. On the examining table, the head ceased its ghastly noises, and the eyes rolled down. A bit of the pale liquid that must act as its blood spilled from the corner of its mouth, a thickening drool.

As Vanderpool began stuffing the monster's mouth with garlic, I raised the ax for a final blow to the back of its head, opening a passage into the skull. The brain glistened within its skeletal nest, deep red with blood and wrinkled far more times than any human's I had ever seen. I took some garlic from Henrik and inserted it into the skull.

It was growing dark when we secretly buried the creature in two different spots on the grounds of the hospital. Vanderpool wanted to keep the head as far away from the body as possible. The entire time that we spent digging, the monster haunted me: Its awkward shamble toward me on new feet, head hanging from shoulders, those surprised, dead eyes. Interspersed with these memories was the image of my young son's face as he reluctantly took the pieces of skin in his mouth. I had fed part of this obscenity to Kris. Certainly, I had done so only to improve his health, but I had now witnessed the beast in all its fearsome glory, seen the power that had returned it to life. What had I done? Had I introduced the devil's own evil into my son's body? Had I lost his soul for him?

When the holes in the ground had been re-filled, I was sweating more from anxiety than from exertion. I immediately begged off a drink with Vanderpool, claiming that I needed to see my family right away. He understood, allowing me to return to my hearth, and I fairly ran all the way home.

I entered the little house to find Mathilde and Kris already in bed. The fire had been lit, probably in anticipation of my return, and it cast ominous, flickering shadows throughout the room. I observed a glint out of the corner of my eye and turned to see Kris's sliver cross dropped carelessly before the hearth, catching the light of the fire. I held the symbol of Our Lord in my fingers, stroking it, knowing that this abandoning of the cross was no accident.

Tears were in my eyes as I walked to Kris's little room. He lay asleep in his bed, curled into a fetal position, cuddling a pillow. The moonlight was brilliant, illuminating the area enough for me to step around his little toys and the tiny chair that I had carved for him. I tried to remain silent, but a board creaked beneath my clumsy foot, and the boy rolled over, wiping the sleep from his eyes.

"Father?" he mumbled.

I sat on the edge of his bed, "Yes, it's me, Kris. How do you feel?"

I stroked his hair, and he settled back into his mattress, peering up at me with his pale blue eyes. He took a deep breath and released it, grinning with the sound of the air leaving his lungs.

"I feel wonderful, Father. That medicine you gave me really, really works. I even ran a race today against Lars, but he won. I will win the next one, you'll see!"

It had succeeded! The creature's tissues had mended the boy's weak lungs, had even allowed him to run without having to stop because of the pain. The Nosferatu may have been a monster, a minion of Satan himself, but he had, albeit unwittingly, cured my child. It was nothing short of a miracle.

With a sob catching in my throat, I clumsily wrapped my arms around my boy, and he returned the embrace. I had forgotten that I still held his cross, and when it touched the side of his shoulder, there was an awful hissing sound and the smell of searing flesh.

Snarling, he threw me away from himself. Such was his strength that I flew several feet and landed on his little chair, breaking it. My brief joy shattered. When I looked up, his eyes were glowing red in the moonlight, and some aspect of his face had become unfamiliar, infused with lust.

I had infected my son with the Nosferatu's flesh, and I had to be responsible for the terrible deed that I had done. Looking into his demonic face, I realized that this was no longer my Kris. This was some incarnation of the beast Vanderpool and I had murdered just hours earlier.

"Oh, Father," he whispered, his word muffled by the sheer size of his canine teeth. "What have you done to me?" He touched his bare shoulder, and I could see for the first time the cross-shaped burn etched in his skin. He stood up on the bed, his demoniac figure all the more horrible for its diminished size. "You have hurt me with that wicked necklace in your hand. You should toss it away, so that it doesn't harm me again."

He stepped to the edge of his bed, and I crawled back towards the doorway. Beneath my fingers, I felt the broken chair legs, and I grasped for one, praying that it would be sharp enough.

Kris looked down on me, his face filled with sadness. "Throw it away, Father, so that we may be together. For so long, you've struggled to be a good father to me. You made me a chair and gave me a necklace, but you never really loved me. You're not even certain you have the ability to love, are you? But I know you can, Father. I know you can love. All you need to do is remove the barrier to your heart. Put aside that cross, so we can be together. Put me, your son, first, before all else, in the true, unselfish love you have always longed to give—and I have always hoped to receive."

In that moment, I wanted nothing more than to do what he asked, to be, finally, a good and loving father, a father whose words were not awkward and whose embraces were not clumsy. Yet as I opened my hand to release the cross, I remembered Kris's words on receiving it: *Now I know that if I should die while wearing my cross, I shall be with God. I'll never take it off.*

"You are not my son!" I shouted. There was a rustling behind me.

"Oh, yes, I am, Father. I am your son in every possible way. You made me. You created me, helped me to rise above my little breathing problem and become what you see before you. Now, fling that damned cross away and let me near you."

There was another sound behind me as well as a flicker of light. Mathilde was approaching the doorway with an oil lamp in her hands. She glanced at me, smiled curiously.

"Why Abraham Van Helsing," she said, "what are you doing?"

The beast took advantage of my distraction, hurling himself through the air with an enraged, wolflike growl. I rotated back to the creature, whose red eyes blazed as though the fires of Hell were inside his skull. His lips pulled back to reveal fangs fully two inches long; his hands reached forward with clawlike nails.

"Kris!" Mathilde cried.

Without thinking, I brought the chair leg up to my chest, pointing the end at the little figure. The creature's eyes flared wide, and he fell upon the jagged chair leg. His body spasmed with a crazed ferocity.

I flung him away. His legs kicked, back arched. A mixture of blood and that strange, pale liquid gushed from his mouth. The chair leg had pierced his heart and run him through. The jagged end clattered against the floor in time with his gyrations.

Behind me, I could hear Mathilde screaming and screaming. I assumed she was going into a state of shock, but I couldn't take my eyes off the little boy with the piece of wood sticking out of his chest. Eventually, he stopped fighting and lay quietly. Mathilde stopped her screaming, and the only sound in the room was a phlegmatic breathing from my son. Bubbles of blood popped on his lips. When he finally turned his head to me, his eyes were once again that lovely shade of blue. He was my son, and he said the words that will haunt me for the rest of my miserable days on this Earth.

"Pappa . . . I'm afraid . . . I'm afraid of dying."

I left him there, and I took Mathilde by the hand, leading her to our bedroom and forcing her to sit on the bed. I didn't think she could understand, but I told her that I would explain everything later. Then I went out back to the wood pile for our ax.

Kris lay still, his breath soft, the chair leg jutting obscenely from his chest. Trails of the pale liquid crisscrossed his cheeks. It ran from his eyes as tears. He looked up at me. "Pappa . . . you *do* love me. I always knew. . . ."

I wanted to tell him so myself, but the words refused to come to my lips, halted by the terrible sight that lay before me. His eyes sought encouragement, sought comfort. But I could find none to offer. He had said he did not fear death, knowing he could be with God. Yet I did not see how he could go to God now, after what I had done. After what I was going to do.

I separated the boy's body from his head and stuffed his mouth with garlic, my breath coming in terrible sobs.

Returning to the hospital, I awakened Vanderpool and confessed the entire story. Instead of rebuking me, he tried to soothe me, telling me that there was nothing else that I could have done. We found a place at the asylum for Mathilde, and we buried Kris in two distant graves. With our sad tasks completed, we attempted to go on with our lives.

Afterwards, I explained to the neighbors that Kris had finally succumbed to his weakened lungs, and that his death had driven my wife insane with grief. It was a believable tale, and it worked on the people of Haarlem. All of them were kind to me in my shattered state, and I appreciated their attempts to dispel my morbid melancholia. I often wondered if they would treat me in a similar fashion if they knew the truth. I suspected not.

I visit Mathilde daily at the hospital, often taking meals with her. She stares at me as though she does not realize who I am or in what prison she now resides. She has never spoken another word.

I understand what she has done. If only I were able to forget the terrible things I had seen, the terrible things I had done. I remain conscious of my deeds, reliving them nightly, and wake each morning to know that every second I spend alive is a mockery of God's will. How could He desire such an outcome? What purpose could this infernal knowledge serve?

So, I grow older, living the life of a scholar who is actually a child murderer. I watch my darling wife wither away to a shell of her former self. I hide myself in various studies, masking my pain with science and philosophy in a vain attempt to escape the guilt that holds me prisoner. I await the judgment of Our Lord, surely a terrible fate, and I bide my time until He decides to illuminate me to the purpose of this dreadful ordeal.

I grow older.

And I wait.

Alone.

The Tomb of Fog and Flowers

C. Dean Andersson

✠

Dr. Abraham Van Helsing shifted his weight in a wingback chair, uncomfortable in every position. He maintained clinical detachment only by taking deep steadying breaths. Emotional uninvolvement was always essential for the good of his patient, and for his own protection, but it was even more critical than usual in the current case.

He sat observing an elegant woman of middle age. Upon a couch of cordovan leather near his chair, she lay comfortably on her back with eyes closed. Her blond hair, frosted with silver, spread pale against indigo silk pillows. A dressing gown of forest green silk enclosed her like a cocoon. His dearest wife. Anna. Insane.

Inside his cherished book-lined study, burgundy drapes of thick damask silk held daylight at bay, muffled the voices of people passing on a busy Amsterdam street, dulled the sound of horses' hooves striking cobblestones as clattering carriages bustled about their business. From a single gas lamp turned low, burning in a brass fixture on the wall over his chair, came all the light he needed for this vital session.

Did he hold hope that hypnosis was the key, the final one, the only one left to unlock the secrets swirling in his wife's brain? The key to return her sanity? He felt he had little choice. Hope, slim hope, was all he had left.

He lowered his voice to speak in soft, soothing, almost husky tones as he leaned near her. "Now go ahead, Anna, follow these feelings that cause you to toss and turn, to moan and cry out in your sleep, follow these strong feelings back to their origin. Go ahead. You are safe and secure at all times. I am with you always. And when you reach your compelling dream, you experience your emotions as if you are watching someone on a stage. You see your dream upon a stage with you safe and alone in a small theater."

Beyond the room's closed door he heard footsteps as a servant or possibly one of Anna's nurses passed by.

"Any sounds you hear beyond my voice and this room simply lull you deeper into relaxation." He waited until he was convinced nothing disturbed her. "Go ahead now, Anna, follow your emotions back into your dream and tell me what you see upon the stage."

Silence from Anna's lips, but she moved her head away from him, as if to reject his command.

Good. He felt encouraged by any response from her.

He sat still, so very still, and he watched her, his bushy red eyebrows knitted together in a frown of concentration. How he remembered the early fire of their relationship, how busy years pursuing his career and analytical science cooled it, how the death of their son extinguished it. Now he felt that closeness again, even pursued it as he searched in her clouded mind for the Anna he loved.

That Anna's mental decline began after their son's death there was no doubt. Three years ago this month. August. Three long years.

Anna felt strongly that Paul should not go on that fateful climbing excursion. But Van Helsing believed she was always overly protective of their son. Paul was nearly seventeen, strong, healthy, and well trained in climbing lesser ascents. So he took his son, his only child, with him.

At least Anna did not see Paul fall, did not hear that final scream, that heart-wrenching sound that still echoed in Van Helsing's memories, jerking him awake from dreams where he fell with his son toward jagged rocks and snow. But their Paul, their wonderful, brilliant son, was never found, left alone, abandoned, lost in some snow-filled crevice. Surely the lack of Paul's body to bury contributed to Anna's grave condition.

At first she grieved and blamed him for Paul's loss. Then began nightmares she could never remember, and with them came her delusion that Paul was still alive and desperately needed his mother. The fantasy became a fixation that dragged the rest of her mind into that chaos of unreality.

Van Helsing resisted a deep sigh as he quietly slipped a heavy gold watch from his vest pocket, a gift from Anna long ago. With a gold fountain pen, also from her, he noted the time in a leather-bound journal he leaned against his right knee. Half past noon. He knew better than to allow painful memories to overwhelm the present.

"Anna, you are floating on the sound of my voice, so relaxed, so comfortable, so safe. Now imagine your dream as a play on a stage. You sit alone and safe, so very comfortable. Now go ahead. Imagine the play and tell me when the action begins." He held out little hope that she would speak, but even a little hope was a lot to him now.

Anna slowly turned her head toward him.

He froze, feeling his heart beat faster in anticipation.

She swallowed. "Yes, I see." An expression of unease, then fear, crossed her features. "A woman . . . me . . . alone, in a small room, in a strange house. There is a narrow window, open and dark with night, moonlight shining through. Spiderwebs hang in the corners. Dust is everywhere. All is quiet. So very quiet."

Van Helsing closed his eyes in silent, profound relief, then quickly made efficient notes in shorthand as he slipped totally into the necessary clinical detachment. "What do you feel about the woman on the stage?"

"She, no, I want to run away. I fear what lives in the house, people who crumble to dust if touched."

He puzzled at her words even as he quickly jotted them down in his journal. What could the dark, silent house and its inhabitants represent? Perhaps a tomb?

In a whisper she said, "But *he* lives in the house, too, so I must stay. I must wait. I will never abandon him."

She fell silent.

Van Helsing glanced up from his notes. "Anna, you are safe. I am with you. Tell me, for whom do you wait?"

She tossed her head as tears slowly leaked from the corners of her eyes. "For my son, of course. For Paul."

Van Helsing stared at her, totally transfixed, then closed his eyes in despair. It was, as he feared, dementia based on grief, for which he felt responsible. Guilt cut deeply into him. For all his fine reputation for knowledge, he had not been able to save his son, and now he feared the worst for his wife. She was imprisoned in a tomb, awaiting her dead son's return.

"You are safe and relaxed, my dearest Anna. This is a play you watch, and your feelings are safely at a distance." His voice cracked with emotion, and he stopped speaking, reached for the all-important detachment so he could continue.

She took a deep, ragged breath, relaxing slightly. "Are you . . . playing a game, Paul? Hiding from me? Where are you? Wait! There you are! Oh, Paul! How tall you are, and . . . so much older?" A sob broke from her trembling lips. "Who *are* you? You're not Paul!" A louder sob. And then silence, a thick, heavy silence.

Van Helsing tensed. Her strong emotions might bring her spontaneously out of hypnosis, but her emotions were also crucial to discovering important clues. "Anna, what is happening on the stage now?"

"She asked me a question."

"She? Who is she?" He noted that the other woman could be a projection of Anna's own needs, a part of her.

"She informs me that I may see Paul again, but only if I answer a question. Correctly. And I even know what she will ask. She asked it so many times before. Yet I never know what to answer." Anna tossed her head back and forth as tears ran down her cheeks. "I never know what to answer. Never!"

"What is the question?"

"What should . . ." Anna's voice trailed away, then she took a deep breath. "What should I answer?" She clenched her fists, her eyebrows drawing together as she concentrated. "Only one chance! One chance alone." Sweat glistened on her furrowed brow.

"Relax, Anna. You are safe. I am with you. Continue. Tell me the question."

"I want to see Paul! She is going away. No. Come back." Pain filled her voice. "Don't go! Give me time to think!"

Van Helsing felt his own sense of panic rise along with that of his wife. So close now. He had to reach her, get the question now, before her mind closed to him again, before the vital opportunity was lost. "Go ahead, Anna, share the question and lift your burden."

Anna lashed out. "She never gives me time to think! There are so many things I want to do, to know, to experience. With him. One day is not enough!"

Desperate to relieve her frustration, Van Helsing leaned forward. "Anna, tell me what the woman asks. Tell me. Now."

And finally, Anna replied, "If I gave Paul back to you for one more day, what would you do?"

Van Helsing felt the blood drain from his face. Clinical detachment evaporated completely as he remembered a dream fragment of his own. A woman asked him the same question. But how had he answered? *Had* he answered?

He exerted control over himself and leaned back. He inhaled deeply, held it, and then slowly exhaled. He repeated the calming exercise twice more.

How could he have experienced the same dream as Anna? Or had he? As the great pioneer in hypnosis, Charcot, had taught him, the hypnotist must guard against being influenced by the very suggestions he gave his subjects. And he had heard it said that souls and memories could do strange things under hypnotic trance. But for now it was time to let Anna rest from her ordeal.

Van Helsing began the process of bringing her out of hypnosis. Slowly and gently, he counted upward from one to ten. When she opened her eyes, it pained him to see that she again showed no conscious recognition of who he was, lost in her inner world once more, waiting for Paul in a tomb. But Van Helsing saw into that tomb with hypnosis now, an important first step. And he could take the next step without her, investigate the shared dream by following his own memories.

He called for her nurses, supervised her return to her room, made certain she was resting comfortably, then hurried back to his study and closed the door.

He extinguished the gas lamp and drew open the drapes. Sunlight flooded the room. He moved past his wingback chair and the couch. Behind a wide mahogany desk strewn with papers and books, he settled into a comfortable barrister's chair of dark mahogany and cordovan leather.

He opened his journal, reread what he had written about Anna's session, added additional notes with his preliminary analysis and speculations.

Someone knocked on his study door. "Dr. Van Helsing?"

"You may enter, Gretta."

The door opened to reveal Mrs. Gretta Van Mettle, his housekeeper of many years. Though stoutly proportioned, she stood straight-backed, prim and proper, always immaculately groomed, wearing the patient expression he knew so well. How disconcerting it would be to see a single hair out of place on her head, a sign of chaos triumphant. Yet he also remembered her hair, now silver, had been a rich auburn when she'd entered his service after his marriage to Anna. Gretta had loved Paul and grieved dearly for him.

"Your noon meal is ready, Dr. Van Helsing." He had never been able to get her to call him anything but "Dr. Van Helsing," though he had tried.

"Thank you, Gretta."

"I will see that it is warmed. The noon meal has been ready since noon."

"Of course." Gretta disapproved of not taking meals on time. He knew she was also concerned about Anna, and about him. He suspected that she and most of the servants thought his work dealing with the minds of patients was little better than superstition, not fitting for good Christians, a common notion, even among many who called themselves scientists.

"Very good, Dr. Van Helsing." Gretta nodded, then quietly closed the door.

He returned his attention to his journal.

His training also included self-hypnosis, and now was the time to use it. He began working on the specifics of his plan to investigate the shared dream but paused after a few moments, suddenly aware of a sweet scent perfuming the air. He sniffed and frowned. Flowers? His room contained no flowers, and the windows were closed.

"Dr. Van Helsing." He jerked his head up. With a shock he saw a tall woman standing across the room in front of the closed door.

A cloak of crimson velvet covered her from shoulders to feet. Fair hair framed her striking face in a thick tangle that hung to her waist. Her hair shone with golden fire in the sunlight from the windows. Her intense blue eyes held his gaze.

He fought to regain his composure, stood, cleared his throat. "Young lady, you startled me. Gretta should have announced you." How had she entered his house and then his study without Gretta or someone else noticing?

"You do not recognize me?"

Eyes narrowed, he regarded her, intrigued. He noted that in spite of her exotic appearance, she spoke his native Dutch without a trace of an accent. Looking as she did, she could be part of a circus or a member of some traveling troupe of performers, though he had heard of none in the area. "No, I certainly do not recognize you. Do you or someone you know require a doctor's care?"

She smiled, a slight movement of one corner of her rose-tinted lips. "To help your wife you must accept realities your science condemns. I will see you again, after midnight."

Her image wavered, became unfocused, merged with the sunlight pouring through the window.

She was gone.

The scent of flowers swiftly faded.

He looked at the empty room, astonished. He struggled to find an explanation. She must never have been there at all. A hallucination. Very vivid. Extremely real. He felt a tingle of fear. Was insanity waiting in his future, too? It was a fear shared by many doctors who studied mental illness and knew insanity could strike anyone.

A knock came on his door. "Dr. Van Helsing? Your meal."

He took a deep breath to steady himself. "Enter."

As Gretta came into the room, Van Helsing moved several books from the corner of his desk to clear a space. He saw that his hands trembled. He quickly placed them behind his back.

Gretta efficiently set down the tray. "If I may say so, the food is quite delicious today, Dr. Van Helsing."

"Thank you, Gretta. Please see that I am not disturbed this afternoon."

She gave him a searching look. "Very good, Dr. Van Helsing." She closed the door as she left the room.

Van Helsing lowered himself into his chair. He looked at the food but had no appetite after his recent experiences. A dream he seemed to have shared with his wife. A visitor who vanished before his eyes. Fear he might be slipping toward insanity returned.

Gretta often suggested he was working too hard, needed rest. Her common sense might surpass his renowned learning.

He sat thinking for a moment, opened his journal to record the hallucination, started with what had come first. The aroma of flowers. A familiar scent. Not roses.

Lilacs.

The scent had been of lilacs.

The realization summoned a childhood memory of a picnic in the country with his mother, a green meadow, lilac bushes nearby, bees buzzing amongst the fragrant blooms. After their meal, his mother read to him from a children's book of legends and fairy tales. He snuggled closely against her, warm and full, listening to her voice, looking at the pictures. A Witch, half alive, half a corpse, disturbed him. She called herself Old Granny when she tricked her way into people's homes. But a different picture enthralled him, a woman with hair of gold like his mother's, *a woman wearing a crimson cloak.*

He still had the book.

He hurried to the bookshelf near the door of his study, pulled an old book from the shelf, searched for the legend about Tannhäeuser, found the illustration showing the Goddess Venus. The similarity to his visitor was obvious.

Fear of encroaching mental illness returned. Had three years of guilt been more than he could bear? He fought the fear by telling himself he was making progress toward a rational explanation that might help his wife.

His mind had evidently created a hallucination based upon a childhood memory. And his visitor, representing a projection of his subconscious, had said that to help his wife he had to accept realities his science condemned. But what realities did it mean? The realities accepted by the insane? Was he telling himself the only way to help Anna was to become insane himself?

Worry about his mental stability stabbed him again. What if he did fall insane? Who would help Anna then? Who would help him?

He returned his old children's book to the shelf, looked out a window, sought reassurance in the reality of the bustling Amsterdam street. But tears blurred his vision. Paul was dead. Anna was insane. And he might be losing his mind.

He rubbed his temples. A headache was coming. He knew he needed to take Gretta's advice and rest. But he thought again of Anna. Resting could wait.

He sat down at his desk and first recorded the hallucination of Venus and the relevance of the children's book, then revised his procedures for continuing Anna's treatment and planned a self-hypnosis session to investigate their shared dream. As he worked he forced himself to eat some of the cold food.

By the time the clock in the foyer chimed four, he was satisfied with his plans. But his headache was worse. Before subjecting himself to self-hypnosis, he must rest.

He walked upstairs to his bedroom, shut the door, removed his brown worsted jacket, unbuttoned his matching vest, loosened his collar and tie, pulled the drapes closed, and stretched out on the bed he had once shared with Anna. He thought of her now in the bedroom downstairs, attended by nurses, lost in her inner world. A wave of sadness engulfed him. "Anna," he whispered.

A knock on his door awakened him. "Dr. Van Helsing?" It was Gretta. The light that edged above his drapes had dimmed. How long had he slept?

"Dr. Van Helsing? Are you all right?"

"Yes, Gretta." His headache was gone. He rose, ran a hand through his hair to smooth it down, opened the door. "I was resting."

"Very Good, Dr. Van Helsing. The evening meal is ready. Will you be coming down?"

"Certainly. In a moment." He began buttoning his vest. "As soon as I am presentable."

After he had eaten, he told Gretta he would be working late in his study and bade her good night.

On his way to his study he checked on Anna. Her nurses were pleased to tell him she had shown more appetite than usual and had eaten nearly all of her evening meal. Now she was sleeping peacefully. The news encouraged him.

When he entered his study he saw that the servants, possibly Gretta herself, had drawn closed the drapes. The sight comforted him. Since childhood he had preferred windows be covered after dark.

One night when he was four or five years old, he'd heard a sound outside his window. It made him think of a dog walking in dead leaves. But he remembered thick drifts of winter snow lay on the ground. And the next morning he saw no tracks.

After that first time, no matter the season, the rustling came nearly every night when he was getting ready for bed or sometimes after he'd been tucked in. But it only came when he was alone.

While the faint rustling grew louder he would be afraid to move lest movement reveal his presence to whatever approached. And when the rustling stopped, he knew the quiet meant the walker was waiting outside his window for him to see it and it him. To prevent an accidental sighting, he drew the drapes closed over the single window in his bedroom before each sunset.

One night his family returned late from an outing in the country. He hurried to his bedroom to make certain the drapes were closed. But they were not.

As soon as he entered his bedroom the sound began. Too late to close the drapes, he turned to run from the room, but before he reached the door the sound rushed louder to the window and stopped.

He froze, his back to the night-blackened windowpane. He could feel whatever was there looking in at him, willing him to turn and see. He fought the silent command, gritted his teeth, clenched his fists. But as he stood, terrified and trembling, into his thoughts crept a certainty about who was looking in. He could see her in his mind, the Witch from his story-book, Old Granny, half alive, half a corpse, her nightmare face close to the pane. And he knew then what made the sound, yellow bones poking through the decaying flesh of her feet, rustling the dead leaves that always covered the ghostly path she walked.

Time stretched on and on as he struggled to resist Old Granny's will. Finally the sound began again, slowly faded, and was gone.

He raced to the window and jerked the drapes closed. He had won! Or so he first thought. For though the sound never came again, he soon realized that because the Witch had caught sight of him, she could now visit whenever she pleased.

He often felt her presence in his room as he was falling asleep, knew she was standing hunched over at the foot of his bed, willing him to open his eyes and see her. But he never gave in. After he reached adolescence, her visits became less frequent and eventually stopped.

Van Helsing shook his head at the potent memories as he used a wooden match to light the gas lamp above his desk. Such things had deep power in childhood and, unless remembered and understood, could produce hidden influences in adulthood. This he knew. But he also knew that somewhere inside him was a child-self still terrified of the Witch.

He sat at his desk and pushed the childhood memories away, recorded in his journal the nurses' encouraging report about Anna. Then he reviewed his plan to investigate the shared dream with self-hypnosis.

When he was ready to begin the session, he closed the door, turned the lamp's flame low, placed his journal within reach on the chair near the couch, removed his jacket, loosened his tie and collar, unbuttoned his vest, and lay back. He relaxed, breathing deeply and slowly.

The clock in the foyer chimed the hour. But it did not stop until it reached twelve. Which could not be right. He had just lain down to start his session. At the latest it should only be eight o'clock. He noticed how quiet it was. Even the street sounds outside were absent.

He drew his gold watch from his vest pocket. Midnight.

Four hours? He must have fallen asleep instead of inducing hypnosis. He was obviously more tired than he had realized. Then he noticed a scent of flowers. Lilacs. But soured, decaying.

He sat up. With the gas flame burning low, there were disturbing shadows in the room. An image of the Witch came into his mind. Outside the windows, a faint rustling began.

He listened, incredulous.

The sound grew louder, louder, then stopped.

Years of scientific training and education evaporated. He was suddenly a child again, terrified, afraid to move.

But the mature man rebelled. He would not be prey to a hallucination spawned by a storybook! He could not give in to insanity.

Driven by a burst of sudden anger he rose to his feet and flung back the drapes.

The Old Witch was there. But no. It was not the Old Witch. It was worse than that.

He cried out, a strangled sob.

Anna crouched on the sidewalk beneath a streetlamp, her hair an unbound tangle, her feet bare, wearing only her nightdress. Her eyes were closed. She turned and walked away.

"Anna!"

Van Helsing ran from his study. The front door stood open. He raced outside, saw Anna down the street, called her name. She ignored his call, as he might expect, and disappeared around a corner. He pursued her.

The summer night was warm. Nothing else moved on the dimly lit Amsterdam street. The sleeping city might as well have been deserted.

A dog barked in the distance. Another answered, farther away. An old Dutch saying came into his mind: When dogs bark at night, Death is near—Death in the shape of Dame Holda, after whom Holland was named. He had read she was related to other Death Goddesses of legend, like the Scandinavians' Hela, who was half dark, half light, half alive and half dead. He had never made the connection between Holda, Hela, and Old Granny before. He reminded himself to note it in his journal even as he increased his pace, desperate to reach Anna.

There were fewer streetlamps on the street down which she had turned, but a waning moon had risen half full and gave enough light for him to see she was still far in the lead. He pushed himself to move faster, thought how scandalous it must look, the great Dr. Van Helsing running down the street without his jacket, vest unbuttoned, tie and collar loose, in pursuit of his wife.

Why could he not catch Anna? No matter how fast he moved, she moved faster, as if it were all a dream.

Could it be a dream? Could he still be asleep on the couch in his study? No, he rejected that idea. He was sweating, breathing hard, experiencing physical stress. As much as he might wish it, this was no dream!

Anna turned onto another dark street. He suddenly knew where she was going. Of course, he thought. *Of course*. She was going to Paul's tomb.

Through the midnight streets of the silent city he doggedly pursued his wife, until finally he arrived at the cemetery where the Van Helsing family crypt sheltered Paul's empty tomb.

He saw no sign of Anna. The iron cemetery gate stood open. It should have been locked. Had vandals or thieves been at work earlier that night? Might they still be inside, a danger to Anna? He hurried through the open gate.

Down a tree-lined pathway he ran. The night air was cooler in the cemetery amongst the trees. Overhanging branches dimmed the moonlight, made it hard to see as he ducked low-reaching limbs here and there, was battered and scratched by others. The smell of cedar and yew was strong. A bird fluttered wildly overhead, disturbed on its night perch by his passage.

He emerged from the path into an open area where family mausoleums rose in the moonlight. He found the Van Helsing crypt. The entrance yawned darkly. Like the cemetery gate, the door to the crypt should have been locked, but it was standing open. He thought again of vandals.

He approached the doorway, heard a sob, then weeping, inside. He wished for a lamp or candle, but did not have with him so much as a wooden match.

Van Helsing hesitated at the entrance. The weeping continued. Perhaps she had awakened from sleepwalking and found herself lost and confused in the dark. He must be careful not to startle her further, to reassure her all was well.

"Anna." The weeping stopped. Silence. "Everything is all right. I am here with you now."

A faint rustling sound began, grew louder, came toward him from within the crypt. Not now. Not another hallucination!

He fought the old fear, stood his ground as the rustling drew closer. A chilled breath of air carried a scent of death from within the darkness. Foggy tendrils of mist coiled around his feet and legs. He strained to see into the dark, could but barely glimpse a form approaching the doorway.

"Anna." He had not meant to whisper. He steadied himself. Cleared his throat. "It's all right. Come outside."

The rustling stopped.

"Enemies fear what you can become."

What could she mean? What dementia was she experiencing now? The voice hardly sounded like Anna's. "It's all right, Anna," he repeated. "Come home with me now."

"But your enemies are also mine, and they fear me, your Old Granny, in all my many forms."

Old Granny? A chill passed through him. Why was Anna using that name? "Anna, come outside. We must go—"

"I have watched over you, protected your precious soul, kept you safe and alive."

"Anna, what—"

"Anna never left her bed. In her shape I lured you here tonight. This tomb is sacred to you. Your guilt has made it so. A suitable place to choose your destiny."

Had a part of Anna's mind separated from her normal personality? He had seen that happen to other patients. This other part of her mind might provide new clues to her treatment. "Can you tell me, then, what I can do to help Anna?"

"As earlier I told you, to help her you must accept other realities."

Fear clutched at him. No one could know that but him. He was closer to madness than he had imagined if all this was a hallucination. He felt disoriented and confused. "You could only know what was said this afternoon if you are also a projection of my subconscious."

"Or, I might be one of those realities you must accept. At least your science believes in the reality of the power of dreams. And you think you shared a dream with Anna. But your dream was different. Remember *your* dream. Be there, now!"

Memories stirred, conjured the dream, a picnic in a green meadow, lilac bushes nearby. The Goddess Venus appeared, slipped her crimson cloak from her shoulders, stood naked in the sunlight, became the Anna he remembered from their wedding night. They embraced, kissed, made love on the warm, green grass. But when the loving was over, an icy fog settled around them, hid Anna from his view. A winter wind howled, whipped his hair, and blew away the fog to reveal who had taken Anna's place.

The Witch grinned at him. Her face, framed by a tangle of white hair, was pale and alive on one side, dark and decaying on the other. And she asked, her voice a ragged whisper, "What would you give to have Anna back for one more night? Would you give your Old Granny a kiss?"

The memory stunned him. Anna had dreamed of seeing Paul, but he had dreamed of seeing Anna, and his dream, remembered incorrectly during her hypnosis session, could have subconsciously triggered the hallucinations he had experienced that afternoon and this evening.

"Give your Old Granny a kiss."

New fear surged through him. The voice from the tomb was now a dry whisper, Old Granny's voice from his dream.

A pale hand reached from the doorway followed by a second hand dark with decay, bones peeking through tattered flesh.

Van Helsing drew back, inhaled sharply. The nauseating stench of death filled his nostrils.

"As I open my arms to you, open your mind to realities both seen and unseen, like the Earth, always half in light, half in darkness. Like me. Overcome your fear. Accept my reality and your destiny with a kiss. Your reward will be Anna as she used to be, with you again. But if at dawn she still needs to be with Paul more than with you, for your love's sake you must let her go. Step now into my arms. Defy your fear of my darkness. There is more to me than that."

This was true madness, he told himself. If he gave in to it his hold on sanity might slip entirely away. But even a madman's hallucination might give him knowledge to help Anna.

"I will risk submitting to this madness if you reveal the answer Anna must give in her dream to see Paul again. I want her agony about that to be at an end. And I want to remain sane long enough to find a way to tell her."

"When the time comes, you will know what to say to her. But what if I am not a hallucination, Abraham Van Helsing? What if you knew beyond doubting that I am as real as anything you've ever known, as real as life and death? Would you still give me a kiss?"

"Compared to madness, I would prefer you to be real."

She laughed, the ragged cackle of a storybook Witch. "Then step into my arms. Your destiny awaits!"

He stared at the dead hand, fought to overcome his repulsion, forced himself to take one blind step, two, another into the darkness between her outstretched arms.

The stench of decaying flesh became mixed with the perfume of lilacs as her arms closed around him. The decaying arm felt like ice through his clothing, the living one fire. Something spider soft touched his face. He jerked back. The arms held him. He made himself stop fighting. He surrendered.

Fire and ice touched his lips, warm, soft flesh on one side, cold bone and teeth on the other.

A vision possessed his mind. He saw a beautiful blue and white sphere floating in a sea of black amongst the cold, hard light of countless stars. One half of the turning globe was bathed in sunlight, the other half hidden in darkness. With a feeling of joy and awe he understood he was looking at the Earth from far, far above.

From out of the fathomless depths beyond the world a vast cloud of gray mist and lightning appeared and shrouded the Earth.

He found himself standing atop a hill. Overhead churned a gray, sky-spanning cloud out of which two swirling columns of cloud descended, one pale and burning with white light, the other black, shot through with crimson lightning. Their rumbling shook the Earth.

The black cloud disgorged monsters upon the Earth. The white cloud sent forth beings almost human in appearance. They lured Earth's native humans into battle first against the monsters and then each other.

Van Helsing held a sword and a shield. Upon the shield was an image of the Earth and beneath it the face of the Old Witch. She stood beside him atop the hill and pointed a gnarled finger at the battle. "Help me save this world and its children!"

Van Helsing broke away from the nightmare vision as the arms released him. He gasped and staggered back, into the moonlight. The fog swirling around him thinned, snaked back into the crypt as the Witch's arms withdrew into the darkness.

"I am proud of you, Abraham. We have made a good beginning this night. Go home and be with your wife as of old, at least until dawn." The whispered words grew fainter. "Your love for her can give you strength and keep you sane as we fight the monsters of the dark and . . . the light."

The rustling began again, now sounded to him as if a multitude of ghostly voices whispered together. The whispering faded away and was gone. The scent of death and flowers no longer hung in the air.

Van Helsing steadied himself against the cool stones of the doorway, breathing heavily. For a moment he was possessed by a certainty that all he'd experienced had been absolutely real. He struggled to push the mad feelings away, reminded himself that hallucinations did not rule out the possibility he might really have followed Anna there. She might still be inside the crypt. He had to find out.

"Anna? Dearest?" He stepped through the doorway into the darkness, moved blindly forward, arms outstretched, calling her name. He carefully felt his way throughout the single room, made certain it was empty.

He must go home, see if she was there, find out if he had hallucinated everything. But if she was not at home, the authorities must be notified, a search organized.

He hurried from the cemetery, looked for Anna as he went, saw no one on the deserted streets.

The front door of his home stood open as in his haste he had left it. He closed the door and locked it, crept through the foyer past the loudly ticking clock, past his study door near the stairs, headed to Anna's room to see if she was there.

"Abraham?"

He stopped.

Anna stood at the top of the staircase. She looked down at him, her blue eyes bright and aware. She wore a lapis dressing gown trimmed with gold thread. Her hair was neatly arranged in a chignon at the nape of her neck. "I dreamed an old woman told me to wake up and wait for you here. She frightened me. Are you all right? Where have you been?"

His heart pounded in his chest. It was as the Witch had promised. And if this was true, what else of that night's experiences might also be true? Old Granny and all she had said to him, *real?* If he was not losing his grip on reality, reality was far different than he had been taught. But exploring such possibilities could wait. Only one thing mattered now.

He hurried up the stairs, resisted his need to crush Anna in his arms, afraid of upsetting her further. He took her hands gently in his own, felt her warmth, smelled her familiar scent of lavender, raised her warm, fragrant hands and then kissed each fingertip, making the moment last.

"Abraham, I don't understand what has happened. Why was I downstairs in the guestroom with a nurse? I could not wake her. Have I been ill?"

"Anna, come into our room. There are still many hours until dawn."

Upstairs in their bedroom, they held each other close. They talked and kissed as if all the wounding years were mere phantoms. Just before dawn they made love, the rich, vibrant love of two kindred souls, love made bittersweet because from talking both knew they were saying good-bye, perhaps forever.

With the rising of the sun, Anna fell into a deep sleep. When next she awakened, she would be lost to him again. But difficult as that was to accept, accept it he did, and more, much more than he would ever have thought possible.

Most importantly to him, Anna now understood how to answer the question in her dream. As Old Granny had promised, while they talked it came to him to tell her she was looking for the answer in the wrong place. The answer was not in her mind but in her heart. When next the dream came, she could answer correctly and again be with Paul. She would toss and turn in anguish no more.

He stroked her hair, now long and loose. He watched her sleep with a faint smile on her lips.

There was something else he had also known to tell her. One day can last forever, in a dream.

He leaned down and gently kissed her forehead.

"Give my love to our son."

So Far From Us in All Ways

Chris Roberson

LETTER, FROM FU ZHENG LEI, HUNAN PROVINCE, TO HIS EXCELLENCY, THE IM-
PERIAL MINISTER OF EXAMINATIONS, THE FORBIDDEN CITY, BEIJING
(translated from the Mandarin)

Your Excellency, forgive my impertinence in addressing this missive
directly to you. At the urging of my uncle, Governor of Hunan Province
and cousin to His Imperial Majesty Xianfeng (scion of the Qing dynasty,
son of heaven, may he reign ten thousand years), I am writing to explain
my absence from my scheduled Jinshi national examination, and to beg
your indulgence in allowing me another attempt. My uncle, Governor of
Hunan province and cousin to His Imperial Majesty, thought it might be
beneficial if I were to explain how it was that I came to miss my scheduled examination, as the circumstances were most unusual and unavoid-
able. My uncle, likewise, suggests that recounting the events could prove
instructive for me, and help mould me into one who might in future better serve the Dragon Throne.

The difficulty arose on the road from Changsha, en route to Beijing
and the Forbidden City.

ABRAHAM VAN HELSING'S JOURNAL
(translated from the Dutch)
1 Sep. 1860. Zhengzhou.—Left Tianjin by junk boat, morning of 25th August, and after a journey of five days, four onboard and one additional by horse-drawn wagon, reached the rural city of Zhengzhou. Unfortunately, my employer's agent, whose health I was sent afield to tend, could not wait my coming. Arriving too late to help the poor devil, I was able to do little more than supervise the packing up of his body to be shipped, first to Tianjin, then back to England for burial.

I have been in the Orient only a relatively short time, and this journey marked my first real foray beyond the protection of the English Concession in the treaty port city of Tianjin. Within the Concession, guarded by English troops, the narrow streets packed with the regional offices of dozens of leading English international firms, my life has not been much different from my years spent studying in London. But beyond those protective walls lies the alien landscape of China, mysterious and threatening.

I have had occasion, these last months, to question the wisdom of quitting my native Holland for such a strange port. I've not felt at ease since stepping off the packet boat on the Tianjin docks, surrounded by the odd customs and incomprehensible jabber of the natives. Even within the confines of the English Concession I am surrounded by foreigners and never hear my native tongue (though at least there, with my admittedly limited facility with the British tongue, I can comprehend and make myself understood). Still, after the loss of my wife and son this past winter, I could not remain any longer in Amsterdam. Each street corner I turned, each park bench I passed, only served as a reminder of happy memories, and brought to mind the grim, miserable state of my life without them. When the invitation from my former classmate arrived, I saw it as a chance for escape. A fellow student from my days studying medicine in London, he had gone into business and established himself in international trade. With the cessation of the Opium War and the opening of Chinese ports to European powers, my former classmate's business was one of many new regional offices in the Orient, and his branch in the north port of Tianjin was in need of a physician. In a trice, I resigned my teaching position at the University, packed my bags, and made arrangements for immediate departure.

In the months since, there has been little call for my specialized skills, beyond treating the occasional laceration or fracture, prescribing a poultice for a rash induced by some exotic nettle, or tending to a victim of dysentery. This journey into the hinterlands was to be the first real test of my medical abilities, and due to the slowness of the transportation, I arrive too late even to unlatch the clasps on my bag. I will, at least, be able to serve my patient in some small regard by escorting his body back to civilization, to be shipped to his family overseas, who do not even know yet that they should grieve.

2 Sep.—Intolerable. Upon arriving at the docks, after a long dusty wagon ride from the company offices at Zhengzhou, I was informed there were no boats for hire, at least none that would be willing to head downriver. Through the broken English of the dockmaster, I learned the reason. In the days since I traveled upriver aboard the junk, the river's mouth has been seized by Taiping rebels, and it is not safe for travel, either for Europeans or for those Chinese loyal to the Qing emperor.

It was apparent that my only option was to travel the long distance back to Tianjin overland. I was directed to a caravan heading north, under the protection of imperial troops. As I understood it, the caravan was transporting weapons and ammunition to the capital city, to be distributed to loyal troops in the northern provinces. There was but a single large cart in the train, all others traveling on foot, but there was sufficient room for both my luggage and the casket holding my charge's body . . . at any rate, there was sufficient room after I had asked several times, and punctuated each request with an ample outpouring of the local currency. The casket, an airtight box of cherrywood, packed in lye and salts, was lashed securely on the cart under a heavy canvas tarp, with the dead man's head by the driver's seat and his feet near neat rows of crated muskets, balls, and powder.

I had little money left in my purse, but was happy to give what little I had to the master of the caravan, to secure for myself a place at the dri-

ver's seat. The rough plank of the cart was unforgiving and hard, but I
would rather pass the next week with a bruised backside than wear my
feet down to the ankle by walking the hundreds of miles to our destination.

It appears I am not the only member of the company to have performed this calculation. I will be sharing the driver's seat with a young
Chinese scholar, who has some smattering of English, while the cart's os-
tensible *driver* will be walking before the cart horse, leading him on a
rope.

If nothing else, then, there may be some conversation had, to pass the
time.

Later.—I shall endeavor to write in as neat a hand as possible, despite the
jars of this rugged road, that I can later read my record of this journey.
Though why I should want to do so, in future times, I am now hard
pressed to say.

My young companion, the scholar, is a Manchurian bureaucrat named
Fu Zheng Li. He is on his way to the capital city of Beijing to take some
form of examination. Naturally, he speaks no Dutch, as does no one else
in the company, but he knows a smattering of English, learned from the
missionaries in Hunan province, he says, in his childhood. I know barely
enough Chinese to inquire after the location of the privy, but am a fair
hand at English, though in the awkward phraseology of one accustomed
to the more regimented and reasonable syntax of the Dutch language,
and so Fu and I are able to communicate between us without especial
difficulty.

Fu explains that, with many of the shipping channels and imperial
roads under the command of separatists and insurgents like the Taiping
rebels, most traffic from city to city and province to province has shifted
to rough rural roads. Merchants, bureaucrats, and scholars, who otherwise
would travel in some measure of comfort, are forced to trudge through
clouds of dust, under the not-always-diligent watch of imperial soldiers
unable to secure for themselves any more attractive posting.

In our small company, besides Fu and myself, are four merchants,

three bureaucrats, and two scholars, all watched over by a half-dozen soldiers. The soldiers, despite Fu's protestations to the contrary, seem quite
alert, their hands never straying far from the hilts of their swords or the
muskets slung over their shoulders, their eyes always scanning the sur-
roundings for potential threats. China, it would seem, is in the midst of
some considerable unrest, even more than I might have guessed, and a
lack of attention might bode ill for one's chances of survival.

LETTER, FU ZHENG LEI TO THE IMPERIAL MINISTER OF EXAMINATIONS
(continued)

Considering the state of the countryside, and the dangers posed by in-
surgent forces preying on loyal Qing subjects both on the imperial roads
and on the waterways, my uncle considered it best that I travel to the capital overland, and had passage secured for me among a caravan carrying
military supplies from Hunan province, where such were in abundance,
to the capital, whence they would be distributed throughout the northern
provinces. As the Taiping rebels held Nanjing and roamed the surrounding countryside with impunity, the caravan was scheduled to bear more or
less due north before turning to the east in the northern reaches of Shanxi
province.

Given my station, having passed my Xiucai degree provincial examination at the age of eleven years, and my Juren degree provincial examination at sixteen years, on my way to my Jinshi degree national examinations
when not yet twenty years, I was afforded some small comforts among
the caravan. My close relations to the governor, and his relations to the
Dragon Throne, might also have helped my position. While the other
scholars and merchants traveling under the caravan's protection, then,
walked alongside or behind the horse-drawn wagon, I was offered the
wagon-driver's seat.

I rode alone on the wagon seat for many days, until, just past the city
of Zhengzhou, a foreigner joined the caravan and inauspiciously bribed
his way into the favors of the chief soldier in the caravan.

This foreigner, a Dutchman, was a physician of some sort, escorting a
coffin to the city of Tianjin. He was taller than most of the company,
strongly built, with a deep chest and thick neck. His wide face and square

chin seemed more suited to a field hand than a man of medicine or philosophy, and his large, jutting nose and mobile, bushy eyebrows made him seem like some sort of primitive. His hair was a mess of reddish wire, and his large eyes were a blue so dark as to almost be black. He spoke no Chinese, but passable English, and so I was able to communicate with him, having learned some measure of English from foreign religious zealots who traveled to Changsha in my youth.

He was crude, with little of substance to share, and I was loath to surrender the solitude I'd enjoyed on the ride previously.

ABRAHAM VAN HELSING'S JOURNAL

3 Sep.—Stayed overnight at a small shelter along the roadside, presided over by a graven image of the Buddha, the god of these heathen peoples. With such considerable distances separating the cities and towns in this wide land, over the generations the Chinese seem to have established an elaborate network of way stations and shelters along the country byways, separated by the rough distance of a day's travel. I am grateful for these brief respites, in which I can pry my weary backside from the knotty plank of the cart's seat and sleep stretched out under a roof, with no fear that the skies might open up and pour down on me. There was no rain last night, but storm clouds have been gathering since late yesterday afternoon, and I think we've little chance of escaping a drenching.

I've gotten to know my young companion in our short time together. Over our humble meal last evening, a weak soup stock and a chewy stalk of some form of vegetable, he told me some little bit about his background. Throughout our talk, his eyes shifted to the rest of our company, sitting a distance away, in the protection of the shelter, and to the soldiers, who patrolled the road leading to and from our position. It seemed that his words were for me alone, and that he was wary of any other's overhearing. Perhaps it was the use of the foreign tongue which insulated him from propriety, and freed him to confide things to a stranger he'd never utter to another.

"My parents, they are dead," Fu explained. "From an early age, I was a member of my uncle's household. My uncle, he is the governor of Hunan province since I was a child. He is a proud Manchurian, and he re-

fuses to admit that his distant relations, those who have controlled the
Dragon Throne for generations, have led the kingdom of China into disgrace."

"Disgrace?" I worked at the tough, sinewy fibers of the vegetable
stalk, trying unsuccessfully to soften it in the soup stock.

"Disgrace," he said, nodding. "Yes, and even ruin, it might seem. After the shaming loss of the Opium Wars, the Qing emperor and his advi-
sors, they have conceded ports to European control, opened lucrative
financial opportunities to Europeans, allowed Europeans the freedom of
the countryside, to roam as they will. Now, in the countryside, there is
unrest, rebels and insurgents sprouting up like weeds after a spring rain.
Threatening the honest Chinese laborer. Threatening the stability of the
Chinese bureaucracy. Threatening the legacy of millennia of history."

My young companion paused and looked across the open space to the
merchants, bureaucrats, and scholars huddled in the shelter of the way
station. The flickering light of the candles inside cast moving shadows
across his face. His magnetic eyes, narrowed and flashing with the light,
gave his lean face an almost feline appearance. He slowly nodded.

"In order for China to regain her former glory," he said, "she will need
strong, new leadership."

With that said, he set down his bowl, turned his face away from the
light, and lay on his side, silent until morning.

Later.—We have ridden without pause since first light, Fu and I side by
side on the driver's seat, the rest of the company trudging through the
dusty ruts of this country road.

Some time past noon, the silence that had hung over us for hours having grown oppressive, Fu and I struggled to find some meaty topic on
which we could converse.

"Fu," I asked, "what is this examination you are en route to take?"

"Jinshin." Fu paused, searching for the appropriate English term. "It
means, Presented Scholar. It is the highest of three levels of imperial examination, the first two being the Xiucai . . . it means, erm, Flourishing
Talent, and the Juren, it means, I suppose, Elevated Person. To join im-

perial service, in the province, one needs at least to have attained the Xi-ucai rank, but to serve in the capital, truly to prosper in the service of the emperor, one must become a Jinshin. Presented, it means that one is presented to the emperor himself. It is a very high honor."

"Three ranks of academic achievement. Quite like the Western system of education, with the Bachelors of Arts, Master of Arts, and Doctorate. In English, I suppose you might say that you are on your way to becoming Doctor Fu, Manchurian scholar."

"Yes," Fu said, nodding, "something like that." He pointed a long-nailed finger at my chest. "Like you, Doctor."

I smiled, and nodded in return.

An awkward silence filled the space between us, and I realized we'd exhausted the usefulness of the topic. As I searched for anything to say, Fu charged into the fray.

"Doctor," he said, "do you have a wife?"

My hands tightened on the edge of the seat's plank, my knuckles white.

"I had a wife," I answered, "and though she is lost to me now, I suppose in the eyes of Mother Church she is my wife still."

"Doctor, do you have any children?"

My throat constricted, and unbidden came the mental image of my wife and son lying still on the cold tile of our entryway, their eyes wide and sightless, contorted faces bloodless and pale. From the hidden recesses of memory came the impression of something else there, some dark figure slipping out the door, a blood-stained hand, fingers pale and long as snakes lingering on the doorframe for a brief instant before curling out of view. But such a thing, it is not possible. Reason does not allow it.

"No," I managed to choke out the word. "Not anymore."

My face tight, I turned my attention to the monotonous road ahead and ignored any of Fu's questions or comments for the remainder of the day's journey. I hadn't the strength within me to speak further.

Behind us, beneath the lashings and the canvas tarp, lay the coffin of the dead man, always at our sides, silent participant in our disjointed conversations.

LETTER, FU ZHENG LEI TO THE IMPERIAL MINISTER OF EXAMINATIONS
(continued)

On the third night out from Zhengzhou, stopping under a moonless sky at an unmanned way station, the caravan was surprised by strange noises from the dark forest. Shuffling, rustling, something unnatural. We huddled in the shelter in the protective circle of candles, the foreign doctor off to one side, smoking a strong, tightly rolled cigar that fouled the air and offended the senses. Later, we slept restlessly under the sheltering eyes of a stone Buddha. In the morning, one of the guards, who had been posted as picket through the night, was found dead, torn into a dozen pieces, several of which appeared to be missing.

ABRAHAM VAN HELSING'S JOURNAL

4 Sep.—The caravan went on, after the soldiers had dealt with the remains of their fallen brother's body. The company is unsettled, walking closer together, their eyes darting at every sound.

There is scattered talk among the bureaucrats, merchants and scholars, only occasional words of which I'm able to catch. Their chatter continues unabated, in whispered tones, as though afraid something out in the rushes and the hedges might overhear. In the days previous, the company has been mostly silent, with only brief outbursts of laughter following what must have been jokes or ribald tales. The slow, steady susurration of whispered voices today, I must confess, has me somewhat unnerved.

Fu has translated for me the meat of the others' speculations. Some say that it was a wild beast that got to the soldier, while others hold it was some form of phantom or spirit, and that the soldier succumbed to its wiles before becoming its meal. Those who hold the attacker was a wild beast argue that the supply of weapons and ammunition in the cart should prove ample protection, if used properly; those who hold it was a phantom have no such hope.

I couldn't understand what wiles a phantom might have, and explained my confusion to Fu.

"In China, spirits, they often take the form of an attractive woman." Fu kept his eyes on the road, a slight blush rising in his cheek. "In this form, they seduce men, drowning them in the . . . sensual pleasures until they are helpless, and then consume them, body and soul."

Fu paused, and then released a slight sigh. "I do not think, for my part," he said, "that it sounds like such a terrible bad way to die."

Having been raised on stories of rotting ghosts and unquiet spirits, and not knowing the touch of a woman until I was nearly Fu's age, I was forced to agree.

LETTER, FU ZHENG LEI TO THE IMPERIAL MINISTER OF EXAMINATIONS *(continued)*

The sun set on the fourth night, and the company was left uneasy. Still out of reach of any established town or village, the caravan stopped at another way station. Vandals, though, had defaced the small statue of the Buddha within the shelter, removing the head from the stone body. This seemed an inauspicious omen. The members of the company sat huddled, exchanging nervous whispers, in the shadow of the headless form.

ABRAHAM VAN HELSING'S JOURNAL

4 Sep.—I write by firelight, my fingers almost numb from cold and fear, but I want to record my thoughts and impressions before sleep and forgetfulness drive them from me. As though I could sleep tonight. The swift stream beside us gurgles like a drowning man, and the stranger who saved us keeps a wary watch, and I am undone. But enough. My recollections, before my fear consumes them all.

We had arrived at the way-station, and sat huddled within the shelter in restless anticipation, fearful of the falling of night. We ate in silence, feeling vulnerable in the dim circle of candlelight, the shadow of the headless icon dancing on the far wall, unsettling.

A sliver of a moon rose in the sky, and there came from the forest sounds of rustling, of movement. The pickets had been placed closer in tonight, the soldiers well in sight of the shelter. In the flickering candlelight that broke from the entrance, the assembled company could see the tense bodies of the soldiers, their swords and muskets at the ready. The canvas-covered cart was parked a few dozen feet from the shelter, alongside the road, while the cart horse was tied to a nearby tree. Storm clouds gathered overhead.

A strong wind blew in across the treetops, guttering the candles' flames. For an instant, the soldiers were swallowed by shadows. When the wind died down and the flames snapped back to life, burning bright once more, the soldiers were nowhere to be seen. Gone. All gone.

The wind began to pick up again, and the temperature dropped suddenly. A storm was almost upon us. A lightning flash in the distance, and the faint peal of far-off thunder, clouds sliding across the slender moon.

The candles were blown out completely in a sudden blast of cold, dry wind. Another lightning flash, and all of us huddled in the darkened shelter saw, framed briefly in the open doorway, a lurching, stiff-limbed horror, arms outstretched, ruined mouth open wide.

It was some monstrosity of which I'd never dreamt, and yet there was for the briefest instant the frisson of recognition. I hadn't the opportunity nor the inclination to explore the sensation of familiarity, as the monstrosity drew nearer, and fear choked off my thoughts. The stiff-limbed horror advanced with an odd, jerky gait toward the quivering company, filling the small shelter with a faint green luminescence.

Fu was on his feet immediately, sidling along the darkened wall toward the entrance, and escape.

"Doctor," Fu called from just beyond the entrance, beckoning to me. "Come on."

As the lurching monstrosity advanced on the wailing merchants and bureaucrats, I steeled my nerves and slipped through the entrance, following hot on Fu's heels. But the movement had caught the monster's attention. I suppose that it reasoned the livelier meal was the tastier, and that two fleeing were livelier than the huddled masses before it. He pivoted on unbending joints and started after us.

LETTER, FU ZHENG LEI TO THE IMPERIAL MINISTER OF EXAMINATIONS
(continued)

I raced through the darkened forest, lightning marking my path. The foreign doctor followed close behind, lumbering and wheezing as he came. The strange, monstrous figure was close at our heels, bounding along on unbending knees. The path we followed through the dark forest was difficult to see, and whipping braches and thorns stung us as we passed.

The monster was almost upon us, our final moments at hand, when a figure jumped out of the darkness before me. In a lightning flash I glimpsed his clean-shaven head, yellow robes that shined like the sun.

This newcomer jumped between us and the advancing monster, pulling a woven bag from his belt and shaking out a handful of glutinous rice into his palm. He muttered a quick incantation over the grains, the words of which the wind carried away from my ears, and then threw the rice directly into the face of the lurching monstrosity. The monster reared back and uttered an insensible yowl, smoke curling up from its desiccated flesh. It swatted at its face with long-nailed fingers, trying unsuccessfully to claw the grains away. In that moment, I recognized the tattered rags hanging from its gaunt frame as the traditional Manchurian burial garb. This was a corpse, given life, or the semblance of life.

The man in the yellow robe turned to me and the foreign doctor, both of us looking on blank-faced in shock and amazement.

"We must hurry," the man said in refined Mandarin. "The creature will not be stopped for long by the rice, and I haven't the strength to fight at the moment." He hurried into the darkened forest.

I glanced over to the foreign doctor, who stood stock still, watching the writhing corpse, his large mouth slack-jawed, his blue eyes wide.

"Come, we must follow," I told him in English, my tone urgent. "Danger."

Considering my duty filled, I turned and raced after the retreating yellow robe. The foreign doctor must have understood, as within heartbeats I heard his lumbering steps following mine.

ABRAHAM VAN HELSING'S JOURNAL

4 Sep. Later.—Fu and I followed close behind the yellow-robed stranger, and he led us to a little shrine along a swiftly running brook. Instructing us through signs and barked orders to seat ourselves near the base of the shrine, he pulled a collection of small bags from the belt of his robe and proceeded to surround the shrine at a radius of a few yards with a circle of iron filings and rice. I tried to enquire after his purpose, but it seems that our benefactor speaks no English, only Chinese. I pleaded with Fu to repeat my questions to the old man in a tongue he could comprehend, but Fu sat quietly shaking at the base of the shrine, his narrowed eyes closely watching our savior's every move.

I wished that I had a touch of whisky to calm my shaky nerves, or even a cigar, but a quick check of my sweat-damped pockets produced only my package of lucifer matches, my other supplies back with the cart. Back with the monstrosity, that strange figure that had lurched out of the darkness, pure evil at sight.

My thoughts spun in tight frenzied circles around the danger stalking the dark night. Would I die here, by strange hands in this foreign land, and be rejoined with my son so soon?

When the yellow-robed stranger had finished his circuit of the shrine and come to sit beside me and Fu, I found my tongue again, and plied Fu once more with questions.

"Who is he?"

Fu left off rubbing his hands together to relay my question to the stranger along with, by the sound of it, several of his own.

The stranger, after a long pause, answered in just a few short words, and then turned his attention back to the deepening shadows beyond the little circle of rice he'd laid.

"Well?" I said. "What did he say?"

"This man," Fu answered, "he is a Taoist priest from the western provinces, and his name, he say, is Master Xi. He says, the creature we escaped, that was Chiang Shih. It means, the Undead."

LETTER, FU ZHENG LEI TO THE IMPERIAL MINISTER OF EXAMINATIONS
(continued)

Master Xi explained the origin of the strange creature, and how this doom had befallen us.

"The Chiang Shih is a vivified corpse," Master Xi said. "Undead, but yet not living. There is in each of us two souls, the higher and the lower. The higher, Hun, is associated with Yang and controls the higher functions of the human self: emotion, thought, passion. On the death of the body, the Hun soul ascends quickly to the heavens, to be among the stars. The lower soul, though, or Po, is associated with Ying, and controls the baser functions: hungers, appetites, lusts. On the death of the body, the Po soul begins slowly to sink to the earth, to be absorbed back into the soil. In the case of violent or traumatic death, or improper burial, the lower soul remains trapped in the body after the higher soul ascends. The corpse of the departed, then, is still driven by the baser passions and appetites of a man, but lacks the guiding instincts and awareness that makes us human. It is a mindless thing, less than animal.

"A century ago," Master Xi continued, "an army was sent by the Qing emperor to the western wilds of Xinjian, to tame that savage Mongol land for the Dragon Throne. Among those who fought, bled, and died for their emperor were seven Manchurian brothers, the bravest of General Zhaohui's warriors. Buried in that foreign land, improperly interred and not revered by their descendants, their lower souls stayed with their bodies, and they rose from their unhallowed graves. Driven by their lower animal urges and the blind instinct to return home, these seven Undead crossed the breadth of China to return to their ancestral Manchurian lands, driven in their mindless, animalistic fashion to their final rest.

"I have been trailing these seven Chiang Shih across seven provinces, saving those hapless victims it is within my power to save, and burying with proper rites those I cannot, so that they, too, do not rise up as Undead. With the aid of my three assistants, I have managed to defeat the Chiang Shih one at a time, so that there is now but one left, but my assistants have all perished in the attempts, and I am left alone. This last, this final Chiang Shih, is the strongest and fiercest of them all, and it is too much for me to handle alone."

When Master Xi had finished speaking, he sat quietly and watched for our response. I translated as much of Master Xi's story to the foreign doctor as seemed appropriate, and he agreed that we had little choice but to assist Master Xi, primarily because without his help, we had little chance of escaping the Chiang Shih.

ABRAHAM VAN HELSING'S JOURNAL

5 Sep.—This morning, in the full light of day, Fu, the Taoist priest, and I returned to the shelter of the way station. The cart and horse still stood, just as they had the night before, but all that remained of the soldiers and our company were scattered body parts and spatters of blood.

"Why is it the Undead consumes the bodies of men," I asked, "but does not touch the horse?"

Fu relayed my question to the Taoist priest, and after hearing his response, answered.

"The Undead, Chiang Shih, they are driven by their lower souls, but still crave a higher soul. The souls of animals, they cannot sate this hunger, but the souls of men can whet their appetites. Nature does not allow the Undead to consume the souls of their victims, but the mere whiff of souls escaping as the lives are snuffed out is enough to satisfy their hunger, if only for a moment."

My first instinct was to check on the state of my charge, the poor unfortunate whose body I was ferrying back to my employer's care. I found the casket in fine condition, the seals untouched, the wood unbroken and secure. The Taoist priest's eyes followed my movements, making careful study of everything I did. Satisfied that the body was unharmed, I crossed myself and gave a brief prayer of thanks for this small kindness. When I turned, the priest's eyes were still on me.

Later.—We three spent the long hours of the morning and afternoon making preparations for our coming conflict with the Undead. We began by burying the victims of the monster with the proper rituals, Fu and I taking the backbreaking task of moving earth and the gruesome task of collecting the remains, while the Taoist priest busied himself with charms and chants, burning incense and marking strange glyphs on little slivers of rock.

During a brief rest, with the sun high overhead, I expressed some reservation about what I considered to be provincial superstition. Whether the bodies of these poor unfortunates were danced and sung over with plumes of smoke, or just planted a few feet in the ground without ceremony, it seemed to me that they posed no threat to anyone in their present state.

At the priest's request, Fu translated my brief outburst, whereupon the priest made a show of walking with thundering steps to the casket lashed to the nearby cart, and with outstretched finger touched his left shoulder, then his right, then forehead, and then navel. Finishing his mimed cross, he turned to me, his expression plain even across the gulf of language. Then he returned to his charms and chants, and finding I could muster no suitable reply, I returned to my digging.

LETTER, FU ZHENG LEI TO THE IMPERIAL MINISTER OF EXAMINATIONS *(continued)*

Nightfall approached, and we made ready. Master Xi gave me what training he could, in the time allowed, which I then passed along to the foreign doctor.

Here is what Master Xi taught us:

When confronting the Chiang Shih, hold your breath; the Chiang Shih cannot see, as mortals see, and detects the presence of the living by scenting the trace of the higher soul in their breath. The Chiang Shih fears glutinous rice, which represents the fecund power of the earth itself, into whose bosom the body of the Chiang Shih should return, to decompose and fertilize future life. The Chiang Shih fears mirrors, and can be controlled if one places yellow paper inscribed in red-ink or chicken blood with holy symbols on its forehead. If part of a Chiang Shih's body is removed or cut off, it will continue to function, apart from the rest of the body. The Chiang Shih fears running water. The only hope in defeating the Chiang Shih lies in immobilizing it first, and then burying it with the proper rituals, cremating it if at all possible, to free the lower spirit to sink back into the earth.

Master Xi assembled our plans, and we made ready. Nightfall approached.

ABRAHAM VAN HELSING'S JOURNAL

6 Sep.—It is difficult to think on the events of this last night, the evening of 5th September, but having come this far in recording the events of my strange journey, I would be remiss to stop short here.

Night fell, and we three readied ourselves. Where the night before had seen a storm, tonight was clear and still.

The old priest, a sword scabbarded in cherrywood in hand, looked to the sky and muttered a few words.

"Master Xi," Fu translated for my benefit, "he says that fortune is not with us. If it had only stormed again, and fiercely, then the elements might have taken care of the Chiang Shih for us. The Undead are often dispatched by particularly loud thunderclaps, their lower souls shocked from the body by the noise."

I followed their gaze to the cloudless sky and shook my head. Our only hope lay in following the priest's plan.

The plan was to lure the Undead into the shelter, which had only one door. Once the monster was within the confines of the shelter, Fu and I, who to that point would be hiding in the corners, would rush outside behind it, pulling with us strong cords attached to the mouths of woven bags hung from the rafters just above the entrance. The bags would open wide and a shower of sticky rice would fall, blanketing the entrance to the shelter. The Undead, then, would be trapped inside with the priest, unable to exit without the burning, searing pain at the touch of the grains. The priest would wield his silver-bladed sword, with a slip of yellow paper inscribed in chicken's blood pierced at the tip. He would then drive the sword through the Chiang Shih's forehead, immobilizing it long enough to perform the burial rituals and cremate the body.

Fu and I crouched in darkness at either side of the entrance, the cords gripped tightly in our hands. The priest stood before the opening, eyes closed, drawn sword in hand.

From beyond the opening came a thumping noise at regular intervals—the same noise I'd heard pursuing us into the darkness the night before. The Undead approached.

I could scarcely watch it enter, lumbering in on stiff limbs, long-nailed hands stretched out to the priest, its presence filling the shelter with a sickly green luminescence.

The priest opened his eyes and spoke the signal word, the single bit of English he knew, learned just for the occasion.

"Now!"

The initial stages of the operation went as planned. Fu and I rushed past the monster, pulling the drawstrings as we went, which opened the mouths of the sacks and carpeted the hard-packed dirt floor at the entrance to the shelter. Then we crouched outside, fearful, watching the priest do battle with the monster.

LETTER, FU ZHENG LEI TO THE IMPERIAL MINISTER OF EXAMINATIONS
(continued)

For the briefest of instants, it looked as though Master Xi's plan would work. The Chiang Shih fought back, parrying his sword thrusts with long-nailed fingers, but still Master Xi pressed on. The battle between priest and Undead raged.

In the final moment, just as it appeared that Master Xi would succeed in immobilizing the monster, the Chiang Shih swatted the sword from his hands and fell on him, claws and ruined mouth and all. The Taoist priest, with a forlorn shriek, fell under the monster's teeth and talons, and was ripped into bloody pieces before our eyes.

ABRAHAM VAN HELSING'S JOURNAL

6 Sep. Later.—I looked to the cloudless sky overhead, wishing on whatever holy thing that might exist, Oriental or Occidental, that a storm might whip out from the ether and a thunderclap drive the damned spirit of the monster down into the earth. Then my eyes lit on the cart, and the casket of the dead man, and I knew our only choice.

The weapons and ammunition of the soldiers, forgotten in the excitement of the monster's attack, were still on the cart, still under the tarp at the foot of the cherrywood coffin.

"Gunpowder," I whispered to myself, as though to hear the word aloud would bring it to my hand. "Gunpowder."

I grabbed Fu's arm, dragging him after me. I rushed to the cart, still parked only a few dozen feet from the mouth of the shelter by the side of the road, and fell to the knots in the dim light.

(continued)

Having consumed what it wanted of Master Xi's body, the Chiang Shih prowled the rice-laid mouth of the shelter like a caged tiger, sniffing the still air for a hint of our breaths. With every pass, the monster's feet grazed a little further into the carpet of rice, and despite the tendrils of smoke curling up from its soles, and the silent grimaces of pain, still nearer to freedom it came. The barrier of rice would not hold it for long, and then it would be on us.

I had surmised that if a thunderclap could dispel the Chiang Shih, then an explosion of gunpowder might serve the same purpose. The foreign doctor was at my side, tearing at the lashes holding the canvas tarp in place, trying to get at the ammunition. The Chiang Shih came ever nearer the freedom of the open spaces, ever nearer attacking and consuming us both. We couldn't get the stoutly fastened knots loose and had no knife with which to cut the bindings. After all our exertions, only a single trailing rope was free, hanging in the dust.

ABRAHAM VAN HELSING'S JOURNAL

6 Sep. Later.—The monster was almost free. There was no time. We'd not got more than a single rope untied, and our time was through.

Fu drew himself up short and grabbed my elbow. "Your light," he said, struggling for the words. "Your flame. Your—" Frustrated, he mimed the action of lighting a cigar.

"My lucifer matches?" I answered.

Fu nodded, fiercely. "Yes, yes, now, matches, now!"

"But we've no time for nonsense, boy," I said. "There's just no—"

"NOW!"

Taken aback, I reached into my vest pocket and pulled out the box of matches. Fu snatched them from my hands, struck one alight, and then held it to the frayed ends of the single rope trailing down from the lashings. It caught fire, and the flame began to climb up its length.

Fu grimly got behind the cart and began to push it toward the shelter with all his might. I hung back a moment, confused, and then in a flash understood the young man's plan. I put my shoulder to it and heaved for all I was worth.

Three things happened at once, my mind scarcely able to take them all in.

The Undead stepped into the shelter's doorway; the cart careered into the open door; and the flame traveling up the cart's trailing rope reached the canvas covering, which caught fire in an instant blaze. In the following instant, there was only deafening noise and blinding light, as the amassed powder and ammunition on the cart caught fire and exploded in a violent fury, catching the small shelter in a blossoming firestorm that burned bright as the noonday sun.

The cart horse, tied to a nearby tree, brayed and whinnied, while Fu and I, knocked onto our backs, could only look on in exhausted awe at the destructive splendor of the blast.

LETTER, FU ZHENG LEI TO THE IMPERIAL MINISTER OF EXAMINATIONS
(continued)

The next morning, and the way station had burned to fine ashes. Nothing of the cart, or the coffin, or Master Xi, or the monster, remained. Of all the caravan that had set out from Changsha so long before, and all that had joined along the way, only I, the foreign doctor, and the cart horse remained.

We sat in silence while the sun rose and climbed the pale blue sky. With few words exchanged, we got to our feet, unhitched the horse, and mounted, the foreign doctor riding behind me. Then we continued up the road to Beijing.

I arrived, finally, a day late for my Jinshi degree national examination, and was sent with the next convoy back to Hunan province in disgrace.

I have returned to service in the administration of my uncle, the Governor of Hunan Province and cousin to his imperial Majesty Xianfeng (scion of the Qing dynasty, lord of heaven, may he reign ten thousand years), but am still desirous of serving the Dragon Throne in a more personal fashion and helping to bring greater glory to the kingdom of China. Perhaps the strangest lesson I've gleaned from my experience is the resolute nature of the Manchurian spirit. Even in death, the Manchurian will not cease to fight, will not surrender. If we remember that, then perhaps we might someday rule the world.

Again, I thank you for your kind indulgence, and await your response.

ABRAHAM VAN HELSING'S JOURNAL

31 Oct. Tianjin.—I've had neither the opportunity nor the will to update this record since the early morning hours of 6th September, the morning following the conflagration. During the long journey back to Tianjin, my mind was simply too numb to compose rational thoughts, and upon my arrival at the English Concession, I was greeted with too many questions regarding the ultimate disposition of the body of my charge to have a moment's reflection.

In the end, my employers and the British authorities in Tianjin reached a compromise and recorded the unfortunate gentleman as "Lost Through Misadventure." Never mind that a certificate of death existed, showing him dying of native disease in the township of Zhengzhou, and that his body was on the manifest of a caravan lost en route. There was no body, and no chance of his return, and so his family back in England was simply told that he had been "lost," and that was an end to the matter. Still, they look at me with suspicion, and none accept the truth of my story.

Of the young scholar Fu, I have seen nothing since our arrival in the capital on horseback. He was greeted with no small dismay by the imperial wardens, as he had evidently given insult to the examiners by missing his scheduled appointment, and compounded the offense by arriving in a sorry state in the company of an uncouth foreigner.

I could not help but pity the young scholar, yet I felt certain that he would persevere. Though we spoke little in our solitary journey to the capital, on the long nights by the roadside we forced conversation, anything to fill the terrible empty silence of those dark spaces.

I had made mention, on one of these nights, that we in Europe have legends of creatures similar to the Undead of our shared experience, but that men of science and learning such as myself do not give them credence. I wondered aloud what difference in environment or circumstance might give rise to such unnatural monstrosities in one geographical locale, but not allow them in another, as I am certain we have no such in the West.

Fu, after a long silence, began to speak in response, but it was almost as though he were answering some question that had not been asked. He had a faraway look in his eyes, the flickering light of our fire reflecting his eyes back to me like a cat's.

"I could not help but to feel some small pride at hearing the accomplishment of the seven Manchurian brothers in life," he said, "seven champions of Xianjian, even if they were responsible for such horrors after death. They had been, in life, true warriors of the Manchurian spirit. With more like them today, China might prove better equipped to stand against foreign intervention and insurgents from within."

Fu fell silent, and after a time I asked him whether his opinions on the presence and influence of foreigners in his country was common.

"No," he said simply. "Those of my mind, we patriots, must pander to the soft whims of those in authority over us. To gain prestige, to gain position and influence, we flatter and coerce. But someday, perhaps, with enough of us in high bureaucracy, matters will change."

He looked at me across the flickering fire as though seeing me for the first time, and his eyes narrowed.

"And come that day, Doctor, I would hope that you are gone from this land. Far away when that day comes."

I shivered, and could not help but agree.

But I need not wait for Fu's promised rise to power to force my decision. I have arranged to return to Amsterdam as soon as possible. I hunger to be away from here, and my only sleep is fitful.

In my dreams, I am haunted by the memory of that strange, unearthly creature, lurching after me in the darkened Chinese woods. Strange, then, that in my dreams those woods become, at length, the pristine entryway to my home back in Amsterdam, and that instead of the young Manchurian Fu by my side, it is my wife and my young son fleeing for their lives.

And every time, just before waking, the monster overtakes my wife and son, and I alone survive, but before I can turn and face the creature, I awaken with a chest-rattling scream.

I had hoped to escape my demons by coming to the East, but have found that there were only other demons here, waiting for me. I look forward to returning home, where at least the memories which haunt me will be happier ones, and reason still holds sway.

Sideshow

Thomas F. Monteleone

"So," said Detective Robinson. "You've been caught at this before?"

"After a fashion, yes," said the professor.

"You're a *monster.*"

"Actually, I'm not."

"We'll leave that to the judge and jury," said the detective.

The professor smiled. "After you see what I have to show you . . . I think not."

And thus continued the conversation that would change the life of Detective Sergeant Marcus Aurelius Robinson.

Forever.

He was in Chicago, Illinois, to attend the opening of the 1893 Columbian Exposition. The New York City policeman was among the thousands who paid their fifty-cent admission that day, but he was no tourist. Working homicide out of the 303 Mulberry Street station, Marcus had tracked a killer across half the country. And despite the rigors of endless weeks of train travel, Marcus was glad to be far away from the political sewer his beloved Manhattan had become. Chief Byrnes was about as corrupt as you could get; and Dickie Croker was still pulling all the Tammany strings.

It just wasn't a very good time to be an honest cop, and Marcus was a God-fearing member of the Madison Square Presbyterian Church. Marcus was a different kind of policeman, but his essential morality wasn't the only reason. He was also fairly well-educated, having graduated high school in Brooklyn, and still taking night classes at the New York University at the age of thirty-seven. As a boy, he'd always been attracted to science and a general tinkering with machines. Too bad he'd never mastered the mathematics to become the engineer his father had said he should be.

But his interest in science persisted, even after he fell into police work, and he became convinced the job of solving crimes could be enhanced by using the tools of science. After reading the pioneering work of Sir Francis Galton, he'd become one of the very first New York detectives to use fingerprints as a means of tracking down perpetrators. Indeed, in the breast pocket of his tweed waistcoat, he carried blown-up photographs of two very clear prints he'd taken from some of his latest crime scenes. Talcum powder had revealed the imprints on a mahogany desktop and the black granite handle of a cleaver. When he found his man, those prints would seal his guilt tighter than a waxed letter.

And that man was here in Chicago.

Marcus had tracked him from his atrocious and horrifying butchery in Battery Park, then far south through autumn and winter, just missing his witchcraft ritual killing in Chestertown, Maryland, and the arson burning of an entire family outside of Baton Rouge. Then, up the Mississippi, he was shocked to find his target listed as an "attraction" of the Exposition.

As he stood within the gates of this world's fair, looking at the collection of beautiful, neoclassical buildings, Marcus was impressed. New York might have its tall buildings, but there was nothing to compare to this. It was such a spectacle, such a collective monument to the daring of a country rushing headlong toward the next century.

Marcus could feel the energy and power of the moment, pulsing through the crowd that surged around him like a massive amoebic creature.

Approaching a kiosk, Marcus saw attendants handing out fliers to the passersby, and as he grew closer, he realized they were hawkers selling maps for two cents a piece. The Columbian Exposition was surely big enough to warrant a map, and Marcus would have loved to spend the time seeing all its incredible attractions—from a ride on the great turning wheel built by George Ferris to the Electric Scenic Theater to the Sliding Railway—but there was only one show he needed to see.

Purchasing the map, he saw it revealed an impressive number of attractions, ranging from spectacular triumphs of architecture to *divertissements* as minor as snake charmers and Sioux war-dancers. But only one arrested his attention, and when he located it on the map, Marcus oriented himself in the crowd so he could head off in the proper direction.

Marcus allowed himself to be swept up in the current of people funneling into the Midway Plaisance. Each attraction seemed more exotic and beguiling than the one before. As in a novel by Verne or Swift, Marcus felt carried away to a place that defied the rational and the possible. An Italian basilica's shadow crossed the huts of a Javanese village; the music of a Viennese music hall collided with the fifth-note chants of a Shinto shrine; the rich aromatic spices of the East India Bazaar fought the stench of Hagenbeck's Menagerie.

The Exposition's Midway was a tapestry of wonders, and he felt small and inadequate before its grand scale. Why had Destiny chosen this place as his stage to take on such evil? He prayed he was up to the task. He watched a pair of Chicago policemen approach a sandwich vendor, take their pick of his lunchtime offerings, and walk off without giving the vendor as much as a tip. So many of his comrades, it seemed, simply didn't care about the trust given them.

About two-thirds of the way down the immense arcade, on the right, Marcus saw the stately Lecture Hall of Science, surrounded by a family of tents, under which stood smaller exhibitions of a variety of disciplines. Strings of electric lightbulbs blazed against and behind the painted canvas of the tents, creating eerie effects.

As he threaded through the onlookers, he finally reached his objective—*Professor Agamemnon's Traveling Emporium of Oddities & Marvels.*

". . . and your eyes will not be deceiving you!" a barker was saying into a megaphone he held to his narrow, hawkish face. He swung it back and forth, aiming it at the milling crowds as if it were a weapon. "Twenty-five cents, ladies and gentleman! Twenty-five cents to see the stuff of your dreams . . . *and* your nightmares! Take that as fair warning to all the women—this exhibit is not for the faint of heart!"

"Excuse me," said Marcus. "I'm looking for the 'professor.' Is he here?"

The barker was short, wiry, caricatured by a pompadour glistening with too much pomade. Although dressed in a spiffy walking suit, he looked uncouth. "You'll see him soon enough—he's part of the show. Two bits, and you'll see him."

Marcus enacted a patronizing smile, wasted on the feisty little man, and passed him a quarter from his watch pocket. "No doubt, sir. Thank you."

Waving him into the tent, the barker dismissed him without a second glance. And that was just fine. Marcus had no intention of identifying himself as a New York detective, demanding to have Agamemnon dragged forth. Stunts like that usually ended up with the "mug" running out the back door, into the slimy underworld, and the copper with nothing but empty cuffs.

Marcus entered the tent.

A calliope textured the air with dirgeful phrases. Low wattage electric bulbs, well positioned to create dramatic shadows, revealed a maze of museumlike display cases. Lots of expensive polished oak and thick-paned glass. But there was something odd about the place, something not immediately definable. More of a feeling than a conviction. Marcus believed he'd become a good detective by trusting such feelings.

The exhibit was already crowded with patrons, very few of them women. As Marcus threaded his way down the aisle, he tried to see past the heads and shoulders of those gawkers pressed close against the glass-walled cabinets. He caught glimpses of specimens in laboratory jars—a goiter the size of a peach basket, a human skull sliced up like a boiled egg, a foetus with *three* heads.

And he'd just gotten started.

The exhibit had been laid out like a topiary maze, funneling Marcus and the other patrons through a labyrinth so cunning, he soon lost all sense of direction. And as clever as the layout might be, there had also been great thought in the way each exhibit was presented. With each turn, each twist, Marcus encountered a specimen ever more ghastly than its predecessor. And also with each turn, he felt himself growing more angry at his quarry's audacity—peppered among these exhibits could very well be the remains of the madman's victims. The image of that sliced-up skull wouldn't leave him.

When he reached the life-size blowup photo of a Borneo man carting his elephantine testicles along in a wheelbarrow, he almost burst into horrified laughter. A woman behind him swooned.

"This is perfectly ridiculous!" said a man who punctuated it with a proper *harrumph!*

And then, as if on cue, the calliope music increased in volume and tempo, ending in the triumphant entrance of a tall, angular man in black evening wear. His opera cape swirled as he stepped forward to the edge of a small proscenium that formed the cul-de-sac of the maze. All the wandering patrons had gathered here like goldfish in a collecting pool, and they all looked a bit surprised to have been transformed into a little audience.

Total silence as everyone's attention fell upon him. He smiled, but Marcus found it to be the most wholly insincere greeting he'd ever seen. He found himself instantly loathing him.

"Welcome, my friends! I am Professor Agamemnon, and you have just seen a smattering of my collection of oddities and marvels! Where these come from, I have collected *thousands* more. Each time you visit me, I promise you a new surprise!"

Agamemnon paused, paced across the small stage, then back again. There was a mock-theatricality about it, perhaps self-parody. Was it all a game to him? Marcus sized up his quarry. The professor's leonine mane of silvering hair seemed too thick and robust for a man his age. And yet, there was also an ageless quality about him. His complexion, though ruddy, had not a line or crease. A pair of ice-blue eyes reflected the electrics like polished gems. The eyes of a killer, thought Marcus.

"The show is, as they say, *fini*, but I would be honored to entertain a few of your comments or questions."

"Where did you find such horrors?" asked a short, stocky man to Marcus's left.

"I have been a traveler of the world for most of my days," said Agamemnon. "I have seen much."

"It looks like you've *taken* much as well!" said another gentleman, which sent a ripple of nervous chuckles through the assembly.

"I have taken nothing, sir! Everything you see here has either been donated or is on loan from universities, museums, and medical centers around the world. I exhibit them for the greater enlightenment of humanity."

A flurry of other questions ensued, and the professor entertained them for another few minutes of lively banter before directing everyone to the exits and bidding good-bye. With a flourish of his hand, Agamemnon disappeared behind the purple velvet curtain on the small stage. Marcus shuffled himself in and out of the dwindling crowd until he was the only one remaining.

Then, without hesitation, he bounded up to the platform and pulled back the curtain. Other than a small table with a pitcher of water and a drinking glass, the small space was empty. Marcus stepped off the back of the raised stand and followed the canvas partition until it led to a flap that opened on the rear flank of the tent. Beyond this stretched a long alley formed by the façade of the science pavilion on one side and the long row of exhibitors' tents on the other. Was it the only exit? The only route of escape?

Parked along this passageway were a variety of wagons and trailers that had been used to transport people and gear. One of them, looking like a refurbished railway caboose on large, spoked wooden wheels, was identified by a small plaque as the residence of his prey.

After ascending a small fold-down stoop, Marcus knocked on the door.

"Yes?" said a voice through the wood panel. "Who's there?"

Another rapping, then: "This is the police, sir. Would you mind opening up?"

Marcus heard no reply or sound from inside. For an instant, he wondered if there might be another door, and the killer had escaped.

That's why he startled just a bit when the door was yanked open from the inside and Agamemnon was staring down at him. If the man was nervous, he gave no indication. "Good evening, officer. I recognize you from the show."

In a long practiced motion, Marcus had peeled back his tweed jacket to reveal his shield pinned to the pocket of his vest. "I'm Detective Robinson, sir. I have some questions to ask you, if you wouldn't mind."

The professor smiled tightly, pulled a watch from his vest pocket and glanced at it. "I assume it cannot wait until my last appearance later tonight?"

"You would be assuming correctly."

And then a strange thing happened. As the man surveyed Marcus, he felt something oddly violating in the look of those icy blue eyes. It was as if the professor prepared to deliver a very bad diagnosis. An expression of grim determination so subtle, so . . . matter-of-fact . . . but it *scared* Marcus silly. There was no other way to describe it.

"Very well. Please come in. It's small, but private."

Marcus nodded and entered the wagon warily. He was not sure being *alone* with this character was a good idea. He knew he'd have to deal with the Chicago cops when he arrested Agamemnon, but that didn't weaken his resolve to get as many answers as possible from this psychopath beforehand. The interior was furnished in a kind of battered opulence. There was an old-world look to the fixtures—lots of brocade and velvet upholstery, a marble-topped little table, sterling bric-a-brac. Marcus tried to be subtle as he checked for places where his prey might conceal a weapon. He took note of another door at the opposite end of the wagon. An escape hatch? Both men took seats on each side of a table that served for dinner as well as correspondence.

"I have been following you for several months," said Marcus. "Chestertown, Baton Rouge, now here's where I finally caught up."

"And the reason for your doggedness?"

"I think you know," said Marcus.

"You may be correct."

"Do you know anything about the death of Arthur van der Jaegt?"

Agamemnon pursed his lips, nodded. "Yes, Detective, I know of it. Most assuredly more than *you*."

"Then you admit your crimes? Tell me what you know!"

The professor shrugged, raked his fingers through his thick silvery hair. The hair made him look like a tortured composer. But he didn't seem tortured at all. "That's a possibility . . . if you give me sufficient reason."

Reaching into his jacket, Marcus produced the photographs, placed the sheets in front of the other man.

"They are called 'fingerprints,'" he said. "I found them on the edge of the desk in the financial offices of Arthur van der Jaegt north of Battery Park. They were also on the handle of a kitchen cleaver, which had been used to *dismember* him."

The man across the table absorbed this information with no outward emotion. "All right," he said.

"You were in Manhattan at the time of the murder, Professor. Your traveling show was set up in Battery Park."

"Yes, that's true."

"And on the evening of his death, you were seen leaving the home of Mr. Van der Jaegt through a back door which opens onto an alleyway."

"By whom?"

"A reliable witness, who shall be revealed in due course." Marcus found himself running a finger across his mustache, a habit he'd been powerless to stop. He believed it to be an indicator of anxiety, weakness. But why would *he* be anxious? This "professor" should be the one worrying, with his fingerprints condemning him.

"At the time of trial, no doubt . . ." Agamemnon was smiling openly now.

"How dare you be so smug!" Marcus was having trouble controlling what his wife always called his righteous indignation. He looked suspiciously around the dark interior. He hadn't noticed how shadowed everything had become. Was the oil lamp growing dimmer?

"Let me finish it for you, Detective. You obtained more fingerprint samples from my wagon—the latch, the door, a pane of glass, perhaps? Am I correct?"

"Yes," said Marcus. He couldn't stop himself.

"And they are a match for the others . . ." It was not a question. Agamemnon's expression revealed ennui rather than fear. "And then, the final pieces of your puzzle: you found the *same* fingerprints at the murder scenes in both Chestertown, Maryland, and Baton Rouge, Louisiana. Both stops for my road show."

"That's it! You're done, mister. . . ." Marcus was fed up with these theatrics. He pushed back from the table, stood up, and reached around for his service revolver, which he kept in a holster nestled in the small of his back. "Now listen up, Professor, or whatever your real name is . . . I'm afraid I must place you under—"

"Detective Robinson, please. I am not planning on running from you. When I am finished, if you *still* wish to arrest me, I shall go quietly. Willingly."

And the funny thing was . . . Marcus *knew* he was telling the truth. He believed this strange character, and he had no idea *why*. Marcus lowered his weapon, which had become heavy and awkward in his grip. He reseated himself, held his weapon as it rested gently on the table, pointed at his quarry's chest. "All right, I'm listening. But make it fast."

"You are convinced your collection of matching fingertip impressions from the various murder sites will prove to be mine, and you plan to haul me in to get copies of mine." Agamemnon held up his hands to illustrate his declaration.

"Of course," said Marcus, unable to hide his anger. Never in all his days of interrogating criminals had he ever suffered through something like this. . . .

"Well, I can save you the trouble of making the prints, Detective. They *will* match mine."

"So you *admit* to killing all those people?"

"Yes . . . and *no*."

"What?"

"Your phrasing is not quite right."

"I'm tired of playing games, mister."

"This is no game. And you are not the first to connect me to this sort of thing."

"You've been caught at this before?"

"After a fashion, yes," said the professor.

"You're a *monster*."

"Actually, I'm not."

"We'll leave that to the judge and jury," said Marcus.

Agamemnon smiled. "After you see what I have to show you . . . I think not."

"I don't need to see anything more!" He was more angry at himself now than Agamemnon. Why hadn't he already clapped this killer in cuffs? "How could you think you'd get *away* with it—leaving that odd wagon of yours in the park for all to see? Making a spectacle of yourself?"

The professor smiled. "Several reasons. One, I've been doing it for a long time, and no one has ever noticed. Two, it's easiest to hide something by placing it in plain view, officer. And three, I don't really care if I am caught."

Marcus was mulling over the man's odd response when there was a sudden pounding at the door, followed by, "Five minutes, Professor!"

Standing, Agamemnon nodded in a most European fashion. "Excuse me for a moment . . ."

Marcus stood, pointed his revolver at the back of Agamemnon's head. The admitted killer ignored this as he opened the door, whispered some instructions to his slick-haired assistant, and then returned calmly to the table. "Kenneth will act in my stead for the evening's remainder," he said. "Now, I think we have the time to make things clear to you."

"It's already clear to me," said Marcus. "I don't mind telling you I've about used up all my patience."

Agamemnon smiled. "That's all right . . . from here on out, you won't be needing it."

"And what's that supposed to mean?"

"Come with me, please."

The professor headed to the door at the opposite end of the caboose, opened it and held it for his guest. Marcus stood, holding his gun, but no longer pointing it at Agamemnon.

Did he trust this odd duck?

Well, yes, as much as he might be loath to admit it, he *did*. And that was making him very uneasy. Slowly, he reholstered his weapon and exited the wagon.

The professor led him down the temporary corridor formed by the outer wall of the Science Pavilion and the long row of tarpaulin-walled exhibits. They stopped at a second large tent, where his host paused to throw a switch, illuminating a string of dim bulbs that ran the length of a pathway between large cabinets, trunks, and other enclosures.

"Follow me," said Agamemnon.

Marcus did so, but he didn't like it. Trust or not, he was glad to have the service revolver in his hand. The lights were just strong enough to stir up long, distorted shadows; the interior assumed the feel of a gallery more grim and potentially disturbing than the public exhibit he'd already seen.

That observation proved more than correct.

Agamemnon directed his attention to what looked like an armoire. Taller than a man, double doors, stout wooden beams holding it together. The professor unlatched it, swung back both panels.

"Good Christ in heaven!" Marcus said, unable to control his shock. "What in blazes—?"

He was staring at the remains of some sort of creature. Skeletal, yet partially mummified, shreds of leathery flesh sank into its contours. It looked as if a combination of horrors—an insect or a crustacean, but bipedal; with desiccated eyes the size of teacups; razored teeth set into a low-slung mandible. A thing from the darkest nightmare. Marcus stepped back from the cabinet where it hung suspended like a ghastly suit of clothes.

"This is an Ollifyx . . . it is quite real."

"There's no such animal," said Marcus.

"I beg to differ. You are looking at it."

"This is one of your carnival pranks. . . ."

"You doubt what you see?"

"I'm an educated man," said Marcus.

"Then you should understand what I must tell you."

"Go on."

"What the philosophers call 'existence' is a bit more complex than most have suspected. To put it as simply as possible, there are many . . . 'realities' that occupy the same time and space. If you can imagine it, myriad worlds operating side by side (although that's not quite right) and most times never, ever influencing any of the others."

Marcus knew there was nothing he could say at this point. He tried to keep from looking back at the horror in the upright cabinet, and gestured for his host to continue.

Which he did: "There have been several of your people who have entertained this view of the universe. Helena Blavatsky is one; another is a young man named George Gurdjieff. But the truth, Detective Robinson, does not require the verification of a few enlightened humans, does it?"

"Well . . ."

"The truth simply *is*," said Agamemnon. "This creature is a denizen of another plane, a parareality, but it learned to live here—on what is called a human plane—by changing its appearance."

"Appearance or actual structure?"

"Good question, Detective. Believe it or not, its actual shape and structure! This is where *all* your myths of werecreatures have come—"

"Can such things be?" Marcus whispered the idea.

"Indeed."

Marcus paused to ponder this, then: "When you mentioned Madame Blavatsky, you said 'your people.' Am I to take it to mean you're not . . . I don't know how to say this . . . one of 'our people' . . . one of *us?*"

Agamemnon smiled. "You are very good at your job, sir."

"You're not answering me. Are you human?"

"I am indeed, otherwise you would not have been able to obtain a fingerprint, remember? Of the pararealities, there exist more than one human plane."

"Is that a good thing?"

"Such things transcend good and evil. They simply *are*." Gesturing at the Ollifyx, Agamemnon said: "The man you called van der Jaegt was one of these beings. Only by dismembering it did I keep it from returning to its True Form."

"You expect me to believe that?"

Agamemnon nodded.

Marcus forced himself to stare at the remains. There was nothing about them that suggested fakery. He'd seen plenty of dead in his job. This thing looked like the goods.

"You know, Professor, I've always felt that when someone's killed, there's always a motive. Granted you killed van der Jaegt, and just for the sake of argument, let's say he was one of these 'Ollafixes,' what's in it for *you*? What are you getting out of it?"

"I like you, Marcus. You ask good questions."

"I'd like *you* better if you gave me good answers."

"Oh, I intend to . . . but first a few questions of my own. Have you ever, say, been walking through a meadow, and happened to look down? Deep, into the grass and loam, and suddenly there's a whole other *world* down there? Or all the teeming life that can be found in a puddle of mud? Or a cup of seawater?"

"Sure I have," said Marcus, trying to get a bead on where this was leading.

Before continuing, Agamemnon closed the cabinet and directed Marcus farther along into the storage tent with a nod. He stopped before a large chest, lifted the lid so that dim slivers of light and shadow eerily defined two rows of very large glass jars.

Then he paused. "All right, then you've probably imagined there might be beings who look upon this world, this world of humans, in the same way we humans regard the insects or some smear of germs?"

"Well, sort of. . . ." Marcus did not like admitting to thoughts that doubted God's placement of man at the crown of creation. The logic twisted into places that made him physically uncomfortable.

"And when some of these superior creatures stumble upon you, they *might* ignore you, while others give in to the urge, as a child might kick down an anthill, to *disturb* this reality."

"I should tell you . . ." said Marcus, who now fought the urge to hyperventilate—overwhelmed by a sense of decompression, a cloying fear of running out of oxygen. "I should say that sounds *very* unsettling. 'Disturb' in what sense?"

"You do *not* wish to know. But a fate *far* worse than any anthill ever suffered, I assure you."

Marcus felt light-headed, but he was tough, and he meant to fight it. This man had shaken him, and he didn't know what to believe.

"But you still haven't explained why—"

"Wait," said the professor.

Reaching into the chest, he lifted one of the large jars for closer inspection.

Marcus felt his breath and his saliva abruptly squeezed into his throat as he involuntarily gagged. He felt dizzy, disoriented, as he stared at the head that floated in the cloudy, yellowish liquid as if in a swirling atmosphere.

It was not just *any* head, but one uncommonly familiar, yet hideously loathsome. Larger than a human head, its flesh seemed to radiate an internal heat, making its distinctly scarlet color almost glow. Its configuration was triangular from its wide brow down to a pointed chin. Despite what must have been a violent decapitation, its mouth was parted in a demonic grin. And that observation brought Marcus back to its crowning aspect—a set of almost comically bovine horns.

"Lucifer himself! That *can't* be!" His voice a shallow rasp, a whisper dying.

"Not at all. What you see is an example of a being whose types have been drifting from their own plane to this one for so long, their True Form has been seen enough to be incorporated into human myth."

Marcus understood what the professor was telling him, but believing it was another story.

"What you say shakes my . . . my faith. I can't accept this," he said, but there was a part of him that already had. "You're telling me this whole world of grace and sin is less than this bunch of tents in a carnival, that we're just a *sideshow*?"

"To some, yes. Not to others."

Marcus tore his gaze from the demon-being head. "Really? Like who?"

"Well, like *me*, and others like me."

Agamemnon carefully settled the jar into the chest.

Marcus had no desire to see what gigged and bobbed within the liquids of its neighbors. He forced a small grin to his face, but he felt like an actor. "So, finally, our story rolls around to *you*, and motive, of course. . . ."

"There are those from my . . . plane, who have appreciated the kindred spirit of species. They believe there are poisons in the earth that seep from one parallel to the other, and must be neutralized no matter what plane they occupy. Along the way, they believe this plane of humans more than worthy of saving, not only from itself, but from parabeings which would bring about its destruction."

"Mighty nice of you," said Marcus. His attempt to be sardonic sounded flat and stupid even to him, and he was immediately embarrassed. "I'm sorry. Go on. But why? And why *you?*"

"Not just me or my kind. We have help. There are internecine alliances you would never imagine. My assistant, Kenneth, is from a reality wholly different from mine or yours—but he shares our need to rid the various planes of the ones we call 'rogues.' Others help perhaps more out of boredom than anything noble, or perhaps from an abiding curiosity about the wonders of the universe. My own race is very old, and we have left marks of our achievements in the dust and frozen wastes of many worlds, many realities."

Marcus realized he was far past the point of parsing this man's tale into what was real and what was not. It was like a high-stakes card game—either he was all in or all out. Regarding the man he'd come to arrest, Marcus averred he did not look like a liar or a killer. There was more to him. "No doubt, you're no professor, and I'd wager the name's not Agamemnon, either."

"Correct on both points. Although I often change my name, I usually retain the professor persona."

"So what *is* your real name?"

"You could not pronounce it."

"So you chose an easy one like 'Agamemnon'?"

The professor shrugged.

"Saying you're so advanced and different is easy. I've seen nothing in you to prove it. I came to arrest a killer—you. I have to be certain you are not the absolute evil I sought."

"I thought I was doing a reasonable job." The man gestured farther down the aisle of lockers and crates. "There is much more to see."

"They *could* all be fanciful constructions." Marcus voiced this objection, despite a gnawing in his gut that *knew* it was true.

"Well, there is one way to totally convince you. . . ."

"All right."

"When my assistant is finished with the crowd, he will allow you to see his True Form."

"He'll 'allow' me? What's *that* mean?"

"His kind has developed a way to camouflage their appearance—he *makes* you see him as a human."

"What? You mean like 'mesmerizing'?"

"Something like that."

"And he'll let me see him *what?* . . . As he really is?"

Agamemnon nodded. "If I tell him to, yes."

"All right, I'm game. I *want* to believe you."

"I know you do. I appreciate that. Now, I have more . . . 'specimens' to show you," said Agamemnon. "Would you like to move on?"

Holding up his hands, Marcus shook his head. "I think I've seen enough of this kind of thing. Let's go have that talk with Kenneth."

"Very well." Agamemnon turned and began to walk back toward the exit and the path to the exhibition tent.

"A few more questions 'til then, okay?"

"Of course."

"Why the traveling show?"

"It gives me an excuse to be anywhere I need to be. Remember—things are best hidden when left in plain view," said the professor.

"Plus you can keep the evidence of your 'noble work' without anybody getting too suspicious," said Marcus.

"That too. I suppose. Yes."

"Chestertown, Maryland? Why?"

"Popular legend would call her a witch. Very dangerous. They have the ability to produce violent psychoses in humans. Her elimination most likely saved an entire town."

Marcus nodded, feeling the weight of his experience pressing down on all his police instincts. He should *not* be believing such outrageous claims. The suspect had started out sounding like the biggest loonie Marcus had ever collared, but now, he was seeing the unexpected logic of Agamemnon's claims. And even though he found the transition from skeptic to believer troubling, it was also beginning to feel inevitable.

"And Louisiana? Let me guess—we simple folk would call them zombies, right?"

Agamemnon shrugged. "Depends upon the legend. These were flesh-eaters, cannibals. Either dead or alive. Burning is the only solution for their kind."

Marcus remained silent for a moment. "This talk is *insane!* Surely you must realize how absurd it must sound to me?"

"Certainly, but all the cultures of your world are full of tales of monsters and other boojums. Lots of weird, unexplainable phenomena."

"Not so unexplainable after all . . . according to *you*," said Marcus. Everything he'd ever learned as a policeman told him to just cuff this nut, and be done with it. But . . . he couldn't do it. There was the troubling evidence of the professor's previous "work," which could not be explained away. Marcus needed to know more, all there was to tell.

"All right. Why Chicago?"

"There's a well-known legend among the Sauk and the Winnebago . . . both northern Illinois tribes. It's called the *Wendigo*, and the Indians say it means 'that which destroys man.'"

Marcus raised an eyebrow. "Were they right? The Indians?"

"Absolutely. A hideous being."

"And you have the means to dispatch it?"

"I've done it before. In Minnesota. I have its skull back here," said Agamemnon, waving his hand in the direction of the storage tent behind them. "Want to see it?"

"In due time," said Marcus. They had reached the conflux of tenting which formed a corridor to the Emporium exhibit. "I haven't forgotten what you said about your assistant. I'd rather see his 'true form' you promised me."

"Are you *sure* that's what you want?"

The professor looked at him with those ice-blue eyes, and Marcus felt as if a white-hot needle had pierced his spine. But he forced himself to nod.

"Very well," said the professor. "Right this way."

They turned a few corners, until they encountered the assistant locking things up and covering the displays under velvet cloaks. He watched as Agamemnon approached the oleaginous little man, and spoke to him in a language totally unintelligible. The two of them exchanged a few more lines of gibberish, and then slowly, the man called Kenneth turned to face Marcus squarely. For an instant, there was an impish grin on his thin lips.

But that, along with everything else, disappeared.

Like an image in a shimmering wall of heat off a desert basin, the figure of the diminutive barker wavered, then dissolved. His hair became hundreds of undulating tendrils which may have had little grasping cups along their pale, pink, rat-tail lengths. His head had become the tip of a conical body bristling with lesions that oozed like bedsores. The thing looked half alive and half botanical. But more than anything, it looked *diseased* and virulent. Marcus turned his head just as he began to involuntarily vomit.

"Oh . . . my . . . God . . . that . . . is . . ." Marcus said, staggering, try to recover. He gasped for the right word but it would not come.

The image began to waver again, to glimmer for an instant before being replaced by the thing known as Kenneth.

"I am so sorry. I guess I wasn't ready for that," said Marcus, pausing to clean his face with a fresh linen handkerchief.

"I would be shocked if you were." Agamemnon nodded to his assistant, who slipped away without a word or gesture.

Pausing for a moment to collect himself, Marcus reined in the calamity of thoughts in his head. Either he was facing a demon from Hell, or this man was telling the truth . . . and Marcus didn't know which was *worse*. In either case, this was no simple murder.

"Are you feeling all right?" said the professor.

"Well enough," said Marcus. "But I'm thinking there's only one more thing I need to close this case."

"What's that?"

"I'll need to go with you."

"What? Where?" Agamemnon wore an expression of curious amusement.

"I'd like to see this *Wendigo*. Actually, I think I'd like to *kill* it."

The professor nodded, allowed himself a small grin. "You know, you've probably heard this, but you really should be careful what you wish for."

"If I could do this thing *with* you . . ."

"You would finally believe me."

"No, no. I cannot *not* believe you, but it would definitely be the final nail, so to speak. Plus I cannot stand by and not attempt what must be one of the most challenging adventures imaginable! This would be the capstone to my greatest 'case.'"

"Very well," said Agamemnon, as he checked the latches on a nearby cabinet, then began walking toward the exit. "I can arrange it. You're not the first one to ask me to take him hunting."

"You said you'd been caught before," said Marcus. "Is that when it happened?"

"Yes, that's right . . . in England, a few years back. Some fool writer of melodramas. Actually, he was quite smart, and he *begged* to accompany me on a mission in the *Balkans,* of all places. Afterward, he asked me if he could write me up in one of his fictions, and I agreed. . . .

"Most likely nothing will come of it."

Hero Dust

KRISTINE KATHRYN RUSCH

✠

Weigh'd in the balance, hero dust
Is vile as vulgar clay
—LORD BYRON, "ODE TO NAPOLEON BONAPARTE"

· I ·

THE WEATHER THAT SUMMER was frightful. Much later—nearly 200 years later—he learned that the amazing storms with their torrential downpours and terrifying lightning shows occurred as a meteorological reaction to the eruption of the volcano Tambora in Indonesia.

But on those nights in 1816, which he spent leaning against the wall of the villa listening to the voices echo from the veranda, the weather seemed like some special gift from hell. The rain was warm and powerful, the worst he had seen in his young life, hitting the bare flesh of his arms so hard that he sometimes worried the water would bruise him, and the lightning so bright that he sometimes had to scuttle backwards to avoid being seen by the storytellers gathered in a circle on the stone tiles.

Bram was not supposed to be there: George Gordon Noel Byron, the Sixth Baron Byron, had his doctor, John Polidori, rent the villa so no one would know that the famous poet planned to spend the summer on the shore of Lake Geneva. But Bram wasn't there to see Lord Byron—he had never heard of the man before that May. Bram had come because his mentor had ordered it.

His mentor—a man whose name Bram never spoke, not even now, because heroes, Bram had been taught, worked in silence and were not—should not ever be—remembered.

The stars say a power will emerge near the summer solstice, his mentor had said. *I have heard from two other sources as well. The world shall change at the Villa Diodoti on the shore of Lake Geneva in Switzerland in the last part of June. One of us must be there. We must see if we can harness that power and use it for good.*

Because the augurs weren't always correct in their timelines, Bram arrived in Geneva before the spring solstice, and planned to leave after the autumnal equinox. He had little money and no friends, never before having been outside of the city of Amsterdam.

But he managed. And he found the Villa Diodoti, hiding in its gardens when the only renters it would have all year arrived.

He can still remember his shock when he realized he was dealing with the world's most famous poet, Lord Byron, and his not-quite-as-famous friend Percy Bysshe Shelley, and how Bram's own confusion grew when he learned these two men and their party would spend their summer writing, telling stories, and making merry.

At that time, Bram could not see how a summer full of poetry and declamation would change the world.

Now he cannot imagine the world without that summer, without that change, without the lightning and the rain and the competitive ghost stories—and the truths buried therein.

· II ·

B RAM SITS IN the back of the large classroom, his head resting against the wall, his eyes closed. His hands are folded on the metal desktop, his legs spread out before him, ankles crossed.

Once he stood in the well at the base of the long flight of stairs, his arms resting on the podium, his hand clutching a stick of chalk. He had found his best assistants that way, teaching things that could no longer be taught—phrenology, and other types of medicine now discredited.

The students he'd met there, men who were willing to steal corpses so that they could dissect them and study anatomy, had the perfect elements to help Bram in his fight to stop the Undead.

But modern students were not like that, and Bram's qualifications as a teacher had vanished along with the nineteenth century. He had never thought when it became clear that he did not age like other men (*it is because,* his mentor said to him, *you know how to believe in impossible things*) that he would outgrow his education and, in some ways, his usefulness.

The students file in, coming down the long flight of stairs, taking seats near the back so that they won't be near the teacher. Bram doesn't open his eyes until the last student sits. Books slam open, and conversation grows around him. He misses the dry familiar scent of chalk dust, buried these days beneath the chocolate bars and apples and McDonalds hamburgers that the students insist on bringing to class.

The Oral Fixation of the Twenty-First-Century College Student. Freud would have had something to say about that. Bram would have, too, once, back when he was Abraham Van Helsing, M.D., D.Ph., D.Lit., etc., etc.

But he had been forced to drop that name in 1897, after Bram Stoker had published his still-famous novel. Stoker lived up to his agreement to conceal all the names involved—all except Van Helsing's, of course, claiming that the world needed to know such an heroic man existed.

How will they find you, man, if they discover a great evil that must be vanquished?, Stoker had said the day Van Helsing confronted him with a copy of the published book. *Will they just come to you? I think not.*

But that was how it had worked from time immemorial: the augurs, combined with science and knowledge, would send someone—once his mentor or his mentor's mentor, and finally Bram—to the right place to do the right thing; everything else would simply get in the way.

This lecture hall is filled with more than a hundred students, most of them young, most of them with tattoos and piercings and multicolored hair. The styles have changed so many times in Bram's long life that he no longer thinks anything odd.

The class is one of a thousand he has attended at colleges and universities all over America. Each one has a similar title: The Hero in Literature; The Hero's Journey; The Hero in History.

Most are unimaginative, using Joseph Campbell as their base. Some are fascinating but useless to Bram. Still, because of these classes, he has read some of the world's classics. He has learned of acts of heroism the world over, and throughout time, and he has learned—as the students have learned—that men are often flawed.

But he has not found what he's seeking, and he doubts he'll find it here. He has thought of approaching already proven heroes—men who have saved a life or achieved what the world once thought impossible.

He does not, however. He knows that each man has his place. There are different types of heroism, and his is a dark form. He needs someone who will steal a corpse to learn how to save a man, not a man who will do everything he can to prevent the corpse from being stolen.

So the only thing he can think of is to approach men who study heroism, to see if they've seen that remarkable courage in themselves or in someone else—to see if they've looked for other, nontraditional kinds of heroism.

This small university is his last attempt at this tactic. He has heard, through colleagues, through friends, through websites and articles and bulletin boards, that this place has a star professor, one who seems to understand more than all the others, who can impart that which no other teacher can:

What it truly means to be a hero.

So Bram is here, not to learn (although he will: he always does) but to observe.

And to hope that this time, at last, he will find his successor.

· III ·

THE POET AND his friends started with a collection of German ghost stories in the dark of a long clear night that came after a gloriously

beautiful day. At first, the days in the middle of that June were radiant—
sun against a high blue sky, reflecting on the pristine waters of that mountain lake.

The writers, their friends, and family seemed to be taking a holiday.
They didn't notice Bram. He gardened, telling everyone he was hired by
the owner of the house, and no one questioned him.

He had a room for the night not far from the villa. He spent little time
in that room—what with getting up at dawn to hurry to the garden, and
going to bed after the stories were through. Sometimes he slept only an
hour or two—and never realized that this, too, was training for his future.

When he went to Switzerland, he had been indentured for five years.
He was barely sixteen years old.

Odd that he can remember those years with such clarity. Later years
blur—particularly the World Wars. They seem like one long war, and he
must remind himself that there was a period of silence between, a period
in which evil rebuilt itself and started anew.

Sometimes, he thinks he has never gotten past that sixteenth summer,
when he saw the pieces of his life for the first time. It took nearly a
decade for them to fall into place, but the pieces—the pieces sparkled
before him, like sunlight on that high mountain lake.

· IV ·

"OUR DEFINITION OF heroism changes." The young professor's voice
booms out of the loudspeakers placed around the lecture hall. "After 9/11, we started to recognize the everyday heroism in firefighters—
people who risk their lives every time they answer a call. The New York
City firefighters became weary of the label after a while. For months afterward, they appeared on television, claiming they weren't heroes—
they were just regular guys."

Bram squirms in his chair. How many times has he heard this varia-
tion? He represses the urge to sigh. A young woman sitting next to him
fiddles with a textbook. She is petite, dark-haired, and as disinterested as
he is. She keeps scanning the book before her. On the cover, black lettering tames the bright yellow background.

Out of the corner of his eye, he thinks he sees the title: *Heroism for Dummies*. Bram blinks, looks, realizes his mistake. *Graduate School for Dummies*. She isn't paying attention to the lecture, and he has heroism on the brain.

"But what are heroes if not regular guys? We elevate the brave among us, and assume they lead perfect lives. Then we tear down the pedestal when we realize they're made of the same vulgar clay as the rest of us."

"Vulgar clay" caught Bram's attention. He peers down at the young professor. The man has not only read Byron; he remembers enough to quote Byron.

A shiver runs down Bram's back. Byron. Bram always has such mixed feelings about Byron. The Byron of his memory is not the Byron who lives through history.

The historical Byron is a romantic figure—larger than life, with black, black hair and beautiful eyes. He is both strong and sensitive, brooding and playful—the man who gave the world the concept of the gothic romance hero, also known as the Byronic hero—and the man who unwittingly became the model of the modern vampire—tall and suave and smart, a rich man with no soul, who must steal the life of others in order to live.

Byron himself would have laughed at the characterization.

What is a writer, after all, he would have said, *but a creature who steals the lives of others in order to survive?*

He would not have minded the characterization, no matter how exaggerated it was. The Byron Bram observed was a too-thin man with a ghastly pale face. He looked sickly, even though he was not.

His voice had no beauty to it. Too nasal, too harsh, nonetheless, it compelled. Bram can hear it now if he so chooses, reciting lines from a poem, or reading aloud someone else's.

But Byron was the instigator, the man who suggested the gathering tell each other ghost stories every night, the man who saw the world as a competition between himself and everyone else—particularly his friend Percy Bysshe Shelley. The real Byron had a quick mind, a cutting sense of humor and an insecurity so vast that it hid itself behind arrogance, for only arrogance could hide Byron's most obvious flaw—his unwieldy club foot, which gave him a slight limp and often forced him to cut adventures short because of the pain it sent along his leg.

The real Byron intrigued Bram more than the romantic myth. And it was that Byron who told a fragment of a story, a story he would never finish, about a nobleman named Augustus Darvell who contrived to return from the dead.

That fragment did not impress Bram when he heard it. He thought it weak and self-indulgent. And yet, it was the Byronic tale, as usual, that had the most lasting effect on Bram's life—and on the lives of so many others.

The young professor does not have a compelling voice. Even though it is warm and rich and amplified to an uncomfortable degree by the speakers, it does not have the bewitching quality that Byron's voice had. Few people have such a voice, as Bram has learned in his quest.

Few people need it.

Still, he can scarcely wait to escape. Clearly this young professor is not the man that Bram has heard about.

"Studies have shown," the professor is saying to an increasingly less attentive class, "that heroes are rare precisely because they are heroes. In other words, heroes have an innate disposition to run *toward* danger when any sensible person would run *away*—"

Suddenly, he has Bram's attention again. Bram leans forward in his chair, braces his elbow on the curved desktop, and squints. The young professor has brown hair that curls over his collar. He wears blue jeans and a white shirt with the sleeves rolled up, an obvious attempt to be as comfortable as his students.

". . . follows a bell curve. Most of us fall in the middle. When trouble occurs, we look for help. The lower end of the bell curve are those people who freeze in an emergency, and the upper end are the heroes, the ones who seek out danger. These reactions come from a genetic predisposition and can only be changed slightly—the reactions happen from the subconscious, the animal brain, and not from the conscious mind at all . . ."

The animal brain. Bram used to call it the child-mind, but later learned that wasn't exactly accurate. Much of what he'd called science a hundred years ago wasn't exactly accurate.

". . . so," the professor is saying, "the hero sees danger and rushes to end it, with no thought to himself. Or herself."

Bram leans back in his chair, mulling the words "rush toward danger." He rarely rushed. Usually he walked, slowly, knowing he was risking everything.

Even that first time he walked into a crypt. Bram was barely eighteen, reedy and frightened. He clutched a stake in his right hand, and an axe in his left. Around his neck, he wore a cross and a chain of garlic flowers.

The stench of the white blossoms made him ill but he went on, opening the door, stepping into the darkness, his mentor behind him with the lantern whose light cast shadows on the crypt wall.

Bram's conscious mind told him he was being foolish, that he should run and quickly, that this dank, foul tomb was no place for a young man with a scholar's brain. Yet his feet did not listen. He walked forward, his heart pounding and his breath coming in quick gasps, as he approached the resting place of his very first Undead.

"You all right, mister?" The young girl sitting next to him touches his arm. "You looked a little gray there for a second."

Bram blinks. It takes him a moment to leave the past—a sign that he is getting old—and to remember he is in a college classroom, listening to yet another lecture on heroism and its necessity to the human race.

"I was just thinking of something else," he says, and his voice sounds rusty, as if he hasn't used it for a long time.

The girl laughs. "Aren't we all?"

The professor is still talking, but he has moved away from studies and into literature itself—starting, as they all do, with Homer.

"You're not taking this class, are you?" the girl asks.

Her face is narrow, with large eyes and a generous mouth. Her slightness and the intelligence in those eyes remind him of Percy Bysshe Shelley's lover, Mary Godwin. Intelligent and gentle at the same time.

"I'm just sitting in, listening," Bram says. "Hoping for something different."

"That would have been last semester," the girl says. "Professor Miller is new. The guy who used to teach this class—Professor Addison—he got hired away by Yale."

Yale. Bram has been to Yale, but he cannot remember how long ago. He even listened to a hero lecture there, but that had to be nearly a decade ago, before the arthritis in his leg made movement difficult and let him know that finally his body had started aging again, that his time would be limited after all.

"Too bad, too," the girl is saying. "I heard he was just brilliant. We were going to use his text, but Professor Miller doesn't want to. These guys are so jealous, aren't they? Like they're in some kind of competition for our minds or something."

At that moment, the bell rings. The professor finishes his sentence, but no one listens. The class rises out of their seats as if they're one body, gathering papers and laptops and coats.

The girl stands and cradles her books to her chest. She looks around for her purse, finds it, and slings it over her shoulder.

Bram starts to stand, slips and falls heavily into his chair. He closes his eyes against the pain. He is useless, and he has not found someone to replace him.

He has managed, over the years, to get the information out—to use fiction to explain how to destroy vampires—but he cannot get people to believe such creatures actually exist.

To believe in them enough to fight them, anyway.

"Are you all right?" the girl asks again.

He forces his eyes open, then makes himself smile. "I'm fine."

She's standing near him, waiting for him to clear the aisle so that she can leave. But she is too polite to say so.

Her concern touches him.

He puts down the desktop and stands carefully, not losing his footing this time. He slides out of the row of chairs, waits, and offers her a hand to help her onto the steps.

She looks at him as if he has made an alien gesture, then she smiles, and places her hand in his own.

Her fingers are warm and small. How long has it been since he's held a woman's hand? How long has it been since he has touched a woman, except in an emergency?

Although it is hard for him to think of this creature before him as a woman. She is perhaps eighteen, barely at the beginning of her life, and he has lived two hundred years more than her.

He wonders if she would believe that—if her soon-to-be-college-educated mind will allow her to take in the fantastic as well as the scientific.

She slips her hand out of his, but remains beside him on the stairs. Except for the professor, who is still gathering his notes, they are the last people in the extremely large room.

"Are you sure you're all right?" she asks. "You seem upset or something."

"I am not finding what I'm looking for," he says, "and I am getting weary."

She tilts her head to one side, her glossy hair swinging over her shoulder—such a modern, American movement. "What are you looking for?"

His back straightens. He has waited almost a decade to hear that question, and now he hears it from the mouth of a young girl who is just embarking on her life.

A girl whom, like all the rest of the fair sex, he is sworn to protect.

· V ·

HE KNOWS IT is the birth of the vampire story which was the seminal event of that soggy June two centuries ago that changed the world, but Byron's fragment, as he later called it, was unremarkable. Flat, and dull, and without much imagination.

However, no matter how hard Bram tries, he must force himself to remember Byron's compelling voice recite that fragment of a story. Bram might have forgotten that story altogether if he hadn't been so stunned at Byron's knowledge of the Undead—knowledge that John Polidori expanded upon when he used that fragment as the basis of his novella, the one which introduced a vampire named Lord Ruthven who was so clearly Lord Byron that no one seemed to notice the fictional vampire was the first to reveal what factual vampires were actually like.

No, what Bram remembers of that June is Mary Godwin, her reedy voice, shaking as she sat down across from her soon-to-be husband, Percy Bysshe Shelley

Your tales of ghouls and goblins, she said, *and that horrid discussion about discovering the principles of life have given me nightmares. This nightmare gave me an image, and it is a ghastly one.*

Her voice gained strength as she began to turn her nightmare into a story—not of ghosts, but of a thing that seemed alive, and was not. Or had been alive, and then died, and came to a sort of life again.

As she spoke, her face had a paleness to it, the wide eyes, the uplifted chin revealing the naked throat, made Bram think of vampires, even though at that point he had not yet seen one, only heard of them.

He had thought, as he watched her move her pale hands in the candlelight, that she, more than anyone else, would be the vampire's desired mate.

· VI ·

"MAY I BUY you coffee?" he asks the young girl, knowing her generation's predilection for the sweetened, creamed and overly strong drink. It reminds him of Vienna before the war—the First World War—a city that was then filled with coffee drinkers who liked to talk too much about nothing important, and later a city that became the home of so very many Undead.

The girl gives him half a smile, and he knows she will say no. Why should she say yes? Even though she cannot guess his age, she knows that it is at least three times hers. People that young have no interest in the old.

"Oh, what the hell," she says. "I don't have a class right now, and a double-tall sounds good."

He smiles in return, gives her a slight bow, which makes her laugh, and then follows her up the stairs. She won't let him carry her books or her laptop, saying she is used to the weight.

He is astonished still at the independence and the strength of these young women. He knows that the culture has given them permission to be so; he also knows that they no longer have a real imperative to be feminine, have children, and raise a family.

But he finds this new breed of female unfathomable, and this girl is no different from the others. Her tight blue jeans are too short at the hips, and her shirt is cropped too high, revealing her stomach. Her hands are covered with rings, and she has a small tattoo on her left shoulder, just barely visible through the thin fabric of her shirt.

Bram looks away. This new openness embarrasses him. He cannot change 150 years of training as quickly as he would like.

The coffee shop is part of the student union, only a few buildings from the one he has been trapped inside. The girl orders her double-tall and he orders a simple espresso, hoping that the barista behind the counter makes it correctly.

The girl leads Bram to one of the tall round tables. Its surface is sticky. She grabs a napkin and wipes it off before she sets her books or her coffee down. Then she grins at him.

"You finishing up your degree?" she asks.

"No." He smiles in return. He likes her grin. It is infectious. "I have too many useless degrees as it is."

"Yeah," she says, setting her laptop, backpack and purse on the chair beside her. "My dad says any degree above a bachelor's is useless. No one really cares."

"It depends on what you wish to do," Bram says. "Some careers require degrees."

He remembers her *Graduate School for Dummies* text. Perhaps she is slightly older than he thought.

"And sometimes a person turns into a perpetual student, staying in college because it's safe, not because she has a game plan." She sips her coffee, then extends her hand. "I'm Clarissa, by the way."

The good old-fashioned name surprises him. He takes the hand, holds it as if he is going to kiss it, then releases it. "Bram."

"I never met anyone called Bram before." She leans back in her chair. "If you're not taking classes, what are you doing here?"

That question again, framed differently, but with the same meaning. He surprises himself when he says, "I am searching for someone with an open mind."

· VII ·

HE FINALLY SPOKE to her seven years later in London. Mary Shelley, by then a widow and the acknowledged author of her novel *Frankenstein or a Modern Prometheus*, attended the first play made from her work.

Bram was free then, no longer indentured. He was in London on other business and went to the play out of curiosity, not realizing she was going to be there.

Instead of watching the play, he watched her—an old habit that came back easily. She sat with a small smile on her face as all three acts unfolded—wincing only once, when the assistant shouted, "It lives! It lives!" a line too overwrought to be in her finely tuned novel.

After the show, people surrounded her, asked her opinion, and she was diplomatic. "I was much amused," she would say over and over again.

Bram hung back, as he was wont to do in this woman's presence, and sought some sign of the girl he had seen in Lake Geneva.

Finally, the crowd departed, and she turned to her companions, asking one of them to hail a hansom cab.

At that moment, Bram stepped before her, bowed at the waist, and introduced himself as a student and fan of her work.

"I was in Lake Geneva when you wrote the tale," he said. "I worked in the garden."

Mary Shelley stood just inside the doorway of the theater. The light revealed her face. Even though she was only twenty-three, she had frown lines and her girl's body was long lost to children and despair. He had heard that she supported herself now on her own writings, having no money or recognition from her husband's estate.

"I thought I had seen you before," she said, but there was no joy in her tone. Her memory of those days did not seem like a pleasant one.

"That was a strange summer," he said.

"Yes." She glanced over her shoulder. "Sometimes I feel like I created my own vampire. 'It lives, it lives,' even though, at times, I wish it would simply die."

He stood in shock, not knowing how to respond. She tapped him lightly with her gloved fingers.

"Pay me no mind," she said. "The world is not what I thought it then, and I am no longer a girl whose illusions were being shattered, but a woman who knows more of darkness than she ever cared to see."

She stepped away from him and to the cab waiting curbside, its horse thin and bony. No longer the mistress of a rich man traveling with an even wealthier one, she could no longer afford to travel in her own coach. He wondered if she would have been able to afford a ticket to a play inspired by her own novel or if she only came at this late date because of the charity of R. B. Peake, the play's author.

Bram wanted to ask her, indeed, he wanted to spend much more time with her. They were of an age, and he too had become disillusioned, learning more than he cared to know about the violence that haunted the night.

But she got into the carriage before he could call to her and didn't look out the window as the carriage drove away.

And although he thought of her often—still does, almost daily—he never saw her again.

· VIII ·

"D O YOU BELIEVE in stories?" he asks the girl, this Clarissa with the classical name and such a familiar face.

"Stories?" she asks, looking confused.

"Do you believe they have the power to transform, even to save?"

"Is that why you're going to the hero classes?" She tilts her head again. It's an endearing maneuver. "You're looking for stories that save?"

He waves a hand. "No. No. I'm talking about fiction—that inside its apparent untruths there are actual truths. Do you believe this?"

"Sure," she says. Her tone humors him. "Why?"

"I look for the impossible." He hasn't spoken of this in nearly a hundred years. "I look for people who have the capacity to believe in the impossible. And the first step in finding those people is finding people who accept that there is truth in fiction."

"I don't see how that relates to heroes," she says.

"Ah," he says. "Heroes. They always believe in the impossible."

"They do?" She grabs some artificial sugar, rips the top off the packet, and pours it into her coffee. "Professor Miller was saying that heroics is a matter of destiny—heredity, if I heard him right. Like we have no choice."

"We always have a choice." The fact that Bram is sitting before her is a choice. The fact that he has had a long life is a choice—it is just not one he can make again.

"I suppose," she says, in a tone that tells him she does not believe him.

He sips his espresso. Close. Not quite right—the beans had a bit of a burnt flavor—but good enough.

"If you were to choose now," he says, "what kind of life would you have?"

She gives him a wistful half-smile. "It wouldn't be this."

"What would it be?"

She shrugs. "Something unusual. Something adventurous."

"Something heroic?"

Her eyes seem to light from within. Then she looks down. "That's just silly."

"It is not," he says. "We can be whatever we want to be."

"What makes you so sure of that?" she asks, her eyes still downcast.

"I've lived it. I've lived a thousand impossible things."

She looks up at him. "I had a hunch you'd be interesting," she says. "You have that look."

He does not expect her to take the conversation in this direction. "What look?"

She shrugs. "I dunno. Like a guy who's lived."

Lived. He smiles at that. He has lived a good and long life. He has enjoyed much of it, too, even though most of it brought heartache and loss.

He nods toward her book. "Are you applying to graduate school?"

She puts a restless hand on top of it, her fingers tapping against the black lettering. "I don't know. I'm hoping something else will come along."

She is the first candidate—the only candidate—he has come across in more than a decade of searching. He doesn't have much time left. He would rather train a new scholar—an expert in matters impossible—than leave the world without one.

Yet it is hard for him. Even though he knows that women are strong, he is still a product of his upbringing. He doesn't want to risk her.

Then he realizes why she looks familiar. She has that edge, that darkness, he saw so many years ago in the young Mary Godwin—another woman who did not know what she wanted to do. A woman who taught him about the power of stories, enough so that he later sought out a writer to tell the tale of how to kill vampires, so that people could become familiar with the methods.

He had chosen Stoker, but all that time he had been thinking of Mary Shelley.

Mary Shelley. At that point, she had been dead for forty years.

"It won't, though, will it? Unless I choose."

He blinks again. The girl is speaking, and he has to concentrate. His wandering mind—the worst part of his old age.

She was saying that something else won't come along unless she chooses it.

He smiles at her. "What would you say to a few months spent talking about stories?"

"Where would we talk?" she asks, and the suspicion of her generation—the fears of perverts and murderers and all kinds of man-made horrors lurks behind her eyes.

"Here," he says, trying to seem as harmless as possible. "I'll buy you a cup of coffee every afternoon for an hour of your time."

She frowns slightly. "What kind of stories?"

"The best kind," he says. "Stories of impossible things."

She studies him for a moment, and her thoughts are as clear as if she says them aloud. She thinks he is a lonely old man. But she finds him interesting. Her curiosity wars with her training not to give time to strangers.

"Why me?" she asks after a moment.

"Because," he says, "you ask questions."

"Is that all?" she asks.

He shakes his head. "Because you also remind me of a woman I used to admire."

That seems to appease the girl. It certainly fits into her worldview—the lonely old man, trying to recapture his youth.

"Will you tell me about her?" Clarissa asks.

"Eventually," he says, "when I'm sure you'll believe me."

"I'm sure I'll believe you," Clarissa says.

Bram just smiles. He knows, after more than two hundred years, the human capacity for disbelief. He shares it. He is struggling against it even now, all that training which taught him a woman could not succeed him—even though the evidence of his eyes, of his life, disputes it.

"So," she says, "are you going to tell me a story?"

He wraps his hand around his coffee cup. "I'm going to tell you a story about stories," he says. "And how, when the right elements come together, they can change the world."

Remember Me

TANITH LEE

From an explanation of origin by John Kaiine

· I ·

HIS FIRST MEMORY: darkness, fear, and the smell of water—then two
dots of flame, a shape—something which snaked towards him—
and ordinary fear changing to whitest terror.

He was three years old, maybe just four. He would never be sure of
that. Before the first memory was a nothingness, like death, except he
had obviously been alive. And anyway, beyond true death lay another
life. He would come to know that, quite soon.

Years after, he realized he must that evening have been stealing from
the market stalls, mostly things dropped on the ground. He was hungry,
and he had lived like that, stealing, or begging. But there were other
thieves and beggars in the grey little town below the mountains, and they
had no compassion for any small weak dwarf-thing called a child. So they
set on him, and then, getting the taste for it, chased him. He would have
run down past the squat cathedral, along roughly cobbled alleys, towards
the river, and there crawled in at one of the flood drains that ran away un-

der the town. His adult pursuers were too big to get in, or else he had already lost them and only been too afraid to know he had. Certainly they
never followed.

In the flood drain he lay until dusk closed the shutters of the sky against
the world. Perhaps he slept, exhausted, there on the shelf just above the
water. Rats sometimes swam by below, but none of them troubled him.
Later too, he would think he could just recall the rats. Did he believe the
red-eyed thing which was suddenly sliding towards him was itself a rat—
a great rat, a king of their kind, come after all to tear him into pieces?

He had no name, and nameless and alone, he waited, the child, whimpering, for the last cruelty and the final blows.

"Whaar tiss thiss?"

So it sounded to him—language he knew, but sibilant and also gut-
teral—an accent. Till then, he had heard only one accent, that of the
townspeople.

The voice spoke again. The same words. Now the child knew what
they meant.

"What is this?"

He found he had shut his eyes. He opened them, and looked, because
surely even a rat king could not speak any human tongue.

A man's face, close to his, very pale, the skin extraordinarily clear and
fine, so *pure*. It might have been carved from whitest ivory, and was hard like
that, too, with strong narrow bones. It reminded him of the face of one of
the saints, probably seen, though not properly remembered, in some religious procession. The eyes were dark. And the voice . . . that was dark, too.

"You are a child," said the voice, deciding.

He could say nothing. He stared. In his brief life, everything had been
anyway quite strange, and often senseless. Unkind also. And so when the
man stroked back his hair, with a hand that was the perfect companion to
the pale, carved, saintly face, the child did not struggle or try to run away.

"What are you doing here, child? You crawled in and lost your bearings, did you? You're too young. Unripe fruit. Only scavengers and weak-
lings, or those themselves childlike, take your kind before they are
grown. Come, I'll lead you up out of this place."

The saint who had entered the flood drain like a serpent, and whose eyes of shining scarlet were now black as ink, swept the child into his arms. The saint had a curious, not unpleasant smell, like a plant recently pulled from soil, the moist earth still scattered on its leaves. His breath had been wholesome when he spoke, for, as the child would come to learn, he had flawless teeth and lived on a flawless nourishment. Any corruption eventually smelled on such breath had more to do with the rot of the soul.

But what happened next was bizarre enough. At the time the child count not grasp it, it was like those events which happen in dreams. Afterwards, he would be used to it, and to many similar actions. He would think them all usual, indeed, *enviable*.

There was a kind of rush—a sort of flight, inside the drain. Either the stones gushed back, or the man arrowed forward, the child borne with him. Then wet and darkness opened in an O of brilliant lesser dark. The sky was there, streamered with windblown stars. There was a scent of coming storm. Underfoot, the muddy bank of the river, and close by, one of the ugly little humped bridges, and not so far away, the few leering narrow lamps of humankind.

"There then. Here you are. Go back to your kin, little child. Go back and grow up. Twelve or so years, that will do. Then maybe we shall meet again."

Turning, the man, in a swagger of black garments, left the child, there on the ground.

The child stood rooted to the mud.

He saw above him the sky, and nearer the miserly lamp-stars on the banks of the river; he smelled the stink of *people*, and heard the murmur of their heartless minds. From the cathedral, midnight struck.

Then a shadow flicked somewhere under the bridge. Probably it was nothing, only a stray dog perhaps, as desolate and desperate as he, but it woke up again the child's terror.

And with a noiseless cry, he came unrooted from the mud and ran after the tall figure that walked so incredibly swiftly away from him.

"Papa!" cried the child, aloud then. "Papa! Don't leave me—" Where in God's name—yes, God's—had he learned that name *papa*. He never knew. It simply rose in his mouth as the tears rose in his eyes.

But the stranger paused, a hundred yards away along the bank. Then, turning, he came back—and was there beside the child, impossibly, at once. Down from the tower of more than a man's height, he gazed at the boy standing crying before him. Perhaps the man was bemused—or *a*mused. It could not have happened often, this.

"Why call me back? What do you want?"

"Papa," said the child.

"I'm not your papa. I doubt you have one. What is the matter with you? Go away."

But neither of them moved. And presently the man leaned down and picked up the child again, raised him high up in arms like steel, looked at him with eyes like ink.

"What shall I do with you?"

The child flung his own arms round the neck of this saint. He seemed to have been born, the child, in those moments. New-born, of *course* his first cry had been *Father! Father!*

The saint laughed. *A*mused, then.

"I am named Schesparn. Don't call me *papa*. Say my name."

The child said the name.

"Come then. You shall go with me."

THAT night-morning, they went east of the town. The mountains, which then encircled and shut the boy's universe, were as ever immense and craggy, and now blue-veined with starlight. At first he thought they would fly right over them—for of course, they travelled in the air. But Schesparn only went a little way, some twenty miles, maybe. They moved by a form of levitation, or merely juxtaposition, one place to another. There was no changing of shape, not then, for Schesparn carried the child in his arm, and *needed* an arm, to do so.

The estate lay along a lizard-tail coil of the river, deep among pines and then the lighter woods of birch and ash. The house was a mansion of ornamented, decaying stonework. Vast windows glared like beautiful outraged eyes, all glass gone, only the iron lattices or webs of leading still in them. Not a single light showed.

The storm came in those minutes, catching them up, and the old house too. Clouds like huge masonry figures lurched low overhead, cracked with lightnings. Then the storm had passed. Only a white fluttering was left behind in the sky.

Although they had travelled quickly, summer dawn was not so distant. In at one of the wide casements Schesparn bore his charge, and dropped him gently on a floor like watery agate.

Rather than disturb, the lack of lighting encouraged the child. He had only ever been taken into the lighted areas of mankind for some type of punishment. Although he did not remember in after years, the moment of the eyes in the drain being his first adhesive memory, at three or four, no doubt he did recall that lit rooms meant nothing good for him. He liked this domestic darkness therefore, instinctively. He liked the darkness and pallor of Schesparn, the only person who had ever shown him care or any interest.

Then some of the others came.

First was a woman. Her name was Stina, he would learn shortly. She glided forward over the dry watery floor, and she was pale as Schesparn, dark of eye as he was—and, like him, for a second her eyes flashed red. Her mouth was red, too. By the lightning flicker, with innocent acuity, the child saw both the real colour and what it must be, for it ran down her white chin, over the pearly column of her neck, in at the bodice of her gown. But out of her mouth slipped a long tongue, and took the colour away from her face, yes, even off her chin. A white hand attended to the rest, and then she licked the hand, with eager grace.

After Stina, three others entered. They were all men. Every one of them had a likeness to the others, despite some differences of build, hair colour or eyes. The woman too was like this. They might all have been of one family. They *were*.

"Is *that* for us?" one of the men asked Schesparn.

"No. Unripe."

"True. But perhaps, *sweet*—I've never tried lamb or veal."

They laughed.

Fearless now, the child also liked their laughter. He laughed too.

And then Stina said, "How brave he is! Look, how trusting. Come here, little boy, come to Stina. Let her see you close."

"Go then," said Schesparn. "She won't harm you. Not yet."

But the child had been peeled of fear, at long last. So he went directly to Stina, who crouched down, and looked deep into his eyes. And when she smiled, her teeth were clean and her breath had only a warmth on it, as if she had just eaten a little roast beef and drunk a little wine.

"You are a nice child, I think. Not pretty. But look at your forehead and your skull. A head for intelligence. Oh I had to leave a boy like you, he was my darling—so long ago . . ."

She took his hand. He gave it.

The man who had asked if the child was 'for' them also walked over. He had dark red hair. He said, "What's his name?"

Schesparn said, "I think he has none."

"I will *christen* you then," said the other man, whose own name, the child would learn, was Mihaly. "I will call you Dracul—*Dragon*."

Pleased, the child looked at him. Never ever had there been such benign interest, such involvement, from others.

These others sighed and whispered. Some more had come in. They were like ghosts made flesh—never, *never* the other way about. And then, their leader entered.

His name was Tadeusz, for so they addressed him, respectfully and at once. He was older in his looks, his hair grey streaked thickly with white. Yet his physique was like that of a robust man of twenty-five. They all, male and female, older or younger, had firm and perfect faces and bodies, which the child—"Dracul"—would come to see through the years, both costumed and bare.

Tadeusz looked in turn down at the child. After an age, he spoke. "You do not know where you are, where you have come. But one day you will be one of us. I choose you, for Schesparn has chosen you. Those we love and keep we never choose lightly. Be aware, we are not kind, as you think us, little boy, little Dragon. We are so different from anything you know, so changed from what we ourselves once were, that we can hardly be expected to abide by the codes of men. But *you* shall be safe among us." He raised his head. He was like a great wolf, striped with ice, yellow-eyed.

The others nodded. All of them were there by then, all the family that lived in that house. "Now I will give you your first lesson. You must learn, my dear," said Tadeusz quietly to the child now called Dracul, "to sleep by day. Soon the sun will rise. Though some of us may bear it, it is never easy, and some of us it would sear away. Therefore, by day, we slumber. Learn to love instead the night, little child. Night is day to us. And now to you, also."

The child minded none of that. His life had had no patterns. Now it did. He looked adoringly up at Tadeusz. Father first, then mother. Now grandfather, the patriarch and ruler of the house. How the boy had come by such instant physical categorization, he could not ever know, as even then he had no memory left of a beginning. But certainly Dracul knew, at last he had come home.

He was used only to sleeping without comfort, and on hard surfaces. So to find somewhere to curl up in the carved, pillared and otherwise generally empty mansion, was simple. Besides, he knew that here, no one would hurt him. That was a luxury.

Why had he been at once so sure? They had mesmerized with their hypnotic eyes and touches. They had, their kind, great power over his. Just as they could control wild beasts, they could, largely, control savage humanity.

But also—he believed them. Especially Tadeusz, the Old Wolf.

Probably, as he was to think, the child, two decades after that night, had *actual* wolves adopted him and shown him some kindness, he would, like other feral children of whom he later heard, have trusted them, become one of their own.

Sunlight streamed in across the floors, cut little shafts between the columns behind whose bases he had elected to place himself. He woke now and then. But he had slept through days before, having nothing else to do.

As for his name, he prized it, turning it over and over in his mind, even asleep, like a precious jewel. He did not yet, although they had, apply the name to himself. He merely considered it his *possession*. It was the first.

When the sun set, he woke and was thirsty. But he had already found
a large room, a hall or court, where a fountain played into a basin. He
went and drank the water, which tasted dusty. Leaves had blown in at
windows and the open roof, perhaps only last autumn. Some lay in the
basin. Frugal with always starving, and having eaten, the day before, a
piece of cheese rind and a rotted plum, he did not think of seeking food.

The crimson sky darkened. He knew they would soon arrive, come
back from wherever it was they had gone to. He knew infallibly, and
maybe they had told him, sunset was dawn to them.

Schesparn and Stina came first. They brought another woman, young,
with ash-blond hair, who was called Medestha. Stina said to Medestha, as
they were coming in, "You understand, *this* one is not for the usual purpose?" And the blond head nodded. The two women washed the child's
face at the basin, and combed his hair. Then they played games with him,
having brought a hoop, a ball, and three little bats. Soon the red-haired
Mihaly came in, and he had a dead rabbit, which he skinned, then
handed to the child a small portion, raw and dripping. "We do not cook
our food, Dracul. Be like us. It's much healthier for you."

The child—Dracul—took the meat. It was like nothing he had ever
known—rich and succulent, savoury and sweet together. He sank in his
teeth, and they watched him, the blood running down his chin. It did
him, the raw fresh flesh, the blood, great good.

· II ·

DRACUL LEARNED THEM, his companions, like a book. First their faces
and names, next their ways, swiftly their magicianlike talents and
abilities.

He knew, having been instructed by them inside that second day-
night, what they *were*—Streghoi—Nosferatu—Oupyrae—Varcolaci—
Vampires. The Undead.

Did that mean anything at all? Had he ever heard them spoken of among
the haunts of men? Not knowingly, ever. And why was that? Because no
men, nor women either, had ever spent any time with this boy, save to ill-

treat and chase him with stones. He was as alien to his own race as were his hosts at the mansion—though, like them, he too had been human once.

Now, naturally he altered. Loving them, enthralled, petted, protectively taken on "excursions," he aped their manners, longed to be as they were. All that, even despite seeing, after the shortest while, examples of their more terrible—and grosser—acts. But how could it not be so with him? What had humans, also terrible and gross, shown him, or offered? This demonic wolf pack was his family now. And they had promised, from the first, one day he should be one of them. Just as initiation, the rite of passage, was held out before all valued and aspiring males. As was quite normal, he feared it, did not properly grasp what must occur, yet *longed* to be ready and to be made like the rest of his new tribe.

After the first, Dracul seldom went out diurnally. He was trained inside a week to sleep day long and wake at sunfall. His skin paled and grew clear almost as theirs, from the "healthy" diet of bloody raw meat, and juicy fruits—for orchards raved about the upper edges of the forest, pomegranates and peach trees, and higher up the stony sides of the land, orange trees lit bright with moon-washed globes. His night vision strengthened. He saw as he had never done—a snake like black silver in the silvered black of grass—a tiny flaw inside an emerald ring, shaped like a milky hand.

He saw too, shown without reservation, their acts of miracle and magic. How they might *disintegrate* to pass through some obstacle, like snow or mist, how they might raise themselves into the air, or drift across a sky in human, or in other, form. He saw them *change shape*, to bats—wolves— and puzzled as to how it occurred, as if their bodies parted like curtains to let the *other* creature out. He asked Sraga tenderly if it hurt her to change herself in this way. And Sraga laughed. "It itches," she whispered in his ear. "Then one *scratches*."

"How can she explain," said Faliborv. "You will come to know."

"Will I do it right, when my time comes?" worried the anxious child. "How will I know *how?*"

"Your body will be refined and wonderful by then, like ours. Your body will know how, by itself. It's simple to us to do these things, simple as breathing. We are immortal. We are gods, Dracul."

They were gods. For sure, they were the gods of Dracul. And cruel as gods, uncompassionate, avidly noncompunctious and amoral.

They preyed on all the villages and towns scattered, flea-like, through the tree-furred landscape, and up the flanks of the mountain crags.

Sometimes they took Dracul with them. He rode the winds with one, or two or three of them. Arpaz took the child most often, as if on a hunting trip, and showed him first a narrow house against the wall of a church. The church was beautiless, vegetable in aspect, yet it fascinated Arpaz, as such buildings sometimes did the vampires.

"Do you smell the incense, Dracul?"

"No."

"That sweet smoky smell—sickening—yet irresistible . . ."

"No, Arpaz."

"One day you will smell it. Nothing is finer than to *take*, right beside one of these shells of their God, who does so little to protect them." But, passing by the church on the way to the narrow house, Arpaz, gliding like a shadow through shadows, ducked his head aside as if at a blow, where the old crucifix of ancient wood angled from a tree. Arpaz would not look at the God, though he spoke of him with scorn. Nor would he pass any closer to the church than the house.

In the house, a woman was. She was young and fair-haired, and she slept.

Arpaz drifted to the window, the boy somehow borne with him.

The girl on the bed stirred, uneasy, flinging one arm, brown from summer daylight sun, across her face.

Arpaz purred to her then like a great cat, sitting there in the window embrasure, purred and hissed and slipped over like velvet into the room, and covered the girl up against the night like her blanket. There was no real movement, not like the struggling plunging scenes of human sexual activity Dracul had sometimes glimpsed, in horrified disbelief. The girl sighed, and her long plait of hair slid over and along the floor, and then a little vermilion thread dripped down into it. That was all. They went five nights in a row. Once Stina joined them, once Cesaire. The last night there were two big rough men waiting in the room, but Arpaz stood below purring in the dark, having sensed them, and going up, the men too were tranced to a comalike sleep. Then Arpaz choked. He sneezed and hawked and spat on the floor, backing away. "Dracul, darling," he moaned, leaning at the wall as if he might faint, frightening the boy, "do you see there, those stinking bulbs and flowers—gar-gar-garlic—move them away, throw them out on the street for me—" Dracul rushed to help Arpaz. Once the allergy-causing flowers were gone, Arpaz recovered himself. He stared, his eyes burning like red-green coals, at the unconscious maiden. "You shall pay for that," he said, and going to her casually, tore out her throat with his clean white teeth.

Schesparn also took Dracul "hunting." He had a penchant for caves, tunnels—doubtless why the child had first met him in a flood drain. Travelling this way, rather than having any real sense of forward momentum, Dracul seemed to see the stones instead melt off them in a maelstrom. In towns, emerging from under the earth, Schesparn bent over drunks in alleys, or sleeping guardsmen even, in their barracks, three together, while the boy stood watching in admiring astonishment. Schesparn required the blood of men for his sustenance. Mostly, however, the vampires had a preference for victims of the gender opposite to their own.

Dracul was privy to the suborning, by handsome Cesaire, of a female goat herder on the hills. Cesaire enjoyed the seduction, it appeared, as much as the conquest, and drew the procedure out, meeting the girl twice under the stars before finally overwhelming her. As she sank into his arms, the arch of her white neck offered to him like a slice of moonlight, Cesaire remarked, lingeringly, "How I adore the reek of goat on her. How earthly she is. How utterly human."

Chenek and Faliborv were more violent. They would often work together, waylaying young women straying home too late from some mortal tryst or other fleshly business. They felled these prey animals with harsh blows, or leapt down on their backs from trees like panthers, pinning the women to the ground, stifling the screams only fitfully, allowing legs to kick: a form of rape.

Béla hunted always alone. Mihaly was the same. But these were the two who hunted beasts also, sometimes for themselves, and always for the child. In the end, as he grew older, they taught Dracul the ways of ordinary hunting for survival. Though they could, like all their kind, call and draw wild beasts to them, they took a keen interest in the ordinary hunter's skills they had, presumably, possessed in their prevampiric existence.

Nevertheless, lessoned to hunt, Dracul was still envious of that knack of drawing deer, wild pig, and birds of any kind, by the inexplicable charismatic spells of vampire magic. It was Tadeusz himself who drew the wolves to the mansion on certain nights of the full moon. Huge packs would stand, a grey-black tide of pelt, crystalled with eyes, singing their eerie, breaking hymns at the sky. Then Tadeusz, the old leader, would walk among them, stroking their heads, so they whined with pleasure and bowed to him like favoured human courtiers.

The pursuit of human blood, in the case of Tadeusz, the boy, even as years passed, never saw.

Dracul was nine before Stina permitted him to accompany her. Of course physically virtually unaging, she was beautiful, a girl still, and hand in hand they walked on a dusk riverbank, until a dark young man came striding from the fields over the hill.

"Oh come to me, my dear," called Stina, "come to me. Here I am. Come and kiss me, beloved."

The young man turned, and his eyes clouded and brightened, both at once. As he went into Stina's embrace, Dracul felt within himself a new and distinctive urge. It was sexual, but he did not realize that. He thought, with pride and some relief, he too was now coming to desire the drinking of blood. But he was patient and modest. He kept the awakening to himself because he had yet to become a god.

LONG before that, in the first year he was with them, Tadeusz had decreed certain matters must occur in Dracul's life.

He called Schesparn and Dracul, and the three of them went to a library high in a square stone tower.

"Since you are, in some manner, his guardian, Schesparn, you may teach him the rules of our life, our needs and codes." A look passed between them. It was the compact of something, but Dracul did not know what. As he grew older, he came to see, he thought, that Schesparn would be the one to change him, alter him into the being of a vampire. The process stayed always mysterious to Dracul. For although it involved some of the acts of blood he saw the others perform on humans, there was more to it, naturally. Many of those the vampires fully drained did change, rising from graves and deathbeds, becoming a *sort* of vampire-thing—but it was a moron, a kind of automaton, mindlessly lusting for blood, filthy and stinking, with matted hair and the claws of a lion. The soul seemed gone, so much was plain, and the ghastly machine easily trapped. Usually the native village, or other community, settled these zombies swiftly.

In the making of a true vampire, where soul and flesh fused to create an immortal of barely imaginable powers, other rites must additionally be carried out. It was done only for those they loved and wished to keep by them, and seldom done lightly.

Why had the vampires decided to rear the child for this signal honour? Some sentimental thing perhaps, both in Schesparn, and most of the tribe . . . Stina missing her lost son, Mihaly wanting a boy to teach hunt-ing—human foibles somehow remaining in the luminous material of vampiric life.

Yet Tadeusz, the leader? More gentle, more *implacable* than any other of the band, he had not accepted Dracul, nor allowed him to keep such a name, out of special fondness.

As it seemed to Dracul—a parade of years later, and no *longer* Dracul—Tadeusz had noted something in the randomly rescued and worthless child, some quality of steel, of *self-will*. But at the start of it all, the boy had not known even that he had a self, let alone any will at all.

In the library, nevertheless, it was Tadeusz who began to forge the child from clay to iron and bronze.

"*I* will teach you books, Dracul. If you can read, you may learn any-thing. See, here—" His white hand swept across the dark air of the room, describing the cranky ebony shelves, piled high with masked, secret blocks: books, to one who could not yet read. Dust was thick there, and the webs of spiders. Beetles had eaten a way in at certain tomes. Despite that, there was enough. More than enough.

Tadeusz taught the child to read. He did it hurtlessly, and by a method of hypnotism, Dracul presently thought. For one moment he stared at a page covered by an unknown alchemy of symbols—*next* moment he had begun to decipher them. Words—sentences—mental landscapes having no borders.

Nor was it only a single language that Tadeusz lavished on the child. Latin and the purest Greek he gave him, High German, Russian and French. English too, an outlandish teeming tongue, made apparently from an amalgam of all others. "Be advised," said Tadeusz to the child, "sometimes, when you speak to a man in a language that is his, and not your own, it is wise to make a few little slips. If that time is also fraught or dangerous, you may wish to speak gauchely and clownishly, too. For that way he will in turn say and reveal things to you he might not otherwise attempt. And you will likely, if you must, catch him out. Or, if you may rely on him, that you will learn also. The wise are often best served by appearing imperfect, nor too clever. The higher you ascend in one region, the better to frolic and seem ignorant elsewhere."

Dracul relished these lessons. But he loved *all* the lessons, including the killing of animals for his food, Cesaire and Stina's seductions, Medestha's childish wiles upon other children scarcely older than Dracul had been himself.

Dracul had been a land burning up with drought. And now the drinkable rain fell on and on. Cascading water for thirst. One day—blood.

He did not confide in Tadeusz, not dreams, nor questions, beyond those of the student. Dracul loved and respected Tadeusz, half feared him, in the way it is possible to fear someone also loved and respected and trusted—fearlessly.

But he loved them all. They were his kin. And he, was theirs.

Twenty years on from then, or was it thirty—forty—a *hundred*—he had driven her mad, literally mad, the human woman he had taken to himself. With *his* nightmares, *his* regrets, *his* rages, anguish—his *erudition*. His *strength*. With all that remained of love, respect, and fearless fear.

FROM his seventh year, Dracul slept by day, as they did, in a grave.

He had been shown the scrolled stone boxes, filled with earth, containing always elements of their indigenous soil. At sunrise, the lids were lowered, either that or the bed of stone lay in some vault, far down, where daylight never penetrated.

The sun was wasps and scorpions to the vampire kind. It could burn them, tear them. If very vital they might endure it, but never for long. Some would perish in less than a minute should the light fall on them. It was like acid.

One day-night, then, when he was seven, he lay down with Sraga in her box. This had been done to accustom him to such a resting place, before he should have to do it alone. She smiled, and put her arms about him, and slept instantly, as if her life had ended. Sleepless an hour, Dracul stayed looking at her.

Without doubt, they slept—*like the dead*. You could not rouse them. They were helpless at such couchings. Initially, Dracul did not like to believe this, and surely they never said as much. But it was obvious enough.

When he was twelve, Dracul had it proved to him, anyway. The event was, at that time, the worst incident of his life.

The vampires spread their activities over a wide area. Travelling in air or mist, running as wolves or flying as bats, they maintained so colossal a territory, they usually eluded too much specific attention.

But Cesaire had fixed on a particular family, and these lived in the nearest village of all. First he had the daughters, all four of them. Then the mother, who was still young and good-looking. All five pushed up from the graveyard with earth in their nails and blood between their fangs, and were put down by the village priest, an irate old man, part crazed, and full of energy.

Following that, the brother of the sisters set out after Cesaire. No one else would go with him. They were too afraid, even the yowling, hammering priest. But the younger man, a sturdy woodcutter, got through the forest and the birches, and climbed up from the river, the mountains above like silver in the morning light.

The crumbling mansion and wild estate were known of a little. The woodcutter found his way. He got into the house by climbing the face of the carven stones—rather as a vampire might have done it—and stepped through one of the casementless windows, to spring down in the hall.

All was deathly silent, the twelve occupants asleep. The priest had tutored the woodcutter well, and besides, this man had witnessed the curtailment of the zombie second lives of his mother and his four siblings. He had stakes with him of sharpened ash wood, his ax, haft good as any hammer, and a cavalry sword that had lain in the church for a century, rusty but serviceable. Round his neck hung an aromatic garland of garlic, and his mother's silver cross, which she had thrown off for the vampire.

It seemed he knew not only Cesaire was in the mansion. He thought he might get one or two more, if they were present—he had brought five stakes, the same number as his familial dead. He knew that a vampire slept by day. What he did not know was that one of the vampire tribe was not yet vampiric, and slept by day only from choice and habit.

Dracul woke from his human slumber, hearing a noise in the house which normally, from dawn till sunset, was silent. He believed some big animal had got in, and decided, for once, to get up and hunt it, since it had been foolish enough to attract his notice. But the light was so shrill in his streaming eyes, for some while he could barely see. In that condition he almost came to reckon it would be better to leave the animal alone. After all what harm could it do? Dracul's kin were safe under stone lids or behind vault doors. For the furnishings of the mansion, a handful of antique chairs, cabinets, beds, they were very few, and anyway eaten by moths and damp.

Then though, he heard a sound deep down, down where the vaults were, under the house. And it was the note of something metallic striking, and next of a door opening. Only one animal could undo such a door.

Dracul ran down the stairways of the house towards the vault, and coming into the blessed dimness, could see again. He had been very quiet, having peerless teachers in that as in so much else. The thickset man bending over Cesaire's grave box had not heard anything beyond his own racing heart.

For Dracul, he himself was transfixed. Yes, he had beheld other people—mortals—frequently, when he was in company with his kindred. But *never* any human thing in a position of power over a vampire.

Dracul stood leaden, unmoving. As if helpless in a stupor, he watched the woodcutter heft one of the ash stakes. There was no lid to this box. They were in the vault. Only the light the villager had made, three small

wavering candles, illumined Cesaire, lying there handsomely cataleptic
in undead sleep. Dracul could have made him out by now, in any event,
with no light but that of his own night vision.

But the woodcutter lifted the ash stake high. Although Dracul had
heard the modus operandi described, en passant, by the vampires, who ef-
fected no dread, he had never *witnessed* it. This time his mind was slower
than his eyes, his body slower yet.

The plunge of the stake, even that, though it horrified Dracul, did not
quite bring all his faculties together. Cesaire's scream of fury and agony
did so. Dracul bounded forward. Then everything was there at once. He
saw Cesaire's wide-open *knowing* eyes, locked like rigid jewels in his im-
mobilized face. *Saw* Cesaire's body already spasming, the hands ripping
at empty air. *Heard* the smash of the ax haft coming down as the pointed
shaft was hammered home, right through the heart.

A spout of blood burst from Cesaire's chiseled mouth. His eyes grew
cloudy—just like the eyes of certain victims of the vampires, when the
love-spell-trance enveloped them. Then his eyes went blank. He was—
no longer there.

The woodcutter still had not noticed another running up to him. He
swung the cavalry sword and lopped off Cesaire's fine head. It lay there
on the pillow of earth, marble pale, absurd in its charm and loathsome-
ness. Then one of the remaining four ash stakes thumped into the woodcutter, back to chest. He half turned, gaping, and saw, judging by his
look, a sort of imp—a monster—before the world fell over into darkness.
No vampire, the stake had not even needed to pierce his heart, only his
intestines. He was humanly dead in minutes.

Dracul did not look at that. He was lying in the grave-bed by then,
with Cesaire, holding the dead vampire in his arms, weeping, howling.

He knew it was no use to try to wake the others. By day, once they
slept, it was almost impossible to do so. Only Tadeusz, he had gathered
from their talk, had sometimes been awake by day. But Dracul had never
learned where the leader lay down to sleep. In that insane hour, Dracul
vowed he must find out. For of them all, surely Tadeusz might yet have
saved Cesaire. Yet Dracul knew also from the talk, the lessons, that these
two reductive strokes, the heart-stake, the decapitation, as with sunlight

and burning in fire, were the only deaths a vampire must avoid. They were final.

When the others appeared at sundown, looking for Cesaire and for the boy, they found Dracul, there in the vault. Cesaire lay smooth, his head replaced against his body, face wiped clean of blood, eyes closed.

The woodcutter, Dracul had hacked in pieces, employing the man's own ax. As a last statement, Dracul had stuffed his mouth with garlic, and stabbed the silver cross into one of his eyes.

THE event of Cesaire's execution was in fact another lesson. When it happened, Dracul did not understand this. Or if he thought it valid instruction, then of another meaning completely. Grieving for Cesaire he found, to his vague surprise, a novel estrangement from the others. For they, after the first shouts of calamity and distress, did not seem to suffer much. Nor Sraga, either, whom Cesaire had made his own and personally altered to the vampire condition, only two or three decades earlier. Tears had run down her face. They were tinged with blood, like palest rubies. But it lasted only moments.

As this—what was it?—*indifference*—was borne in on the boy, he became deeply offended. Somewhere in his unremembered past, he must have seen human funerals, and more recently observed the laments of persons who had lost relatives, lovers or friends to the vampires. Human beings had this quality. Those they cared for that died, they mourned. Yet the Nosferatu, it transpired, were with their own kind also heartless, callous. Rather as they left the butchered woodcutter to rot and rats on the vault floor, they cast Cesaire out of doors, into the sun, and let it burn him up. Like emptying a pail of slops.

Dracul took his problem to Tadeusz.

The boy was taller now, tall and thin, hard and strong. He confronted the old wolf leader of the pack, courteous and overawed as always, by Tadeusz, but with scorched affront.

"Didn't they love him?"

"Yes. Cesaire was ours."

"Then why—*that?* Who do none of you—"

"It is a fate any of us may share. Yet, too, we have no vast fear of death, for it is nearly forever avoidable among us. Humankind demonstrates hysteria at human death, but this is a form of panic, for each of them knows he too, today, tomorrow, or in fifty years, must experience the same extinction."

"You tell me it's cowardice then, not sorrow."

"To a degree."

"What then do *I* feel? You promise me immortality, yet I still mourn Cesaire."

"You are yet human, little Dragon. Listen. Mihaly named you after a very great and mysterious member of our universal family. It was his joke, perhaps, though affectionate enough. And you may grow to reap the name. That one you are named for was a great warrior, and a noble and intellectual scholar, a rare combination. At his changing, he became less and also far more than he had ever been. Yet, even in his human state, before vampiric prowess came to him, it is said he had no fear of death, and both gave his enemies to it, and faced it out himself, laughing. Laughter is king, Dracul. Misery is only negation. Laugh, Dracul, and loudly, in the face of fear and death, or desolation. Give the dead no tears of yours. They, none of them, nor yet Cesaire, can use them. Nor yet can you."

Dracul—named for some legendary warrior-scholar of the vampire horde—went out and roamed the midnight woods, laughing, *yelling* with laughter, till his throat bled. In the hour before dawn he returned to Tadeusz and knelt at his feet. "You were right."

But then he asked Tadeusz where he lay through the daylight hours. Because, if ever this occurred again, Dracul would run to the place and rouse Tadeusz, who might then intervene.

"Ah, Dracul. If it is only the stake, then sometimes it is possible to save us. But the severing of the spinal cord—head from body—after that, it is finished. But I will show you my bed. If you need me, I will try to wake."

It stood behind a secret wall in the library. It was dark as pitch in there, and smelled of moist earth and green plants, and some other tindery scent, like a cedar scorched by lightning. Maybe that was the odour of Tadeusz or his slumber, for it was always there, in that cubby behind the books. Dracul knew, for he went there twice, by day, about a month after Cesaire's slaughter, and looked for Tadeusz, and found him lying asleep, and the scent was more rich. The leader slept with his eyes open, like a golden snake. Yet *he* was not behind them. Since vampires did not die, did they perhaps instead die in some temporary manner while they slept? For it was obvious, they went far off. To bring them back took the trumpet of sunfall, or the throes of personalized true death. Dracul, seeing the patriarch, the grandfather and king of his adopted life, did not believe he could be woken after all, only by a human boy, however frantic the demand.

· **III** ·

UNTIL HE WAS eighteen, or nineteen, they waited.
     That was a proper age for him to alter to their condition, they told him, when—as after his fourteenth year he did—he grew urgently impatient to be as they were. Once changed, he would age very little, and very slowly. He must accordingly reach manhood, before the ordinary process was stopped.

The day-eve of his birthday, that was, where Tadeusz had fixed his birthday, for he himself did not know it, no more than if he was eighteen or nineteen—Dracul could not sleep. He prowled the hills, looking at everything with sun-inflamed, sore eyes, for the very last. Five, six, or seven nights were needed for his transformation. After that, he would probably never see the sunlit earth again. He thought he was not sorry. He was eager for godhead, and a magician's powers.

That night they had a breakfast feast, in which Dracul joined. Fresh human blood had been collected in a large crock. Next, goblets of tarnished silver were filled with it. Everyone drank deep, Dracul with the rest. Accustomed to the raw bloody meats they had reared him on, he did not mind the blood, was only a little disappointed that it did not yet thrill him. In the past, sometimes, one or two of them had awarded him a sip of blood, smeared on their fingers from a victim. He had been like a child given as a treat a sip of alcohol. He had failed to see much in it. Which had not yet been rectified, but soon, now, would.

Tadeusz spoke some words. Excited and nervous, Dracul barely heard them. Then Schesparn came and led Dracul into one of the smaller stone chambers.

There was an old bed there, its canopy long eaten away and posts fallen. Mice rustled in the depths of the couch, but Dracul had no fear of mice or rats. Presently he would be able, if he wished, to command them. He lay down.

Schesparn sat by Dracul, and stroked back his hair.

"So it is to be now, my friend. Are you content?"

Dracul nodded. He was alight with expectancy, already running before he had assayed a single step.

Schesparn murmured, the purring chant that soothed and controlled. Dracul tried to sink into it, to allow it to do its work. But he had seen this done, listened to it, so often—partially he had become *immune*. Nevertheless, he turned his head, offering the vantage of his neck, the vein there, to be milked.

Perhaps he, or could it be Schesparn himself, misjudged? They knew each other too well. Trusted too much. Or perhaps it was not that at all, could never be only that. The sharp teeth, like great needles, pierced inward in one snapping bite. And at once on the pain, from which Dracul had not flinched, came an awful drawing, a tugging of darkness, and the young man felt his very psyche come loose inside him, and begin to unravel up through the two wounds in his throat. He had anticipated much, something wonderful—*spiritual*—even, he later thought, *sexual*, for he believed he had seen versions of both transports happen in the vampire's victims, yes, even sometimes those Chenek and Faliborv had forced. There were neither now for Dracul. It was only horrible—*disgusting*—and it filled him, he who had looked for anything but fear—with sheer primal terror. For it was death itself he felt fastened there upon him. Not a friend and mentor, not his rescuer, his "Papa," nor even his brother or lover. *Death*, stinking of corruption and the repulsive muck of a grave.

So Dracul fought. He did it without thinking. It was spontaneous. But Schesparn, far gone already in his own trance, the ecstasy of drinking living blood, struck Dracul randomly a solitary blow, that had behind it, naturally, incredible strength.

Disabled then, swimming in unspeakable swirlings of pain and miasma and horror, Dracul lay, till Schesparn was done with him. And after that, the others came, like ghosts. One by one each of them sucked out a little more of his life. Tadeusz the leader, first, a moment only. Mihaly, Béla, the hunters, slower. Medestha with a childish little murmur of enjoyment, Faliborv rough, biting him again, Chenek strangely mild, perhaps bored. Last, Sraga, then Stina, Dracul's too-young mother. They had done this because they honoured and cared for him. It was a ritual act, not greed or sadism—but in the nightmare, he no longer knew that. And even when Stina . . . The feeling and sense was of death, still, of a reeking mouldy corpse, its breath raucous with foulness. And once she too was finished, her cold stony hand on his forehead. "It's done for this night. Sleep now."

And into sleep, as into death, he tumbled—screaming, but in silence, dying but yet alive.

DRACUL woke at noon. The sunlight pouring in beyond the columns that guarded his box, cut through his eyes like knives. He writhed from the earth bed and threw up on the floor. Then he wept. He kneeled snivelling on the flagstones. Shivering, he dragged himself to the dim hall where the fountain played, and drank the water on and on, a river of it, unable to get enough, until once more he vomited. Then out into the sunlight he staggered, the sun right overhead like a boiling spear, its razor-beak in his brain.

Five or six more nights. He must be brave, and patient. The prize would come to him. Had he really never grasped he must suffer to achieve his longed-for goal? But he knew, Dracul, he *knew*, it was not the suffering, not even the *dying* that he feared.

How had this happened? He loved them. They him. Yet—*instinct*—or less even than that. *Humanness.* He was human, perhaps more so than most. It was his humanness. It would not let him go, he who had thought of himself, since the age of three or four, as the kindred of vampires, and a student-god.

Push it down. Hold himself in fetters of steel, and allow the process of god-making to take place. Even then, half lying on a tree, whimpering from sun, nearly blinded, Dracul knew he could not.

Yet he tried. That night he tried, and when Schesparn came to him again, Dracul saw the face hover above him, and it was not that of Schesparn, nor any saint, but of a fiend. And Dracul shouted aloud. "Hush," said Schesparn, "be still." And he sang the purring chant, and now it did not work at all, and despite the fetters of steel Dracul had attempted to put on himself, again he lashed out, and the cuffing paw of the undead smashed him down into oblivion. Much that was Dracul did die then, though it was not yet any fleshly death. It was his love that died, and sympathy, and belief. Later there would come to be what he thought a greater and better belief, one that resided not in men or monsters, but in a single God, brilliant and distant as another sun. For with everything else this young man had learned, he had learned that the Devil existed. And if that were so, God also must exist. One had only to claim Him, and reach out.

When Dracul woke the second day, again at noon, he rushed into the sunlight and let it sear him till he fainted. If the steel had not been able to hold him quiet, still it was there. He had lost his faith and his name. Who was he? A *man*—a *man* of flesh and *blood*.

He knew them too well. Recognized all their charms and spells and tricks—had even gained some of their knack for himself, not noticing, beside the vastness of their talents, that his abilities, now, were something remarkable in a mere human. Oh, he had been well taught.

That afternoon, he walked again among the trees. As if bidding farewell to some beloved, he began to mourn for the loss of day, even though it hurt his eyes, for the greenness of the leaves against sunshine, the colours of fruits in solar light.

Long before sunfall, which had been dawn, he had found an ultimate solution. Deranged as he suddenly was, he thought he heard them laughing, his tormentors, as they slept in their tombs, musing on how they would drain him dry. No, it had been only their game, to keep him, like a favourite calf, letting him grow to his fullest deliciousness, before seeking him with cleavers. Make him their own? Never. He would become what all the other human things had become that he had seen. A mindless automaton, addicted to blood, less than a beast, and, since probably the soul did stay trapped within, damned for all eternity.

In after years, when he had another identity, had *become* another—that was, as he thought, become *himself*—he brooded and wrestled over and with his past, both his time of living among Satan's creatures and his action finally on that last day. Reasoning it through, in ghastly dreams and waking nightmares, he came to see that he had had no choice. For he had only been englamorized, could never have loved them—must in fact have *hated* them, and their vile deeds, yet been unable to see it, like treasure stored in darkness, until they attacked him. Beyond that day, of course, he must *always*, therefore, hate them. Hate them best of all the world, both natural and supernormal. And when he had reasoned it all out, this ranting mental hell, which by then would have driven his wife to madness, it would in turn have driven him, at last, quite *sane*. But all that was in the future. All that was yet to come.

As the sun westered over the mountains, he went into the house. He found what he needed very easily. The legs of the ruinous old chairs were simply enough refashioned, for though leeched of so much blood, he was fit and tough and not at all near death—they had told him, it would be a formula of seven nights. There were even some ready-prepared weapons, carelessly left lying about, from the previous drama years before. Not to mention a rusty sword.

One by one, he went to them, the young man who had been Dracul. One by one he eased up the lids of the boxes, or stole into the shadows of the vaults where they lay. It was always the same. It did not shock him, the outcry, the eyes, the blood, the severed head. He had seen it before with Cesaire, after all. *He* had at this time no compunction. It was a dirty job which, as with the emptying of night-soil, must be done to make existence a cleaner place.

He visited Tadeusz last of all. Schesparn had been the first, and Stina the second, Mihaly the third. When Undracul drove in the final stake, the open wolf eyes of Tadeusz closed instead. Out of the ancient lips issued, not a shriek, but a breath, carrying two words.

It was this curse of Tadeusz's which would haunt the man who killed him, long, long after he had become that other studious, secretive self, who was called Van Helsing. Those two words would also catapult him onward, into freedom, into hell and out of hell, towards a future that was all to do with explaining and tidying the past. *"Remember me,"* Tadeusz breathed as his life went out of him. Van Helsing's own life became then itself a tomb, the words carved in its granite. He had murdered eleven helpless beings who had perhaps, probably, loved him. If it was not to be his fault, it must be theirs—they and their kind. *Remember me.* Van Helsing, who had learned every lesson perfectly, would never forget.

A Letter from the Asylum

KRIS DIKEMAN

✠

THE CIRCUMSTANCES OF *my newfound clarity are so unremarkable as to make any right-thinking person laugh. Indeed, they make me laugh, and my thoughts are only just returned to reason. A late-summer storm, such as Amsterdam is prone to, a violent clap of thunder, and the startled trustee dropped my meal of thin gruel across the damp, straw-covered floor. The slow-witted girl fled my cell, slamming shut the great wooden door, and did not return with more. She feared to confess her blunder to the grim grey sisters who watch over the women's ward of the asylum.*

I liken my awakening to a morning in Amsterdam: the sun moves slowly, burning the haze from the canals, revealing the city one narrow street at a time, houses and shops appearing gradually until the fog is vanquished and the city is revealed entire. So was my mind uncovered, bit by bit, as the narcotic mist shrouding my senses melted away.

For a while I slept. When I woke—sick with hunger, head throbbing—the storm had passed, and clear moonlight illuminated every part of my cell. I count heaven merciful that I was as yet not entirely in my perfect mind as I took in the damp unwholesome stone, the filthy straw. Worst of all the smell—urine, mold and decay, the stench of madness. How long had I been in this place? Time had no definition. I tried to stand on unsteady feet, stumbled and came up hard against a stinking bucket, and as I took in my reflection in the foul effluvia, the last vague wisp of fog flew from my weary mind. I slumped against the wall and wept my despair into the cold uncaring stones.

I have grown old. My hair, once long, lush and yellow, now completely white, and ragged as the very straw I lay upon. My face, lined and ruined, my eyes haunted and filled with despair.

In the two days since the storm I have eaten almost nothing, stealthily tipping the bowls of gruel into a fetid pile of straw at the furthest corner of my cell. I am light-headed and beset by a pervasive nausea; I cannot last in this wretched state for many days more. But having reached this precious morning of clarity, I am determined to hold on, to resist a return to the fog of man-made madness. And so I make my testament, in this most costly ink. I will serve as my own Ariadne, this covert memoir my slender thread of all that was once dear to me. I must not let his memory slip away again. He is too precious.

I remember the night the stranger came.

I was in the kitchen, my son Hendrick at my feet, playing with our little black cat as I prepared our evening meal. Perhaps because of what came later, I see this moment with perfect clarity—my home, my child. My life.

All at once I became aware of a rank, unwholesome smell; a heavy mist was spilling in under the front door, covering the threshold. Immediately there came a thunderous pounding at the front door. Hendrick burst into tears, and our little cat scurried to the corner, howling piteously. I was filled with a terrible presentiment of evil. I picked Hendrick up in my arms, then took up an iron skillet and brandished it as a weapon, though against what, I could not have said. The knocking came again, a violent fusillade, and we were all three—cat, babe and witless woman—atremble with fear.

"Anna?" My husband stood in the doorway that led down to his workshop. "For heaven's sake, what are you doing? Someone is at the door, why are you standing there? What is making him *scream* that way?"

"I . . . Abraham . . ." I could scarcely form words. *Don't let it in*, I wanted to cry. *Send it away.* But whatever dark force held me in its thrall, my husband was unaffected. He pushed past me to the front door, exasperation clearly written on his handsome face.

"It might be one of my students, Anna." He reached the door and lifted the latch. I threw the pan to the floor and, clutching my son, rushed up the narrow back stair to our bedroom. I set Hendrick down, shut the door and took up a chair to wedge against the jamb.

I stood, eyes wide, heart racing, distracted with terror. I heard my husband's voice, sharp and interrogative. And then the stranger spoke.

All changed in an instant. In the moment that voice, rich and heavy-timbered, reached my ears, my panic faded. Hendrick stopped crying and began to laugh. I might have laughed with him, so completely had my fear vanished. I pulled the chair aside and carried my son downstairs. We followed the sound of that magical voice like the doomed rats of Hamelin.

"Ah, my dear." Abraham smiled. "Come and meet our guest. I have spoken of the Caliph to you, I am sure. We met during my last trip to Egypt. He's arrived in Amsterdam this very night. He has journeyed all the way from Egypt to work with me and help with my research."

The man's skin was as pale as milk after the cream is gathered away. His eyes were shaped like almonds, and colored a deep golden hue. He was lean and lithe, dressed in rich, flowing black robes embroidered on their hems with bands of silver. His hair was full and black, shiny with some exotic pomade. He took my hand and kissed it, and his lips, like his fingers, were wonderfully cool.

"I am so very happy to meet you, Madame Van Helsing," he said, in liquid accents completely foreign from the heavy tones of Dutch. "And this is your so-perfect son, I presume?" Hendrick leaned towards the stranger, reached out his little hand and tugged hard on the flowing robes. The Caliph and I laughed together at my son's wide, foolish smile. Then Abraham gave a gentle pull at the back of my apron, releasing my hand from the Caliph's grasp. Hendrick lost his grip on the hem of the robe and began to howl in indignation.

"Yes, this is our little prince, what do you think of him? A fine set of lungs, eh?" Abraham was smiling, but I knew the baby's crying set him on edge. I shushed Hendrick and, excusing myself, returned to the kitchen as Abraham led the Caliph down to his workshop in the basement.

The frying pan lay where I had flung it moments earlier. I hung it again in its proper place above the stove. What disorder had seized me? What had possessed me to flee upstairs in that unseemly way? I heard the men below, calling out to each other. The Caliph's boots rang on the stone floor of the cellar. Abraham was at his most winning, I could hear it in the very timbre of his voice, without needing to understand the words. When it suited him, my husband was a charming man. He wanted something from this stranger.

I prepared dinner hoping the Caliph—hungry from his long travels— might take some satisfaction from the meal I would serve him. I waited in the kitchen well past my usual hour, but the men worked long into the night. At length, head nodding, I gathered Hendrick in my arms and went upstairs, leaving covered dishes on the table. Several hours later, Abraham came to bed.

"Did the Caliph enjoy dinner?" I asked, as my husband entered our bedroom and lit the lamp.

"He was not hungry. It was just as well." He began to dress for bed, a wry smile on his face. "I hoped, in time, your cooking might improve."

"Will your friend stay in Amsterdam a while?"

"He will be with us for some time. I've invited him to stay with us, but he insists on taking rooms in the old city."

"Thank goodness," I said. "The house is so small! Where would he have slept—" The stinging slap across my cheek threw me back against the bed. I did not cry out, for fear of waking Hendrick.

"I will convince the Caliph of the necessity of his staying here. We resume our work early tomorrow morning. Good night, Anna."

The next morning I prepared a breakfast fit for the King, and Abraham gave me a warm smile as he threw down his napkin. But the Caliph did not eat more than a mouthful. He arrived early, before the mist was fully cleared off the canal, and straightaway after breakfast he and Abraham removed to the workshop and stayed there most of the day. Again I heard their voices, laughter, the sound of the Caliph's boots. At certain moments the scent of his pomade drifted through the floorboards, and I knew he was standing directly below me. At other times the aroma wafting up was sharp and unpleasant, one of my husband's many strange decoctions. I amused Hendrick by tossing bits of sausage to his kitten while we ate our lunch. The day passed slowly, and in the course of my chores, I found myself pausing several times near the cellar door. The men finally emerged just before sunset. Abraham clutched some sheets of foolscap, closely covered on both sides in his thick, spiky handwriting.

"I must go to the chemists' shop, Anna." He dropped into his armchair. He took the glass of port I offered him, drained it in a breath, and sighed heavily. I plucked the sheets of paper from his hand and picked up my shawl.

"You are tired, my dear. I will go."

"No, no, you must not go alone," my husband said, though he made no move to rise. "During my constitutional early this morning I overheard some workmen gossiping in the street. A woman was brutally attacked last night in the old section of town. I will go myself." He rubbed his temples and sighed again.

I smiled. "The shop is only a little ways down the canal. And I so enjoy helping you with your work."

The Caliph suddenly lifted Hendrick up in his arms. "I will accompany Madame Van Helsing," he said.

Abraham rose quickly. "There is no need. I will go myself."

The Caliph laughed. "You have worked hard today, dear professor. Allow me to serve you, sir."

As I tied on my shawl, I saw Abraham frown, and to avert the coming quarrel I quickly hurried out into the street. The Caliph, with squirming Hendrick in his arms, had to stride quickly to keep pace with me. After a moment he laughed again. He had an easy, lovely laugh. It showed his strong teeth to good effect.

"Do not be distressed, Madame. When I return to the workshop, I will flatter your husband so shamelessly, he will forget and forgive our willfulness."

"The professor is not used to being contradicted."

The Caliph lifted his free hand to the mark on my cheek. The edge of his silk robe brushed against my hair. "So I see."

I felt a flush stain my cheeks. I quickened my pace. "He is a good husband. He works hard. I try to be a help to him."

"If he is as good a husband as he is a scientist, then he is a fine spouse, indeed. Fine enough even for you, Madame."

The remainder of the journey was made in silence. We reached the shop as the chemist was raising the wooden shutters in preparation for closing, but the Caliph's persuasive smile allowed us entry. The men pored over Abraham's long list while I held Hendrick's hands to stop him reaching for the brightly colored bottles that crowded every surface.

Our errand complete, we walked back to the house at a more leisurely pace. The sun was now fully set, the night breeze blew cool, and as the cathedral bell struck the hour, the Caliph gave a small shiver. Hendrick toddled for a while between us until his tiny legs grew tired, whereupon the Caliph swung him up to ride upon his shoulders. I saw the sidelong glances of the passersby and wondered what they thought of us. We stopped for a moment to watch the lamplighters at their work, and from the chemist's parcels the Caliph drew forth a small phial of amber liquid, which he presented to me.

"Oh, sir, I . . ." I blushed again, more fiercely this time.

"It is a trifle, Madame. A perfume essence the ladies of my country find amusing."

The aroma was redolent of the east, cinnamon, myrrh, sandalwood. The fragrance of a mysterious land, captured in a bottle. I thanked him, and placed the phial in my apron. Perhaps the perfume stimulated his memory, for as we continued along, he began to speak of Egypt. His expression became melancholy as he described the sun-drenched landscape, the enigmatic pyramids, the pure, undefiled desert.

"The sun, the beautiful sun," he said, and smiled sadly. "I would give much to feel the hot sun of Egypt upon my skin again." He held his hand up before him. His long fingers were as pale as the ivory keys of my mother's piano; the nails a milky, opal blue.

"I do not understand," I said. "Surely you met my husband in Egypt? Did you not leave your homeland to journey here?"

The Caliph frowned. I had overstepped myself; he was offended.

"You owe me no explanation, sir," I said. "Excuse my womanly curiosity."

We stopped walking for a moment, and I reached out for my son. He took Hendrick from his shoulders and passed him to me. Then the Caliph put his hand on my arm, and I gazed deeply into those extraordinary golden eyes.

"My dear Madame, it is I who must be excused. You think me displeased at your kind interest in my pitiful state, but indeed I frown only in contemplation of my misfortune. I am"—he struggled for words—"afflicted . . . with a terrible condition. You see the pallor of my skin, my unnatural complexion; the sunshine of my native land is anathema to me. I must shun the warm embrace of the sun. Here in this cold northern clime, the insipid, pallid coin that hangs in the sky can do me no harm. But the strong, rich light of Egypt is denied me. This is what has brought me here, to this cold and sodden place, to your husband. Pray for me Madame, that he may rid me of this curse. I am a desperate creature."

He was almost weeping; the hand that lay upon my arm trembled. *Surely heaven will help this poor man*, I thought. Filled with pity, I tried to offer him some words of comfort.

"My husband's thirst for knowledge is unquenchable, sir," I said. "He will stop at nothing to unlock the great mysteries of nature. If anyone can solve the dark riddle that binds you, it is he." I saw that my words did give him solace, and I was glad. In a moment, he was composed again.

"Thank you," he said. "You give me hope."

"You took a great deal of time about your errand," Abraham said when we returned home. He took the parcels from the Caliph, inspecting them closely. "Did that fool have everything you needed?"

"Yes indeed, Professor, it is a most excellent shop." With a deep bow to me, the Caliph allowed my husband to usher him down the cellar steps, and I knew I would see no more of them that night. I went to the kitchen to prepare dinner.

The next several days followed the same pattern. The Caliph and Abraham spent entire days in the workshop. I had played the role of the grass widow before, and I knew Abraham would not rest until the mystery of the Caliph's strange malady was solved. I prepared meals, tended our home. I often heard the men's voices raised, in anger and frustration. Their work did not go well.

I was allowed to leave the house only during the day. The madman whom Abraham had heard the workmen speak of was terrorizing the city. Women were attacked, children lost in the dead of night—the town was in a panic. A woman's lifeless body was found not two alleys from our very door, pale and cold upon the cobblestones, but no mark of violence upon her.

The Caliph was distant; often he entered and left the house without offering me even a word of greeting. There were no more walks by the canal, and I suspected he regretted his earlier familiarity. His drawn face and unhappy demeanor confirmed my earlier suspicions—the work was not progressing.

Late one night, nearly two weeks after the Caliph's arrival, the sound of shouting and a crash of broken glass from the cellar told me some crisis had been reached. Abraham rose early the next morning and hired a hansom cab to take him to Utrecht, in search, he said, of a rare metal oxide the local chemist could not provide.

"I will be home late, Anna. If the Caliph arrives, please tell him I will see him tomorrow. A day apart is the best thing for us both."

I was alone in the house with Hendrick. Our little black cat had been missing for several days, and by mid-morning on the day of Abraham's errand, Hendrick was frantic for it. Knowing how the baby's cries affected Abraham's nerves, and having searched in every other place I could think of, I resolved to take advantage of my husband's rare absence to search his workshop. I was loath to leave Hendrick alone upstairs, and so I carried him down with me and bid him hush while I searched.

I felt a small frisson of excitement as I lit one of the oil lamps and entered my husband's sanctum sanctorum. The low tables were crammed with bottles and medical paraphernalia. Bunches of drying herbs hung in profusion from the low beams, giving the room a musty, medicinal scent. There were dozens of heavy, leather-bound books, their bindings crumbling with age. Papers and notebooks were strewn everywhere, covered in symbols, some mathematical, others more arcane. Most were drawn in my husband's distinctive style, a few in a lighter, more elegant hand. Within a huge jar of cloudy liquid a vague shape pulsed and twitched in an odd semblance of life. Hendrick reached out to touch it, and I hurried past. Suddenly a foul smell, as of an abattoir or knacker's yard, assailed my nostrils. From the shadows by the far wall came a low rustling, and a sibilant hiss.

"Kitty?" I whispered. I felt foolish, but was determined to try, for Hendrick's sake. I held the lantern higher. "Are you there?"

"Hello, Anna." The Caliph stepped from the shadows. I gave a shriek and dropped the lantern. He reached forward and caught it with uncanny speed, and presented it to me, as he had the phial of perfume. Here in the darkness I found the gesture less charming.

"Sir, you frightened me." I tried to steady my voice. "Why are you here?"

"I am waiting for Abraham."

"He's gone to Utrecht. He is in search of some rare chemical."

He leaned forward and offered Hendrick a fingertip to tug on. "He's gone to Utrecht, but not for any chemical. He's gone for his old friend, the priest. The man of science will change partners and parlay with the man of God. Abraham is finished with me. He's learned all he can, and now he means to destroy me."

"What are you saying? My husband is no monster. He has respect for all life. He would never hurt anyone, least of all someone who came to him for help."

The Caliph's laugh was hollow. "Respect for life? This is how much respect for life your husband has." He motioned for me to hold the lamp higher. "Look."

The cat was laid out in a grotesque parody of crucifixion, its paws brutally nailed to the table. The damned creature's eyes glowed with a strange golden light; its teeth seemed multiplied in its tiny mouth tenfold. It looked at me with murder in its mind and struggled wildly to free itself, its body quivering with the effort. I took a step away, so that Hendrick relinquished his hold on the Caliph's finger.

"Oh, horrible!" I cried. "What have you done? How can it live so?"

"Your words are truer than you realize, Anna. It cannot live so. It *does* not live so. It is as I am. It is undead."

I took another step away from him. "You . . . you are mad."

The Caliph took the lantern from my trembling hand and held it close to his face. His skin shone in the reflected light, pale and luminous as the moon. "I am Vampire. Nosferatu. I am dead but not dead. My true name is Sekwaskhet Nedjes, servant of the great Queen Nefertiti. I have walked the earth for centuries beyond memory, searching for a cure for my curse. I came here to Amsterdam to find the great Van Helsing. He welcomed me into this house, knowing what I am. He understood my ravenous hunger. All that matters to him is knowledge, his research. But I am his great failure."

A wave of pain passed across his face, and I thought of his words by the canal: *I am a desperate creature.* And in my ignorance I had hoped heaven would show mercy to one so beautiful, so pure. How little I understood.

"There is no cure," he said. "I shall never see the desert at noontime. I shall never feel the warm sun of Egypt on my skin again." His eyes glowed golden now, stronger than the lamp in his hand. He moved towards me.

"Come with me, Anna. I can make you like me. You will stay young forever. He does not deserve you." He moved closer, the silken whisper of his robes like the rustle of wings. My mind was clouded by a heady perfume. *Egypt,* I thought. *The desert night, warm and inviting—*

Then Hendrick stirred and whimpered in my arms. At once I was aware of a noxious vapor heavy on my skin, raw and fetid like a foul disease, the stench of a charnal house. The Caliph's teeth, sharp and pointed like an animal's, were inches from my child's bare arm.

I stepped back. "I cannot go with you." My voice sounded small and very weak.

"Do you think Abraham loves you?" His exquisite mouth twisted into a sneer. "He presented you to me, that first night, as though you were a glass of wine. He was desperate for my secrets, for what I might show him. You are *nothing* to him."

"Did you think I do not know that?" I said. "What do I care if he loves me or no? He gave me my son. What can you offer me that is worth more than my child?"

My child. My child. I set down my bloody pen. I am empty, hollowed out, not from hunger, but remembrance. A bowl of gruel—laced, I am sure, with laudanum—sits beside me on the floor. The sisters suspect me of mischief. I can hear them outside the door, whispering. I cannot allow them to take my memory from me. I must finish.

"Get out," I said. I tightened my grip on Hendrick, and he began to cry. "I do not know what you are, monster or madman, but get out of my house."

The Vampire's handsome face was transformed into a mask of feral rage. "You refuse me?" he cried. "Then you are lost. If you will not abandon him, I will find another way to teach Van Helsing the price of failure." And with hideous force he struck me a shattering blow across the face.

Must I continue? Why not stop here, before I reach the irrevocable truth? Or write myself a new ending. A new memory, of a happy child, to carry with me. But it is too late now. The memories will not stop.

When I woke, my head was throbbing. The front of my blouse was soaked through with blood. I lay on the floor of the cellar, a pile of straw beneath my head, Abraham's coat spread over me. The Caliph was gone. My husband stood before the table, bent low over something I couldn't see.

"There, there, my dear one," he said. He held a thick piece of wood, its end sharpened to a wicked point, high above his head.

"Abraham? What are you doing?"

He turned. His face and neck were covered with scratches and clotted blood. Tears, the first I had ever seen my husband shed, streamed from his eyes. "Anna. Forgive me. This is my fault. I invited him into my home."

Our home, I thought, and pulled myself upright. Pain racked my body. I took a shaky step towards the table. "Where is Hendrick? Keep him away from the cat, don't let him see what you've done."

Abraham made a movement with his arm to ward me off. "Oh, Anna, please, I would spare you this."

There was a low cry behind him. I lurched forward, pushing him aside, and he fell to his knees, praying. For a moment I thought his mind unhinged. Then I looked at the table.

Its skin was an unearthly white, the color of milk after the cream is skimmed away. Its eyes were purest gold. With its tiny, starfish hand— the one not pinned to the table by a metal spike—it held the cat's severed head. Its gore-streaked lips sucked at the bloody fur of the animal's neck.

I turned to Abraham and damned him with every vile word I knew. I beat at him wildly, and rent his face with my nails. I keened like an animal as he took up the stake and began to recite the Lord's Prayer. And when my husband drove that stake through the heart of the monster that once was our child, I fell to my knees and cursed God.

Later, much later, he threw the body into the canal, like so much refuse. Taken in the night, he told the magistrates. The final victim, it was said, of the fiend of Amsterdam, and of course that was true.

Abraham had me committed here after my second suicide attempt. I spent months pounding my hands into bloody pulp against the stone walls, screaming for my child, and for vengeance against the Caliph.

I lay down my pen. That is my story, my life, the thread that will draw me back again and again to sanity. My child thrown into the canal, all my love not enough to save him. His tiny starfish hand reaches out to me. His tongue laps at the cat's neck.

Why do I need these memories? To what life am I clinging? He will never come back. He will never come back, no matter how much I remember.

I rip the pages of my memoir again and again, then reach up to the high barred window and offer the pieces to the wind. If this terrible memory is all that I can have of him—my boy, my lovely boy—then let me forget everything, forever.

In my weary heart, I have forgiven Abraham. He truly does love me, after all. Why else would he make it so easy for me to forget?

The bowl is in my hand. I will drink. I am drinking. I want to forget.

My Dear Madame Mina

Lois Tilton

✝

I SAW THE *Count lying within the box, deathly pale; and the red eyes glared with the horrible vindictive look which I knew too well. Then the eyes saw the sinking sun, and the look of hate in them turned to triumph.*

But, on the instant, came the sweep and flash of Jonathan's great knife. I shrieked as I saw it shear through the throat; and blood sprayed from the wound. The scent of it made me frantic, so that I would have rushed forward if the Holy circle had not prevented me.

Hearing my cry, Jonathan started up, and the anguish on his face was unbearable to witness. He groaned aloud, "Oh, my God, the mark is still upon her brow!"

The Count's curse—his terrible curse was still upon me!

But the Count himself, almost in the drawing of a breath, had crumbled into dust and passed from our sight, leaving nothing of himself but a red haze shimmering in the last glowing rays of the sun before it sank below the mountaintop. Yet even in that moment of final dissolution, there was in the face a look of peace, such as I never could have imagined might have rested there.

At that moment I resolved to seek an end to this unholy existence, to seek that same eternal peace, for I fear there is no other route to salvation for me now.

November 8

No! I will not let you destroy yourself, my dear Madame Mina!

I do not apologize for violating your privacy, reading your journal, for you have written it out in longhand, as if you meant your words to be a Last Testament.

But you must not think that Van Helsing is so easily defeated. There are other methods, other solutions we have not yet tried, now that you are no longer in thrall to Count Dracula. In that much, at least, our quest has succeeded.

Yet your peril can not be denied. The infection is in your blood and I have seen the signs of it: the slight lengthening of your incisors; and once or twice, at sunset, a flash of red that might almost be the reflection of the sun as it strikes your eye. The same signs, just as they appeared in your poor friend, Miss Lucy! I will always blame myself for failing that sweet young woman. Yet I thank God that now, with you, I have a chance to redeem myself.

The main thing now is to keep you apart from Harker. You know that contact between you is no longer safe, for the insidious nature of this curse is the perversion of pure, sanctioned love to something foul and un-holy. I have watched you, these last days, reach out to him, then pull away as you regain control over the dark impulse. It is Harker we can not trust—dare not trust! He will feel it is his right and duty as a husband and a man to interfere, to attempt to protect you, which we must prevent at all costs, both for his own sake and for yours, dearest Mina.

For the moment, nothing else can be done, not until we have reached Veresti. It will be a slow journey, for as our own poor horses are now food for the wolves, we must use those belonging to Seward and poor Morris, which are spent from their long chase. And we must carry the body of Morris with us, as well, for I would not by any means leave him to lie there in that unholy ground!

Until then, I will expend every effort, spare myself nothing, never re-lax my vigilance over you, my dear Mina.

November 18

Now, my dearest Mina, we must act at once! Harker will be the undoing of all my plans unless we can be away before tonight. Surely you must have seen how he has grown ever more jealous when I have insisted on placing myself between him and you in the carriage, in order to prevent what we both know must never take place. I even believe he would have fought me, if he did not respect what he considers to be my great age. But now that we have come to an inn, I know that he will insist on being alone with you in your bedchamber, and that I will never allow!

Fortunately, there is a chemist's shop nearby. I have sent Seward and Godalming to arrange for poor Morris's burial in hallowed ground. Now I must only persuade Harker that this bottle contains the drug I use to keep sleep at bay while I keep my vigil over you, that *on no account* must Madame Mina be left alone and unwatched once the sun has set.

But, my Mina, the hardest task will then be yours, once sleep has overtaken your other guardians, for you must convince your Jonathan, for his own sake and for the sake of your soul's salvation, that you have gone where he may not follow. I have written the letter on your typewriter. You must sign it in your own hand, and we will place the sheet of paper in your journal, marking the last page, so that he will find it there when he wakes, and understand your intent:

Dearest Jonathan, by the time you read this letter, I will be gone. It is too late to save me by any other means.

You must know that despite the Count's death, his unholy curse still lingers in my blood. I fear I must share my dear Lucy's fate, but I will not see the holy love between us corrupted so as to damn you, as well.

I have placed myself in the hands of good, dear Professor Van Helsing. Who better than he to save me, as he saved my dear friend's soul? It will be an act of mercy. I long for release from this torment!

Pray for me, beloved Jonathan. It is the best, the only aid you can give me now.

November 20

Oh, how deeply you sleep, my dearest Mina! Beneath the black veil, your face is pale to transparency, like wax, with the blue veins running beneath the surface. Even your lips have no color. A sleep like death, I might fear, except for the regularity of your breathing.

I cannot blame you for weakening at the last, the most crucial moment as we left the inn, by calling out to Harker. You were exhausted, and you have suffered much. Fortunately, he was too deeply under the influence of the chloral to respond, so we were able to make our escape without hindrance.

You may rest now, at last. Sleep. As always, I will keep watch over you. I have made all the arrangements. You are travelling as Mrs. Morris, a young widow, whose husband was tragically murdered by bandits at the Borgo Pass. The black veil and widow's habit will discourage impertinent questions along the way, for it is only natural that you are insensible with grief.

I, as your old uncle, am a respectable escort for a young woman in your tragic situation. There are some advantages to being a man of my age, "the good, dear old Professor." Oh yes, recall that I have read your journals, and I know what you young English people call me among yourselves: the quaint old Professor with his funny way of speech. Even your husband was not so jealous—not at first—to see you alone in the carriage with me, when we set out in our pursuit of the Count.

It was on that journey that my admiration for you, for your sweetness and bravery, grew to become something more. To see how you persevered in spite of the threat of damnation, even with its mark branded upon your brow—by my own hand!—yet none of your own, true, goodness was ever lost! I could almost think the Evil One himself might have had pity and repented his work, had he seen you as I did then. That impulse a true man has, to guard and protect those of your sex, has become my entire purpose. And I am still a true man, Mina, not so old as you think me—no! Not so old that I can not be your true protector, and I hope perhaps in time to become more to you than that!

These have been such bitter years for me, dear Mina, such lonely and barren years! My wife—that dear woman I took my marriage vows to love until death will part us—her body is still alive but it is only empty flesh. So many years. My poor Mathilde!

But I am a man, and every impulse and power I have as a man—so long without an object! I will confess it now, to these pages alone, that there was a brief time when I would have given all my love to your sweet friend, poor Miss Lucy. But that is past and she is at peace now in her grave, taking with her a small portion of my heart that will ever be hers. All the rest is turned to you now, my Mina.

November 26

How wonderful is the telegraph! I have wired ahead just now to make arrangements for our arrival in Amsterdam. There is one place where I know I can take you in complete confidence: the Convent of the Poor Sisters of Saint Margaret, who have had the care of my Mathilde for so many years. The Sisters have great faith as well as goodness, which will be necessary in the work of exorcising the evil that has taken possession of you.

I have also wired my good friend and closest confidant, Monsignor Hubertus, for he will have to perform the Rite. It is the Monsignor, you must know, who has provided me with my supply of the sacred Host and the dispensation to use it as I have done; his knowledge of the demonic kind will be essential in what we must do.

I now wish I had insisted on the Rite when our poor Miss Lucy was first afflicted with this same evil, instead of treating it as we did—as a *medical* matter. I grieve to think that we might have saved that poor, sweet young woman's life, if only we had known then what we do now—knowledge obtained at such terrible cost! For the physical manifestations—even the loss of blood—are but symptoms, while the true cause is the infection of the soul, which no medicine is capable of casting out, but only the Holy power of God's Sacrament.

I am anxious for our journey to be over. I admit I am slightly uneasy at those unguarded moments in your sleep, when you have called out Harker's name. I know you, my Mina; I know what courage and resolution you possess. And I have already seen you, once or twice, watching me as I feigned sleep. How easily you might make shift to slip away and send a wire to him, only the message: *I live!* This I must prevent at all costs! Never will I relax my vigilance, not until you are safe in the good Sisters' care!

November 27

It is a miracle!

I must weep, I must laugh! I am overcome!

I am bereaved and freed, in the same moment!

People stare at me; they believe me a madman. I have read the telegram, how many times I cannot say. The words do not change; I must believe them. My Mathilde, my poor Mathilde is dead! The good Sisters have been frantic for so long; they did not know how to contact me, for I was gone to the ends of the earth, but it is over at last!

She who was once everything to me! The vows we took, I never broke them, though there was nothing left of the soul I once loved. The end could have come at any moment, of course, but to have it come now—to learn of it only now! I can only believe it is a sign to me, that the time of my loneliness is over at last!

Oh, my Mina, my beloved Mina, I am free! In all truth and honor and in the sight of God, I am free once again to bestow my love, my heart, my whole self, having never betrayed my first vow!

My heart is trembling, I can not believe it still, it is too wonderful!

But I must, I must compose myself. These pages help me gather my scattered thoughts. There is so much to do. This is not the time, no, I must think of what must be done, as soon as possible, no time to delay.

The good Sisters will be ready to receive you as soon as we arrive in Amsterdam. You will occupy the room that *she* did for so long, but I have given instructions to have it newly furnished and certain other alterations made, for your sake. And any other thing you wish, of course, my Mina— you have only to ask! The prospect is pleasant and quiet, overlooking the Convent's garden. Mathilde loved to walk among the flowers there—

No, I must not turn my thoughts that way. Monsignor Hubertus, too, my good friend, will meet us in the Convent at our first convenience. It cannot be too soon.

I must write here again, for I have not sufficient command of myself to speak to you at this moment.

Of course you noticed my agitation when I returned from the telegraph office. I was ready then to tell you of my news, my hopes, but before I could speak, you leapt at once to your feet with a cry of joy. "Jonathan! It is a wire from my Jonathan!"

It was the sharpness of my disappointment that made me reply so coldly, "No, it is not your Jonathan. I have just now received news that my beloved wife has died in my absence, while I was gone to put an end to the Count."

Then of course you apologized and offered me your condolences, but my heart, which was so tender and full of loving hope, was too wounded to allow me to accept them. I had expected something more from you by this time, Mina. I have my whole heart to offer you. Am I never to have the slightest return?

November 28

So much to do now that we have arrived, that I have no leisure to dwell upon such matters as I wrote of yesterday. I am returned to myself again; only these pages will know of my disappointment. And the sweetness of your condolences, your efforts to comfort me in my bereavement, have by now won a return of my feelings toward you. I have your compassion, at least that much of your heart. And perhaps—I can hope—more will grow from that in time.

There was no Harker waiting for us at the station when our train pulled into Amsterdam, though I saw you glancing at the faces on the platform, searching. I could not help wondering if you had somehow managed to send him word of our destination, despite my vigilance. As a precaution, I ordered our cab to deliver us to a hotel, before taking another to the Convent.

The good Sisters welcomed us with all the warmth and kindness I had known from them in the past, and showed you at once to your rooms. I saw you looking at the bars on the windows, to which I had ordered crossbars fixed, so that they formed that Sign of the cross which the evil cannot pass. But I only pointed out the garden below, saying, "Of course it is all brown now, but you should see it in the springtime, when the tulips bloom!"

These words alarmed you. "Surely I will not remain here for so long!"

I pressed your hand to reassure you. "Of course we must hope it will only be necessary for a few days, until the Rite is performed."

"When will it be?"

"I have asked Monsignor Hubertus to meet us here tomorrow, if you have no objections."

"Let it be as soon as it can be!" you exclaimed with an edge of desperation in your voice that Sister Agnes noticed, giving me a significant look.

We left you to rest while we retired downstairs to discuss your situation. "This is not a case like my poor Mathilde," I assured her. "Mrs. Morris has borne this evil affliction with such courage that it has earned the admiration of all who know her."

"But this is not the same young woman you travelled to England to treat, at Dr. Seward's request?"

"No, that was Miss Westenra, whom we were unfortunately not able to save. Mrs. Morris, her true friend, had come to assist us in our investigations, and fell victim to the same diabolical monster who destroyed poor Miss Lucy." The Sister crossed herself fervently, hearing these words. "Him we did manage to destroy, at great cost," I went on, "but the infection remains in her, and will ultimately destroy her if we do not act. Here, better than anywhere else, we will be able to guard her."

"Then there is still danger?"

"There is," I said gravely. "The foul curse placed on Mrs. Morris, though she was without fault or sin, has at some times almost a will of its own. Under its influence, she is likely to forget that her poor, brave husband was killed by the vampire Count Dracula, and she imagines herself the wife of another man, a Jonathan Harker."

"Another of those unholy vampires?"

"No, or at least he is not yet so far gone, though he, too, bears the infection and will doubtless become one of the Un-Dead in time, if not destroyed. It is a tragic case. He was a young solicitor who was sent to assist the Count in his purchase of property in London, and returned a madman, not responsible for his own actions. He was, at the time I was summoned to treat Miss Westenra, a patient in Dr. Seward's sanitarium, from which he escaped to do the Count's bidding, to bring young women to him, for the monster always needed new victims, fresh blood. Mrs. Morris was taken by him, and her delusion is the consequence. When possessed by it, she will do anything in her power to escape and go to Harker, wherever she imagines him to be."

Sister Agnes crossed herself again, kissing the crucifix of her rosary and uttering a brief prayer for divine aid.

"Yes," I cried, "if only we had been able to keep Miss Westenra in such a place as this, with such protection, we might have saved her! Guard Mrs. Morris well, Sister Agnes!"

November 29

I spoke privately with Monsignor Hubertus after I brought him to see you this morning, to obtain your consent to the Rite. I must say that he was greatly and favorably impressed by your courage and your resolve. He was most interested, of course, in the brand upon your brow, made when I pressed the Host to your forehead. "You are quite right, my old friend," he told me, "this is a demonic manifestion. We must proceed at once with the Rite, to cast out the evil."

It will be tomorrow, then. I will fast and pray the night through, to prepare. God's will be done!

November 31

Oh, my dear Mina, my poor dear Mina, it is agony for me to see you so inconsolable! There is nothing I can say to ease your distress. It is not your fault! No one could say so, no one who knows your sweet purity and goodness. You are the victim; you have committed no sin!

I had hoped, I had prayed, that the exorcism would cast out the curse! Both the Monsignor and Sister Agnes say they have never before witnessed such courage and resolve as when you commanded us to continue the Rite, despite the Holy water raising such terrible blisters each time a drop of it touched your flesh! It was torment to witness, to hear your cries, and yet you endured the ordeal with the fortitude of a Holy Martyr. We were the ones to abandon the effort, not you, for we could not bear to inflict more pain on one who never deserved such suffering.

But how am I to convince you now that all hope is not yet dead? Despair, too, is a sin. And suicide, a most mortal sin. Do you not recall that suicides are accursed? In times not long ago, they were buried at a crossroads *to keep them from rising again as the Un-Dead!* Is this a risk you wish to take with your immortal soul?

Perhaps I can use your own words, written in your journal that I know so well. Will you not recall how Lucy Westenra made herself open to the evil influence of the Count by *seating herself at night on the tomb of a suicide?*

You accuse me unjustly. I do not default on my promise, nor do I regret it. If the day does finally come when all hope is at an end, then indeed I will give you the mercy I gave that poor young lady, and drive the liberating stake into your heart. I will promise it again if you ask me, I will swear to it on the Holy cross, on the Most Blessed relics of Saint Margaret, on the grave of my own beloved wife. But now, while we still have hope and life, you must not ask me to be your murderer, to destroy the one living thing most dear to me.

I cannot trust you as long as you continue in this state of despair. I fear that you will take matters into your own hand and do what is irrevocable. Perhaps you will forgive me when you wake, for what I have done. After the influence of the sedative has worn off, after you have recovered from your ordeal, I hope you will return to your own, sweet, *reasoning* self, and accept my consolation in the spirit in which it was offered.

There is one more factor to consider; a decisive one, if Sister Agnes is correct. I suspect yours is no longer the only soul to be lost. Is it the truth? Are you with child?

If it is so, you must see how it changes everything! This innocent soul in your care, would you condemn it to the darkness forever, without the Grace of God's Sacrament? Even the most vile and depraved murderess can plead her belly to the law, for every innocent soul, unborn, has such a claim on its protection. Can you deny this to your own child?

December 1

Your accusations are hurtful. I had hoped you would understand the sedative was only for your own good, to keep you from harming yourself while you were in such a state that you could not take responsibility for your actions. I must remind you that a woman in your interesting condition, even without the terrible shock and distress you have endured, is always subject to vagaries of mood, to tempestuous and mercurial passions, sudden outflows of tears. *Hysteria,* you know, is derived from the Greek for "womb." At such times, a woman needs the support of a man's more rational mind and steadfast will.

Dear Mina, I had hoped to be able to declare myself openly to you by this time, to reveal myself as one who hopes to mean more to you than merely a physician and protector—as you now for some time have meant everything to me! It pains me to have this quarrel between us. I wish you could believe that I have only your good at heart. I have in mind an experiment, with the assistance of the Holy Sisters, which might well flush the infection from your blood. If you would only have faith in me!

But I see that you need more time for reflection upon your situation. Perhaps then we can be better friends again, as we once were.

I know that with all your troubles, so grievous, my own concerns must mean little to you. There is no need to tell you that I went today to my Mathilde's grave. It is only a short walk across the churchyard. As we had always planned, she is buried next to our own dear son, who was taken from us too soon. You do not need to know how long I wept there, how many tears I let fall onto the cold, bare earth. Such is the human heart, that can always surprise us anew. For so many years, I had thought her dead to me, yet the sight of her grave tore open a fresh, raw wound.

It is in your power, Mina, to bring solace to my wounded heart, to restore to me the domestic happiness I have been so long deprived of. Why must you continue to thrust me away?

December 2

So you acknowledge, at least, that I am right—you are with child. There is certainly nothing unusual in your being ignorant of your condition, given the shock and distress you have had to endure most recently. Many young women, newly married, are not aware of these symptoms, and I believe the pregnancy can not be yet of long duration. Be assured that you will be well cared-for here, by the good Sisters.

It is not true, as you accuse me, that you are a prisoner in this place, as if you were a criminal or a madwoman. I acknowledge that I have sealed the door to your chamber with the Sacred Host, and the window as well, recalling Harker's exploit at the Count's castle, which you might well decide to emulate, knotting together your bedsheets. But it is the demon within you that is imprisoned, not your true self. If the evil were not present, you could pass through that door as free as any other. It is not locked.

I only wish there were more trust between us. This morning Sister Agnes came to me with a note addressed to Jonathan Harker, that you had given her in secret. Of course she placed it directly into my hand, without telling you. There is no use causing you more distress by making you believe you are held here *incommunicado.*

So now I can read just what you think of me: "Professor Van Helsing, who used to seem so kind and good and wise." Now you call me your abductor, your jailer, who has confined you in a strait-waistcoat and kept you insensible with drugs! Such hurtful words! *I fear Professor Van Helsing may have gone mad. If he were not so old, I might almost believe he has abducted me with dishonorable intent!*

This, then, is my return for my all my devoted efforts on your behalf, to be so hated and reviled!

December 12

Sister Agnes has come to me again. She is gravely concerned. You have been denying that your name is Morris; you continue to insist that you are truly Mrs. Jonathan Harker, of Exeter in England.

You know we agreed from the beginning that Harker must believe you dead, that no other way can we prevent his interference in your treatment. Do you imagine he would have been able to stand by, unmoved, during the Rite, hearing your cries of pain as the Holy water blistered your tender skin? No man could! Even I, after years as a physician, could scarcely endure it!

The good Sister believes your delusion is increasing to a dangerous degree; that you must be more carefully monitored, lest you contrive to evade your watchers and do yourself a fatal injury. The Sister has much experience in such matters, and of course I can not contradict her.

But I will beg you to be reasonable, that we may proceed to find a cure for your affliction. I would not wish to force it upon you, without your consent.

December 19

I am greatly pleased to hear of your improvement! Sister Agnes tells me that you have at last agreed to the operation. How good they are, the Poor Sisters, to offer you their own blood! But it is for the sake of your soul's salvation, a Holy cause.

With the failure of the exorcism, I have had to return, however reluctantly, to the search for a medical solution. My plan now is to drain the tainted blood from your body, while at the same time transfusing into it the pure, clean blood of the good Sisters.

Sister Agnes says you tell her you have no other choice, that unless you consent to the transfusion, you will never be allowed to go free from this place. The good Sister asks me what we must do if, after the operation, you insist on leaving the convent and returning to Exeter, to find your imagined husband, Jonathan Harker. I answer that once you are truly cured, that delusion should be dispelled. Yet privately, in these pages, I must admit that I would have no valid grounds to keep you here if my efforts do succeed in lifting the vampire's curse.

This is my terrible dilemma: if I succeed in my purpose, if I save you, then you will return to *him!* Yet if I fail . . .

No, I cannot fail, I will not admit the possibility. But how I want to cry out, "You are dead to him now! He has seen your letter, he believes you at peace in your grave! Let him go, my Mina! Do not try to come back to him from the dead!"

In two days, I will attempt the operation. Perhaps, afterward, there will finally be an opportunity for me to speak the words that lie locked within my heart.

December 21

May God forgive me! If you die, if I have killed you—

It must have been the transfusion, a reaction to the transfer of blood. There is no other explanation. I prepared everything with such care, sterilized the equipment, defibrinated each ounce of blood before I introduced it into your veins.

Of course I stopped the transfusion as soon as I felt the rate of your heartbeat increase so dangerously, but it was still too late! You entrusted yourself to my care, and this is the consequence! I only hope you will live to grant me your forgiveness.

December 23

Still no improvement. It is now two days, and the fever continues unabated. The blood in your urine is certainly a sign of kidney damage. I begin to fear the worst, but I will not leave your side, not until I can be sure.

I am watching alone for a time, acting as your nurse while the good Sisters are at prayer. They have given you constant attention, but they are weak themselves, from blood lost to the transfusion. They need rest, even Sister Agnes the indefatigable.

The fever makes you restless; you toss and moan incoherently. Your skin is dry and flushed, making the brand on your forehead appear almost incandescent. While I was tending you, placing a fresh cold compress on your brow, I noticed the corner of a notebook protruding from beneath your mattress. As I suspected, it was a diary written in shorthand. I will keep it a while, for you will not be able to write anything more in it now. Perhaps—unless God hears my prayers—never again!

December 25

Thank God! You have opened your eyes! Only for a second, but the first sign of consciousness, of any improvement in your condition. On this Holy day, God has given us the gift of hope!

I think the fever is diminishing. Your pulse—yes! It is less rapid!

Sister Agnes moistens your lips again, and you sigh, you form a word: *Jonathan!*

The Sister shakes her head. "Still delusional."

But I tell her it is too early to tell if there has been permanent damage to the brain, and the most important thing now is to bring down the fever.

Now you have opened your eyes again and recognized me. You speak my name. "You must promise . . . if I die . . . you must swear."

And of course I swear again what I have promised you before, in the event of your death, to do what is necessary to ensure your salvation. But your lucid gaze, your coherent words, have confirmed my hope that you have passed through the crisis. I think I will soon have sufficient confidence in your recovery to leave your side for a while. It has been four days, and I fear not even drugs can keep me awake much longer, without impairing my judgment.

December 28

My heart grows cold every time I realize how close my error came to killing you. Only today I read in an issue of *The Lancet* that blood transfusions are now regarded by many physicians as carrying too much risk to perform, except in a few life-threatening emergencies, because of potential reactions such as you suffered.

Yet I no longer know how I can save you. Exorcism has failed, and now transfusion is out of the question. I had considered, at one point, that a direct infusion of Holy water into your veins might destroy the vampiric infection, but I hesitate to attempt it after witnessing how much pain even a few drops caused you.

Indeed, you are still so weak that any amount of shock or stress could prove fatal. I now fear to attempt any more untried operations, after failing so often, with such dire consequences. At least until after the birth of the child, which must yet be many months away.

December 30

I have obtained a manual of shorthand, to aid me in deciphering your new journal. After reading your letters, I thought I was prepared for the worst. But this first entry!

I now believe that Doctor Van Helsing must have murdered Jonathan before we left Veresti. What other reason can account for him failing to answer my letters? Why does he not come to take me from this place?

Now I have come to an entry that has made me forget all else:

I wish I could determine the date this child was conceived. If only I could be sure it was before October—that horrible night in October!

Oh, wise Mina! Once again, you see the truth before any of the rest of us!

You are right, the date could be crucial. If the conception occurred while you were already infected with the taint of vampirism, then what is the state of the child? Of its soul? Medicine knows there are conditions which can be passed from mother to child, in the womb. What if this evil is one of that kind? In that case, no matter when the conception took place, perhaps the same danger might yet exist.

If only I could be sure! I must consult with Monsignor Hubertus. He will know the answer, if anyone does.

January 4

I have now spoken at some length with Monsignor Hubertus. It is a difficult matter. On the one hand, it can be argued that we should take no chance, that we should destroy the evil in the womb. This would be the safest course.

Yet what if this child is innocent? We would be committing the gravest possible sin, sending an innocent soul to death, without the benefit of the Sacrament.

"And we must recall," he said, "that the Sacrament washes away all sin, all evil."

So we must hope. For we are now resolved that the child must be allowed to be born.

January 12

Sister Agnes was gravely concerned, that in your madness, if left unwatched, you might attempt to destroy the child. She bid me come to see if you could not be brought to see reason, or at least to have faith in the power of God's Sacrament.

I began by saying, "You know it is a sin to destroy such an innocent unborn."

"Not innocent! *You* know what it is! What it must be!"

You raised your hands to strike your belly, but I grasped your wrists so you could not harm yourself. "Not so! Not so, dear Mina! This is not Dracula's child! It is your own!"

Then Sister Agnes added, unwelcome, "And your dear husband's child, as well! If you can not want it for your own sake, dear lady, think of him! The child is now all you will have of him!"

But you only struggled against my hold on your wrists, crying, "Jonathan! Oh, Jonathan!"

I bid Sister Agnes leave the chamber, telling her, "I fear it is no use. You can hear for yourself—she is not rational."

I was resolved to be alone with you so that this once I might finally speak from my heart. "My dearest Mina! You must forget Harker! Only consider, how reckless and precipitate a man he is! Would he allow you to remain here, to receive the care you need? Would he ever allow me to come near you again, when I am the only one to do what may become necessary, in the end?

"And the child! Would he pause to reflect what the nature of such a child might be? Would he be able to recognize the signs of damnation if they appeared, or do what must be done in such a case?

"Forget him! Put him entirely from your mind, forever! Let *me* care for both you and the child, when it comes. It will be as dear to me as my own dead son once was. And you—" In my passion, I brought your hands to my lips, but you recoiled; you pulled them away with a strength that surprised me, given your condition.

"You forget yourself, Professor! You forget that I am Jonathan's wife!"

May God forgive me, but in my desperation I resorted to a lie. "You *were* his wife, my poor, dear Mina."

"What do you mean?" she demanded.

I took the words from your own journal. "In Veresti. I had to prevent him at all costs from following us. The dose I gave him—I had to be sure he would not awake."

"Then it is true! He is dead!"

"I did it for your sake, my Mina! And now we are both free to find a new happiness—in each other. No one else can care for you as I do. My Mina, my dearest Mina!"

But even as I spoke your name, I could see as you drew away from me, such an expression of shock and horror that I knew all my hopes must be dead. Writing these words now, I can see how I damned myself in your eyes. Thus I am punished for my lie, for I can never confess it. You would not believe me, and you will now loathe me forever, when I only meant to set you free to accept my devotion. I must resign myself to being hated where I once wished to inspire only the deepest affection, and to endure the loss of that domestic happiness I have been wanting for so long.

Outside your door, I called Sister Agnes to me. "You can hear how she is hysterical. Reasoning with her is impossible. I fear we must resort again to sedation, for her own sake, as well as the sake of the child."

February 28

Patient's condition is deteriorating. Sister Agnes reports that she refuses food. In addition, there is considerable oedema of the feet and ankles. I no longer find blood in the urine, but I fear this may be due to aenemia.

Except for the anaemia, however, I note with interest that the progress of the vampiric symptoms appears to have ceased. The stigma on the forehead has not faded, yet the elongation of the eye teeth does not seem increased. I must take regular measurements, to be certain, but it appears that some of my treatments may have been efficacious to a degree, after all, in arresting the condition, if not reversing it.

Under other circumstances, I might like to repeat the experiments, but not now, when the child's condition must be my first concern.

Fortunately, the pregnancy appears to be progressing normally. The swelling of the womb is quite noticeable now, and with a stethoscope, I can detect a foetal heartbeat.

Complete bed rest must be continued—restraint, if necessary—and she must be made to take nourishment, whether she wishes it or not.

April 2

Maternal condition continues to deteriorate. Anaemia and hypotension, with oedema of the extremities. Despite forced feeding, weight loss has progressed so that there is a hollow appearance to the face, with the shape of the skull to be seen beneath the skin.

On the advice of Sister Agnes, I have brought in Doctor Van Zandt, who specializes in difficult obstetrical cases. He could not be encouraging. He fears the strain on the heart will prove too great; and he suggested, in order to save the mother's life, that I consider sacrificing the child. Religion, I explained, made this option unthinkable.

"Then it must be left in God's hands," he said at last, though he did not seem entirely to approve. "But you say she is a madwoman, after all, and the child may yet survive." He paused, as if in doubt. "I suppose it is her husband she keeps calling for?"

"Her husband was killed several months ago. I fear it was the shock that undid her mind, for she cannot accept that he is dead."

"I see," he replied, accepting my explanation with no more questions. He then advised me not to rely on too-heavy sedation, as it has been reported to cause damage to the developing brain of the foetus. So I am glad I decided to consult him; yet I think there will be no need to have him here again. I will tell Sister Agnes to employ stronger physical restraints, in place of the drugs.

I fear that her cries, without the sedation, will be distressing to the rest of the establishment here, but it can not be helped, for the sake of the child. Perhaps we can find some other way to quiet her. I wish I were able to consult my old friend, John Seward, about the means he employs in his sanatarium, but he is too close to Harker now. I fear betrayal.

May 14

Maternal condition grave. Anaemia extreme. There can be no doubt that the heart is starting to fail, and I fear now for the kidneys as well. I have pricked the flesh with a lancet, and only clear fluid seeps out, no blood. It is almost impossible to draw blood, even directly from her veins.

I might almost think her dead, if not for the eyes, that still follow my every motion. The presence of the feeding tube in her throat, at least, keeps her silent these days. I could not bear those screams.

I wish I could be more sure of the date of conception. I may have to take the child before it has come to full term. Fortunately, its growth continues, the heartbeat is still strong, and the foetal movements quite vigorous.

June 1

My son! This date must be one of great rejoicing and great sorrow. Rejoicing, of course, at your birth, but sorrow at the death of your poor, dear mother.

I will leave this journal as my legacy to you, in case one day certain questions come to be resurrected, that you may understand how I acted always for her own good, and the sake of her soul's salvation. First, be assured that your mother was certainly one of the finest creatures of God's creation, with all a man's intelligence and courage, yet the pure sweetness and goodness belonging only to the best of women. Through no fault of her own, she became afflicted with a dreadful curse, which proved in the end to be fatal.

I was forced to watch her condition deteriorate, able to do nothing but comfort her, while she slowly wasted away. There finally came the time when her heart could no longer support the burden of carrying her child. I was forced to operate in order to save it—to save you.

As soon as I opened the womb, she expired, with no more than a faint sigh and only the slightest effusion of blood. It was then that I acted to fulfill the sworn promise I had made her, at her own urging, for the sake of her soul's salvation. I cut open her chest and removed her heart. At that moment, I witnessed what I will always regard as a divine miracle, for the hateful brand, which she had borne upon her brow, faded instantly away! And at the same time, an expression of blissful peace came over her dead features, as pale and stainless as new-fallen snow, which regained much of the sweet beauty that I had long since come to love.

I knew at that moment the curse was lifted! She was saved, and free, and with God.

It was for the sake of her soul that I completed my task by severing her head, then filling the body cavities with garlic, which has the property of repelling the evil, in case it might seek her out again in her grave. Thus she was buried, next to my own dear wife, at this convent where she was so kindly sheltered in her last, sad, days.

I will always regard you as her most precious legacy to me, the gift of domestic happiness that we could not find together in her life, the consolation of my loneliness and sorrow. Such joy I felt at your birth, seeing you sound in limb, in ruddy health, with a strong, lusty cry!

Although I failed in the end to preserve your mother's life, as I had earlier failed with her poor, dear friend, Miss Lucy, I rejoice that I now have another chance to redeem myself. I place my first hope, of course, in the Holy Sacrament of Baptism.

Yet if it fails, as I most fervently pray it will not fail, then I will expend every effort to save you from the fate which took her from me. At all costs, I will not allow it to take my own beloved son.

Ardelis

Sarah Kelderman

✝

When I was a mortal I liked watching the gypsies dance. They danced in a circle, around a towering bonfire, and their voices and laughter and music spread out into the darkness, into the trees and up into the sky to the moon. I crouched in the brush, and thorns scratched my arms, and the ground was cool. The dirt left indents on my knees.

The gypsies sang up into the sky as they danced and played their fiddles and drums and little tambourines. The women wore colorful skirts and their hair was long and black and highlighted orange from the fire. The men laughed and danced on their toes, and everyone drank, and I wanted to join them.

I wanted to step out of the brush and feel the warmth of the fire on my face and arms, and dance around with them and raise my hands up to the sky. The music pushed the darkness and silence that was everywhere else around this clearing away. The moon above was full and white, and its light shone down on the field, and the laughing and singing and dancing of the gypsies embraced it.

They danced and sang all night, until the treetops let the moon sleep and a faint light shone in the sky. For three more nights they stayed and danced and sang up to the moon, and each night I watched them from my hiding place in the brush. They left on the afternoon of the fourth day, in their painted wagons and with dogs barking behind them, and when they were gone I stepped out of my hiding place in the woods and stood in the center of the clearing, in front of the still-smoking fire.

Night was just falling, and the trees cast long shadows over the clearing, on the indents of wagon wheels, on the remains of cooking fires, on an empty pot left behind, and I heard the gypsy music in my head.

The music was loud in my mind, as was the singing and the laughter, and I danced around and around the fire and left my blond hair to fly with the wind.

And I felt what they must have felt, and my life was as strong as the wind through the tree branches and the shadows across the grass, and I danced in a circle, holding up the hem of my gray dress and imagining it was as colorful as the dresses of the gypsy women had been. I twirled and raised my arms up to the approaching night.

NIGHT was a time of silence and stillness, when the villagers slept and the wind and the moon ruled the world, and my memory of my mortal life was only a small fragment of what my mortal life had actually been, limited to those nights so long ago at the gypsy encampment. I sat in front of a table covered in scrolls, and the candlelight flickered over my slender fingers and long, sharp nails as I read.

I went outside my house, which was half buried in the earth and covered with the roots of ancient trees, and out into the yard, where stone had been laid down centuries before and vines spilled over a crumbled wall. Flower buds, black in the night, dotted the vines and poked through crevices in the wall. In one corner rainwater had accumulated, and the water was black in the silver moonlight. The water didn't reflect the moonlight. The water didn't reflect anything anymore, not since Zola and Caprice had come.

I gathered the power around me and my body shrank and the world turned red and my outfit—a colorful skirt and a white blouse—spread out above and hid the sky. As a moth I flew out into the night, into a red world of sound and scent, and where I went moths came to me and died, falling from redness to darkness, as I sucked away their power of being, and for a brief time I ruled the night.

The villagers slept, and I smelled their life, their blood, and lights flickered ahead in the redness. The villagers slept, but not all did, and the light attracted me—light from candles and dying fires—and I fed on blood.

I loved the night.

When I returned, Caprice and Zola were usually home, or rematerializing in the silver moonbeams. Specks of silver dust twirled around and around until Caprice appeared and then Zola, and I was usually naked and covered in blood, and their mouths were smeared with it.

Caprice was taller than her sister and in all black—she blended with the shadows, and the silver moonlight made the red blood on her white face gleam. Her hair was dark and fell down her back. Zola was shorter and her face less severe, and she wore white. She giggled too much. She giggled as we stood there.

"Stop," said Caprice.

Zola stopped and looked at the stone at her feet. "But what we heard!" she burst out. "About the Romanian prince. Oh, imagine his blood and warmth. His power!" Zola giggled again, and she put a hand to her mouth to make it stop.

"Go inside, Zola," said Caprice.

"But! Caprice—"

"Inside now!"

Zola pouted and frowned, but did as her sister commanded, brushing her dark hair behind her shoulder as she walked. Zola was a fool. Caprice was the strong one. They lived with me in my half-buried under-the-earth house, and their presence had made the loneliness go away.

"What Romanian prince?" I asked.

"The one the villagers speak of, Ardelis. He has power, my sister, great power. He is strigoi like us. His name is Voivode Dracula." Caprice smiled, and the moonlight made her dark eyes gleam silver. "He kills and makes blood seep into the earth. His power is through the slaying of mortals."

"And you want that," I said.

Caprice licked her lips.

"Yes, Ardelis, my new sister. The villagers say we can travel up the thread off spools as the women sew and journey to the moon. They say in tales that we can eat away at the moon and make it bleed. I want the power to do that if I someday wished. Will you come with us?"

I looked over at the black pool of rain water in the corner. The vines that touched the water were brown and shriveled and dying in the night, and I had no desire for power.

"No," I said.

"You are even weaker than Zola and I. We take away the moon and disappear and reappear at will."

And I only transform into a moth, which is something easily captured and crushed.

"What will you do if a mortal discovers you?" Caprice asked.

"They won't," I said. "I won't leave here."

I knew nowhere else and could remember nowhere else, but the clearing where the gypsies danced. The night could hide me and the sweet, damp-smelling earth, and I wanted no power. I shared the night with the moon and the wind.

When Caprice and Zola left, disappearing in swirling dust and moonlight, I went to the black water and knelt before it. I couldn't see my reflection. Caprice and Zola had taken away the power of moonlight too much from this place. Dead moths littered the stone and floated in the empty water, and I was afraid. My fear had kept me from leaving with Caprice and Zola. This was my home, but the loneliness returned and I was empty inside.

Off in the darkness and moonlight I thought I heard the gypsy song, and the laughter, and longing rose in me. A longing like my mortal longing had been, the loneliness I now felt emphasizing it, and I put a cold hand to my cold chest, covered in now-cold blood from my latest victim, and I turned away from the song, which was like an echo in the night I loved.

It was a life I could never feel again, but yet I wanted it, and I went into my home and fell into the earth and slept to forget it.

My sleep lasted centuries.

Until one woke my senses.

❧ ❧ ❧

HE spoke aloud to himself. His accent was strange and his speech difficult at first to understand. He was above my darkness, standing in my
house, and through the damp earth I smelled him.

I smelled his mortal life and his mortal, sweet, warm blood, and I was
hungry. For the first time in a long time I felt the damp earth around me
and tasted the dirt in my mouth and the moisture from it, and up above
that man walked and spoke, and his life enticed me.

"What is this, I wonder!" he said, his voice excited. "This dust must
have been paper at one time, and the water outside reflects no light."

He paused in his speech.

"Why is that, I wonder, yes. I will bring samples of both back for analyzation."

More movement from above, frantic this time, and the smell of his blood
intensified and I reached up my hand through the earth, up towards him,
and the earth moved as I pushed it. I wanted his life, and the gypsy song
echoed in my mind, and I remembered Caprice and Zola leaving to find
Voivode Dracula. Caprice had wanted power enough to eat away at the
moon and make it bleed if she wished.

The loneliness came back too, and I choked on the earth. I longed for
that man above. I needed him. I couldn't go back to sleep now, not while
the longing for blood coursed through my starved, empty veins.

Everything above was still. The man was gone, but I pushed up
through the earth, upwards and upwards, until my hands broke through
the surface and then my head, and I breathed in cool air and sighed.

I stood up out of the earth, and my rotted clothes fell from my shoulders. The room was full of cobwebs and dust, and a stream of yellow light
shone in through the opening to outside. The light burned my eyes, and
I turned away. My table was covered in piles of dust. Time—centuries, I
assumed—had eaten away at the scrolls and the table, and the ground
was covered in rat droppings.

The air was cool on my mud-covered skin, and the scent of that man
filled my little room. His scent was on the table, where a tiny bit of dust
had been brushed away and his fingers had left a trail, and the lingering

smell of warm blood perfumed the air. I wondered how long it had been, but it didn't seem to matter.

When night fell I stepped out into the yard. The vines had grown. They now consumed the wall and the stone on the ground, and the buds that grew from them were silver in the darkness and the moonlight. I crushed black vines and silver buds under my feet as I walked, and the trail he had made across the vines was red with the scent of blood and life.

The black rainwater was stagnant in its corner, and dead vines floated on top of it.

I held my arms up to the sky and touched the cool darkness with my fingertips. The moon was half hidden behind the tree branches—obviously Caprice hadn't the desire, or maybe the power, to eat away at it yet—and I could hear moths flying through the night, flapping their wings and looking for light. I licked my lips and drew the power to me, and the world shrank and turned red.

I flew through the night, the darkness cool on my wings. The scent of the man was strong and I followed it, my hunger growing. I wanted him. Caprice's lust for power and my only memory of my mortal life no longer mattered, and the sounds of the night surrounded me. Crickets chirped, the wind whispered through the grass, and an animal scratched against bark as it scrambled up the trunk of a tree.

The world was different. I sensed more mortals out in the blackness, and strange noises I had never heard before. The scent of blood came at me in a wave as I flew. There was so much blood out in the night. It became difficult to separate his scent from all the others.

A light shone ahead, a dot of it out in the redness, and it grew brighter and bigger, and the scent of the man stronger, until I came to a partially open window and inside there he was.

HE paced back and forth before a desk covered in manuscripts and quills and spilled ink that was as black as the reflectionless water.

There were other strange instruments and display cases of different insects. The light reflected on the glass and on the silver pins stuck through their lifeless bodies. A dead rat lay on a table next to the desk, disemboweled and pinned down. A dead bird lay beside it, its beak cut off and its eyes poked out. The blood of the rat and the bird smelled cold and rotten.

The man muttered and paced, stepping over an open bag.

On a table beside the bird was a circular piece of glass with a handle on it, and a phial of the black water from my yard, and before that a tiny plate with the dust from the ancient scrolls spread across it.

The man muttered and paced and tapped his fingers to his chin. His hair was brown and unkempt, and his clothes were dirty.

"Reflectionless, no matter what is shone upon it!" he said, stopping, but then continuing his pacing and the scratching of the stubble on his chin.

"I wonder!" he said.

He was so close, just beyond the glass, and his life was strong, but fragile. The display cases of insects reminded me of how any mortal could crush me and destroy me in my moth form, and I turned and dropped to the blackness below the window, and I became Ardelis the strigoica again.

The night was silent and the wind cool, but for inside where I sensed the warmness of the man and where I heard him pacing and muttering in excitement. The blood scent filled my nostrils and made my mouth water.

I went through the partially open window and a wind followed me and blew the candle flame out.

THE darkness was immediate. I stood before the man, and he pulsed with life and the blood burned red through him, and he stared at me, his eyes wide. I raised my earth-encrusted hand to his face and ran a finger down his cheek.

He flinched upon my touch. Drool seeped from the corners of my mouth.

"Your life is beautiful," I said. "You awoke me."

I stepped closer to him, and he followed me with his eyes. The blood radiated from him and enfolded me in its scent, and my veins screamed for it.

"Who—" He swallowed. "Who are you?"

I grinned and stepped nearer, until my face was right before his and the smell of his blood was thick in the air.

"Who are you?" I whispered, touching his face and running a hand down his neck, which was nothing but a shadow in the darkness.

"Abraham," he said. "Abraham Van Helsing."

I put my mouth to his neck and brushed his tender skin with my teeth, and he sighed. Saliva dripped from my mouth, and I bit down and tasted his blood—warm and sweet—and I drank, putting a hand on his shoulder and pushing as I bit down harder.

An object at his neck caught the moonlight, and it burned me. A cross. I shrieked and jumped back, blood dripping from my chin. The power gathered around me, and I shrank into redness and flew out the window and back into the night, Abraham Van Helsing's shouts taking a long time to fade away behind me.

THERE were mortals all around, more than there had ever been before my sleep, and I drank from a different one that night before I flew back to my home and trembled in the darkness of my yard. The vines shook in the breeze and cooled the blood that covered me. The mortal Abraham Van Helsing—he had told me his name because I had asked, for some reason—haunted my thoughts.

I wanted him. I wanted his life. He had awoken me and he had taken the dust that had become my scrolls and the water that accumulated in my yard. He put insects in display cases and cut open rats to analyze. He killed life to study it. He took things to analyze them. He had told me his name and I had asked. I trembled at the thought of him, yet I wanted him. The taste of his sweet blood still lingered on my lips, polluted by the bland blood of the other mortal I had fed on. He was different from any mortal I had ever come in contact with, and my thoughts were on him as I went back under the earth and slept.

I woke to his presence above and his scent, and I trembled in the earth, the hunger for him rising, and I couldn't believe it when he began calling out for me. His voice sank beneath the earth.

"You are here, yes?" he asked.

No mortal had ever come in search of me, and I rose out of the earth. It was night out. He held light dangling from his hand, a flame beyond glass, and his eyes gleamed in excitement when he saw me. A bag rested by his feet. I stepped back.

"You are a vampire," he said, his voice shaking with excitement. The light danced.

"Strigoica," I said, the word *vampire* foreign.

"Oh! Yes, yes," he said, looking around and laughing, and blood and life came from him in a wave, and my mouth watered. "Strigoi, that is one of the many names that the people of this country call you."

The blood drew me, and I stepped closer to him. The puncture wounds on his neck still looked fresh. He stopped laughing. Silence surrounded us, and the blood.

"That cross. You don't like it very much, do you? You are a child of the Devil." The light was still.

I didn't want to answer him. I wanted to ask him why he was here. I wanted to run or turn into a moth and fly away, but yet I wanted to stay, and I trembled.

"You analyze things. Why?" I asked, my voice below a whisper, and I swallowed.

"To know about them, of course. Knowledge cannot be attained without reason and the studying of an object and the analyzation of it. You dislike the cross, yes?"

I nodded.

"And you want my blood."

It wasn't a question.

I lunged at him. The light fell to the floor as I sank my teeth into his neck and drank. Warm blood ran down my throat and fed my empty veins, and there was no cross around his neck. He analyzed things for knowledge. He stuck pins through insects to gain knowledge about them, and I sank my teeth in harder.

I sucked away at his life, the blood sweet and warm, and then I smelled something other than the blood and life. The scent made me pause in my drinking. It sickened me and made bile rise in my throat, and I stepped back, choking. He held a white bulb in his hand and laughed as he held it up to my face, and I gagged.

"The folklore of the villagers is proven true. Garlic is not to your liking. Do you also disembowel children and cut off their lips, child of the Devil?"

I fell to my knees from the garlic scent. He took another bulb from his pocket, unleashing another wave of the scent. The air became thick with it, and it ran down my throat like water, and I clenched my hands around my neck. The power was around me, and I shrank from the overpowering scent of garlic and rested on the earth.

His big hand obscured the world from view as he reached down and picked me up. I fluttered my wings against his warm, garlic-scented flesh.

The needle gleamed in the tilted light as he spread my wings against a piece of wood. His face was monstrous and high above. The gleaming needle stung as it pierced through my moth form, and the top of a glass jar swallowed me. The world beyond was distorted, and I couldn't move. The pain was paralyzing as my glass prison shifted and Abraham's hand concealed all and a lid was screwed into place above my head.

Then Abraham's smiling face was looking in at me and his laughter was magnified. His ugly face was distorted and demented, his big nose flaring, one nostril higher than the other, and his eyes were watery from excitement. His upper lip was turned up, exposing giant yellow and rotting teeth. I couldn't believe I had ever wanted this horrible, hideous thing, and my red world intensified.

He laughed as he lowered my glass prison and darkness engulfed me.

THERE were loud noises, and the darkness rocked back and forth, and my conversation with Caprice came back. Her talk of my weakness fed my anger. My fear of leaving my home to go with them and gain power fed my anger. I had let a mortal capture me, and now that mortal—Abraham Van Helsing—would analyze me and place me into a display case, next to other insects, behind glass.

The noises were deafening—loud, clanging noises, and there were mortals everywhere, outside the darkness and the glass I was trapped in. The smell of garlic overpowered their sweet scent. The noises were maddening, and the scent of garlic sickening, and I was weak.

Where was he taking me? I hung limp on the needle and in the darkness, and against the movement of the darkness I slept and dreamed. No mortal of the past would have ever gone in pursuit of a strigoi and captured one—save for the magicians that could supposedly drive us into jars and trap us and burn us, but Abraham Van Helsing was no magician. Perhaps he was what this new loud world considered one—with all his talk of knowledge and reason. Perhaps he was a new and horrible version of a strigoi, with how he fed on the lives of things living.

I wondered if he believed we could eat away at the moon, like the villagers believed, or had believed before my long sleep. I wondered if he meant to throw me into a fire and burn me, and somewhere above the darkness all became still and silent.

THE darkness was opening and orange flickering light shone through and around it the redness, and above the sickening scent of garlic I smelled him. His blood was boiling, and beyond his blood I smelled the innocent, potent scent of a little baby.

Abraham Van Helsing reached in with his giant hand and pulled my glass prison out into the light.

"Hello, my demon child!" he said, his face pressed to the wall of my prison, his nostrils turned up as before and his yellow, rotting teeth exposed. He set me down on something. Color was distorted, and the light flickered and was red and Abraham's massive form paced—a brown, demented thing in redness.

"How is it you exist," he said, putting a hand to his protruding chin. His body blurred across my vision. "A melding of the ancient world and the modern world this must be—an old creature of species made new by modern science. There will be a coexistence between science and ancient, superstitious beliefs, and you will be the first one experimented on and analyzed."

His face became level with the jar. His giant eyes watered and gleamed.

"If only I could take you out of that jar and you could tell me what you know—"

"Abraham!"

The voice came from somewhere else, the place where that sweet-smelling baby was, and Abraham stood and looked towards the door.

"*ABRAHAM!*" the woman screeched again, and Abraham glanced down at me one last time before leaving and closing a distorted, blurred door behind him.

A melding of the beliefs of the ancient world and the modern world— the modern world of knowledge and reason and the ancient world where the villagers believed we strigoi could travel up thread and eat away at the moon and make it bleed, and gypsies danced and sang and embraced the moon. I didn't want to be the experiment. I didn't want to be analyzed. I wasn't like the insects behind his display case!

A girl had entered the room. Her blurred form knelt by the door, where a pile of Abraham's books rested. She picked one up and lip-read the title to herself. She looked up and glanced around. Her gaze rested on me, and she stood and walked towards me and my glass prison.

Abraham's book was nestled in her arms as she stood before me, and her blood scent was overpowering and her face distorted and looming, but she wasn't as hideous as Abraham. Her eyes were large and gleaming, like Abraham's eyes, but younger and full of curiosity instead of malice. Her blond hair was tied back. She touched the wall of my glass prison with a pale finger and ran it down the side. Her life leaked through the glass and enveloped me, and I knew this must be his daughter.

She reached with her hand—which was white and slender, the veins deep blue beneath the skin—and picked up the jar and held me to her face, her lips parted. I had to move. I had to do something. She had to free me. I gathered up the little strength I had and fluttered my wings, beating them against the looming walls of glass, and the noise was like a frantic whirlwind.

She gasped, her eyes widening, and she set me down. A thud echoed through the whirl of wind, and her blurred form was backing up and running away, and the door slammed shut behind her.

As Abraham analyzed me I made no acknowledgment of his presence. I hung limp behind my glass world as he mumbled to himself and shone bright lights on me and put crosses up to the glass that burned me and crushed bulbs of garlic in the air, and I grew weaker. He brought in dead moths from outside and cut them open and spread their smeared, black insides over the table. He never unscrewed the top of the jar. He kept me prisoner, and often while he leered through the glass at me, mumbling to himself and scribbling things down in his book, that woman yelled for him. Whenever she did he left at a run.

I heard pots smash and glass shatter in other rooms, and him and that woman—his wife, I assumed—fighting. One day a baby cried—the baby whose sweet scent I had smelled the first time Abraham had taken me out into the light—and Abraham stopped his reading and left the room.

I wondered if he loved that baby. I wondered if he'd be sad if I drank the life out of it to gain strength again. The baby's scent was innocent and pure. The blood would be delicious. Whenever the baby wailed or the woman screeched, he left, and when he came back I silently asked him if he loved the woman and if he loved the baby.

Abraham Van Helsing, I would say, do you love that wailing baby? Would you be sad if I made its blood spill from its little fragile neck, its fluttering heart stop beating?

I hated Abraham Van Helsing. One day he brought me outside, into bright sunlight, and let me sit there, and the sun was bright white and searing, and he scribbled words into his book of experiments as I hung in pain. I knew he loved the baby. I knew he was afraid of his wife. I wondered if he acknowledged his daughter at all.

He called me the Devil's child or spawn of Satan, and when he took me back inside I watched him cut open a mouse and poke at it with silver gleaming instruments and stare at it through that round glass with the handle.

His disregard for life was maddening. His arrogance was maddening. He poked at the insides of something dead and yet wore that silver cross around his neck and called me the Devil's child.

Abraham's daughter had not returned to the room. Just when I had given up hope that she ever would, I heard voices above the darkness Abraham had stuffed me in. One of the voices was hers, and the other I didn't recognize.

"We have to do it! Come on, Jette!" said the unfamiliar voice.

"Arabella—"

"It was even your idea."

"It was not my idea!"

"You're the one who stole the book about vampires from your father. You're the one who read that passage about how they kill vampires over there by driving them into glass jars and burning them. Besides, this is probably just a normal moth."

A sigh came from Abraham's daughter, whose name was Jette.

"But . . ."

"You know you want to!"

There was a silence, and then laughter, and then Abraham's daughter said, "Okay, but let's do it tonight."

The voices faded away, and I hung immobile in the darkness until later when I heard them again and my darkness shifted. Beyond the glass and the darkness I heard the sounds of the night, mingled with muffled whisperings from Jette and her friend Arabella. Farther and farther out into the night they took me. Finally we stopped and all was still. An orange blur rose to the sky before me as I was lifted out into the night and set down on the ground.

THE orange blur rose up and licked at the blackness above and pulsed with crackling life. The noises of the woods were all around. Creatures scurried under brush, and owls hooted, and this wood was different. It was newer and smaller, and the night held little power or meaning. This place was foreign and strange and far from my own home and woods.

Instead of the wind and moon dominating the night, the flames from that fire dominated the night. The heat from it enveloped my glass prison and strangled me, and the fire wasn't the same as the fire at the gypsy camp had been. Instead of embracing the moon and wind and night, this one drove them away and made them small, like the woods and night were small here. I blamed it on Abraham.

His daughter—Jette—stood before the fire, silhouetted by bright orange, and another girl, who I assumed was her friend Arabella, stood beside her. Arabella's hair was brown and wild, and the orange blur made it appear on fire. Jette's hair was tied back and covered with a white lace bonnet. Both wore plain skirts and colorful jackets.

The burn of the fire intensified, and the girls laughed and spoke words that the fire overpowered, and Arabella began to dance. She raised her arms over her blurred head, the fire rising even higher than her fingertips, and she twirled in a circle. She danced around the fire, disappearing behind it and reappearing, her face an orange glow. Her laughter rose above the roaring of the fire.

"Come on, Jette!" she said, taking Jette's hands and pulling her, and they both danced.

Around and around the fire they danced, two blurred figures silhouetted in orange light, and they laughed. Jette held out the hem of her skirt and twirled, and Arabella raised her hands to the sky, and I heard the gypsy music.

I was at the gypsy camp, watching those long-dead gypsies dance and laugh and play their fiddles and tambourines and embrace the moon with the overpowering feeling of life. I danced around the remains of a charred and smoking fire, holding out the hem of my gray dress, like Jette was doing with her skirt, and dancing in a circle with the wind through my hair and the approaching darkness sliding through the tree branches behind me.

Arabella's and Jette's lives were strong, the scents suddenly choking, and I longed for my mortal life. I longed for life and freedom and the clearing with the gypsies on that night so long ago, and I hated Abraham for waking me. I hated the fire, and I hated those two blurred girls, whose mortality and ability to feel these things taunted me, because I could never feel that way again and wanted it. I was a dead thing who fed on life, and I wanted theirs.

I imagined their blood, spilling down the throat I had in my woman form, and feeding my shriveled, empty veins. I imagined sucking away the last of their blood and lowering them to the earth as they took their last breath. Jette's blurred form disappeared behind the fire and Arabella reappeared.

The fire burned the walls of glass, and I wanted my freedom.

Jette reappeared, and Arabella's blurred hand reached down for me, and I hovered over the reaching flames.

"Wait, Arabella!" Jette's voice floated from the blackness all around. "Maybe we shouldn't."

"It's just a moth if it isn't a vampire, isn't it? What's the problem? And it was your idea in the first place anyway."

There was a silence, besides the crackling of the orange, burning inferno below.

"Okay, do it." Jette's voice was quiet.

Arabella dropped me, and the flames closed in around me, and the jar cracked. Smoke blackened the inside of the jar, and heat scorched my fragile moth form. Once again I could feel the power, and I rose, frantically reaching upwards and upwards for cool air and the night. The orange flames burned my flesh as I rose, and I screamed. The needle stuck from my chest, coursing through all my organs as I rose, until it popped out and fell to the flames below. The wood I had been pinned to fed the fire.

I stood up straight. The fire licked my feet and legs and my hair was alight with fire. The pain was weak in comparison with my anger. Flesh burned and hair burned, and I burned as I stared out at Jette and Arabella. Jette trembled and stepped back, and her face—the features too much like Abraham's for my taste—was pale and her eyes wide.

I stepped out of the fire. My hair was gone, and fire caressed the top of my head and sizzled. The skin on my feet and legs bubbled.

"Your lives are beautiful," I croaked. Smoke filled my lungs and throat. "Your father is the one who awoke me," I said to Jette.

Jette screamed. Arabella stood still, her mouth partially open. Her wild hair, much like the hair of the gypsy women, blew in a cool breeze. The blood perfumed the night, rising above the smell of burnt flesh and hair, and I wanted their lives.

I lunged at Arabella, clutching her shoulder with one hand and running burnt fingers down her smooth, shadowed neck. She didn't pull away. Jette cried out. Life pulsed beneath Arabella's neck. The blood was red beneath her skin, and I put my mouth to her soft neck and bit down. She gasped as blood filled my mouth, and I drank frantically, sucking away her life and mortality. The blood burned down my throat. It made my weakness less.

I lowered her to the earth as I sucked out the last of her blood and life, and her eyes glazed over and reflected the orange fire.

The flames rose to the sky, and blood dripped from my chin, and strength filled me and I wanted to stand up and howl into the night.

Jette was gone. Her scent disappeared into the blackness of the woods.

I couldn't rest until I had destroyed Abraham Van Helsing and his modern beliefs. I hated him for waking me and trapping me so he could examine me. I hated how he studied rats by disemboweling them and insects by sticking pins through them and trapping them behind glass. No one at the time of my slumber would have ever done that, and I would make him pay for doing it.

The anger burned, and I now realized why Caprice had wanted power—power to destroy any mortal, power to feel life, power like that of the moon in the sky.

Arabella's body was cold when I gathered the power and shrank to my moth form again. Moths fell dead as I flew out into the night, following Jette's blood scent, which was much the same as her father's had been.

The trail wound red around the trunks of trees and over water that glistened on tall, silver blades of grass, and the scent of mortal blood was strong. The people of this place were many and everywhere. Light shone in the distance, a small dot of flickering light, and it drew me on, pulling me towards Jette's scent, and Abraham's scent, and the scent of that baby

Abraham loved so much. I no longer wanted Abraham. I wanted that baby, and I wanted his daughter who could still feel life.

The light came from behind a window, and I flapped my wings before Abraham's study. He paced within the room, holding an open book in his hands and reading from it. Garlic perfumed the air and crosses hung on the walls within, and I flew higher, up to more flickering light, though this light wasn't as strong, and I smelled Jette.

She was just beyond the window, a black shape asleep among shadows and an almost burned-down candle.

The window was open and I flew in, landed on the floor, and became Ardelis the strigoica again. The wood floor was cool on my bare feet, and the shadows were comforting. My hair was long again and rested on my shoulders, and my skin was healed. Arabella's life had restored my immortal form.

Jette was asleep on the bed. She breathed deeply, and her breath made the sheets rise and fall. She breathed, something I didn't have to do, and I hated her for it. Her hair was spread across the pillow. Her face was pale and innocent, and the scent of her life intoxicated the air.

I went to her and sat beside her on the bed and ran my hand—the skin white and healed, and the nails long and pink again instead of burnt black—down her bare arm.

Her eyes flew open and she opened her mouth to scream, but I put a hand over it and the scream died away beneath my cold flesh.

"Shh," I said, putting a finger to her soft lips.

Her eyes were wide and she trembled, and goose bumps covered her arms.

"Arabella!" she finally gasped.

"She's dead, but shh, your life is beautiful." I touched her face. She bit her lip and her eyes filled with tears. Her eyes were too much like Abraham's, and I resisted the urge to scratch them out.

"Please go away!" she gasped.

"No. How would you like to never die, daughter of Abraham?"

"I—I don't understand," she said.

A tear fell down her cheek, gleaming in the soft glow from the candle, and I wiped the tear away and smiled.

"You soon will," I said.

Her blood enveloped me, and I bent my head to her neck and bit down. She cried out and struggled, but I held her down as I drank away the life she had that reminded me of the gypsies, and she grew limp in my arms. I lowered her head down to the bed. Blood dripped from her neck and stained the white pillow. Her eyes rolled back, and her face was white. The last of the candle went out, and we sat on an island in darkness. Beyond the window the moon was full and surrounded by stars.

I cut my neck with a sharp nail and knelt to Jette's mouth.

"Drink," I said, putting a hand under her head and urging her up to where my blood—warmed by her own—dripped to the blankets. "You freed me."

Her dry lips touched my neck and she drank, and when she was done I laid with her until she too became a child of the Devil, as Abraham referred to us.

It was a baby son that Abraham loved, and Jette was more than willing when I suggested she drink away the life of her baby brother. It only saddened me that I wouldn't be able to feast on Abraham's baby, but this would be better. My last glimpse of Jette was of her leaning over the crib of her brother and reaching down for him with white, wraithlike fingers. Her hair haloed her face in the shadows. Her eyes were large and brown and gleaming. She wore a long white gown, and the moonlight shining through the window made it translucent. She really was a beautiful strigoica.

I turned from Jette and went out into the dark hall and stepped down the staircase. The smell of garlic polluted the air, coming from beneath a door where an orange light glowed.

It was the room where Abraham had tortured me. I smelled him behind the door, his blood weak in comparison with the garlic.

Above a baby cried, and I smelled the baby's spilled blood. It made my mouth water.

Abraham's wife screamed from upstairs, her voice loud and rising with the baby's wails. The door to Abraham's study flew open, emitting a wave of garlic, and I gagged.

His hair was unbrushed and dirty and his eyes bloodshot, and the cross he wore around his neck was partially shadowed in the dim light. He recoiled at the sight of me, and I licked my lips and smiled.

"Will you analyze and torture your daughter now? Will you drive a stake through her heart and cut off her head and fill her mouth with garlic? I know you like dead things. I know you like causing it. The baby you love is near death right now. Will you love him when he's a dead thing like me?"

The wife screamed and screamed. The baby was silent.

"Child of the Devil! What have you done!" cried Abraham, and he pushed past me and ran up the stairs, and I heard a thud and the wife's screams, and then Jette's soft voice, her words lost to me.

"No!" The shout was Abraham's.

The night was beautiful as I stepped outside, and the air was perfumed with the scent of approaching rain showers and sleeping, beautiful life. The cobblestones were wet and the tree branches shook in the cool breeze, and above the spreading tree branches rose the full moon. It glowed white, and I imagined traveling up thread and eating away at it and making it bleed, and the blood seeped out into the night sky and ate away at the stars. This was something Caprice had wanted power enough to do if she someday wished.

I gathered up my own weak power, and as a moth flew out into the darkness to find my sisters.

Abraham's Boys

JOE HILL

⚜

MAXIMILIAN SEARCHED FOR THEM in the carriage house and the cattle shed, even had a look in the springhouse, although he knew almost at first glance he wouldn't find them there. Rudy wouldn't hide in a place like that, dank and chill, no windows and no light; a place that smelled of bats. It was too much like a basement. Rudy never went in their basement back home if he could help it, was afraid the door would shut behind him and he'd find himself trapped in the suffocating dark.

Max checked the barn last, but they weren't hiding there either, and when he came into the dooryard, he saw with a shock dusk had come. He had never imagined it could be so late.

"No more this game," he shouted. "Rudolf! We have to go." Only when he said *have* it came out *hoff,* a noise like a horse sneezing. He hated the sound of his own voice, envied his younger brother's confident American pronunciations. Rudolf had been born here, had never seen Amsterdam. Max had lived the first five years of his life there, in a dimly lit apartment that smelled of mildewed velvet curtains and the latrine stink of the canal below.

Max hollered until his throat was raw, but in the end, all his shouting brought only Mrs. Kutchner, who shuffled slowly across the porch, hugging herself for warmth, although it was not cold. When she reached the railing she took it in both hands and sagged forward, using it to hold herself up.

This time last fall, Mrs. Kutchner had been agreeably plump, dimples in her fleshy cheeks, her face always flushed from the heat of the kitchen. Now her face was starved, the skin pulled tight across the skull beneath, her eyes feverish and bird-bright in their bony hollows. Her daughter, Arlene—who at this very moment was hiding with Rudy somewhere—had whispered that her mother kept a tin bucket next to the bed, and when her father carried it to the outhouse in the morning to empty it, it sloshed with a quarter inch of bad-smelling blood.

"You'n go on if you want, dear," she said. "I'll tell your brother to run on home when he crawls out from whatever hole he's in."

"Did I wake you, Mrs. Kutchner?" he asked. She shook her head, but his guilt was not eased. "I'm sorry to get you out of bed. My loud mouth." Then, his tone uncertain: "Do you think you should be up?"

"Are you doctorin' me, Max Van Helsing? You don't think I get enough of that from your Daddy?" she asked, one corner of her mouth rising in a weak smile.

"No, ma'am. I mean, yes, ma'am."

Rudy would've said something clever to make her whoop with laughter and clap her hands. Rudy belonged on the radio, a child star on someone's variety program. Max never knew what to say, and anyway wasn't suited to comedy. It wasn't just his accent, although that was a source of constant discomfort for him, one more reason to speak as little as possible. But it was also a matter of temperament; he often found himself unable to fight his way through his own smothering reserve.

"He's pretty strict about havin' you two boys in before dark, isn't he?"

"Yes, ma'am," he said.

"There's plenty like him," she said. "They brung the old country over with them. Although I would have thought a doctor wouldn't be so superstitious. Educated and all."

Max suppressed a shudder of revulsion. Saying that his father was superstitious was an understatement of grotesquely funny proportions.

"You wouldn't think he'd worry so much about one like you," she went on. "I can't imagine you've ever been any trouble in your life."

"Thank you, ma'am," said Max, when what he really wanted to say was he wished more than anything she'd go back inside, lie down and rest. Sometimes it seemed to him he was allergic to expressing himself. Often, when he desperately wanted to say a thing, he could actually feel his windpipe closing up on him, cutting off his air. He wanted to offer to help her in, imagined taking her elbow, leaning close enough to smell her hair. He wanted to tell her he prayed for her at night, not that his prayers could be assumed to have value; Max had prayed for his own mother, too, but it hadn't made any difference. He said none of these things. *Thank you, ma'am* was the most he could manage.

"You go on," she said. "Tell your father I asked Rudy to stay behind, help me clean up a mess in the kitchen. I'll send him along."

"Yes, ma'am. Thank you, ma'am. Tell him hurry, please."

When he was in the road he looked back. Mrs. Kutchner clutched a handkerchief to her lips, but she immediately removed it, and flapped it in a gay little wave, a gesture so endearing it made Max sick to his bones. He raised his own hand to her and then turned away. The sound of her harsh, barking coughs followed him up the road for a while—an angry dog, slipped free of its tether and chasing him away.

When he came into the yard, the sky was the shade of blue closest to black, except for a faint bonfire glow in the west where the sun had just disappeared, and his father was sitting on the porch waiting with the quirt. Max paused at the bottom of the steps, looking up at him. His father's eyes were hooded, impossible to see beneath the bushy steel-wool tangles of his eyebrows.

Max waited for him to say something. He didn't. Finally, Max gave up and spoke himself. "It's still light."

"The sun is down."

"We are just at Arlene's. It isn't even ten minutes away."

"Yes, Mrs. Kutchner's is very safe. A veritable fortress. Protected by a doddering farmer who can barely bend over, his rheumatism pains him so, and an illiterate peasant whose bowels are being eaten by cancer."

"She is not illiterate," Max said. He heard how defensive he sounded, and when he spoke again, it was in a tone of carefully modulated reason. "They can't bear the light. You say so yourself. If it isn't dark there is nothing to fear. Look how bright the sky."

His father nodded, allowing the point, then said, "And where is Rudolf?"

"He is right behind me."

The old man craned his head on his neck, making an exaggerated show of searching the empty road behind Max.

"I mean, he is coming," Max said. "He stops to help clean something for Mrs. Kutchner."

"Clean what?"

"A bag of flour, I think. It breaks open, scatters on everything. She's going to clean herself, but Rudy say no, he wants to do it. I tell them I will run ahead so you will not wonder where we are. He'll be here any minute."

His father sat perfectly still, his back rigid, his face immobile. Then, just when Max thought the conversation was over, he said, very slowly, "And so you left him?"

Max instantly saw, with a sinking feeling of despair, the corner he had painted himself into, but it was too late now, no talking his way back out of it. "Yes, sir."

"To walk home alone? In the dark?"

"Yes, sir."

"I see. Go in. To your studies."

Max made his way up the steps, towards the front door, which was partly open. He felt himself clenching up as he went past the rocking chair, expecting the quirt. Instead, when his father lunged, it was to clamp his hand on Max's wrist, squeezing so hard Max grimaced, felt the bones separating in the joint.

His father sucked at the air, a sissing indraw of breath, a sound Max had learned was often prelude to a right cross. "You know our enemies? And still you dally with your friends until the night come?"

Max tried to answer but couldn't, felt his windpipe closing, felt himself choking again on the things he wanted, but didn't have the nerve to say.

"Rudolf I expect not to learn. He is American, here they believe the child should teach the parent. I see how he look at me when I talk. How he try not to laugh. This is bad. But you. At least when Rudolf disobey, it is deliberate, I feel him *engaging* me. You disobey in a stupor, without considering, and then you wonder why sometime I can hardly stand to look at you. Mr. Barnum has a horse that can add small numbers. It is considered one of the great amazements of his circus. If you were once to show the slightest comprehension of what things I tell you, it would be wonder on the same order." He let go of Max's wrist, and Max took a drunken step backwards, his arm throbbing. "Go inside and out of my sight. You will want to rest. That uncomfortable buzzing in your head is the hum of thought. I know the sensation must be quite unfamiliar." Tapping his own temple to show where the thoughts were.

"Yes, sir," Max said, in a tone—he had to admit—which sounded stupid and churlish. Why did his father's accent sound cultured and worldly, while the same accent made himself sound like a dull-witted Scandinavian farmhand, someone good at milking the cows maybe, but who would goggle in fear and confusion at an open book? Max turned into the house without looking where he was going, and batted his head against the bulbs of garlic hanging from the top of the door frame. His father snorted at him.

Max sat in the kitchen, a lamp burning at the far end of the table, not enough to dispel the darkness gathering in the room. He waited, listening, his head cocked so he could see through the window and into the yard. He had his English Grammar open in front of him, but he didn't look at it, couldn't find the will to do anything but sit and watch for Rudy. In a while it was too dark to see the road, though, or anyone coming along it. The tops of the pines were black cutouts etched across a sky that was a color like the last faint glow of dying coals. Soon even that was gone, and into the darkness was cast a handful of stars, a scatter of bright flecks. Max heard his father in the rocker, the soft whine-and-thump of the curved wooden runners going back and forth over the boards of the porch. Max shoved his hands through his hair, pulling at it, chanting to himself, *Rudy, come **on,*** wanting more than anything for the waiting to be over. It might've been an hour. It might've been fifteen minutes.

Then he heard it, the soft chuff of his brother's feet in the chalky dirt at the side of the road; Rudy slowed as he came into the yard, but Max suspected he had just been running, a hypothesis that was confirmed as soon as he spoke. Although he tried for his usual tone of good humor, he was winded, could only speak in bursts.

"Sorry, sorry. Mrs. Kutchner. An accident. Asked me to help. I know. Late."

The rocker stopped moving. The boards creaked, as their father came to his feet.

"So Max said. And did you get the mess clean up?"

"Yuh. Uh-huh. Arlene and I. Arlene ran through the kitchen. Wasn't looking. Mrs. Kutchner—Mrs. Kutchner dropped a stack of plates—"

Max shut his eyes, bent his head forward, yanking at the roots of his hair in anguish.

"Mrs. Kutchner shouldn't tire herself. She's unwell. Indeed, I think she can hardly rise from bed."

"That's what—that's what I thought. Too." Rudy's voice at the bottom of the porch. He was beginning to recover his air. "It's not really all the way dark yet."

"It isn't? Ah. When one get to my age, the vision fail some, and dusk is often mistake for night. Here I was thinking sunset has come and gone twenty minutes ago. What time—?" Max heard the steely snap of his father opening his pocket watch. He sighed. "But it's too dark for me to read the hands. Well. Your concern for Mrs. Kutchner, I admire."

"Oh it—it was nothing—" Rudy said, putting his foot on the first step of the porch.

"But really, you should worry more about your own well-being, Rudolf," said their father, his voice calm, benevolent, speaking in the tone Max often imagined him employing when addressing patients he knew were in the final stages of a fatal illness. It was after dark and the doctor was in.

Rudy said, "I'm sorry, I'm—"

"You're sorry now. But your regret will be more palpable momentarily."

The quirt came down with a meaty smack, and Rudy, who would be ten in two weeks, screamed. Max ground his teeth, his hands still digging in his hair; pressed his wrists against his ears, trying vainly to block out the sounds of shrieking, and of the quirt striking at flesh, fat and bone.

With his ears covered he didn't hear their father come in. He looked up when a shadow fell across him. Abraham stood in the doorway to the hall, hair disheveled, collar askew, the quirt pointed at the floor. Max waited to be hit with it, but no blow came.

"Help your brother in."

Max rose unsteadily to his feet. He couldn't hold the old man's gaze so he lowered his eyes, found himself staring at the quirt instead. The back of his father's hand was freckled with blood. Max drew a thin, dismayed breath.

"You see what you make me do."

Max didn't reply. Maybe no answer was necessary or expected.

His father stood there for a moment longer, then turned and strode away into the back of the house, towards the private study he always kept locked, a room they were forbidden to enter without his permission. Many nights he nodded off there and could be heard shouting in his sleep, cursing in Dutch.

"STOP running," Max shouted. "I catch you eventually."

Rudolf capered across the corral, grabbed the rail and heaved himself over it, then sprinted for the side of the house, his laughter trailing behind him.

"Give it back," Max said, and he leaped the rail without slowing down, hit the ground without losing a step. He was angry, really angry, and in his fury possessed an unlikely grace; unlikely because he was built along the same lines as his father, with the rough dimensions of a water buffalo taught to walk on its back legs.

Rudy, by contrast, had their mother's delicate build, to go with her porcelain complexion. He was quick, but Max was closing in anyway. Rudy was looking back over his shoulder too much, not concentrating on where he was going. He was almost to the side of the house. When he got there, Max would have him trapped against the wall, could easily cut off any attempt to break left or right.

But Rudy didn't break to the left or right. The window to their father's study was pushed open about a foot, revealing a cool library darkness. Rudy grabbed the windowsill over his head—he still held Max's
letter in one hand—and with a giddy glance back, heaved himself into the
shadows.

However their father felt about them arriving home after dark, it was
nothing compared to how he would feel to discover either one of them
had gained entry to his most private sanctum. But their father was gone,
had taken the Ford somewhere, and Max didn't slow down to think what
would happen if he suddenly returned. He jumped and grabbed his
brother's ankle, thinking he would drag the little worm back out into the
light, but Rudy screamed, twisted his foot out of Max's grasp. He fell into
darkness, crashed to the floorboards with an echoing thud that caused
glass to rattle softly against glass somewhere in the office. Then Max had
the windowsill and he yanked himself into the air—

"Go slow, Max, it's a . . ." his brother cried.

—and he thrust himself through the window.

"Big drop," Rudy finished.

Max had been in his father's study before, of course (sometimes Abraham invited them in for "a talk," by which he meant he would talk and
they would listen), but he had never entered the room by way of the window. He spilled forward, had a startling glance of the floor almost three
feet below him, and realized he was about to dive into it face first. At the
edge of his vision he saw a round end table, next to one of his father's
armchairs, and he reached for it to stop his fall. His momentum continued to carry him forward, and he crashed to the floor. At the last moment,
he turned his face aside and most of his weight came down on his right
shoulder. The furniture leaped. The end table turned over, dumping
everything on it. Max heard a bang, and a glassy crack that was more
painful to him than the soreness he felt in either head or shoulder.

Rudy sprawled a yard away from him, sitting on the floor, still grinning
a little foolishly. He held the letter half-crumpled in one hand, forgotten.

The end table was on its side, fortunately not broken. But an empty
inkpot had smashed, lay in gleaming chunks close to Max's knee. A stack

of books had been flung across the Persian carpet. A few papers swirled overhead, drifting slowly to the floor with a swish and a scrape.

"You see what you make me do," Max said, gesturing at the inkpot. Then he flinched, realizing that this was exactly what his father had said to him a few nights before; he didn't like the old man peeping out from inside him, talking through him as if he were a puppet, a hollowed-out, empty-headed boy of wood.

"We'll just throw it away," Rudy said.

"He knows where everything in his office is. He will notice it missing."

"My balls. He comes in here to drink brandy, fart in his couch and fall asleep. I've been in here lots of times. I took his lighter for smokes last month and he still hasn't noticed."

"You what?" Max asked, staring at his younger brother in genuine surprise, and not without a certain envy. It was the older brother's place to take foolish risks and be casually detached about it later.

"Who's this letter to, that you had to go and hide somewhere to write it? I was watching you work on it over your shoulder. 'I still remember how I held your hand in mine.'" Rudy's voice swooping and fluttering in mock romantic passion.

Max lunged at his brother but was too slow; Rudy had flipped the letter over and was reading the beginning. The smile began to fade, thought lines wrinkling the pale expanse of his forehead; then Max had ripped the sheet of paper away.

"Mother?" Rudy asked, thoroughly nonplussed.

"It was assignment for school. We were ask if you wrote a letter to anyone, who would it be? Mrs. Louden tell us it could be someone imaginary or—or historic figure. Someone dead."

"You'd turn that in? And let Mrs. Louden read it?"

"I don't know. I am not finish yet." But as Max spoke, he was already beginning to realize he had made a mistake, allowed himself to get carried away by the fascinating possibilities of the assignment, the irresistible *what if* of it, and had written things too personal for him to show anyone. He had written *you were the only one I knew how to talk to* and *I am sometimes so lonely*. He had really been imagining her reading it, somehow, somewhere—perhaps as he wrote it, some astral form of her staring over his shoulder, smiling sentimentally as his pen scratched across the page. It was a mawkish, absurd fantasy, and he felt a withering embarrassment to think he had given in to it so completely.

His mother had already been weak and ill when the scandal drove their family from Amsterdam. They lived for a while in England, but word of the terrible thing their father had done (whatever it was—Max doubted he would ever know) followed them. On they had gone to America. His father believed he had acquired a position as a lecturer at Vassar College, was so sure of this he had ladled much of his savings into the purchase of a handsome nearby farm. But in New York City they were met by the dean, who told Abraham Van Helsing that he could not, in good conscience, allow the doctor to work unsupervised with young ladies who were not yet at the age of consent. Max knew now his father had killed his mother as surely as if he had held a pillow over her face in her sickbed. It wasn't the travel that had done her in, although that was bad enough, too much for a woman who was both pregnant and weak with a chronic infection of the blood that caused her to bruise at the slightest touch. It was humiliation. Mina had not been able to survive the shame of what he had done, what they were all forced to run from.

"Come on," Max said. "Let's clean up and get out of here."

He righted the table and began gathering the books, but turned his head when Rudy said, "Do you believe in vampires, Max?"

Rudy was on his knees in front of an ottoman across the room. He had hunched over to collect a few papers that had settled there, then stayed to look at the battered doctor's bag tucked underneath it. Rudy tugged at the rosary knotted around the handles.

"Leave that alone," Max said. "We need to clean, not make bigger mess."

"Do you?"

Max was briefly silent. "Mother was attacked. Her blood was never the same after. Her illness."

"Did *she* ever say she was attacked, or did he?"

"She died when I was six. She would not confide in a child about such a thing."

"But . . . do you think we're in danger?" Rudy had the bag open now. He reached in to remove a bundle, carefully wrapped in royal purple fabric. Wood clicked against wood inside the velvet. "That vampires are out there, waiting for a chance at us? For our guard to drop?"

"I would not discount possibility. However unlikely."

"However unlikely," his brother said, laughing softly. He opened the velvet wrap and looked in at the nine-inch stakes, skewers of blazing white wood, handles wrapped in oiled leather. "Well, I think it's all bullshit. *Bullll*shit." Singing a little.

The course of the discussion unnerved Max. He felt, for an instant, light-headed with vertigo, as if he suddenly found himself peering over a steep drop. And perhaps that wasn't too far off. He had always known the two of them would have this conversation someday, and he feared where it might take them. Rudy was never happier than when he was making an argument, but he didn't follow his doubts to their logical conclusion. He could say it was all bullshit, but didn't pause to consider what that meant about their father, a man who feared the night as a person who can't swim fears the ocean. Max almost *needed* it to be true, for vampires to be real, because the other possibility—that their father was, and always had been, in the grip of a psychotic fantasy—was too awful, too overwhelming.

He was still considering how to reply when his attention was caught by a picture frame, slid halfway in under his father's armchair. It lay facedown, but he knew what he'd see when he turned it over. It was a sepia-toned calotype print of his mother, posed in the library of their townhouse in Amsterdam. She wore a white straw hat, her ebon hair fluffed in airy curls beneath it. One gloved hand was raised in an enigmatic gesture, so that she almost appeared to be waving an invisible cigarette in the air. Her lips were parted. She was saying something; Max often wondered what. He for some reason imagined himself to be standing just out of the frame, a child of four, staring solemnly up at her. He felt that she was raising her hand to wave him back, keep him from wandering into the shot. If this was so, it seemed reasonable to believe she had been caught forever in the act of saying his name.

He heard a scrape and a tinkle of falling glass as he picked the picture frame up and turned it over. The plate of glass had shattered in the exact center. He began wiggling small gleaming fangs of glass out of the frame and setting them aside, concerned that none should scratch the glossy calotype beneath. He pulled a large wedge of glass out of the upper corner of the frame, and the corner of the print came loose with it. He reached up to poke the print back into place . . . and then hesitated, frowning, feeling for a moment that his eyes had crossed and he was seeing double. There appeared to be a second print behind the first. He tugged the photograph of his mother out of the frame, then stared without understanding at the picture that had been secreted behind it. An icy numbness spread through his chest, crawled into his throat. He glanced around and was relieved to see Rudy still kneeling at the ottoman, humming to himself, rolling the stakes back up into their shroud of velvet.

He looked back at the secret photograph. The woman in it was dead. She was also naked from the waist up, her gown torn open and yanked to the curve of her waist. She was sprawled in a four-poster bed—pinned there by ropes wound around her throat, and pulling her arms over her head. She was young and maybe had been beautiful, it was hard to tell; one eye was shut, the other open in a slit that showed the unnatural glaze on the eyeball beneath. Her mouth was forced open, stuffed with an obscene misshapen white ball. She was actually biting down on it, her upper lip drawn back to show the small, even row of her upper palate. The side of her face was discolored with a bruise. Between the milky, heavy curves of her breasts was a spoke of white wood. Her left rib cage was painted with blood.

Even when he heard the car in the drive, he couldn't move, couldn't pry his gaze from the photograph. Then Rudy was up, pulling at Max's shoulder, telling him they had to go. Max clapped the photo to his chest to keep his brother from seeing. He said go, I'll be right behind you, and Rudy took his hand off his arm and went on.

Max fumbled with the picture frame, struggling to fit the calotype of the murdered woman back into place . . . then saw something else, went still again. He had not until this instant taken notice of the figure to the far left in the photograph, a man on the near side of the bed. His back was to the photographer, and he was so close in the foreground that his shape was a blurred, vaguely rabbinical figure, in a flat-brimmed black hat and black overcoat. There was no way to be sure who this man was, but Max *was* sure, knew him from the way he held his head, the careful, almost stiff way it was balanced on the thick barrel of his neck. In one hand he held a hatchet. In the other a doctor's bag.

The car died with an emphysemic wheeze and tinny clatter. He squeezed the photograph of the dead woman into the frame, slid the portrait of Mina back on top of it. He set the picture, with no glass in it, on the end table, stared at it for a beat, then saw with horror that he had stuck Mina in upside down. He started to reach for it.

"Come on!" Rudy cried. *"Please, Max."* He was outside, standing on his tip-toes to look back into the study.

Max kicked the broken glass under the armchair, stepped to the window, and screamed. Or tried to—he didn't have the air in his lungs, couldn't force it up his throat.

Their father stood behind Rudy, staring in at Max over Rudy's head. Rudy didn't see, didn't know he was there, until their father put his hands on his shoulders. Rudolf had no trouble screaming at all, and leaped as if he meant to jump back into the study.

The old man regarded his eldest son in silence. Max stared back, head half out the window, hands on the sill.

"If you like," his father said, "I could open the door and you could effect your exit by the hallway. What it lacks in drama, it makes up in convenience."

"No," Max said. "No thank you. Thank you. I'm—we're—this is—mistake. I'm sorry."

"Mistake is not knowing capital of Portugal on a geography test. This is something else." He paused, lowering his head, his face stony. Then he released Rudy and turned away, opening a hand and pointing it at the yard in a gesture that seemed to mean, *step this way.* "We will discuss what at later date. Now, if it is no trouble, I will ask you to leave my office."

Max stared. His father had never before delayed punishment—breaking and entering into his study at the least deserved a vigorous lashing—and he tried to think why he would now. His father waited. Max climbed out, dropped into the flower bed. Rudy looked at him, eyes helpless, pleading, asking him what they ought to do. Max tipped his head towards the stables—their own private study—and started walking slowly and deliberately away. His little brother fell into step beside him, trembling continuously.

Before they could get away, though, his father's hand fell on Max's shoulder.

"My rules are to protect you always, Maximilian," he said. "Maybe you are tell me now you don't want to be protect any longer? When you were little I cover your eyes at the theater, when come the murderers to slaughter Clarence in *Richard*. But then, later, when we went to *Macbeth*, you shove my hand away, you *want* to see. Now I feel history repeats, nuh?"

Max didn't reply. At last his father released him.

They had not gone ten paces when he spoke again. "Oh, I almost forget. I did not tell you where or why I was gone, and I have piece of news I know will make sad the both of you. Mr. Kutchner run up the road while you were in school, shouting doctor, doctor, come quick, my wife. As soon as I see her, burning with fever, I know she must travel to Dr. Rosen's infirmary in town, but alas, the farmer come for me too late. Walking her to my car, her intestines fall out of her with a *slop*." He made a soft clucking sound with his tongue, as of disapproval. "I will have our suits cleaned. The funeral is on Friday."

ARLENE Kutchner wasn't in school the next day. They walked past her house on the way home, but the black shutters were across the windows, and the place had a too-silent, abandoned feel to it. The funeral would be in town the next morning, and perhaps Arlene and her father had already gone there to wait. They had family in the village. When the two boys tramped into their own yard, the Ford was parked alongside the house, and the slanted double doors to the basement were open.

Rudy pointed himself towards the barn—they owned a horse, a used-up nag named Rice, and it was Rudy's day to muck out her stable—and Max went into the house alone. He was at the kitchen table when he heard the doors to the cellar crash shut outside. Shortly afterwards his father climbed the stairs, appeared in the basement doorway.

"Are you work on something down there?" Max asked.

His father's gaze swept across him, but his eyes were deliberately blank.

"Later I shall unfold to you," he said, and Max watched him while he removed a silver key from the pocket of his waistcoat and turned it in the lock to the basement door. It had never been used before, and until that moment, Max had not even known a key existed.

Max was on edge the rest of the afternoon, kept looking at the basement door, unsettled by his father's promise: *later I shall unfold to you*. There was of course no opportunity to talk to Rudy about it over dinner, to speculate on just *what* might be unfolded, but they were also unable to talk afterwards, when they remained at the kitchen table with their schoolbooks. Usually, their father retired early to his study to be alone, and they wouldn't see him again until morning. But tonight he seemed restless, always coming in and out of the room, to wash a glass, to find his reading glasses, and finally, to light a lantern. He adjusted the wick so a low red flame wavered at the bottom of the glass chimney and then set it on the table before Max.

"Boys," he said, turning to the basement, unlocking the bolt. "Go downstairs. Wait for me. Touch nothing."

Rudy threw a horrified, whey-faced look at Max. Rudy couldn't bear the basement, its low ceiling and its smell, the lacy veils of cobwebs in the corners. If Rudy was ever given a chore there, he always begged Max to go with him. Max opened his mouth to question their father, but he was already slipping away, out of the room, disappearing down the hall to his study.

Max looked at Rudy. Rudy was shaking his head in wordless denial.

"It will be all right," Max promised. "I will take care of you."

Rudy carried the lantern and let Max go ahead of him down the stairs. The reddish-bronze light of the lamp threw shadows that leaned and jumped, a surging darkness that lapped at the walls of the stairwell. Max descended to the basement floor and took a slow, uncertain look around. To the left of the stairs was a worktable. On top of it was a pile of something, covered in a piece of grimy white tarp—stacks of bricks maybe, or heaps of folded laundry; it was hard to tell in the gloom without going closer. Max crept in slow, shuffling steps until he had crossed most of the way to the table, and then he stopped, suddenly knowing what the sheet covered.

"We need to go, Max," Rudy peeped, right behind him. Max hadn't known he was there, had thought he was still standing on the steps. "We need to go right now." And Max knew he didn't mean just get out of the basement but get out of the house, run from the place where they had lived ten years and not come back.

But it was too late to pretend they were Huck and Jim and light out for the territories. Their father's feet fell heavily on the dusty wood planks behind them. Max glanced up the stairs at him. He was carrying his doctor's bag.

"I can only deduce," their father began, "from your ransack of my private study, you have finally develop interest in the secret work to which I sacrifice so much. I have in my time kill six of the Undead by my own hand, the last the diseased bitch in the picture I keep hid in my office—I believe you have both see it." Rudy cast a panicked look at Max, who only shook his head, *be silent*. Their father went on: "I have train others in the art of destroying the vampire, including your mother's unfortunate first husband, Jonathan Harker, Gott bless him, and so I can be held indirectly responsible for the slaughter of perhaps fifty of their filthy, infected kind. And it is now, I see, time my own boys learn how it is done. How to be sure. So you may know how to strike at those who would strike at you."

"I don't want to know," Rudy said.

"He didn't see the picture," Max said at the same time.

Their father appeared not to hear either of them. He moved past them to the worktable and the canvas-covered shape upon it. He lifted one corner of the tarp and looked beneath it, made a humming sound of approval, and pulled the covering away.

Mrs. Kutchner was naked and hideously withered, her cheeks sunken, her mouth gaping open. Her stomach was caved impossibly in beneath her ribs, as if everything in it had been sucked out by the pressure of a vacuum. Her back was bruised a deep bluish violet by the blood that had settled there. Rudy moaned and hid his face against Max's side.

Their father set his doctor's bag beside her body and opened it.

"She isn't, of course, Undead. Merely dead. True vampires are uncommon, and it would not be practicable, or advisable, for me to find one for you to rehearse on. But she will suit for purposes of demonstration." From within his bag he removed the bundle of stakes wrapped in velvet.

"What is she doing here?" Max asked. "They bury her tomorrow."

"But today I am to make autopsy, for purposes of my private research. Mr. Kutchner understand, is happy to cooperate, if it mean one day no other woman die in such a way." He had a stake in one hand, a mallet in the other.

Rudy began to cry.

Max felt he was coming unmoored from himself. His body stepped forward, without him in it; another part of him remained beside Rudy, an arm around his brother's heaving shoulders. Rudy was saying, *please I want to go upstairs.* Max watched himself walk, flat-footed, to his father, who was staring at him with an expression that mingled curiosity with a certain quiet appreciation.

He handed Max the mallet, and that brought him back. He was in his own body again, conscious of the weight of the hammer tugging his wrist downwards. His father gripped Max's other hand and lifted it, drawing it towards Mrs. Kutchner's meager breasts. He pressed Max's fingertips to a spot between two ribs, and Max looked into the dead woman's face. Her mouth open as to speak. *Are you doctorin' me, Max Van Helsing?*

"Here," his father said, folding one of the stakes into his hand. "You drive it in here. To the hilt. In an actual case, the first blow will be follow by wailing, profanity, a frantic struggle to escape. The accursed never go easily. Bear down. Do not desist from your work until you have impale her and she has give up her struggle against you. It will be over soon enough."

Max raised the mallet. He stared into her face and wished he could say he was sorry, that he didn't want to do it. When he slammed the mallet down with an echoing bang, he heard a high, piercing scream and almost screamed himself, believing for an instant it was her, still somehow alive; then realized it was Rudy.

Max was powerfully built, with his deep water-buffalo chest and Scandinavian farmer's shoulders. With the first blow he had driven the stake over two-thirds of the way in. He only needed to bring the mallet down once more. The blood that squelched up around the wood was cold and had a sticky, viscous consistency.

Max swayed, his head light. His father took his arm.

"Goot," Abraham whispered into his ear, arms around him, squeezing him so tightly his ribs creaked. Max felt a little thrill of pleasure at the embrace, the only one he could ever remember receiving. Then his windpipe closed up, and he thought he might be sick. "To do offense to the house of the human spirit, even after its tenant depart, is no easy thing, I know."

His father went on holding him. Max stared at Mrs. Kutchner's gaping mouth, the delicate row of her upper teeth, and found himself remembering the girl in the calotype print, the ball of garlic jammed in her mouth.

"Where were her fangs?" Max said.

"Hm? Whose? What?" his father said.

"In the photograph of the one you kill," Max said, turning his head and looking into his father's face. "She didn't have fangs."

His father stared at him, his eyes blank, uncomprehending. Then he said, "They disappear after the vampire die. *Poof.*"

His father released him, and Max could breathe normally again.

"Now, there remain one thing," his father said. "The head must be remove, and the mouth stuff with garlic. Rudolf!"

Max turned his head slowly. His father had moved back a step. In one hand he held a hatchet; Max didn't know where it had come from. Rudy was on the stairs, three steps from the bottom. He stood pressed against the wall, his left wrist shoved in his mouth to quell his screaming. He shook his head back and forth frantically.

Max reached for the hatchet, grabbed it by the handle. "I do it." He would, too, was confident of himself. He saw now he had always had it in him: his father's brusque willingness to puncture flesh and toil in blood. He saw it clearly, and with a kind of dismay.

"No," his father said, wrenching the hatchet away, pushing Max back. Max bumped the worktable, and a few stakes rolled off, clattering to the dust. "Pick those up."

Rudy bolted, but slipped on the steps, falling to all fours and banging his knees. Their father grabbed him by the hair and hauled him backwards, throwing him to the floor. Rudy thudded into the dirt, sprawling on his belly. He rolled over. When he spoke, his voice was unrecognizable.

"*Please!*" he screamed. "*Please don't! I'm scared. Please father don't make me.*"

The mallet in one hand, half a dozen stakes in the other, Max stepped forward, thought he would intervene, but his father swiveled, caught his elbow, shoved him at the stairs.

"Up. Now." Giving him another push as he spoke.

Max fell on the stairs, barking one of his own shins.

Their father bent to grab Rudy by the arm, but he squirmed away, crabwalking over the dirt for a far corner of the room.

"Come. I help you," their father said. "Her neck is brittle. It won't take long."

Rudy shook his head, backed further into the corner by the coal bin.

His father flung the ax in the dirt. "Then you will remain here until you are in a more complaisant state of mind."

He turned, took Max's arm and thrust him towards the top of the steps.

"*No!*" Rudy screamed, getting up, lunging for the stairs.

The handle of the hatchet got caught between his feet, though, and he tripped on it, crashed to his knees. He got back up, but by then their father was pushing Max through the door at the top of the staircase, following him through. He slammed it behind them. Rudy hit the other side a moment later, as their father was turning that silver key in the lock.

"Please!" Rudy cried. "I'm scared! I'm scared I want to come out!"

Max stood in the kitchen. His ears were ringing. He wanted to say stop it, open the door, but couldn't get the words out, felt his throat closing. His arms hung at his sides, his hands heavy, as if cast from lead. No—not lead. They were heavy from the things in them. The mallet. The stakes.

His father panted for breath, his broad forehead resting against the shut door. When he finally stepped back, his hair was scrambled and his collar had popped loose.

"You see what he make me do?" he said. "Your mother was also so, just as unbending and hysterical, just as in need of firm instruction. I tried, I—"

The old man turned to look at him, and in the instant before Max hit him with the mallet, his father had time to register shock, even wonder. Max caught him across the jaw, a blow that connected with a bony clunk and enough force to drive a shivering feeling of impact up into his elbow. His father sagged to one knee, but Max had to hit him again to sprawl him on his back.

Abraham's eyelids sank as he began to slide into unconsciousness, but they came up again when Max sat down on top of him. His father opened his mouth to say something, but Max had heard enough, was through talking, had never been much when it came to talk anyway. What mattered now was the work of his hands; work he had a natural instinct for, had maybe been born to.

He put the tip of the stake where his father had showed him and struck the hilt with the mallet. It turned out it was all true, what the old man had told him in the basement. There was wailing and profanity and a frantic struggle to get away, but it was over soon enough.

The Black Wallpaper

Kim Antieau

15 Oct.—Today we leave London for the country in the hopes of curing my beloved Catherine of her melancholy. We have not discovered the cause of it as yet, although her physician and I have interviewed Catherine at length.

When Dr. Hawkins finally diagnosed Catherine's lassitude as melancholia, he recommended taking her away from London's nearly constant autumn fog. He was alarmed that I allowed Catherine to read the London newspapers—this meant she was aware of the murders which had recently occurred in the East End. I assured him Catherine was a modern woman and no newspaper article would cause her to blush or faint away.

"Mrs. Van Helsing was my assistant in my medical practice in Amsterdam when we were first married," I reminded him. "I relied on her exceptional brain and steady hand for many years."

After helping me in my practice, Catherine blessed our lives by giving birth to our sweet boy, Abraham. When Abraham was five, we moved to London to enable me to continue my studies with the esteemed metaphysician Dr. Ehrenreich. After a time, he asked me to stay on as his assistant. For many years we have lived happily, the three of us—Catherine,

Abraham, and myself—in a cocoon of blissful domesticity interrupted only by my sojourns to the university each day.

As summer came to a close this year, however, Catherine began calling out in her sleep. I could not understand her words, try as I might. When I awakened her, she had no memory of her outbursts. Then she stopped sleeping regularly.

"A form of hysteria, perhaps," Dr. Hawkins suggested. "You should have consulted me earlier, Van Helsing. As a physician yourself you know these conditions can deteriorate quickly."

And as a physician, I did not believe the diagnosis of hysteria was the correct one. This disease was particular to the Americas and not one with which our European women were often afflicted. I did, however, concur about the melancholy.

I have rented an old English manor house, which shall be fun for us all. Catherine asked if we could please have plenty of trees, flowers, and sunlight.

"Sunlight in October, my dear," I said, "may be difficult to obtain. Most of the blossoms are in wilt or gone altogether. But the trees shall stand tall—I am certain they are covered in autumn color. You shall revive immediately!"

I am looking forward to seeing Catherine's smile once again.

16 Oct.—Catherine sits beside me in the breakfast room, which overlooks the garden. The French doors open and a slight breeze ruffles Catherine's hair as she takes the medicine I have given her. Today she has color in her cheeks. Abraham squirms in his seat. He has finished breakfast but waits for consent to leave.

Finally I look over at the boy and say, "You may be excused, Abraham. Miss Deirdre is waiting to give you your lessons."

"Oh please, Father," says my nine-year-old son. "Can't I go outside? There is no rain!"

Catherine looks up and smiles. "Yes, Father," she says. "There is no rain. We should all go outside and play."

I cannot resist her smile—or the boy's. I motion him to go outside.

"Thank you, sir!" He jumps up, kisses his mother's cheek, then is gone.

Catherine pats my hand.

"Feeling better this morning?" I ask. "You slept well?"

"What else could I do but sleep?" she says. "I am not allowed to read, write, paint, or supervise the staff or my child. Sleep is the only alternative."

"You are supposed to be resting. You need to get your strength back."

"Yes, Abraham. Did you notice the wallpaper in my bedroom? It's so bright. Even in the dark. As if it is constantly reflecting light from some source I cannot discern." She looks around the room. "It is strangely quiet here. And bright."

"You asked for sunlight."

"But it isn't sunlight," she says. "It is just . . . the light hurts my eyes."

She shrugs. Her shoulders look so delicate. She has lost weight and has become weak, so unlike herself when she is in good health.

"Good, that is what we need!" I say briskly. "Light. And pleasant thoughts!"

"By the by, good Abraham," Catherine says, "don't you think it is going a bit too far to tell the staff to keep newspapers away from me? I am not a child."

I blush. "I know. I am trying to do as Dr. Hawkins instructed."

"You are a doctor, too," Catherine says. "Does your intuition tell you that keeping me from the world will cure me?"

I laugh. "I am a man of science, sweet Kate! Intuition is part of a woman's domain."

"My intuition tells me I need to have some activity to keep me busy or I shall go mad! Couldn't I write in my journal?"

"That is a reasonable request," I say. "I will consult with the doctor."

She sighs.

"Dearest, you requested my assistance. Do you not remember? After you had not slept for a week, you put your hand in mine and begged me to help you. That is all I am attempting to do."

"Father!" My son comes running into the room. "Come quick. I've found a yellow-and-green snake!"

"I shall join you," I say.

My son runs outside again. I kiss the top of Catherine's head. "Perhaps you would like to come out with us?"

"As soon as I finish my tea," she says. "Did you find out what happened to the trees?"

"I talked to the vicar last night," I say. "He told me a strange rot came over the trees a few weeks ago, and they had to chop them all down."

"It was so strange," Catherine says wistfully, "coming down the drive and seeing stump after stump of dead trees. Now there are so few trees on the property. Do you suppose it is a sign?"

"A sign of what?"

"That nothing will ever be the same," she says. "I had everything I wanted, husband. And now. I wished for trees, and they were taken away from me. Perhaps it is a sign to remind me that I am now vulnerable, and everything around me is likewise vulnerable."

"Life is not that personal, Catherine," I say. "When we worked side by side in the clinic, you saw sickness strike down the noblest of person yet pass by those lost in drunken debauchery. Illness is of the brain or blood, inherited from our families or caused by our living environment. The trees became diseased. That is all."

"Still," she says, "I feel that all is not right here." She looks over at me and smiles. "Never mind that. Your son awaits you. Go."

"I will instruct the gardener to begin planting more trees immediately," I say to Catherine before I leave, but she is no longer listening, lost in her melancholy again.

CATHERINE VAN HELSING'S JOURNAL

19 Oct.—At long last! I can once more set my thoughts to paper. I cannot honestly converse with anyone here. I feel alone and lonely out in this small town in the English countryside—even though I have seen none of the country. I have been only in this house and the gardens. I wish I could summon back my strength—it continues to seep away since I saw what I saw. But I cannot speak or write of it yet. Maybe not ever. I wish not to think on it at all. Can I hide from the experience? Will the consequences of what I saw then be lessened?

This place is far too big for the three of us and the servants. My husband says he can do his work here. I suspect he will start traveling to London during the weekdays, and I will be left even more alone.

Perhaps I will feel freer with him gone. Not to be watched all the time. During those few moments I am alone with my boy Abraham, I feel myself again. Only then. We sit on the floor or on the earth in the garden, laugh, and tell each other stories. I would do anything for him. For his father, as well. I would protect them with my life. Only just now I feel so physically weak. It is as though I have seen the truth of the world, and my physical body cannot bear it! My mind does not waver, however, despite what the doctor tells Abraham.

I am not sleeping through the night again. I think it is the wallpaper. It is as though a light is on all night in my room. I have asked Abraham to replace the paper. I chose a darker pattern, an almost rosy maroon and gray. They shall put it up soon.

I wish Abraham would sleep in my room, but he says the doctor has told him we must abstain from marital relations. I suggested he simply come and sleep next to me. He thought this was a bizarre request. My poor dear husband! I love him, but he is so conventional.

The vicar and his wife came over for tea yesterday. Why is it I can never remember their names? I shall call them Mr. and Mrs. Vicar instead. Or perhaps not—this might alarm Abraham!

I asked them about the history of the house. They could not tell me much, except that one family owned it for a very long time, and they were prosperous and loved one another dearly. It was sold a few years ago to a gentlemen and his wife; they came only in the summers, and no one saw much of them.

"I'm not certain who owns the place now," Mrs. Vicar said, "but I know the gardener has had a terrible time lately with various plant diseases. There was a blight on the rhododendrons. He had to pull them all up. Then the trees."

"Yes," Mr. Vicar said, "but it has all worked out the better for *your* family. It's much sunnier in here now than it used to be. Quite pleasant."

"Yes," Mrs. Vicar agreed. "Quite."

ABRAHAM VAN HELSING'S JOURNAL

28 Oct.—Catherine is much improved. She was laughing and playing with
Abraham this morning. Perhaps I could go into London for a few days, after all. Dr. Ehrenreich has a brain-fever patient he wants me to examine.
The man was a loving husband one day, and then he became ill. Since his
recovery, he has started drinking and beating his wife and children. No
doubt this case will confirm what I already believe. Men are not evil.
They become diseased—a brain is damaged, so a man's personality is altered. He is not possessed, he has not been cursed, he is a victim of circumstance—and that circumstance is disease.

Catherine seemed particularly interested in this case.

"You are certain a fever caused this change?" she asked me.

"I have not examined the patient yet," I answered, "but from the facts
given to me, yes, I am fairly certain. What other cause? A person's personality and demeanor do not alter suddenly without some organic cause."

Catherine stared out at the garden. My son Abraham sat on a bench
outside reading. She waved to him when he looked up.

"You don't believe in evil?" she asked, turning to look at me.

"I believe evil happens, but it is done by men," I said.

"Not by women?" She smiled.

"Rarely," I said. "Do I believe in an evil such as Satan? You know the
answer to that, my dear."

"What if I told you I have seen evil?" she whispered.

I went over to her and put my arm around her waist. "The doctor told
you you mustn't brood."

"I'm not brooding, husband. I am telling you that I believe in evil as
separate from people, and I have seen it. That is how I know. I don't
think I did believe it until then."

"Catherine, you must stop this. The doctor told you—"

"I think I shall have Abraham read to me," Catherine said abruptly.

"But, Catherine, we were talking."

She stopped and looked at me. "No, I was talking, but you were not
listening. Go to London. Do what you need to do. Abraham and I will
wait for you here."

After this conversation, strangely enough, Catherine seemed cheered.

She laughed and ate dinner with enthusiasm. She even played the piano for us. Chopin, I believe. The new wallpaper was installed yesterday. Catherine has not said a word about it.

CATHERINE VAN HELSING'S JOURNAL

30 Oct.—Abraham has left for London. My son and I are alone with the servants. We will celebrate All Hallow's Eve with them. Maryann says they will make a feast, then a fire outside. I have given them permission to build a fire on the other side of the house, in the clearing. I saw what looked like a fire ring there, so it must have been used before.

I decided not to take the medicines while Abraham is gone. They make me feel strange and dry out my mouth. Last night I stared at the new wallpaper until I fell to sleep. The paper was not as dark as I would have liked, but it was better than what was there before. I cannot remember what color it had been, only that it was too bright.

Abraham tells me not to think "dark" thoughts. He is naive. He believes that life is basically fair and good, and if we are good and decent people, all will be well. He is wrong. I happened to be in a carriage in a neighborhood I did not normally frequent when everything changed for me. When I saw "it." When I understood reality to be different from what I had perceived it to be. I knew in that moment that I was in jeopardy. That both my Abrahams were in jeopardy. Now and forever. Since that encounter I have felt so weak. I cannot shake this lassitude. And I must. Because this evil is not a singular thing. It may be everywhere.

I am afraid part of it may have latched onto me that day, followed me here, and is now in this house. I don't know! I am no longer certain of anything. I still cannot write of what I saw. Perhaps if I did write it all down, the power would go out of the experience. After all, when I think on it, it was such an ordinary occurrence. How could it then make a wreck of my life?

Whatever it was, whatever happened to me, I must rally, so that I can protect myself and my family from harm!

2 Nov.—Abraham Sr. would be quite cross if he knew what his son and I did last night. I ate far more food than anyone should, then went outside

under a nearly full moon and danced around the fire. Everyone sang. I
did not know the words, but it didn't matter. Abraham Jr. was so happy!
He learned the songs right away. They were all very kind to him. Before
we left the celebration, one of the men made a toast to our good health. I
appreciated the gesture. Everyone looked sincere with raised glasses,
cheeks rosy from the fire (or drink), asking that we might be well. I felt as
though I might carry on after all.

I fell directly to sleep that night. When I awakened in the morning and
looked around my bedchamber, all appeared normal. Even the maroon
roses on the wallpaper seemed to be as they should be.

The next day, I felt well enough to explore the house. Abraham Jr. was
upstairs having his lessons, so after breakfast, I wrapped a shawl around
my shoulders to keep off the chill, and I wandered from here to there.
The servants' quarters were below, of course, and I tiptoed past the
kitchen, hoping not to disturb anyone. I opened doors and found empty
rooms. One or two doors were locked. The downstairs was dark and
dank—away from the kitchen—but not extraordinary. I followed the corridor outside to the barn and beyond. I walked past our smoldering fire
ring toward the woods. The sun was bright today. It seemed our autumn
had turned to fall again.

I noticed clumps of grass growing up in a small clearing to the north of
the woods, so I walked toward it. I crouched down to move the grass away
and was surprised to find two headstones. One said, HENRY BLYTHE, CHER-
ISHED SON. I could not discern the birth or death date. The other read,
SARAH BLYTHE, CHERISHED DAUGHTER. Her dates were also obscure. I pulled
away as much of the grass as I could. Then I went back to the house to
find the gardener, so he could put right the little cemetery.

I passed Maryann as I started down the path toward the front of the
house.

"Maryann, I've just found two gravestones for a Henry and Sarah
Blythe. Do you know of them?"

"Aye," she said. "They were the children of the owner. They died in
the pond out back one summer, both of them. It was tragic, madam.
They think one of the children got a cramp so the other jumped in to
help. Although no one knows for sure. They were both just found dead,

floating on the surface. They had the pond drained soon after—that's why you haven't seen it. Then they sold the place."

"Thank you, Maryann," I said. "Could you please ask the gardener to cut down the weeds and make the plots tidy again?"

"Certainly, Mrs. Van Helsing."

As I walked back into the house, I wondered if Abraham had known about the deaths of these children. Had he kept this information from me? Such nonsense: to pretend the world is a pretty place does not mean it *will* then become a pretty place! That is not the Abraham I married.

3 Nov.—I could barely get out of bed this morning. The room was suffused with light. And something else. It was as if the walls breathed. No, that is not quite right. As if the walls panted. Like a mad dog from thirst. I called Maryann into the room, but she heard nothing.

"Is it not too bright in here?"

"Shall I close the draperies?" she asked.

I consented, but it did no good. My son Abraham came into the room then. He hesitated at the door and looked around.

"Mother," he said. "I don't like the wallpaper."

"Neither do I," I said. "Perhaps we can change it."

"What's behind it?" he asked.

I slowly got out of bed, relieved and terrified that Abraham sensed something in the room, too.

"I have wondered that very same thing," I said. I reached out for Abraham's hand. "It's too light in here. I can't see what's behind the paper. I think if the wallpaper were darker, I might be able to tell, don't you think?"

"I don't know, Mama."

At that moment I saw something move beneath the wallpaper—causing the wall to undulate, like leaves do when a snake or mole passes underneath them. Only this movement in the wall sent a chill of terror up my spine.

My son tugged on my hand, and we left the room.

I was certain then that the evil *had* followed me that day and was now lodged behind the wallpaper. I didn't know why. Had I been vulnerable, like someone is before they become ill with a cold? Was this house some-how vulnerable, too? Abraham would want me to know why, would want me to address it all scientifically. Why me? Why now? Why that wall? Per-haps so it could be with me as I slept, invade my dreams? I did not know why. I only knew I had to find a way to protect my son and husband from it. I had to make certain it did not touch our family—any more than it al-ready had.

ABRAHAM VAN HELSING'S JOURNAL

3 Nov.—I am glad to be finished with my work and am eager to rejoin my family. Dr. Ehrenreich and I performed trepanning on the patient. When he recovered his senses, he was quite rational, and his wife said she could see her husband in his eyes again. "Seeing him in his eyes" was a strange utterance, yet I understood what she meant. He was sane again after the treatment. Unfortunately, he caught the meninge and died. His wife said, "I thank you for relieving his agony. At least he has died with the evil wrenched from his soul."

Her words reminded me of Catherine's. I was tempted to explain the science of her husband's disease but decided my neutral words were not what she needed to hear.

I can hardly bear to be away from my own beloved for so long. Tonight we will be together again!

4 Nov.—I should have never gone to London. I was completely fooled by Catherine's demeanor before I left. I fear she wanted me gone so she could indulge in her delusions. That sounds harsh, doesn't it? I do not mean it so. She cannot help herself. She is ill. But they were *dancing* in the moonlight! I suppose that is great sport for someone who is well, but she could have gotten a chill. And a fever would have exacerbated the wildness of her imagination.

Today she told me she wanted to change the wallpaper again.

"I cannot," I said. "We haven't the funds."

"But it is for my well-being," she said. "For your son's well-being."

"I would be indulging your fantasies," I said. "There is nothing wrong with the wallpaper."

"It needs to be darker," she said. "Or tear it down altogether and paint the walls black. Then whatever is there will be gone." She stopped herself. She looked wild. "*Wait.* Oh! I had not thought of that! No, you must *not* take off the wallpaper. Cover it with more. We must keep it all inside."

"Catherine, you sound quite foolish," I said. "What has come over you?"

She turned to me. Her eyes looked feverish, and I felt afraid. Was it more than melancholy that taxed her? I remembered what my patient's wife had said about her husband not being in his eyes. Catherine was in hers. But she appeared quite agitated.

"I must tell you what has been happening," she said. "You must listen to every word and not judge until I am finished. Sit, husband."

I did as instructed. Catherine sat beside me.

"I was coming back from my work at the charity hospital. One of our cases had left the hospital suddenly—she had been severely beaten by one of her customers. I was concerned, so I got her address and instructed a cab driver to take me to it. He did not want to go—at least not with me. 'No place for a lady,' he said, and other such nonsense.

"But I convinced him," Catherine said. "He stopped in front of what looked to be a boarding house. It was quite rundown. The streets were full of people. Drunks, prostitutes, orphaned children, people going to and from work. Like any other place, I suppose, only more lively. It did not frighten me. I asked the driver to go up and see if he could find Mrs. Lansing. He left and—"

"He left you alone in the carriage?"

"Abraham, you must *listen*. I was alone in the cab. But I was safe. I watched the people. It was quite entertaining. And then I saw this man walking toward me. At least at first I thought he was a man. He looked like a man. Walked like a man. He had a black walking stick, I remember, and he swung it back and forth as he walked. He had a tall black top hat. A shiny gold waistcoat. I was certain he was only walking toward the cab to walk beyond it. He did not look at me—until he was right next to the window. Then he turned to me without breaking stride and looked directly into my eyes. What I saw shook me to my very core. His eyes were not human, husband. They were not animal—I do not mean that. They were not those of a wild creature. Not like that. They were inhuman. Unalive. I was filled with this awful sense of dread. As I tried to withdraw my gaze from his, he smiled. I wanted to scream but could not find my voice. In those instants, he took something from me. My vitality. Then he was gone. And I was shattered. I heard the next morning that those two women had been murdered. No man did that, Abraham. Evil did that."

"Men kill all the time, Catherine!"

She shook her head. "This was different. Evil exists. On its own. In a form that is not human. Is not animal. It just is, Abraham. It took from me, and I am afraid part of it has also latched onto me. And now it is here with us. And this evil—this thing—will steal from us. It will take what vitality I have left and crush it. It will steal what makes you my husband and Abraham my son. I believe we must leave this place, Abraham. And we must leave soon."

She was breathing heavily, almost panting.

I poured her a glass of water from the decanter on the table nearest me. Her hands shook as she took the water from me.

"I am not very strong," Catherine said, "and I feel as though I am getting weaker. This morning, before dawn, I awakened and I knew it was in the room with me. I felt this terrible weight on my chest. I could not move. I could not call to anyone to protect Abraham. I could only stare. After a while, I saw something behind the wallpaper. I was able to move then, and I got out of bed. With my hands, I felt around the entire room, looking for it. But it moves faster than I can. If I find it, I will smash it out of existence. But my strength fades, husband; it fades."

"You must calm yourself! Shall I give you something?"

"I have taken your pills, salts, and remedies," Catherine said. "I am not sick!"

"That feeling you had this morning," I said. "The weight on your chest. It is called a succubus dream, or an old hag dream. They often occur when one is suffering from exhaustion. You have exhausted yourself with these fears, Catherine."

"Why didn't you tell me about the children drowning?"

"I-I. What children? Oh. I thought it might disturb you."

She laughed. An almost unnatural sound. "Of course it is disturbing and tragic, but so is life! We must look it in the face. Accept what is. Please, you must get us out of here."

"All right, my dear. I will try to arrange to change the lease."

Catherine shook her head. "Haven't you heard anything I've said?"

"Of course I have," I said. I took her hand in mine and squeezed it. "Don't sleep in your room tonight. Stay with me. Or I'll find you another room."

She nodded. "As you wish."

I am at the end of my wits! This morning Abraham started to come into Catherine's bedchamber, and she yelled at him to stay out. She ran down the hall after him, barely dressed, her hair flying every which way. She looked quite mad.

"You mustn't go near there," she said once she had caught up with him. "That is the heart of it. You must stay away until Father gets us away from here."

CATHERINE VAN HELSING'S JOURNAL

? Nov.—I am not sure what day it is. I write in the dark. I like the dark. I can see. Moonlight comes through the window and falls across this page. Moonlight is safe, too. It has a quiet, inner beauty. It knows. In this darkness, I can see the truth. Abraham is asleep. I left our bed and found the paint I arranged for the gardener to leave for me. He could not find black, but he poured color into color until he had almost black. It likes the brightness: the pretend brightness. Where we can pretend all is well. So I painted the wall black. Each time my paint brush touched the wallpaper, what was beneath seemed to undulate. Frantically, like a fish out of water. That made me happy. Each coat of paint is another wall I am erecting to keep the evil trapped here, unable to harm anyone else. Maybe then we can escape, leave it behind, and be safe.

The paint odor has made me quite dizzy, so now I sit by the open window. I was right, you know. The dark wallpaper allows me to see the wall as it truly is. And something is moving underneath the paper. Sometimes it is shapeless. Sometimes it has the shape of a human. A human who is not quite right. Nauseating in its distortion from normalcy.

Now it is whispering to me.

"Let me out," it says. "Let me out and you will be free."

It is a constant refrain now, in-between the panting. Is it right? Will I finally be free once it is released from these walls?

I shake my head. No, that is evil talking.

It must remain shackled.

But it won't stop whispering.

I fall to sleep.

When I awaken, I hear tapping. I listen carefully. It is as if someone is tapping their fingernails against something. Against the wallpaper—*from the inside!* It is testing the paper. Trying to find a weak point.

So it can tear the wall open and release itself!

I must do something!

ABRAHAM VAN HELSING'S JOURNAL
5 Nov.—I awakened to the sound of something slamming against a wall. Then Catherine's scream. I jumped out of bed—first noticing that Catherine was not in the bed beside me. I ran toward the sound. My son cowered in the doorway to his mother's chamber, crying. Moonlight poured through the window. Catherine stood on the other side of the room heaving the back of a shovel against the wall. She groaned with the effort every time the metal hit the wall.

"Catherine!" I cried, running to her.

"I struck it a couple of times," she said, nearly breathless. She smiled, then laughed. "It's not invincible. It even cried out when I hit it!"

She raised the shovel again, and I grabbed it from her. "That was you, Catherine! *You* were screaming!"

"It's here, Abraham. The evil is here, and it is trying to get out! To get at us. I must stop it!"

"You are acting insane!"

"Give the shovel back to me!"

I glanced at my son. He trembled in the darkness to see his mother thus.

"There is nothing here," I said. "This is all nonsense." I raised the point of the shovel and drove it into the wall.

Catherine cried out. "No, you mustn't!"

I dropped the shovel and grabbed at the now torn wallpaper and began ripping it away from the wall. "See, there is nothing!"

Catherine ran to Abraham.

"Nothing!" I said. "It is just a wall with—"

And then something leaped out of the hole I had created—some *thing* I can't describe, sucking away all the air as it went by me. Then Catherine screamed, strangely, her voice broken and terrified. She pushed Abraham to the floor. I tried to run to them.

"No!" Catherine called. She reached out. She reached out . . . for it.

Put herself between us and it.

Then she screamed again.

Only it was no longer Catherine's voice, even though the sound emanated from her mouth.

I grabbed Abraham and pulled him up against me.

Catherine collapsed to the floor, gurgling, laughing.

Maryann was suddenly at the door holding up a lantern. The light made the shadows sharper. When Catherine looked up at her, Maryann gasped. I put my hand over Abraham's eyes.

Catherine turned to me, and I was filled with a dread I cannot explain. I knew in that moment that my wife had saved us but was now lost herself. She was no longer in her eyes.

The instant I realized this, Catherine smiled.

"Get the doctor," I told Maryann.

I led Abraham around and away from his mother—my back against the wallpaper and Abraham's back against me—until we were out of the room. I heard Catherine get up, heard the sound of tearing as she pulled the black paper from the walls, heard her panting.

"It's free now, eh husband!" She screamed, then laughed. "Now you know you should have listened to her! You'll be next. She never loved you, you pompous man! She felt trapped by you and your life!"

I pulled the door shut and took my latch key from my pocket. My son watched as my shaking hand inserted the key in the lock and turned it.

"What has happened to Mama?" Abraham asked.

"She has left us to save us," I said as we walked quickly down the corridor toward the front door. "When you are older, I will tell you the whole story. She has saved us this night."

I began to weep. The thing in the bedroom continued to cackle and rip paper. Would I tell Abraham my part in his mother's demise?

"You should have listened!" she screamed, the sound of her voice getting more and more distant.

"My beloved," I whispered.

I tightened my grip on her son's hand. "You already know of your mother's sweetness and loving care. But you should also know that your mother was a brave and gallant woman, and all who knew her loved her well!"

Except one.

I had not loved her well enough.

But I would make it up to her.

I swear to you, sweet Catherine. I will make it up to you! I will show people the truth. I will stare evil in the face—and I shall be the victor. This I promise you, my beloved wife.

And just then, as we were about to step outside, the voice that had been Catherine's came to us clearly by some trick of acoustics. She whispered, "Let me out, and you will be finally free."

Brushed in Blackest Silence

BRIAN HODGE

🦋

FROM THE WAY the house was described in the letter two weeks earlier, he's been expecting it to scowl and grimace. Instead, from the road at least, it hardly seems worth a second glance.

I am coming to fear that it may be an accursed place, the Baron wrote, *harboring malice toward those who would exercise even the smallest right of mastery over the property. Yet I am determined to make the most of my investment in it, and the artifacts upon its walls.*

As the carriage clatters nearer, the driver pulling back on his reins, Abraham's first judgment is that the Baron may have a keen imagination for a banker.

It's a country house, no more and no less distinguished than a hundred others he's seen. It stands two stories of brick and adobe, little adorned but for the tall, narrow windows, its garden and grounds nourished by the same stream that feeds a marble fountain, ill maintained of late and green with algae. Close by, a stone well juts from the ground. Farther away, the green tendrils of a small vineyard twine about their arbors.

La Quinta del Sordo, the place has been called for generations. The House of the Deaf Man.

A cluster of white poplars throws some precious shade near the house, an oasis from which the Baron waves and beckons. He looks reluctant to leave it, and Abraham can sympathize. Spain is an arid land. He feels cooked here, the sun a savage cousin to the sun of the north.

Thanking the driver, he steps from the carriage, then takes a moment to stare at the house; imagines that it stares back and then imagines what it might see in him . . . an enemy to repel, an ally to win over. The driver turns back for the dusty road to the east and the sprawl of Madrid, a proud sea of steeples and red-tiled roofs beyond the gentle curve of the Manzanares River. Yesterday Abraham was told at the Museo del Prado that the painter Goya, when he lived here, enjoyed watching the city's washerwomen come down to the river's edge.

He joins the Baron under the poplars. They've done their catching up already, the way old family friends should, over beef and cognac and cigars three nights ago, after Abraham first arrived in Madrid. He learned then that the Baron was a father of four now, rather than three. Sons, all of them. He's seen none of them, nor the Baroness Mathilde, since the wedding nine years earlier. And to Abraham, their titles mean little. Ties between the Van Helsings and the d'Erlangers reach back three generations, to the years before Belgium took her independence from the Netherlands. For all he knows—because he would rather read books of words than numbers—Frederic and his family might still be watching over some of the old investments.

The years between them are beginning to seem wider. Frederic is a dozen years the younger, not yet forty, and seems to have adapted to the dryness and dust of Spain with ease. He's abandoned the frippery of Brussels for a simple linen shirt, dull white in defense against the sun, and the broad-brimmed hat of a country don.

"Two and a half days at the Prado," Frederic says. "Not long, I realize, but . . . do you know Goya now?"

Abraham gives a sharp laugh. "Can anyone know Goya? I knew him little before, and not so much better even now."

"I have two secretaries with me, trying to find anyone who might have known him personally, but this is no easy task. He died an old man and outlived many of his friends, maybe most of them . . . and that was half a century ago. Still," says Frederic, "you do recognize his genius?"

"Not to worry." Abraham claps him on the shoulder. "I declare it almost as emphatically as my own."

"Then I think you'll soon agree that such genius did not come without its price." Frederic rises to his feet. "Come, let me show you."

Francisco Goya has been dead for some forty-five years. It was nine years before that, in 1819, that he set up house here after a long, successful career as a painter not only to the royal families of Spain but of the commonest folk sweating in the fields and streets.

With Goya already past seventy, it would've been reasonable to expect that he might have lived out his days here. But four years later, Spain's affairs of state took their latest in a series of bitter turns, with the despotic reign of King Ferdinand VII, and Goya decided to leave. He deeded *La Quinta del Sordo* over to his sole grandchild, Mariano, and joined the community of exiles in France, to live his last years in Bordeaux. He died in bed at eighty-two, attended by friends, his grandson, and his housekeeper, Leocadia—who was, most believed, his mistress, even though she was forty-two years younger than he, and the mother of a little girl thought to be his own.

Frederic opens the door to the house. Immediately they are in the ground floor's main room, where he's greeted by the first painting, flanking one side of the doorway. It's been brushed directly onto the plaster wall: a pleasant-looking woman in a black veil, leaning on one elbow against some indistinct hummock, perhaps a fresh grave, daubed in yellow-brown ochres and backed by an ornate railing.

"Leocadia. Hers is the kindest face you'll see here," says Frederic. "Although it's said her tongue was shrill enough that had she lived a few centuries earlier, she would have been condemned to a scold's bridle."

"And Goya deaf as a stone! A perfect match. God's mercy takes peculiar forms at times."

On the other side of the doorway, another painting shows two figures rendered in even more somber tones. The first is an old man in a flowing cloak, propping himself upright with a cane; his beard wags down to his chest.

"Is it him?"

Frederic shakes his head. "Not a self-portrait, no."

"But in spirit, maybe so, jah . . . ?"

It's the second figure that gives the painting a sinister air, with an eerie, semihuman form leaning in from the right. With one hand it clutches the old man's shoulder, and its dark cavernous mouth gapes wide next to his ear.

"His demon muse," Abraham goes on, "must shout to make itself heard."

"Maybe you know Goya better than you think."

"I thought myself to be a painter too, once," he says. "Rembrandt reborn, I just knew it. But my brushes, they had other ideas. I couldn't find a single one that wasn't stubborn and willful, with a so devious mind of his own."

They move deeper into the house so he can examine the others, but the place is poorly lit. Its two largest rooms, whose walls became Goya's canvas, were built one atop the other. There's something about them that makes Abraham think of caves, and of men of long ago who used their rough stone walls to sketch ancient animals with a primal grace—as he has, by lantern's light, seen evidence in France and the north of Spain.

The deeper they go, the more he loses himself to the spell of the place. He can imagine the rooms filling with a wet, heavy smell as Goya prepares the walls with gesso, a mixture of plaster and glue that would better hold his oils.

Downstairs, upstairs, these murals are the blackest things he's ever seen. It's not just the preponderance of black paint, although this frequently seems to have been a tactic combined with the poor light of the rooms, as certain images seem to be freeing themselves from primordial tar: Here, a maddened procession of pilgrims winds over the hills of a scorched-looking countryside, their contorted faces showing no joy, only a frenzy of desperation. There, an assembly of cloaked hags makes a rapt audience to the speaking silhouette of a goat. Elsewhere, a pair of depraved and toothless old men sits hunched over a bowl of gruel.

Yet even when Goya employed more vibrant colors, the light of day still reveals something just as dark and terrible: Two men against a blue and white sky, one's head streaming blood, both sunk to their knees in the earth as they batter each other to death with cudgels. And, most enigmatic, the head of a dog rising above a gentle slope and staring forlornly into an emptiness of golden-brown.

He has seen plenty of art with morbid themes. Bosch and the Breughels painted infernal epics; Gustave Doré could not have depicted Dante's Hell any better if he'd toured it in person. Yet for all their demonic invention, they only warned of dangers to an unwary soul.

These works, though, are so very different. They seethe with an energy he has never seen. Only a deaf man could have painted them, Abraham thinks. Only a deaf man would have needed to. They roar with savagery and sorrow; they whisper with recriminations and regret. The brutality in them reverberates from wall to wall to wall.

There are no warnings of torment here. Any warning would come too late.

And to think that Goya painted them for no other eyes, no other soul, but his own . . . then lived with them as daily companions. Until he left them behind.

"Mariano kept the house for some years," Frederic tells him. "It then passed through several owners, but the paintings have remained. I know they're Goya's because they were inventoried after his death by his friend, Antonio Brugada. I bought the house so they might be saved. Oil on plaster, they may not last much longer. For fifty years these walls have drunk the air coming off that river out there. Already most of the paintings show signs of deterioration. I want them saved. They *should* be saved."

"So save them—I agree and approve," Abraham says. "You don't need me for that. My knives are for the body, not for walls."

"The walls," says Frederic, quietly now, as if not to offend them, *"do not wish to turn loose of them."* He walks a slow, wide circle, points at painting after painting here on the second floor. "Look around, Bram. You see what is here. You *feel* what is here. Am I to call a priest? You as well as anyone would know the power of the Church in Spain. You know the things it's done. Their Inquisition wasn't abolished so long ago that there's no sympathy for it left, and they would maybe be as ready to purify this place with fire as they were heretics once."

"And still might again, so permitted," Abraham says. "What has happened here, Frederic?"

The Baron tells him how, after the sale of *La Quinta*, he brought down from Antwerp a gifted conservator, Tobias Gammel, along with a pair of apprentices, to assess the condition of the paintings and begin their salvage. For each opus—fourteen in all—this would mean painstakingly cutting it free along with its upper layer of plaster, then affixing it to a canvas. Thus rescued, their damage could be restored and all of them could one day be properly exhibited, maintained, sold.

"Gammel began here." Frederic points to the hideous pair of old men, the smallest work at less than two feet by three. Abraham can see the initial scorings and primary cut into the plaster down the left side, and some dark stains that have run from it. "It took only two or three minutes from the time he first put in his plaster knife until the hindrances began."

A stinking miasma came wafting in from the river, Frederic tells him, a grayish mist that fouled the air and turned the stomach. They secured the windows, but this only slowed its progress instead of halting it, as the murk sought entrance down the chimney and through the fireplace. They blocked the flue next, and this seemed to make the place fit for work again . . . except what had been mist now appeared to congeal from the walls themselves.

"Black bile," says Frederic. "It ran from the cut in the wall after Gammel went back to extending it."

"Curious." Abraham nods. "There is no such thing as black bile, though. Bile may be yellow, green, brown even . . . but black bile, no, this was an invention of the ancients to explain a man's melancholy temperament."

Frederic steps over to a small table standing amid materials gathered for the work that has been abandoned. He picks up a small, clear apothecary jar, nearly one-quarter full of what must be the fluid from the wall.

"At one point it came in enough quantity to dredge up." He uncorks the jar and hands it over. "If not bile, what is it, then?"

Abraham gives it a sniff; tips the jar to wet a fingertip, then cautiously dabs it to his tongue. Caustic and bitter, it's familiar in taste if not color. He spits it to the floor.

"Jah," he says, "so there is maybe a bit more to the physical causes of melancholy than we think we know."

"Gammel moved to another painting," Frederic goes on. "Not so eager to taste it as you, he thought it might have been some stagnant water collected in the wall that could be drained later. So he tried across the room." Frederic points to the struggling dog. "Once he got his knife in, it was as if the wall took aim and spat at him just as you spit the vile stuff to the floor. It struck him in the eye. We took him downstairs and washed it clean with water from the well, but the damage was done. The eye was useless for the next week, and still not fully restored . . . although by the time the bandage could come off, he was back in Antwerp with no more heart for this job, and who could fault him? By noon of the second day, both his apprentices were dead."

Frederic points to the brighter, sunlit mural of the two men mired to their knees in the earth, fulfilling their destiny to batter each other to death with clubs.

"Like that," he says. "Except they were both free to run . . . and neither did."

This will weigh upon him for a lifetime, Abraham knows. The Baron likes his money but is no miser. He donates to museums, he's a patron to artists and composers; he and the Baroness have founded two hospitals that Abraham knows of, and probably more that he doesn't. Black bile or red blood—Frederic is not a man who could live with either on his hands.

"The man I sent you to talk with at the Prado . . . Cubells," he says. "He's eager to begin work here, as soon as I say, but he has no knowledge of what's happened already. I imagine it would make no difference if he did. He would probably not believe it, but suppose he did . . . still, it is Goya. In Spain, there's a second holy trinity: El Greco, Velázquez, and Goya. It's the honor of a lifetime for him. But I will not send him into harm."

Even between friends, this is much to ask. Abraham has seen many strange things, and they cannot always be understood, much less bested.

"I told you I could never let the place be burned in the same spirit as a heretic," Frederic says. "But if this may be best after all . . . I trust you more than anyone to give an honest opinion."

"You flatter me," Abraham tells him, "but let's see if we cannot keep it from coming to that."

FROM the way the house has been described to him, now that he's beneath its roof, he expects it to try its worst to send him fleeing. To spit at him like a cobra, to turn him as blind as Goya was deaf. Instead, for the first day, and the next, and the next, the house seems content to merely contain him at the heart of its conundrum.

Not that he lives here—he has the hotel for his bed, and all of Madrid for meals. It's just that he cannot stay away.

Upstairs, downstairs, eight walls, fourteen paintings. The house has no need to use tricks, to peel its inhuman apparitions from the walls and send them after him with grotesque faces and savage appetites. No, it's craftier than that. It waits for him to drag a wooden chair from one vantage point to another and let the murals become what they will—windows, some of them, and others mirrors.

Downstairs, on the back wall, one of only two paintings based on a traditional theme: the Titan Saturn, god of melancholy, panicked by prophecy that a son will overthrow him, and caught in the act of eating one of them alive. Abraham has seen the myth depicted before, but never with such savagery. Goya's Saturn is an angular brute, eyes bulging in mad fury and his hair a ragged gray mass. His hands squeeze a pitifully small man who dangles lifeless, the stump of his neck and one shoulder gnawed to raw meat while the other arm disappears into a blood-blackened maw.

Is it fair, Abraham wonders, that some fathers have so many children while others have none left? Is it fair that some fathers can slaughter sons out of convenience while others are condemned to watch their one and only sicken and wither and die? That one father feels his son's blood on his chin while fate laughs at another's failed efforts to save the boy's life?

So many years gone by, and still: *Did I do all that I could for him?*

Next to Saturn is the other painting that bows to tradition: the widow Judith of ancient Israel. She brandishes a large knife as she prepares to behead the enemy of her people, the Assyrian general Holofernes. He sleeps, trusting and unaware; this is their third night together.

Is it fair, then, that so far from home, a husband can encounter such vivid reminders of his wife and the ravaged state of her mind?

So many years gone by, and still: *Did I not do enough for her?*

He visits them all, each vision and vista, and listens to them lament and wail in voices loud enough that even a deaf man could have heard.

At least one Dutchman, too.

"You immortalized hundreds," he tells Goya, across the decades. For this was a man who could paint children and devils, kings and crones, flirtation and insanity, wars and bullfights and pastorals . . . all with equal veracity. In rendering likenesses he illuminated souls. He painted them so well their beauty—or their bitterness—would endure long past the day their bodies turned to dust.

"And I've saved the lives of at least as many—even better, jah? I delayed their return to dust. We both were called by noble professions."

Something he's told his students a thousand times.

"So how is it that such noble men could fail the ones closest to them?"

He puts more questions to the walls; quietly at first, then shouting them in a rage that blows through him like a storm, only to leave in its wake an awkward shame. The house soaks it up, down to the last faint echo, as if to ask him how he expects to bring peace to this place if he has so little in his own soul.

THE Baron has returned for the time being to Brussels, but with only one of his secretaries. The other remains behind, to continue the search for a living link to Goya. After Abraham's first few days roaming to and from *La Quinta*, the man leaves a letter for him at the hotel.

My dear Professor Van Helsing,

I believe, after conducting a considerable number of interviews, over a period of time whose duration long precedes your arrival here, that I have at last discovered a claimant whose professed acquaintance with the Spanish artist Francisco José de Goya y Lucientes appears to be of legitimate merit.

He has in his possession an aged sketch of himself, as a much younger man of course, whose style bears a strong resemblance to that of Goya. I have made a painstaking examination of the signature and am convinced that it is genuine.

His name is Gaspar Zárate, and I have taken the liberty of arranging a meeting for you at your hotel tomorrow afternoon at 2:00 o'clock.

I beg your apologies that I am not able to send to you someone of greater note, as he is a quite small fellow who can have been of no distinction in the artist's life, or in the social order of the day. But perhaps in your inquiry you may find certain anecdotal items of use.

A punctual man, Gaspar Zárate arrives before the two peals of the nearest church bells have faded. Abraham meets him in the courtyard, the floors and iron balconies of the hotel rising around them. There is no breeze here, but it's shaded and cool, made even more pleasant by the jungle of plants bursting from thick clay pots and from rings of earth where the courtyard's blue and amber tiles were never laid. The air smells of onions and olive oil and, somewhere too close, a sluggish drain.

If anything, the Baron's secretary was guilty of understatement. Gaspar Zárate is not just a small fellow—he's a dwarf, around four feet tall, with a forehead that looks too broad for the crinkled little face beneath it. His hair remains thick but unruly, a piebald mix of white and gray.

"Yes, I knew Goya," he says. "But only in his last few years alive. Not here. In Bordeaux. He was ten years older than I am now when he moved there!"

In a hand as brown as a nut, Gaspar clutches a walking stick, and appears to need it, but when he clambers into the chair that Abraham has pulled close for him, he's nimble for someone nearing seventy.

"Some would say he went there to die," Gaspar says, "and it *was* a better place to die than here in those days. But I say he went there to live."

Abraham asks about the drawing.

"You don't believe me? Again, I have to prove myself to some pale, giant man who talks funny?"

"No, I believe you," Abraham says. "I just want to see his work."

"I should start charging coins for this," Gaspar says. He reaches into a pocket of his threadbare jacket and draws out a yellowed paper folded into quarters. As he unfolds it with great tenderness, Abraham realizes it may well be the only likeness of himself that Gaspar owns. When he hands it over, he does so with such an imploring look to treat it with care that Abraham feels compelled to give his hand a reassuring pat.

Abraham lets the opened drawing rest upon his fingertips. It's a peculiar thing, but full of whimsy, the thick paper marked with strokes from the kind of greasy black crayon that Cubells, at the Prado, said Goya liked to use for his everyday sketches while strolling in Bordeaux. That it's a much younger Gaspar is clear; the face is almost a boy's, but with the same sad frontal bulge of his brow. He's raising his arms in triumph, his mouthful of square teeth wide with the smile of a champion. Far stranger, though, one foot stamps down to crush the head of an enormous snake. It's a bizarre use of iconography—the Virgin Mary has been depicted doing the same in countless paintings—yet unmistakably playful.

Abraham feels his heart lighten. Imagine . . . producing such levity after years spent living with the grimmest visions any man ever pulled from his soul.

He raises his gaze to Gaspar, inviting him to explain.

"Goya went to France to live; I went to work," Gaspar says. "The Olympic Circus, Polito's Grand Menagerie . . . the greatest spectacles you could ever hope to see. It was a better life than I could've had for myself here, I'll tell you. Goya loved the circus. And he loved to watch *me*."

"You worked with snakes?"

"No, no. That snake there belonged to an African fellow. He had some big ones, too, made women faint sometimes. No, I was an acrobat. And," he says with pride and mischief, "I performed with a *petomane* quartet."

Abraham nods. He should probably know what this is, but doesn't. Worse, he's afraid it shows.

"We farted. At will," Gaspar explains. "We could even play tunes. They were all big men, the rest of them. I was littlest. They called me 'The Piccolo.'"

Abraham can't remember the last time he laughed with such delight. "And can you, still . . . ?"

"You shame one of us, sir, but I don't know if it's me or yourself." Gaspar rolls his eyes. "Who wants to hear an old man fart?"

Abraham grins, then nods at the paper. "You bested the snake, then . . . ?"

Gaspar sits very still, staring past his dangling feet toward the tiles.

"I never bested anything," he says, quietly now. "There were some men from the audience one afternoon. They caught me alone. They thought it would be funny to take me to the snake wagon, between the reptile shows, and feed me to the boa. They laughed more then than they did during our performance. 'Here's your little piglet,' they kept telling it. 'See how he squirms and squeals!' The snake wasn't interested, but . . ." Gaspar does not look up. The memory seems like a scab that has never mended. "My friend Francisco stopped them. He hit two of them with his cane."

"A brave man," Abraham says, "especially for one so aged."

"Well, I suppose by then, after the war, he had seen enough of what men do to others when they think no one is around to stop them." Gaspar rolls his shoulders. "They probably would've fed Francisco to the python, but then the African came running. He wasn't nearly so gentle with them as Francisco was."

Gaspar wills up a smile, as if to exile the memory. Abraham looks at the drawing one last time; there's nothing more to ask about it. He's already known that Goya continued to work the whole time he was in France, as feverishly as ever, until the last two weeks of his life. Portraits, as always. Lithographs of bulls. A French milkmaid so reposed one could almost hear her thoughts. He knows that. Yet he finds it so heartening to learn that the man who painted the walls of *La Quinta* could later do this simple sketch of a smiling dwarf crushing a snake.

If you could know such lightness after such despair, he tells the artist, *then there must be hope for all of us who confront what God seems to have forsaken.*

He places the drawing into Gaspar's hands, where it's folded as carefully as a flag, then returned to his pocket.

LATER he takes Gaspar out past the city, to the house. Gaspar shuffles from painting to painting, looking them up and down, although less like a visitor to a museum than someone finally meeting acquaintances he has only heard about.

"Not that I'm displeased to see them," he says, "but why do you show these to me?"

"I know you didn't meet Goya until after these were painted and left behind . . . but did he ever tell you anything of his life here? Or about the paintings themselves?"

"The man is fifty years dead, almost, what does it matter?" Gaspar raps his walking stick on the floor as sharply as if he were planting a flag. "Do you ask for yourself, or for someone else . . . that snobby man who found me?"

Abraham tells him about the Baron, how he's bought the house and intends to peel the paintings from the walls. He tells Gaspar nothing of what happened when they first attempted this.

"And what does he want with them then?"

"To exhibit them. To show them as any painting should be shown, when done with such"—Abraham glances at the forlorn dog staring into his mottled void—"skill and power."

"If Francisco meant for them to be seen, don't you think he would've put them on a canvas? He didn't *have* to paint on his walls, you know. He could afford canvases. My friend was a wealthy man. If he chose to paint these on the walls, then they should *stay* on the walls."

"They won't last here, Gaspar. The river . . . she decays them a little more each passing year. Would you rather see them crumble? Would you rather see them lost?"

Gaspar leans heavily upon his stick and does not answer while staring at the floor. When he looks up again, he's on the move, stumping forward and brushing past Abraham on his way to the stairs.

"I'll tell you what I do know," he says, trusting that Abraham is following close behind. "The Goya I knew was more like a child again than any man I ever met. Not like his mind was gone—I mean *free* like a child, before the world expects anything of him. He left his home and his country and all the people who'd made him rich out of their own vanity, and he went to a place were nobody expected anything of him. Almost eighty years old and he couldn't taste enough of the world again. He maybe didn't walk as fast as he used to . . . but he still moved like a man who'd left a terrible weight behind."

They're downstairs now, near the front door, flanked by the house's master and mistress from five decades past—Leocadia on one side, Goya's long-bearded proxy on the other. Gaspar pauses to stare at it in farewell, and the demonic visage that bellows into the old man's ear.

"Of course he painted the things he did," Gaspar says, and bustles out the door. "What choice did he have?"

OVER the next few days they wander Madrid together. He's lodged in the city before, seen plenty of it, but with Gaspar's help he's looking at it with new eyes, seeing details he always overlooked before.

It is the ghost of Goya's Madrid: Here, bullet scars in a wall that's never been repaired; there, a plaza whose air weighs heavy with memories of blood and bayonets; and there, a church bell that tolled to mourn the dead in their rotting heaps—everywhere, echoes of executions and uprisings, the revenants of grief and rage.

Gaspar seems to remember it all, even though Abraham calculates he would have been just two or three years old when Napoleon's armies first seized Spain. His first recollections undoubtedly must be of war, as terrible a war as has ever been fought, years of slaughter and starvation and atrocities . . . on all sides.

They seem so far away from it now, these people in the streets and cafés of Madrid—the proud men with their confident swaggers, the colorful women with their dark flashing eyes, the priests in somber black—and they *are* far from it. For most, it was their parents' and grandparents' war.

But it could happen again, and Goya dared to know it.

The sleep of reason produces monsters, he once captioned an etching, and for this alone Abraham has come to love him.

He feels that he knows the man better now: Goya, haunted by the specters of war and famine, humbled by illnesses and the theft of his hearing, more than once turning from commissioned portraits to use his brushes as his way of shrieking . . . his only defense against the world permitted by the same aristocracy who'd made him rich.

Half a century later Abraham can hear the screams. He and Gaspar may tour Madrid by day . . . but at night he leaves the city to stare once more at the walls.

So what *had* happened at *La Quinta?* Had Goya poured so much despair into its plaster that, after he'd left it behind like an amputated limb, it had festered? Or had some even grimmer business been undertaken?

"That house has a hold on you, I can tell," Gaspar says. "You think of his money and talents and fame . . . and then you see those walls. Are you thinking he was a Faust, maybe? That he made a wicked bargain somewhere along the way?"

They've stopped for the afternoon at a café, out of the heat and the dust, to rest their sore feet. If Gaspar notices the grins and glances from men who pass by the table, puffing themselves up to look larger still beside him, he doesn't show it. Perhaps after so many years, he is blind to them.

Abraham shakes his head. "No, my friend, I don't. I've talked to men who've been accused of it, to other men who freely swore they had . . . but every time, I could find no evidence that devils had answered any such invitation. I think devils take what they can, and leave the contracts to lawyers."

He's drinking absinthe this afternoon, the French way, poured over a sugar cube and into water to leaven the bitterness of the wormwood. It's a tonic that he sometimes permits himself, like a decoction he might brew for a patient. The slow, deliberate ritual of preparing it is intoxicating in itself.

Gaspar sighs as he gazes out the window to the street, the passing women. "He bought me a prostitute once. In Bordeaux. Now that was an act of true friendship."

"I suppose," Abraham says, "that would depend on the whore, jah?"

"But you wonder why Francisco would do such a thing for me, don't you? Why he would tell me anything. Not just me, but *anyone* like me. Don't you?"

Abraham doesn't want to be cruel . . . but yes, he's wondered. The Goya he was told of at the Prado was an ambitious man who didn't shy away from affectations to enhance his stature in society. In such a world, a dwarf was more apt to be a pet than a friend. But, for all that, men change as they stoop and slow.

"Well, even I don't know, really," Gaspar says. "He said I reminded him of one of the other happiest times of his life—not long after he went deaf, when he left his family behind and took up with that Duchess. She was his benefactor for a time, and he loved her, I think . . . before she tired of him, the same as she tired of any man except for the next one." Gaspar rubs the smooth round top of his walking stick. "She kept a man like me. She named him Love." Idly, he now reaches with the stick to tap at the toes of his shoes. "But I think Francisco maybe needed someone to tell things he couldn't even tell the canvas. He knew I'd be safer than most—who would think to ask me?"

"Or perhaps," Abraham muses, "if he had any such things to say, he told them to a friend he knew would always remember, in case someone *did* think to ask."

Gaspar smiles at the thought . . . then frowns. "Those paintings on the walls? He talked of them only once . . . but for a long time. I think he was afraid of them. When he finally seemed ready to say something about *why* he painted them, he stopped. He told me to be glad of my size, that I would be too small to see, maybe. 'Who by?' I asked. He thought awhile, then he just said what a terrible thing it is for a man when the universe notices him. That most go unnoticed, but when it happens, no good can come of it . . . because it is unkind, and will try to destroy that man and his world around him.

"You spoke of devils, and Francisco painted them . . . except I don't think he believed in them anymore. I think he believed in something worse, and hoped he had escaped from it. But whatever it had to do with the paintings, he wouldn't say."

This explains much.

And nothing.

And Abraham suspects that this unlikely confessor has nothing else to tell about the paintings. A pity; he's enjoyed Gaspar's company.

Gaspar seems to sense it too. "Hey!" he cries. "We should go to the bullfights tomorrow! He loved the bullfights. You can't really know Goya unless you've gone to the bullfights."

MUCH later, after the moon is a high icy sliver, he again finds himself back at *La Quinta del Sordo*. His first absinthe, hours earlier, has not been his last. He's known of poets in France who celebrate its derangement of the senses, and maybe that's what he needs now. This house is no place of science, or reason . . . and now, listening to the green whispers of each glass he drank, he wonders if it isn't a place entirely forgotten by God.

A single lantern in his hand, he's surrounded by black—the black of night, the black of the paintings, the black of their themes.

Beside the door, the weariest old man who ever lived leans on his cane, his eyes closed and wearing an expression that could be surrender, or that of a last long flight into dreams. At his ear looms the subhuman face, with its bulbous nose and bellowing mouth, pressing so close the old man must feel the warm mouldy reek of his breath.

Abraham whirls, sure that he feels it on his own neck.

But the house is silent, empty of life.

"I know your secret now," he tells Goya, in a cracked tone that carries far less authority than he would like. "I know what you feared above all. Because I have always feared it too."

And the house is silent, yet full of purpose.

His eyes return to the face on the wall, the horrid muse and all it represents. It is the face of chaos itself . . . that terrible void from which God yanked the world, and into which the world seems so eager to return.

What doctor would not fear such an enemy, once he has acknowledged its power? He's seen it in the growths he's cut from people, which return again and again. He's seen it in the strength of madmen, madwomen; in diseases of the body and disorders of the brain. Its hurricane winds blow armies into war; its softest breaths urge men to feed dwarves to snakes. It steals senses. It destroys innocent sons while robbing fathers of the power to save them.

And it was here, he is certain, that Goya made his stand against it.

Abraham remembers his first impression of these darkened rooms . . . how they reminded him of caves, and the men who decorated their walls with the likenesses of animals. He has heard a theory that these primitives did so out of superstition, to control and appease the beasts they hunted, or that hunted them.

But tonight, at least, he can believe that men and women of all epochs show wisdom, in their way. And he longs for the miracle of five minutes with Goya, so he might ask: *Could* the chaotic forces that put their designs upon a man be appeased, bargained with, if he dredges up enough bitterness and desolation from the chaos of his own soul, and makes of them an offering?

In the flickers of the lantern, he imagines that the lone visible eye of the ugly head blinks . . . languidly, as if in contemplation. His hand darts out to touch the wall and feels only old paint, old plaster.

But the house is no longer silent. From the floor overhead comes the sound of blows, cudgels splitting flesh and breaking bone, and the grunts upon impact. They're soon drowned out by a greater cacophony, a multitude of shuffling and stomping feet, madmen on pilgrimage braying homage in a groundswell of discordant voices.

Abraham imagines it must be the sound of chaos laughing.

He cannot fight this. He wouldn't know where to begin.

But he *can* tell the Baron the place might best be burnt after all.

The pandemonium fades as he hurries away, turning his back for good on the far end of the room, where Saturn squeezes his son in rending hands. The house sends him into the night with a final gale of mockery: the sounds of teeth and lips and tender, tearing skin.

"It's a spectacle worthy of the circus . . . *almost*," Gaspar told him before they reached the bullfight arena, and indeed it is, wilder than anything Abraham expected.

There isn't nearly as much division between the audience and the *toreros* as he thought, men and boys constantly clambering over the wooden barricade to drop into the ring and play a part in the show, taunting and harassing the bulls, then springing from their path. Some escape unscathed, scrambling back into the stands to celebrate with a wineskin. Others are slammed aside by glancing blows from the massive bodies, but injuries are minor.

The bulls, for their part, seem so maddened that they can't decide which way to lunge, and when the *toreros* finally go to work, it's an ugly, brutal business. The bulls race around the edges of their jail, hooves kicking up sprays of sand, and, finding no escape, let themselves be drawn into the macabre dance of hooked horns and flashing cape and saber, until the fight and life are bled out of them. The cheers rise on a tide of cigar smoke and sweat, and while the *torero* basks in the roar, a team of mules is driven in to haul the carcass away, and the sand is raked smooth again.

Gaspar shouts and applauds with the rest. When he slaps Abraham on the shoulder and laughs, Van Helsing sees that he can't conceive of anyone failing to enjoy this. Yet, as with all terrible things that pass before his eyes, Abraham has trouble looking away. His heart is repulsed while his eyes continue to stare. His spirit sinks while his mind hungers for understanding.

He finds little mystery in why they all would find raucous comfort in watching lithe, graceful men vanquish such unbridled ferocity. He just thinks they and their champions are battling the wrong enemy.

"Francisco said he fought bulls when he was very young," Gaspar says during a lull. "Before anyone cared about his art."

"Is it true?"

"I don't know. But if he didn't, he should have."

The tiered stands thicken with more and more people, and the crowd pushes toward the center, late arrivals as well as those from the upper benches surging down for a closer look. Gaspar sputters with indignation and latches onto Abraham's sleeve, tugging him toward the barricades and demanding a perch upon his shoulders. He stoops, reluctantly; he's straddled by the thick little legs, then straightens. The jostling shoulders press them close enough to the barricade for splinters.

In the ring, a trio of fresh bulls has burst through the gate, driven by men on horseback and inciting a renewed free-for-all. They snort and paw at the ground while dozens spill over the barricade; a few strip off their shirts to whirl them like capes. A dismayed groan goes up when a man, too slow, is thrown by one bull, then trampled by another. The people want vengeance now—Abraham feels it crashing over the crowd like a tide, and all around him fists are waving and faces are contorting into hardened masks.

He should never have come here—he knows this now. Because chaos and the mob are indivisible.

Abruptly, the weight slides from his shoulders. At first he thinks Gaspar must have slipped. Abraham turns, ready to lift him to his feet again. But there is no Gaspar, neither left nor right nor behind him. The truth is clear even before the crowd ripples with laughter: Someone has plucked Gaspar off his back.

Abraham catches sight of him twenty-odd feet away, borne high by hands that ignore his flailing arms, his kicking legs, and pass him over the barricade. In the ring, a laughing man grabs him by a wrist and an ankle, then turns toward the nearest bull.

In the fever of the moment, he must seem to weigh little more than a cape.

Abraham knows he's shouting, can see Gaspar's mouth, but cannot hear him over the crowd. Abraham is shouting too, and can scarcely hear himself. He struggles along the edge of the barricade, battered by elbows and shoulders, chins and spittle, until he can no longer move, nor even breathe, the suffocating weight of them all bearing down like an avalanche.

With a crack like the splitting of an oak, the barricade gives way, and dozens of them go tumbling into the sand and onto the shards of wall. His senses are gone, crushed beneath a riot of feet and panic, but he struggles upright, getting as far as his knees before the smell of human sweat gives way before a thick animal odor that wafts in, enveloping as a fog.

He lifts his gaze into another pair of eyes, just inches before him. From behind the broad snout, they stare back, black and full of will and, he swears, recognition.

What a terrible thing it is for a man when the universe notices him.

He thought he had been noticed before. But no.

He has never felt so noticed in his life as now.

"You took my son," he whispers. "You took my wife's mind. Is your greed so great as this?"

He never knew that anything so quick could feel so slow, the horn punching into his side as if slipped in with care to find the perfect excruciating fit. The great black head shakes, then snorts a gust of breath so hot it's scalding.

It withdraws and lets him collapse backward, to stare up at the long face and wet nostrils and the mad ecstatic eyes that first roll, then find him again and hold a level gaze, the snout straining toward his ear, shaping itself into a dark cavernous mouth that seems about to bellow with words that only he will understand. . . .

And might have, if not for the spear that the horseman drives down from above, shearing through the side of the thick muscled neck to release a cascade of blood that showers across him from face to belly.

As it runs down his chin, he cannot help but think of his son and all the failures that seem too great to ever find atonement.

Abraham, my dear friend,

Forgive the tardiness of this letter, as it has only been in recent days that I have learned you have made great strides in your recovery, and so I wish your convalescence continued haste. They may have told you that I looked in upon you personally the week after your grievous wounding, although you may not remember this, for the fevers had rendered you quite insensible, and when you moved, you did so as a man encumbered by a great weight.

I also wish to extend my deepest thanks for your contribution to my project at the House of the Deaf Man. I look forward to the day when you can enlighten me as to what you have done there, for we are plagued by no more maleficence. The removal and restoration have begun at an encouraging pace, and Mr. Salvador Cubells is a man of great abilities.

He has shared with me a tale I must relay to you. It holds that a ser-

vant of Goya's once asked him, "Why do you paint these barbarities that men commit?" to which he replied, "To tell men forever that they should not be barbarians." Whether true or not, I cannot say, but it is the spirit of this response that informs my intention to display the paintings, when ready, at the International Paris Exhibition, where I am convinced they will enjoy the long-overdue reception they deserve.

It is not too soon, I think, to look ahead to the promise of the coming century, and rise to our obligations as men of reason and compassion to do our utmost to lift our civilization above the barbarities of this present century.

It is my great hope that such works as we have rescued will play a part in such a golden age.

Yours in greatest appreciation,
Baron Frederic Emile d'Erlanger

Empty Morning

STEVE RASNIC TEM AND MELANIE TEM

✠

ALL EVENING, BEFORE she stood up and found her balance and began a slow journey across the small room made to seem smaller by multicolored smoke and by the impression of many bodies not entirely visible, before she stalked him and called out his name, she had been watching him. Through the opium haze so dense it did not drift but pulsed, pooled, coagulated, she had traced and traced again his features, his profile, the outline and contours of his head and shoulders and arms, the occasional glimmer of his hands on pipe or glass.

Having wizened considerably, he could no longer be said to be of medium weight and strongly built. His head, though, was still noble, large behind the ears in the shape currently imagined to indicate superior intelligence. His nose, when she caught it in profile, was still straight, the two ridges at his hairline still prominent above bushy brows. Dim blue and violet lights had the intended effect of obscuring the true colors of objects they illumined, but she knew his hair would be gray now rather than red. His eyes would still be large, dark blue, set wide. She had looked into his eyes before, and would do so again, this time with very different purpose.

He sat hunched over his folded hands. He leaned back, rested his head against the pillowed edge of the chair, folded his hands across his abdomen. He looked up to exchange words with someone who paused beside him, then gazed distractedly after the figure as it went on.

He lifted the thin green glass, sipped, set it down, did not drink again for a long time. Others approached him, spoke, drifted away. She had watched him.

Through the fluted syrupy cylinder of her own glass, his silhouette had floated and blurred, emerging into transparency and then sinking once again into emerald murk. Having drained and replenished her drink far less often than he had, she was indeed inebriated. This establishment prided itself on serving only Swiss absinthe, the finest available; the far better and stronger liquors she had once known were now by her own choice lost to her. This was and forever would be the best she could do. With the help for which she had hunted him down, it could perhaps become enough.

An immense holiday was at hand, the turn of a century, but neither the measurement of time nor the celebration for which it provided excuse had relevance to her. She guessed, however, that it would mean something to him.

He was an old man, besotted by opium, absinthe, no doubt laudanum, no doubt memory and dread and all the other maladies she understood were associated with mortal aging. He would be weaker of body, mind, spirit than during their very brief encounter long ago and during the many years thereafter when she had followed him by reputation. But from the throbbing at the base of her belly when he glanced her way, she knew he would still kill her if he knew who she was. And she also knew he, he alone, could save her.

All but certain she recognized this man, she dared not trust what she knew, about this or anything else. "Who—is that?"

Her companion was a long-haired young man who spoke, moved, drank with such studied languor that his recurrent sexual overtures surprised her, and of whom she would soon divest herself though not with as much dispatch as she once would have done. Mistaking the object of her query to be the girl on a nearby chaise whose hair across her face and fingers around the pipe were themselves like smoke, he uttered a name as if it were an obscenity.

"No," she interrupted, suddenly very tired and very bored. "The man behind her, at the corner table, alone. The old man."

"Van Helsing." Supercilious and sure of himself, he quaffed the last of his absinthe, sighed and licked his lips, reached for her.

She pressed her fist into his chest. It was easy enough to keep him at bay without really hurting him, though under other circumstances and in another time she'd not have resisted the urge. "Abraham Van Helsing?" Her constricted throat had turned her voice husky.

"Yes." The young man caught her fist, brought it to his mouth, grazed her knuckles with his teeth in what she supposed he thought was a daring caress.

"The physician and metaphysician?" Blood coursed hot through her arteries and veins, pounded at her throat and wrists, reddened her vision, coppered her tongue. To be so close.

"And world-famous slayer of creatures vampiric." Thrusting her hand away from him, he stood, laughed, swayed. "What utter rubbish." The declaration was meant to be haughty, but he lost his balance and collapsed against the next table, spilling the liquor of the patrons and attracting the attention of those charged with maintaining the decorum of this place. A large man escorted him out. Blue and violet smoke instantly oozed into the place he had lately occupied.

Testing herself, she took time finishing her drink, smoked another pipe. Since her vow—an indefinite span, as was all time for her kind, though for humans it moved and had shape in ways she could only yearn for—she had tested herself on countless occasions, and had not always passed. Now, though quavering, she did hold firm.

At last, fortified as best she could be within the condition she had set for herself (blood was thick here for the taking, blood to satiate, blood to transport, but she would not take it, she would not), she thought to approach him. The smoky girl on the chaise cried out and flung her legs wide, skirt raised. The stalwart guardian of public propriety went to her, momentarily obscuring the view.

Van Helsing was gone from his table. Panicked, she rose, then saw him slowly making his way toward the door. He was the only hope she had of turning away from the thing she had been for so many years. She had little choice but to follow him.

SICK in stomach and head, unsteady on his feet, he stumbled as he left La Fee and reentered the teeming night. Almost immediately he was seized by the sharp cough that lately beset him in the London streets. A hack driver cursed at him, the horses kicking rubble against his shins. A street urchin screeched in his general direction for tuppence, and dropped into his hand a filthy apple he knew better than to eat but absently ate anyway. His head ached, and he noted his hands shook more than usual.

He noted also, and not without a certain sad amusement, that the malaise and despondency which had brought him into La Fee had been deepened by his time there. This was nearly always the case, and yet he went there nearly every night, a typical addictive pattern. As he steadied himself against a grimy wall before turning the first of the three corners between the opium den and his flat, he mused that, for a man of science in all its forms, he had become decidedly irrational.

Once he'd believed the turn of the century would herald the dawning of a cleaner, more scientific era. But now approaching his dodderage, and mere weeks away from that most anticipated event, he saw little evidence of it. England was at war once again, this time with the Boers. The summer had seen the death of his beloved Strauss. And if anything these streets were darker, dirtier, more chaotic. He would not be surprised if the Ripper himself returned. He would not be surprised if Dracula himself returned from the dead.

"Sir? Kind sir?" A woman hailed him from behind. Irrationally, he turned. Heavy perfumes did no more to mask her other unsavory odors than did layers of rags to disguise her gauntness and filth. Even in the near-darkness her trembling was evident. He knew her for yet another harlot desperate to feed the very habit he himself was well on his way to acquiring.

Searching a pocket and then another, he grew light-headed, and his vision blurred a sickly version of absinthe's emerald. Needing both hands now to support himself, scraping his palms on rumpled brick, he shook his head and turned his face away from her.

But she came closer and said his name. "Dr. Abraham Van Helsing." It was not a query.

Drawing in his breath caused him to cough again. "Yes, yes, I am Van Helsing. What do you want with me?" Being thus recognized in public had become increasingly rare; he was both grateful and disappointed.

"My name is—"

He thought she hesitated, although the various substances he had taken into his body this evening and many previous evenings had the attraction of making perception unreliable.

"—Katherine Harker." Another hesitation, as if she expected some response. "We have met."

The surname was familiar but not uncommon, and he discerned no physical resemblance to the Harker he had once known. Doing his best to be, if not quite gallant, at least polite, he reached to tip his hat and discovered it not on his head. Perhaps he had not worn it, or perhaps he had left it at his table where another patron might find and wear or discard it. "Please," he said, "forgive the memory of an old man."

"It was a long time past and a very brief encounter," she said, "and not under the most favorable of circumstances. But it changed my life." She gave a harsh laugh. "More accurately, it caused me to want to change my life."

Social protocol dictated he inquire as to the particulars, and he wished not to be impolite, even to creatures as unwholesome as she. But a wave of sickness overcame him. He swayed. When she caught and held him, he saw her more closely.

No taller than his shoulder, and he was not a tall man, she had dark greasy hair and dark complicated eyes shadowed by dense lashes. Her cheekbones made high cliffs, her lips were cracked and slightly parted, her teeth broken. By nature she might be beautiful, but obviously her current situation was extreme. Her hands shook where they clutched his arms.

"Miss Harker." Saying the name, he suddenly felt as if he could have known her very well. "How nice to see you again."

THE doddering old fool did not know who she was, nor did he care. Although using the name Harker had been a risky self-indulgence, she need not have worried; clearly, he was well past his heroic prime. But she knew of no one else who could turn her into what she longed to be.

Again he stumbled and she caught him, then pushed him away, afraid of her own instincts, afraid of what he might smell on her though she thought she remembered the Master scoffing at human olfactory capacity. Van Helsing looked like a man pondering whether he had wandered abroad in his nightshirt; the image was not as amusing as it might once have been.

"Pleasant to see you as well, sir," she mumbled, glancing about. When a man grinned and beckoned, she took ridiculous offense.

"You ought to be escorted," Van Helsing slurred into her ear. "All manner of rough creatures about. Believe me, I am versed in such things."

Revulsion flooded her throat, belly, groin. The Master had talked like that. "I love you," the Master would whisper or snarl through endless nights of food displayed and denied, through long hours hiding from the daylight, when the hunger he induced in his countless brides kept them awake and nearly drove them altogether out of the dark. "You, most beautiful and most hungry. All manner of creatures are abroad in the night and day. Such as this one, my darling!" flinging bones of cattle or wild dogs and making his arousal clearly visible as the chosen bride scrambled to mine for the little blood still in the marrow.

Often his favorite and his favorite victim, she had at his leering behest more than once trawled like a pig the bloody waste pits behind hospitals for sustenance and, indeed, for pleasure. His and her own. She could taste it now. She could taste it. She bent her head to the old man's neck.

Rather more easily than she would have expected, he extricated himself from what had become almost an embrace as though he knew already what she would beg of him. He still slurred, however, and shambled as he took a step or two away from her. "The night does have its appeal, though, does it not, my dear?"

Was the most honorable Abraham Van Helsing making a dishonorable suggestion? Nearly as weak now with memory and unholy desire as this weak old enemy she desperately needed, she nonetheless caught up with him in a single stride and in the light from a grimy streetlamp examined his face for intention. He looked wasted and ill; she detected no lechery in him, only relief, bafflement, despair. Her fate was in the hands of a baffled, despairing old man.

He was still talking, perhaps not to her. "A woman should not be left to manage the darkness alone. I would rush the night's passage myself if I did not feel such emptiness in the mornings."

"Ah, the mornings," she agreed. "I manage the nights better, too."

A passing hack driver cut his horse with the whip, and although the animal reacted not at all, she nearly swooned to the quick odor of its blood. And to the odor of human blood as well; perhaps the tip of the whip had flicked the driver's forearm, or perhaps she was smelling Van Helsing's blood through thin flesh and vein, a thought she dared not long entertain.

Since the Master's blessed, cursed murder, she had managed a base survival with small meals of rats and bird hearts, once or twice an addict with blood so diluted it was almost not blood, the occasional newborn and its afterbirth, the occasional child weakened by disease. Hunger had made her delirious, and out of that delirium had come yearning for life without the sickness. The blood fever had distorted all memory of her life before the Master had come to her, but what she remembered, what she must have again, surely was better than this. Eventually out of her desperation had come: *Be like him. Be like the destroyer, the only one in the world more powerful than the Master.* She had not since tasted live blood.

Scurrying at the base of a building. Blood, blood everywhere, and the terrible need. The need to eat. The need to keep her vow. The need.

Van Helsing turned into an alley. She followed him.

THE woman seized his face and brought it close to her own to stare at him. Van Helsing shuddered, reminded not only of the madness of his own late beloved wife but also of a butcher appraising a cow. Vehemently she whispered, "I require your assistance, Dr. Van Helsing. Your protection, if you will."

Too tired and inebriated to articulate a refusal, he shrugged and went on. When he missed the grimy doorway to his building, he turned back abruptly and they collided. He felt the surging desperation of her, the decadent ardor. She seemed remarkably strong for a woman, especially a woman in such straits. No doubt she was dangerous. But perhaps for once he would not be alone in the morning, not quite so empty.

At some point on the many stairs up to his flat, he realized she was supporting him with a hand at the small of his back, and he asked himself who was protecting whom. But when she gasped at the rat bright-eyed and –fanged on the landing, he put himself between her and the vermin. He had seen much worse.

Dimly he recalled she had more than once spoken his name, so perhaps she knew who he had been. Dimly he recalled that the name she had given him for herself—he doubted it was truly her name—had meant something to him, suggested something, but it eluded him and he made no effort to chase it down.

The gray cat that now and again shared his flat—which sometimes he indulged himself by thinking of as Fee Verte for its liquid green eyes—hissed and put its back up as they entered. Van Helsing had received aloofness from this scrawny creature as often as affection, but he had not before been the target of its hostility, and he wondered at it. Behind him, she gave a small cry. Pitying what he took to be unreasonable fear, he shielded her from the cat as he held the door open for it to slink out into the stairwell, perhaps to dispatch or be dispatched by the huge rodent gnawing there.

Uninvited, she settled herself onto the settee his wife had, in her calmer moments, so enjoyed for its prim elegance. It was slovenly now and unsteady. He made a vague, belated motion of hospitality, then realized the disorder that had overtaken his living quarters, as if a tide of filth and misery had seeped in under the door, spread and ruined everything. Papers lay scattered like ashes, books sprawled half-devoured. Stench rose from soiled plates and utensils, rotting meat and soured milk and moldy bread and fruit nearer liquid than solid, clumps of stiffened and odoriferous clothing, spilled and long-unemptied chamber pots. He should be ashamed.

He should offer her refreshment, could not think what food or drink he had that would be fit to consume. He should offer her a place to sleep, his own bed the only choice and he would spread a blanket on the splintery floor. He should ask her again for her name. Green smoky unconsciousness overcame him, and he was dimly aware of falling.

SOMEONE laughed outside the battered door, and she started. The hunger in her, tearing at her brain like insects in a feeding frenzy, sometimes made her hear things. Sometimes she felt pursued, and when she was aware enough to know that nothing pursued her but what had taken life inside herself, she was not soothed. Men shouted and cursed in the noisy street below. Church chimes announced the eleventh hour. The despair of the night was young, and, worse, the hope.

Stiffly crumpled at her feet, Van Helsing could not truly be regarded as sleeping, able to be awakened by pleas or threats or by any sort of touch. She considered touching him. She considered kneeling beside him, lying upon him, touching him with open mouth and tongue and then with teeth.

She must move quickly away from him, but her strength was insufficient; she shuffled as far as the confines of the flat allowed. He was her only hope, small and despairing as it was. More than any other creature not like herself, he knew about creatures like herself. He had studied. He had come close. He had destroyed the Master. He could destroy her. She had allowed herself the fancy that he could also save her, teach her how to change her essential nature or at least bear witness while she did so herself. Turn her.

The journey to London had taken a heavy toll, but she had maintained her vow along the way, keeping her distance from villagers and shopkeepers, able to imagine their veins filled with substances other than blood, minimally sustaining herself with raw meat pilfered through unfastened kitchen doors and buried rags from women's monthly bleeding she smelled and unearthed and forced herself to suck. She had heard he was in London and had developed a mighty opium-laudanum-absinthe habit. But once in the immense, crowded, odoriferous, clamorous city, she had been baffled by the search. This evening's serendipity had been a long time coming, and had cost her dearly.

Now here she was, and here he was, and he was unavailable to her. He well might sleep through the night, and the first light of day—even the gritty, overcast, nearly sunless light of London in winter—would cause her further anguish. She would have to find some corner to cower in, and cover herself against the sun's direct and accusing gaze.

She kicked him. He groaned and twitched his shoulder. She hissed his name, shrieked it. He stirred. He began to retch and she stooped to turn his head so his own vomitus would not choke him, thinking she might vomit herself, wondering as she watched the noxious puddle sink into the floor whether there might be anything in it for her. When he seemed to have finished, she wiped his mouth with the end of his own rumpled shirt and sat back away from him. He sank into oblivion again.

Something scratched at the door. She nearly lost her balance as she scrambled to her feet. The scratching came again. She opened the door. Instantly the scrawny gray cat sped past her yowling, claws raking her ankle. The roiling of its small reservoir of blood made her tongue swell. She did not see where in the flat it hid itself, but it would not be difficult to find. Its odor pulsed. She shut the door carefully and turned back into the room.

THAT night Van Helsing's opium dreams were convoluted tales of intrigue and adventure, loss and mourning, evil and great good and the vast territory between. They gave the illusion of meaning. Mostly, they were deep green. Mostly, he was alone.

He emerged to find himself choking on bile, hands turning his head so that his neck seemed in jeopardy, foul breath in his own foul face.

He emerged to the sensation that his flat was underwater, under blood, detritus from his life floating in the viscous fluid.

He emerged to the instantly clear sight of the woman who had called herself Katherine Harker. Crouching near to him, she held the green-

eyed gray cat Fee Verte stretched long and flat across her indecently exposed thighs, its throat and belly slit wide. Her long teeth dripped.

He sank again, knowing it to be delirium. He had seen so much worse.

He awakened again, clutching the petrified claws of a woman whose
name he should know as well as his own, but try as he might he could not
bring it to his lips. Then he looked out to see it was the paw-like leg of a
chair he gripped from where he lay on the floor. His wife howled from her
crouch on the other side of the room, tongue out and mouth slavering, her
once sweet nature parodied in mad laughter.

He struggled to his feet. Surely he could summon sufficient will and
strength to stop what was happening to her, even if it meant beating the
demons from her body, driving them out of her heart with that symbol of
everything she'd once held sacred.

But he was falling. The gravity of all his failures tore him down.

"Van Helsing! Are you injured?"

Her hands were upon him, helping him to stand, the capable hands of
this good woman. But it was that poor woman he'd met out in the street.
What was her name? He wanted to say Harker but that couldn't be.

He saw the redness in her eyes, her gaze flitting away to the corner like
some winged thing, then back again, trying to force him to see only what
she wanted him to see. But he turned his head just enough to find the
gray fur pressed behind the curtain, the streaks of red visible even in the
clutter on the floor, and that crimson kiss on the back of the hand soothing his face.

He felt a moment of true sadness before realizing the death of his only
companion was not the most important implication of this gruesome discovery. He struck her across the face.

She howled. Her back pulled her upward until she was almost his
height, her eyes slitting as the skin of her face tightened.

But instead of attacking him she sprang backward. The shelves behind her splintered, book spines ripping and paper exploding into the air
as if a cage of birds had been let loose in the room. She threw herself over
the chair and into the small table by the window, knocking off his only
photograph of his wife. With a cry he reached for it, but it cracked the
window pane and fell.

"Demon!" he shouted, and scrambled toward the bed for the leather physician's bag he had not seen in months. He pawed frantically at the bed linen, threw garbage and sour garments behind him at the creature he'd invited in, hoping to delay her until he could once again feel the confidence of the spike in his hand and the power of the mallet that could send her back to Hell. For he knew now what she was. Expecting her on his back at any moment, teeth ripping out his throat, he found himself slowing, ready. More than ready.

SHE thrust her hand against her teeth, which instinctively bit down. Her own meat was tasteless and pale but she could not let go. Having come this far, having at last forced herself into his presence, she had been unable to deny herself a simple meal of his pet cat. She was lost. Meaning to call his name, she howled wordlessly around her own bloody flesh.

He was coming for her with mallet and blessed spike heavy in his hands. She wrenched her hand out of her teeth and crooned, "Van Helsing! Don't be shy, Van Helsing." He stopped. "Please!"

With tears in his eyes, he shook his head. "I cannot. I haven't the strength to raise the mallet anymore. It might as well weigh the world."

Diving into the garbage, sewage, wreckage in which he stood ankle-deep, she fed. He groaned but he stood by. With fingernails and teeth she tore out fibers of the threadbare rug, then bits of half-dissolved wood. There was blood in all of it. There was blood in everything. In him, too.

"Stop! Stop it, woman!" Lowering himself to his haunches and then to his knees, he stared her in the face. His broad forehead looked animalistic now. His mouth contorted. "Such a pitiable pair we are." He ripped his shirt down the front and pulled away his collar. "Drink if you must. I myself have drunk quite enough for one evening, and now self-pity inebriates me past enduring."

In the decimated and dingy little flat, a clean space of silence formed. The pair of them were alone in this place at the end of this human century, which would bring neither of them release. Street noise pulsed at the broken window but had little to do with them. Something cleared in her head: a memory of life before the Master. She had sat alone in a room above a street like this one, sat by a broken window letting too much of the cold in, her lover long gone and herself reduced to whoring. And then the Master had come. Despair, preceded only by despair.

"Would you," Van Helsing inquired pleasantly, "like a cup of tea?"

BY the time he had brewed their tea, set it in chipped china cups in a space he cleared with his elbow on the rickety table, tipped the trash off two flimsy chairs and dragged them into an arrangement simulating companionability, she had put the flat into a semblance of order. Having already rid it of much debris, she had only to set its remaining objects right and gather or conceal broken things she had no idea how to organize. In lamplight, presentability was easy to achieve; daybreak, even through the small sooted window, would make more noticeable the hidden things. Daybreak was not far off.

Shakily but with practiced elegance, he gave a small bow and held a chair for her. She nearly curtsied. Disheveled from their earlier exertions, both of them bearing stains of various external substances and bodily fluids not mentionable in polite company, they sat together politely, even comfortably, and sipped their tea. He did not wish for absinthe or opium. She granted no notice to the steady pulse of his blood.

When after a while he stood up, she thought he would leave her or order her away, and she felt a vast sorrow. Instead he leaned, with some difficulty, across the table to pry open the window. The cracked pane wobbled but did not fall out. The air that burst in was almost violent in its sweetness. Sitting down again, he swayed and she reached to hold his arm until he was settled, then eased herself back into her own chair and folded her swollen, shaking hands in her lap.

"A fine morning, my dear," he observed. When she said nothing, he continued, "Uncharacteristically clear and bright."

"Empty," she said.

But it was not yet empty. The sky was pale blue. The sun would very soon rise above gray and brown roofs. Light would stream between buildings and into the room. Then, the morning would be empty.

He was aware of what was happening before she was, although they had both expected it. He saw the first ray of sunshine fall across her tangled hair and set it on fire. He saw her fingertips begin to disintegrate, and then she felt the first pain. "My dear," he said sadly, but he did nothing to try to stop it, knowing he could not. He did not flinch or look away. For that, as long as she was aware of anything, she was grateful.

Fantasy Room

ADAM-TROY CASTRO

S OMETIMES I WISH I did not need to destroy you.

    I wish I could put the necessity aside like any other useless baggage, perhaps not forever, perhaps not even for long, but for an hour. I wish I could take that hour, remove it from the world of ticking clocks, and spend it in a meeting place large enough to contain you, and me, and all the unspoken questions we could only share in such a sanctuary. In such a place it would not matter to either of us that I must destroy you, or that you, given the opportunity, would do the same to me; it would not matter that I am a man and that you are something even worse. In such a place, Dracul, we could cease plotting against each other, and face each other, across a gulf no greater than the width of a drawing-room table: equals, each fully at ease in the other's presence, each content to entertain the questions of the other.

    I think of us together, in that room that does not exist, and in my fantasy we find ourselves dumbstruck by the ludicrousness of our respective positions. We spy each other for the first time and break into astonished, bemused smiles. We each know that this is just an intermission: that when we are freed from this box we will remain enemies until one or the other falls. But that does not bother us. The conflicts of the real world do not matter, here. All that matters, in this place of truce, is the opportunity to enjoy an hour of perfect candor.

Oh, my friend for one hour: the things I would ask!

I would ask you what it is like to see your death not as an inevitability lurking in your near future, but as a threshold crossed and conquered in your distant past.

I would ask you what it is like to experience history as not just a brief chapter, taken out of context, but as a great sprawling narrative, with threads that last decades or centuries, and themes that reverberate throughout entire ages. I would ask you what it was like to stand above the petty issues that afflict every age and follow the parade of history long enough to perceive its shape and form and the hidden drumbeat that gives it purpose.

I would ask you what it is like to stand in absolute darkness, with no stars above you and no cold capable of bothering you, and not feel the uncertainty that comes from fearing the presence of monsters: to know, instead, that you are the greatest of monsters, and that the shadows hide nothing more dangerous than yourself.

I would ask what it is like to regard a pristine young beauty and know that you can claim her absolute devotion, free of willfulness or the possibility that she might someday tire of your whims and abandon you for somebody else: certain that she will be faithful, confident that you can keep her forever; the only price you pay the mere effort of taking her.

I would even ask what it is like to feed: how it feels to sink your teeth into flesh, to taste the salty copper tang of blood, and feel not horror but satisfaction, as the life that once belonged to another flows into yourself, warming you, strengthening you, settling into every cell of you.

In my fantasy, where we are not obliged to threaten each other, I picture you greeting my questions with an indulgent smile at my naiveté. I see you describing the dark pleasures of your existence with eloquence and wit and an enthusiasm that stops short of vulgar braggadocio. I see you enjoying my fascinated expression and taking on the manner of a triumphant explorer describing the wonders of distant lands for a more timid soul never quite adventurous enough to leave the village of his birth. I see affection in your eyes: for who is not affectionate toward those impressed with what they have? I see a shadow pass over your face as for a moment you regret remembering that we will be enemies again when this pocket hour is over. And then there is a moment of awkward silence, as you struggle with a degree of self-consciousness normally alien to your nature: and the mists seem to thicken around you as you grope for the right words to say; and then they come and you face me with open curiosity, astonished by the earnestness of your question.

And you ask, "Tell me, Van Helsing. What is it like to be alive?"

IN my fantasy, I know your question bears a weight quite different from any I have posed. After all, mine came from a man who had never been where you stand now, and yours comes from a creature who once walked this Earth wearing human flesh. Mine were birthed of curiosity over something I'll never have; yours is birthed of longing for something you once had, and lost.

You should already remember what it was like.

At the very least, you should remember the broad outlines. You should know the aches and pains, the sudden lashing pleasures; the moments of cruelty and the moments of uncertainty; the joys and the sorrows; and the awareness, constant at every moment, that whether you waste this time or make every instant count, that your time here is all you are allotted. You should recall the battles you fought, the dreams you had, the hours of boredom and the instants of great searing discovery. You should remember the names, the faces; the issues that seemed so important then. You should remember the details as well: handed a pen and some paper and the time to fill them with words, you could fill a book with an accurate and passionate history of the time before you drew your last breath. Indeed, if you have such an autobiography, I would be delighted to read it. Though I know enough of your history as the Impaler to understand that even in life you were already a monster in human form. I have come to know you, a little, in our time as antagonists, and would be fascinated by the perspective that only such an account could provide.

In my fantasy, what you no longer remember, and what you now ache to receive from me, is the flavor.

What is it like?

I could only answer thus.

You are not a creature of the night, my temporary friend; not in the sense that some of my allies believe. You are not trapped in shadows. You do not crumble beneath the first rays of dawn. As terrible as you become in night, you inhabit daylight the same way as any other man. More than once I have seen you up and about during the day, wandering like any other country squire along the paths that wind through your manor gardens. But even as I watched you ambling, and you lifted your face toward the sky's golden flower, I noticed something about your pale features.

There were no beads of sweat on your forehead, nor on your upper lip. There was no flush of color on your cheeks. Your eyes did not narrow against the glare. Your spirit did not seem brightened by the glory of the day.

You were not warmed.

That, I would tell you, growing eloquent, is what you have lost. You cannot feel anything that touches you. The sun shines down, and you feel no warmth; the girls you turn become your passionate followers, and you feel no love; the years roll by in all their power and majesty and you feel no difference between one day and the next. You see suffering and feel no pity; you commit horrors and feel no shame. And though you have often preached your endless admiration for all the beauties of the night, are those not just words? Do you truly feel wonder beneath a full moon, or awe beneath a sky filled with stars? Or do you feel mocked? Are you not, in fact, most at home beneath a starless, moonless night, which best reflects the emptiness of your unending existence?

I would say that I am alive. I would say that when I feel sadness the very air seems weighted with gravel. I would say that when I feel joy the ground can barely hold me. And I would say that when, many years ago, I possessed the devotion of a glorious young woman now many years gone, it was a gift greater than any your condition could offer: for it had been my words, and my character, and my kindness toward her that had earned the blessing of her heart, and not just a few predatory visits passing along a contagion. I would say that when I felt her heart beat, it was more than just vitality I felt. I would say that part of me also felt the sad promise of the inevitable moment, with fortune many years in the future, when that heart would run down and stop, ending everything she was; and I would say to you that it was this very promise, this very limit on the time we had together, that made our mutual devotion such a blessing.

I would conclude: life needs death to be precious. And that is why you no longer know what it is like.

I then imagine us staring at each other, from opposite sides of our hypothetical meeting table, the words still fading in the empty air between us. I imagine you hesitating, if only a moment, before offering your response. I must confess that I do not know you well enough to hypothesize what that response would be. Because this is my fantasy, I prefer to imagine you shattered, or at least saddened, by the simple truth I have just offered. I recognize, however, that you possess any number of other possible options. You might explode with rage. You might laugh in derision. You might tell me I know naught of which we speak. It would all depend on how right I am, about you, and even then on your own willingness to face unpleasant truths.

But this is the sad thing, Dracul, the confession I would not make to you, ever, even in that fanciful meeting place. That entire self-righteous speech would have been a lie.

For while I am alive, I am also that which you will never be: an old man.

There is still strength in my limbs, and a mind in my head: enough, at least, to pursue you. But those limbs grow cold, day by day, with a pain here, an ache there, a moment of frustrating weakness now and then. Every weight I lift, every stair I climb, every day I drag myself from the bed of the night before, I feel each and every one of the thousand and one ways in which I am less than what I was ten years ago, or twenty. I have trouble sleeping. I have trouble digesting. I have trouble remembering the right words, or the right name to match a face. I need to squint to see the things that were once upon a time as clear as the tip of my nose.

I have even had friends remark that I am not as tall as once I was. They say it is all part of the process of growing old, but growing old is just a euphemism for my ailment. I am dying. I might well live another ten years, or another thirty—always assuming I survive our final confrontation—but I am still descending a long, dark slope that leads to only one place. Every day is another step toward that final end.

And the inevitability that looms large before me does not render my existence, now, precious at all; for the journey to this point has been a tiring one. That glorious young woman I mentioned before is indeed long gone: not dead, I hasten to explain, but gone, the first flush of our devotion toward each other swiftly curdled by all the ways a man and a woman can turn such love into loathing. The memories are poisoned not only by the things she said to me but the things I discovered I was capable of saying to her. The learning on which I built my reputation is also a loss: for my youthful dreams of greatness have given way to the realities of disappointment and mediocrity. The simple pleasures that once filled my days, from fine meals to finer music to the pursuit of love, have all palled. The best food is just a pale remnant of the feasts I enjoyed before, the best music just a rancorous noise, the most sweet love just a treacherous offering, that only a younger man might have trusted. And as for that gift I would have said I most envied of you? The chance to watch the vast sweep of man's history? I have seen enough of that, already. There has been too much ugliness, too much savagery, even without you. I am tired of it.

Like you, I stand in sunlight, and am not warmed. I do not feel the glory of the day. I just feel the nearness of the night, and crave the moment when it falls for good. I provide guidance to fools I respect not at all, in the vainglorious defense of a woman who seems silly and selfish and not worth the effort: all my supposed bravery an act, all my supposed wisdom a farce. I do what I do because the downward slope has deposited me here. It is no less onerous than doing nothing. But I do not care for any of them, one way or the other. And I am not as driven by the need to destroy you as I present.

If we were in that fantasy room, addressing each other during an hour of truce, I would never tell you that I see us as lines converging from opposite sides of the axis that separates us: lines that will meet at that place, and at that moment, revealing us as a pair of dead men who both possess the temerity to mimic life. Such things are not to be admitted to one's enemies. Such things are scarcely to be admitted to one's self. If we admit them at all, it's only because, admitted once, they can never be put aside, until the very moment of death.

Maybe that is when we set each other free.

Origin of Species

A. M. DELLAMONICA

THE VAMPIRE DEVOURED the woman slowly, making it a show. Theater in the park, with a backdrop of hydroccultured flowers. It clasped one of the victim's hands, hushing her as she fought, as she fell beneath him.

As their eyes met, her struggles lessened, cries quieting to sobs as if she was comforted by its lingering gaze. Metal-tipped fangs edged past its lips, closing on her throat. Her fingers twitched as, crooning like a lover, it punctured the carotid and drained her life's blood into the unholy vault of its storage tank.

As the victim's heart stuttered and stopped, the vampire brushed hair from her forehead, as if she were a sleeping child. Then, with a cluck and a glance toward its audience of one, it brandished delicate scalpel-tipped fingernails. Cutting away the victim's uniform, it slit her abdominal cavity, working a hand inside to extract the cooling organs. Slick and red, one by one, it eased them out . . . and swallowed them.

Helpless and despairing, Helsing Seventeen could only watch as the creature brought its bloody performance to a close. He was fresh from the Order's assembly manger, and this vampire should have been his first kill.

Armed with confidence and an array of offensive upgrades, he'd confronted the damned and tattered creature.

He'd lost that fight, in spectacular fashion.

Now he was trapped, all but buried under molten metal—heavy pieces of debris the vampire had torn from the spaceship's upper bulkhead. The beams had Seventeen pinned so that only his head and one shoulder poked above the pile. Even had he wished to, he could not turn his face from the slaughter.

As the beams had fallen toward him, Seventeen had hardened his skin, encasing himself in thick layers of fingernail-hardy-tissue. Thus armored, he had weathered the impact of the debris. The heat was another question: coolant fizzed frantically about his body cavities, protecting the bioccultured tissues of his systems.

He ran his diagnostic catechism, stumbling on the useless preliminaries (*I am a made thing, lacking in spirit or holy essence, and yet you have given me purpose, oh Lord . . .*). The feedback was instant and unsurprising: cells were burning by the hundreds of thousands. There was no recommended escape from this predicament, and his online confessor, Mina, was inexplicably unreachable. He could sense her presence in the ether, but something was frazzing his uplink.

The vampire retracted its fangs, wiping its mouth on the corpse's sleeve. Reaching back to the hydroflorium, it cut free a rose and fixed it in the buttonhole of its ratty jacket. Then it closed the dead woman's eyes and, giving a bow to its helpless foe, sauntered out of the artificial park. It would vanish down one of the ship's endless corridors, losing itself among the crew. Concealing itself among the sheep, until it was hungry again.

"Mina?" Seventeen sent a subvocalized message into the ether, trying to reach his confessor. He could smell his tissues burning; the coolant in his rosary was almost exhausted.

Between imminent death and the fading hope of a helpdesk rescue, a single text packet fluttered, like a dust wraith caught in the breeze of a shipboard ventilation duct. Its label was nonsensical, just a name. "Annie?" Seventeen read it aloud, confused.

The air shivered, warped by heat, and a girl stepped out of the bower of the hydroflorium. She wore a striped dress. Her hair was parted down the middle so it was flat against her head, then braided and bound with ribbons. Her eyes were deep and hopeful, her face sensitive. Her bare feet left no impressions in the short-bladed grass of the park lawn.

"Danger, do not appro—" His words died as, impossibly, the child drifted into flight, rising above the sizzling metal beams to peer into his face.

Oh, dear, Seventeen thought.

"Mina." He subvoked the confession through his faulty etherlink. "I've attracted a poltervirus."

"Don't," the girl whispered. "They'll deactivate you."

"Seventeen?" That was his cyberconfessor at last, Mother Mina Magdelene, reply crackling through a tenuous-sounding ether channel. "What was that? Repeat, please."

"I'll help you get the vampire if you don't tell," the girl—Annie, presumably—said.

The vampire. Seventeen's gaze turned to the ravaged corpse. The sight—crushed daisy petals lying slick on her face, gored neck, the sweep of golden hair mashed into the sod by the print of the vampire's knee—triggered rage subroutines deep in his constructed personality.

If I'd only had time to activate my Bait feature . . . , he thought.

"They'll shut you down and you'll fry," the poltervirus insisted.

"Seventeen, what's your status?"

Impulse took over: he would gamble on his firewalls. "I'm trapped under debris," he told Mina. "All systems are functioning."

"Debris . . . *The Pilgrimage?*"

"Damage to the ship appears minimal. I'll free myself and continue pursuit."

"Acknowledged. Blessings—"

A spatter of hot metal on his face made Seventeen howl, and Mina cut off. A sign he'd chosen wrong?

He scowled at Annie. "Well?"

"*Can* you free yourself, Abraham?"

"Call me Seventeen. And no, I can't. I'm barely fending off melt-down."

She nodded, and through the ether he sensed her accessing forbidden spaceship systems. Then iced coolant gusted over him, an artificial blizzard pouring from a gap in the torn wall. False snow met fiery metal in a hiss, a stench of chemicals steaming. The beams began to cool.

He turned his face upward, uttering a thankful prayer for the chill and blessed relief. Then his flesh tightened with soreness, freezing. He switched off his own coolant.

"Can you seal this area before the vampire gets away?" he asked Annie, steeling himself to ignore the cold with dignity.

She nodded. "Can you get out now?"

"Yes." Seventeen slackened his biocultured flesh, softening the protective outer layer of skin and then reducing himself to a skeleton covered in ground meat, a mush-monster.

Wiggling and oozing, he slid his trapped shoulder through the gap where his upper body had been exposed. He twisted, working to free the cage of his ribs, the basket of curved bones where his weapons rosary coiled like a holy serpent. Slowly he disentangled himself, edging upward to freedom.

He was almost out when the pile shifted. His foot wrenched, sending pain in a sandpaper burn up his leg. Something clamped his ankle, crushing bones, and he was caught again.

Seventeen lunged against the restraint, pulling himself taut, testing. No good—brute strength wouldn't do.

"Stuck?" Annie asked.

"No," he gritted. He jellied the biocultured tissue on his lower leg and pulled it as far from the foot as he could. Loose skin puddled on his calf like the fabric of a sock that had lost its elastic. A few sticky tendrils clung to the intractable bone, pink and glistening.

Seventeen growled. Most of his tissue could transub into dedifferentiated mush, but the bones were his foundation; there was only so much he could do. He drew his blade and, uttering an automatic prayer, chopped—above the joint, close to the malleoli.

The tibula and fibula were severed cleanly, the foot dropping away in a blaze of discomfort. Seventeen tumbled off the debris pile, landing beside the corpse in a drift of flaked coolant. He was momentarily disconnected from himself, seeming to exist only in the ether as he watched his meat-covered frame clutching at the fractured ends of his severed bones, grunting.

"It's *pain*," the poltervirus said, voice awed, as if she was making a discovery.

Her words slammed him back to himself. "Of course it's painful," he moaned, withdrawing nerve cells from the site of the amputation. The agony receded, and he reassembled in the shape of a man, smooth of skin, with two pristine feet. Standing, he pressed down experimentally. The new foot flopped; boneless, it would not bear weight.

Seventeen let the tissues below the bone harden, giving him the support he needed to walk.

"Pain disrupts your etherlink to the Order," Annie said.

"Quiet, child." Taking a hesitant step, he struggled for focus. "Is the vampire truly trapped?"

"Yes." The poltervirus stared up at him. "You mustn't let the Order suspect I'm here. Pain disabled their defenses against my Trojan . . . don't numb out everything, please?"

His voice was ragged. "I shall hardly be fit opposition for a vampire if I stagger about groaning until it returns."

"That's good." She smiled. "You're talking like him."

Superb. A mad poltervirus with free run of *Pilgrimage*'s automated systems.

He circled the tower of the hydroflorium, a column of blooms that stretched to an overhead portal through which shone the cold light of the stars. No sign of the vampire there, nor under the benches that encircled the flowers. He scanned the artificial streambed that circled the perimeter of the park. The water had stopped flowing when the vampire tore the bulkhead down. The pebbles welded to its banks were drying in the full-spectrum light shining on the flowers.

"No sign of the creature in the common green," he reported. There was no reply from Mina.

Corridors led outward from the park like the spokes of a bicycle, all but one of them safely sealed. Shining, neon-colored wards glittered on the surfaces of the lockdown bulkheads, sigils to fend off the Undead. Mina would swear—face pinched in exasperation—that the wards were obsolete, that vampires had moved beyond them. People would persist in their superstitions, though.

One open corridor remained. "Why didn't you seal that?"

"It's where your monster went," Annie said.

"Crew quarters?" He viewed them with concern. Cabins were easy to search, and the vampire had only a few dozen bunks to hide in. Unfortunately, those bunks might be occupied.

He stepped over the threshold. "Seal us in."

She skipped ahead, small black shoes soundless on the deck as the heavy door clamped shut.

The corridor was a standard metal hallway, fifteen feet high, ten across. Its bulkheads were painted to resemble a planetbound neighborhood, with sidewalks and false house facades. Casketbound trees exhaled oxygen and a light scent of apple blossoms into the air. Ornately decorated doorframes surrounded the portals that led into each of the private bunks, a ship-sanctioned venue for crew members to assert some individuality, to personalize their limited territory.

Seventeen limped to the first portal, distantly noting the cherubs on its doorframe as he used the Order's standing warrant to override the lock. It slid open soundlessly, revealing a standard one-bunk configuration: cursory kitchenette, dining table that folded into the wall, a closed portal that would lead to the head. A privacy screen divided the small living area from the sleeping quarters, giving an illusion of space, multiple rooms.

As he stepped fully inside, Seventeen found himself staring at the corpse again: the privacy screen was live, showing an image of the battle-damaged park.

"Seventeen, are you there?" Mina was back online—he had reflexively damped the last twinges of pain coming from his ankle.

"Searching crew quarters," he subvoked. "Please ask Parish Control to shut off the hydroflorium cam on Revelations Deck. Residents are picking up the park feeds."

"Of course." The screen before him blanked.

There was a sudden long cry, neither a sob nor scream but a disturbing fusion of both. A woman.

Seventeen found himself unable to move as the cry came again.

"Hello?" he managed, triggering his catechism again. (. . . *a made thing, and yet buoyed up by God* . . .)

"Are you all right, my son?"

"Her screams . . . bother me," he subvoked to Mina.

"Here—use this patch." The confessor sent a squib through the ether and the distress vanished. "Better?"

"Yes. Thank you."

"Records says quarters on this deck are assigned to astrologists and navigators," Mina said.

"Resident's name?"

The woman lunged into sight, clad in a rose-colored slip and clawing at the head portal. She spotted Seventeen and shrieked.

"Catherine," Mina said.

"It's all right, Catherine." Seventeen brought a gentle sedative from the rosary up through his throat, invisibly lacing the air with the drug as he exhaled. "You witnessed a terrible thing, but the creature has fed; it's no threat to you."

"I've located the vampire," Annie announced, sauntering into view. "It's doubling back this way."

Hands outstretched, Seventeen accessed the counseling ethercache and approached the shaking woman—Catherine—murmuring reassurances. He did not answer Annie, barely sparing her a glance.

Looking wounded, Annie reached for his essence through the ether. "Don't you remember me, Seventeen? We met at Malvern when we were sick. I died and you lived. My father took you in as a sort of pupil . . ."

The story was in his historical ethercache. It almost seemed he did remember. But . . .

"I am not Abraham Van Helsing," he mouthed as the woman broke down in sobs and fell against his shoulder, weeping.

"You could be." Annie pouted with heartbreaking sincerity—a look, he thought, that only a ten-year-old could muster. "Elementary possession physics. If you build a vessel and name it for someone, their spirit will come to reside within."

"May come to reside," he corrected, still voiceless, letting the words form as impressions in the ether and hoping Mina would not hear.

"If the vessel is worthy."

"And the spirit is restless. While we're talking possessics, why should I believe you're Anne Darwin?"

Her ethereal presence splashed against his firewall, playfully looking for weak points. "Where do you think polterviruses came from? Old ghosts, it's that simple. I've had centuries to reinvent myself since your death."

"I have no interest in your history." The drugged woman twitched groggily; this time he had spoken aloud.

Mina's voice, sharp, rippled through the ether. "Seventeen?"

Guiltily, he lied again. "It's nothing. The astrologist is sedated. I'll bless her quarters and lock her in until the area is secured for para-medium access."

"The vampire is relic-resistant; it might break in."

"He's trapped; he'll be looking for me. She'll be safer if I leave her."

"Affirmed. But spray her anyway."

He did, bringing a mixture of garlic and holy water up from his rosary and misting the sleeping woman's body as he tucked her into bed. On his way out of her quarters he sealed the portal again, briefly fingering the cherubs and angels on the astrologist's ornately carved doorframe. Coughing up another spray attachment from the rosary, Seventeen pursed his lips and let a stream of golden paint play over the door, covering it with crosses.

He stared at Annie, willing her to tell him where the vampire was.

"Are you that eager to die? Sweep another cabin as the Order expects. It's coming, I promise you."

Seventeen opened the next portal, which was unadorned.

"Vampires evolved," Annie lectured as he searched the space. It was unoccupied, sterile, appealingly clean and free of clutter. One quick look at the head and the air ducts confirmed the vampire had not been inside. "Can't you accept that a ghost would evolve too? Papa laid it all out for you. Competition, adaptation. Granted, he didn't think it would happen in the spirit world. . . . He didn't believe there *was* a supernatural."

An image whisked through Seventeen's mind: Charles Darwin, eyes sharp, hands clamped white-knuckled on a walnut desk, voice brittle as he denounced the very idea of a caring God.

Uneasily, he checked the historical ethercache, failing to find this event on record. How could he know of it then?

For I am a made thing, lacking in spirit . . . He began the diagnostic again.

"Trouble?" Mina asked sharply. He jumped; he kept forgetting she was tracking catechism hits.

"I am afraid," he told his confessor. It was true. This sense of recollection—of a personal encounter with Van Helsing's mentor—terrified him more than the vampire had.

"Have faith," Mina said, voice so intense he nodded as if she were there.

It was certainly true the vampires of the present day were nothing like those of the prespace era. Sanctioned records showed that his namesake had hunted the creatures to the edge of extinction. And they *had* evolved—that was solid historical fact. Enchanted species mutated more quickly than live ones. As an aged Abraham Van Helsing had shuffled toward death, his daughter was already battling the Undead's next generation, vampires who wore toughened scales of demon-flesh, coal black in color, in hard-to-pierce sheaths from their throats down to their navels.

He remembered seeing one . . . no, not remembered. Someone must have taken a photograph. They were becoming more common by then.

And if the image was in color, rather than black and white?

He set the unease aside, driving it away by thinking instead of the vampire he had just fought: its youthful face, carrion and machine-oil smell, the unexpected and frightening compassion in its eyes.

"Consider the battle just now," Annie said coolly as Seventeen sealed the unoccupied cabin. "Your lovely new weapon, the cage of pure starlight. The vampire had countermeasures, didn't it? And the fog vacuum the nuns were so proud of—ineffectual. Your ability to pass for human, to play bait or victim—"

"I had no chance to test that."

"Seventeen, you are the Order's newest Van Helsing prototype. You're a week old and your prey has already adapted to techniques you've never used in the field."

Suddenly the corridor faded into blackness amid a banshee whine of starving power circuits. Annie remained clear and crisply visible, glowing ectoplasm-green, a shade reminiscent of operating theaters.

"Here it comes," he said, spying a trail of fog on the move behind a potted elm.

"Nothing you do will work," Annie said. "The Order's ethercache has been compromised. This thing knows what you will do before you do it."

He nudged his confessional. "Mina, did you hear? I have it in sight."

"Try out new features L through P," Mina said.

"There's no *point* in this." Annie stamped her foot.

"Affirmative, Mina. But—may I ask?"

"Your questions are always welcome, my son."

"New features A through K seemed to have been anticipated."

"Pardon?"

"When we fought . . . the vampire seemed prepared." It was ridiculously hard to keep his voice even. "Could my specifications have been compromised in preproduction?"

"Whatever gave you that idea?" His confessor's voice was sharp. Annie stuck out her tongue.

"Merely an observation." It wasn't exactly a lie.

"Run your catechism again," she ordered. "And activate feature L."

"Affirmative." Seventeen gagged a capsule up from his rosary, settling it behind his tongue. It was an expanding capsule of jellied garlic laced with genenchanteered nettles, meant to bind the vampire and then cut it to pieces. He limped forward on the stiffened, boneless foot. Let the creature think him weakened. . . .

I am weakened, he thought. *One extremity lost, fraternizing with a damned virus—*

The vampire solidified just within range, a sweet smile on its face, fangs edging through the slit of its thin-lipped mouth.

Annie's right, Seventeen thought. *It's prepared.* He spat the garlic at it anyway.

The vampire shifted back to its fog state, making the transition faster than Order Intelligence claimed was possible. The gel passed through it harmlessly, expanding into a jellied ball. There was a dense smell of restaurant, sizzling spices, as the capsule dropped to the deck.

"It didn't work," he reported.

"And yet we shall persevere," intoned Mina. "Try feature M."

"This isn't working." The vampire was solid again, a knowing expression on its youthful face. Seventeen could smell the rosebud in its lapel.

"Have faith, my son. Should you fail, die knowing that your sacrifice was for a greater good."

"Why, oh why won't you ever let me in? I can help!" Annie threw her ethereal self against his firewall again.

Seventeen let himself stumble, grinding down on the edge of his severed tibia, sending agony through his body and into the ether. His confessor's voice was silenced.

"Please," Annie begged. "Please, Seventeen."

Why not? He was going to die anyway.

He made his defenses porous. The poltervirus did not hesitate, penetrating swiftly to the marrow of his programmed self. She corrupted his historical ethercache, releasing a flood of memories that could not be real. The sustained low screams of his insane wife, so much like those of the astrologist just now. Mina Harker's face, vivid and terrified. Her warmth, so unlike his confessor's clipped reassurances. Successful hunts . . . and unsuccessful ones.

Now he remembered Annie herself, clothed always in her best striped dress, pale and persistent, trying to console, to help. . . .

"Haunted," he murmured. "You haunted me."

"Through all your days and nights," said Annie Darwin.

He remembered her death at the Malvern Spa. The sounds of vomiting, Darwin's rising fear and repeated dashed hopes. They'd talked sometimes, she and he, girl and boy, when they were taking the water cure for their respective ailments. He had strengthened as she wasted, he praying over her bedside, even asking God to take him instead. Finally she was so ill that nobody but family could be admitted to the sickroom.

After she was buried, he'd visited her grave as his own recovery progressed, sometimes reading to her in his heavily accented English.

Annie had appeared to him during the last of his boyish fevers, and she'd never left. Following him to her parents' home on a visit, she had laughed sadly at her father's hard new devotion to science, his veneration of nothing but what he could see with his own eyes, touch with his own hands.

Charles and the young Van Helsing had broken over the invisible world, over the possibility of rapid evolution among the Undead. He had left, and to his surprise Annie had been with him at the train station, on the ship back to Amsterdam, and ever after.

Memories of small joys and great pains ran through Seventeen like a spreading blaze. Triumphs. Deaths and horrors. And faith. Like Darwin, he had lost a child. Unlike him, he had never stopped believing.

The Order had bound Seventeen to Church practice with a billion subroutines, but they had never imbued him with the faith he felt now. His constructed sense of purpose burned away, leaving fervor, leaving determination, passion.

"Yes!" the ghost of Annie Darwin cried.

The transformation took place at etherspeed, in just a fraction of a second. But the vampire was fast too. It was upon him, stroking Seventeen gently, sensitive scalpel-nails peeling little strips of his skin away. It had adopted the shining golden hair of its recent victim, rebuilding itself in her image. Its eyes were pools deep enough to swim in, inviting, calming . . .

"Feature M," Mina shouted through the ether as jolts of pain pushed her away. Seventeen groped to remember what she meant. Ah—injecting chilled holy water directly into the vampire's body cavities. Ridiculous. It had closed the distance just hoping he would try it.

"I used my coolant," he subvoked, not knowing if Mina heard.

He drove his flesh into an orgy of growth, generating a hard pair of spikes that grew from his own palms, pegs made of the hardest tissue he could muster. Milk-white, like fingernails, they formed in his hands, cruelly sharp points. Bellowing, he drove them into the vampire's soft fish-pale palms. It was a crude move, all but a tackle, far removed from the finesse programmed into him by the Order.

The vampire fetched up against a doorway, laughing, and Seventeen pushed harder. They were belly to belly as he pierced the foul creature's hands. The vampire's fangs flashed out, and it bit into Seventeen's face.

Seventeen screamed. Blood flowed over one eye, blinding him as he brought out his arms, dragging the vampire into an outstretched position. Thus spread, he jerked his wrists upward, breaking the spikes free of his arms before hammering at them with hardened fists. It was the work of an instant to force them into the decorative doorframe surrounding the bunk portal.

The vampire ignored its position for a critical moment, continuing to worry at Seventeen's head like a dog shaking a toy. An audible crunch and a white blaze of suffering told him the precious bone case of his skull was breaking.

Moaning now, Seventeen triggered the paint sprayer, spurting gold between his lips to etch an image into the bulkhead around the vampire. He pressed his hands against the vampire's chest, pushing himself backward. The creature bit down, and the hunk of skull broke away, remaining clamped in its teeth as Seventeen pulled away. Flesh and blood hung in strings, dangling between his cracked-open head and the vampire's jaws.

Seventeen dropped to his knees, still directing paint, completing the image.

A cross.

"Please, God," he prayed, spitting up staples to fix the vampire's ankles against the wall.

The vampire began to smoke. It turned to fog but did not drift away. Writhing, it solidified again, keening in distress.

"You put him on a cross? Isn't that blasphemous?" Annie asked.

Seventeen ignored her, kneeling with one hand on the vampire's knee, praying. *It's relic resistant*, he thought, *not faith resistant.*

Not yet, anyway.

"The vampire is transmitting details of your fight to its home ether-cache," Annie reported. "Shall I stop the transmission?"

"Can you trace the cache location?"

"I'm not sure."

Under his hand, the vampire went slack. Looking upward, Seventeen saw an expression take hold on its face. It was the look that had kept Van Helsing going during all those years of his earthly life—gratitude. Another tormented soul released from damnation.

Sighing, the vampire died.

Annie said, "I can't trace it. Not without letting the information about your kill go into its cache."

"Let them have the data," he said. "I'll think of some other way to kill the next one."

"There won't be a next one," Annie said softly.

She was so close that, had she been solid, he could have touched her shoulder. He could remember trying to do so, time after time, in the distant past. "Pardon?"

"If you make a vessel and name it for someone, their spirit can come to inhabit it."

"Basic possessics," he replied, voice faint. "Are you saying . . ."

"Can't you tell?"

And he could. Memories of summer rain and barking dogs, a million details of life on Earth that had long ago been lost to the ship's ethercache, glimmered like sunlight on beach sand. He was truly himself, at long last.

"Extraordinary," he murmured.

"But temporary." Soberly the ghost-child teased his product scriptures out of another off-limits section of the ether. The Order had been evolving its hunters on a strictly doctrined path for some time. Possession was distinctly unwelcome, as was associating with a proscribed poltervirus.

"They'll dismantle you," Annie said. "I'm sorry."

The truth of her words was there in the ether. Seventeen would be dissected and studied. Mina would oblige him to confess that physical pain disrupted the etherlink, that this was what had given Annie access to him.

"They'll find a countermeasure," he murmured.

"I'll find another way in." The child lowered her gaze to the bulkhead, her fragile forever-young neck stubbornly bent. Trying to be brave. Still ten after all these centuries.

"No," Seventeen said.

"You'll join me in the ether?" She began to smile, then drooped at his expression.

"The vampires are out *here*, Annie. But—" He dug his hand into the ruined bioccultured tissue of his ravaged face and surprised himself by crying out. Pain rippled through the ether, breaking up any recall code the Order might issue.

Then he threw up the rosary.

It came in ropey lumps, bringing with it all his weaponry. The holy water, the holographic bishop, the garlic sprayer, the cross painter. He brought it up and wrapped the strands in the dead vampire's pinioned claws, making it look as if the monster had torn his arsenal out of him bodily.

"What are you doing?"

"Necessary sacrifice," he said, as with one last retch his airway cleared. "Annie. My bait feature—I'm supposed to be able to transub into a potential victim, indistinguishable from human."

"I told you, you're compromised. It's seen your specs, it can tell."

"And the Order can too, presumably?"

"What do you—" Her eyes widened. "You want to escape them?"

"Can it work?" He was already softening his flesh again, almost collapsing as his ankle became mere putty. Cool ship's air brushed his flesh as he let some of his tissues leak to the deck, making a ragged stump at the end of his calf and leaving a puddle of himself below the vampire.

She flickered, scanning. "Perhaps if you can escape from here. But if they can't account for you . . ."

"I'll leave them enough of a body to distract them for a time." Aching, unbalanced on his remaining foot, Seventeen groped at the vampire's crucified body, unzipping its organ banks. The murdered woman's organs splashed to the deck: heart, lungs, kidneys, spleen. Puncturing the tank, he released a torrent of her blood. Then, reaching down to fumble through the rosary, he found the incineration bead. Hopefully he could make it appear that Seventeen's genetically enchanteered body had been fried in a final battle with the monster.

"Annie, can you hack me an identity?"

"As many as you need."

His mind raced. If the paramediums carried him out of here, he might escape into the ship's population. . . . "Let the record show I'm another victim from this neighborhood," he said. He pulled the piece of his skull out of the vampire's jaw, leaving behind a burnt cap of skin and hair—his own scalp. Fingering the edges of the bone, he assessed its shape, finally sliding it back into place like a jigsaw puzzle piece.

Then he triggered the bait feature.

Preset tissue drivers took over, modeling an organic brain for him, creating a heart and a pair of lungs where his rosary had been before. Kidneys, stomach, pancreas . . .

Then the process aborted, amid a welter of error messages, leaving his abdomen loose and empty.

"There isn't enough of you to make a whole person," Annie said. "Not if you're leaving all that tissue behind on the floor."

"The Order will need evidence that I died here," he said. The bait program had given him veins and filled them to bursting with tempting reservoirs of blood. He pulled the cells back into his body cavity, dedifferentiated them again, made the vital organs one by one. Then he cut a pair of exsanguination punctures into his throat with the point of his blade.

The pain increased as his body and nervous system became more complex, the connection to the Order becoming ever more and more tenuous. He fought to construct one last burst of false data. The pinned vampire awoke, he recorded. There was a great struggle, and then the mutual incineration.

He could feel Annie working with him, smoothing the edges in the tale, making the story conform to the evidence. Finally they let it go, a single packet of data shooting through the ether, Order-bound.

He hopped back two paces, setting the incineration bead of the rosary manually. With one last look at the crucified vampire, the torn flesh and spilled organs, he tossed the bead into the pile. It flared like a rocket; the corridor filled with a reek of burning meat.

"Your head looks terrible," Annie said. "Like you've been mauled."

"I'll survive." The paramediums would come soon, now that the vampire was dead. If they believed he was human, they would give him a transfusion—one his new laboring heart was desperate for—right away. They'd fix his face, give him a prosthetic foot, and release him onto the ship like any other human. God willing, the Order would be none the wiser.

"It'll work," Annie said, apparently reading his intentions.

"I have faith," Seventeen agreed.

He lurched to the portal of the empty apartment and collapsed there, making himself easy to find.

"Annie," he said. "Can you reduce my ether privileges? Install a regular crew uplink?"

"Of course," she said. For the last time, he sensed her shifting through the caches, marshalling her ethereal resources.

He drew as much of his consciousness into the partial, human-seeming body as he could, pulling against his own firewalls. He strained to load his history, his personality, and the Order's vast knowledge into the newly formed neurons inside his broken skull.

"I've got it all backed up," Annie said. The poltervirus seemed incredibly close at hand. They mingled, just for an instant, and he saw himself through her eyes, a young man in a long-ago time, haunted and struggling with horrors.

"And yet buoyed up by God," Annie murmured, slapping restrictions on his etherlink, blinding him as she squeezed his consciousness into his frail organic brain.

The pain doubled, trebled. He cried out in anguish.

"Rest, Seventeen," Annie said. "The paramediums just reached Revelations Deck."

"Call me Abraham," he rasped, and as he slid into what he hoped would be a temporary state of shock, he saw that the poltervirus's cheeks were wet with another impossibility. She had learned to cry spectral tears.

About the Contributors

C. Dean Andersson is the critically acclaimed, internationally published author of thirteen novels and numerous short stories. In horror, *I Am Dracula* and *Raw Pain Max*, a novel of Countess Bathory, are groundbreaking cult classics. In fantasy, *Warrior Witch*, *Warrior Rebel*, and *Warrior Beast* chronicle the Scandinavian mythos adventures of Bloodsong, a Viking warrior woman. With degrees in astrophysics, art, and business, he is a member of HWA, SFWA, and Sigma Pi Sigma national physics honor society. He has also worked as a television artist, musical entertainer, robotics programmer, and computer software technical writer specializing in mainframe documentation. Visit www.cdeanandersson. com.

Kim Antieau is the author of *Coyote Cowgirl*, *Gaia Websters*, and *The Jigsaw Woman* as well as dozens of short stories. She lives in the West with her husband, poet Mario Milosevic. Her website is at www.kimantieau.com, and her weblog is at www.furiousspinner.com.

William D. Carl has appeared in several horror and suspense anthologies, including *Tales from the Gorezone* and *Dark Streets After Hours* and will soon be seen in Cemetery Dance's tribute to Richard Laymon, *In Laymon's Terms*. He lives in Cincinnati, where he is also a manager and trainer for Waldenbooks.

Adam-Troy Castro is the author of four Spider-Man novels and seventy-five short stories, among them the Stoker nominee "Baby Girl Diamond," the Nebula nominee "Sunday Night Yams at Minnie and Earl's," and the Hugo/Nebula nominee "The Funeral March of the Marionettes." Another Hugo/Nebula nominee, "The Astronaut from Wyoming," was written in collaboration with Jerry Oltion. His short story collections include *Tangled Strings*, *Vossoff and Nimmitz*, *An Alien Darkness*, and *A Desperate Decaying Darkness*. Adam lives in Florida with his lovely and long-suffering wife, Judi, and a trio of neurotic cats intent on reenacting the War of the Roses in the dusty space behind the ottoman. So far, the orange one is winning.

A. M. DELLAMONICA had the kind of action-packed childhood that most people dream of, featuring actual plane crashes and the occasional long car trip. Her fiction first appeared in print in 1986 and—despite repeated washings—remains in circulation in a variety of locales, most recently *On-Spec* magazine. Her next anthology appearances will be in *Alternate Generals III* and *The Faery Reel*. Three other works can be found anytime at scifi.com, and her 2002 *Asimov's* piece, "A Slow Day at the Gallery," is out in *The Year's Best Science Fiction #8*.

KRIS DIKEMAN lives and works in New York City. Her short stories have appeared in *The Book of Final Flesh* and *Yellow Bat Review*. She is currently working on her first novel, *Panspermia*, a story of life, love, and carnivorous plants.

CHRISTOPHER GOLDEN is the author of many novels, including *The Boys Are Back in Town, The Ferryman, Strangewood, Of Saints and Shadows*, and the Body of Evidence series of teen thrillers, and coauthor of the youth fantasy series OutCast. He cocreated, with Amber Benson, the animated web serial *Ghosts of Albion*.

Golden has also written and cowritten a great many books, comic books, and video games related to the TV series *Buffy the Vampire Slayer* and *Angel*. In the comic book field, he has written tales of Batman, Spider-Man, Doctor Fate, and Hellboy.

Please visit him at www.christophergolden.com.

JOE HILL is a past recipient of the Ray Bradbury Fellowship and the A. E. Coppard Long Fiction Award, and has been nominated for a Pushcart Prize. His stories have appeared in *The High Plains Literary Review, Crimewave*, and *Implosion*, and in anthologies such as *With Signs and Wonders* and *The Mammoth Book of Best New Horror*. He has recently completed three books: *The Hallowe'en Companion* for children, *The Evil Kites of Dr. Lourdes* for young adults, and *The Briars* for grown-ups. He lives in New Hampshire with his wife and children. You can learn more at www.joehillfiction.com.

BRIAN HODGE is the author of eight novels spanning horror and crime-noir, most recently *Wild Horses* and its cursed-with-delays successor, *Mad Dogs*. He's also written ninety short stories and novelettes, many of which have been imprisoned without trial in three acclaimed collections, the latest of which is *Lies & Ugliness*. When not writing, he makes ungodly noise, composing and recording dark electronic music for an alter-ego project dubbed Axis Mundi. More of everything is in the works.

NINA KIRIKI HOFFMAN is the author of ten novels, including *A Fistful of Stars* and *A Stir of Bones*. She has written over fifty short stories, some of which have been gathered in two collections, *Time Travelers, Ghosts, and Other Visitors* and *Courting Disaster and Other Strange Affinities*. She has received multiple nominations for the Nebula Award and the World Fantasy Award, and is a winner of the Bram Stoker Award.

SARAH KELDERMAN lives with her musically obsessed husband, Taylor, and their psychotic, catnip-addicted cat, Zak. She is a graduate of the Odyssey Writing Workshop, class of 2001. This is her first publication.

KATHE KOJA writes novels and stories for adults and for younger readers. Her latest novel is *The Blue Mirror*. She lives in the Detroit area with her husband, artist Rick Lieder, and her son.

J. A. KONRATH recently signed a three-book deal with Hyperion. His first novel, the thriller *Whiskey Sour*, will be out in hardcover in June 2004.

He has a wife, three kids (that he knows of), a dog, and a house just outside of Chicago. J. A. currently teaches fiction writing and marketing at the College of Dupage in Glen Ellyn.

Visit his homepage at www.jakonrath.com to follow his progress on his second novel. Email him at haknort@comcast.net.

TANITH LEE was born in 1947 in London, England, and began to write at the age of nine.

Having worked variously in libraries, restaurants and shops, publication by DAW Books in the U.S. made her a professional writer in 1975.

She has since published seventy-five books and nearly 250 short stories. She has written for television, and four of her radio plays have been broadcast by the BBC.

Lee has won the August Derleth Award and the World Fantasy Award (twice), besides being a frequent nominee. In 1999 she was short-listed for the *Guardian* Children's Book Award.

She lives in England.

THOMAS F. MONTELEONE has published twenty-five novels, the most recent of which is *The Eyes of the Virgin*. His third collection of short fiction, *Fearful Symme-*

tries, recently appeared in a signed, limited edition from CD Publications, and his award-winning omnibus collection of columns about writing, genre publishing, television, film and popular culture entitled *The Mothers And Fathers Italian Association* was released by Borderlands Press. Despite being dragged kicking and screaming into his fifties (*and* losing his hair), he still thinks he is dashingly handsome—humor him. With his wife, Elizabeth, and daughter, Olivia, he lives in Grantham, New Hampshire, where the state motto is "Live Free or Die." He picked the first one.

You can visit his website, www.borderlandspress.com/tfm, or email him at tfm@borderlandspress.com.

RITA OAKES is a librarian currently residing in southern New Jersey. A former Air Force brat, she has difficulty answering the question, "So, where are you from?" She attended the Odyssey Writing Workshop in 1998. Her story "By Bayonet and Brush" appeared in the debut issue of *Paradox: The Magazine of Historical and Speculative Fiction* in 2003. She is currently working on a novel of historical horror. Her interests include travel, history, Belgian beer and her cats, Calpurnia and Theodora.

CHRIS ROBERSON is the author of the novels *Voices of Thunder, Cybermancy Incorporated, Set the Seas on Fire*, and *Any Time at All.* His short stories have appeared on *Fantastic Metropolis, RevolutionSF* and *Opi8*, and in the anthology *Live Without a Net* (Roc, July 2003). In addition to serving as associate editor for *International Studio* (Coppervale Press), he is the publisher of MonkeyBrain, Inc., an independent imprint specializing in nonfiction genre studies (www.monkeybrain-books.com).

KRISTINE KATHRYN RUSCH has won major awards in each genre she's written in, from science fiction and fantasy to mystery to romance. The former editor of *The Magazine of Fantasy and Science Fiction*, she has published more than fifty novels. Her latest science-fiction novel is *Consequences* (April 2004), a novel in the Hugo-nominated world of the Retrieval Artist, and her latest fantasy novel is *Fantasy Life* (November 2003), which has some very dark elements.

MELANIE TEM's most recent novels are *The Deceiver* and *Slain in the Spirit*. Recent short story publications include "Piano Bar Blues" in the anthology *Gathering the Bones*, and several of her poems appeared in the anthology *The Devil's Wine*. Her one-act play *The Society for Lost Positives* has been produced in several venues and will be produced in Chicago in 2004. She lives in Denver with her husband, writer and editor Steve Rasnic Tem. They have four children and three grand-daughters.

STEVE RASNIC TEM's most recent novel is *The Book of Days*, from Subterranean Press. His selected poetry, *The Hydrocephalic Ward*, was recently published by Dark Regions Press. He is a past winner of the Bram Stoker, British Fantasy, World Fantasy, and International Horror Guild awards.

LOIS TILTON is the author of six novels and almost one hundred short stories of science fiction, fantasy and horror. Since her first novel, *Vampire Winter*, she has been fascinated with the matter of vampires and the history of vampire litera-ture. Much of her recent work has been concerned with ancient military history and the Trojan War.

THOMAS TESSIER is the author of several novels of terror and suspense, including *The Nightwalker, Phantom,* and *Finishing Touches*. His novel *Fog Heart* and his first collection of short stories, *Ghost Music and Other Tales*, both received International Horror Guild awards. He lives in Connecticut and is working on new stories and a novel.

ABOUT THE EDITOR

Jeanne Cavelos is a writer, editor, scientist, and teacher. She began her professional life as an astrophysicist and mathematician, working in the Astronaut Training Division at NASA's Johnson Space Center.

After earning her MFA in creative writing, she moved into a career in publishing, becoming a senior editor at Bantam Doubleday Dell, where she created and launched the Abyss imprint of psychological horror, for which she won the World Fantasy Award, and ran the science fiction/fantasy publishing program. In her eight years in New York publishing, Jeanne edited numerous award-winning and bestselling authors and gained a reputation for discovering and nurturing new writers.

Jeanne left New York to pursue her own writing career. Her latest book is *Invoking Darkness*, the third volume in her highly praised, bestselling trilogy, *The Passing of the Techno-Mages*, set in the *Babylon 5* universe. Other works include *The Science of Star Wars*, chosen by the New York Public Library for its recommended reading list, and *The Science of the* X-Files, nominated for the Bram Stoker Award. Due to popular demand, her first *Babylon 5* novel, *The Shadow Within*, has just been brought back into print. Jeanne is currently at work on a thriller about genetic manipulation, titled *Fatal Spiral*. She has published short fiction, articles, and essays in many magazines.

Jeanne also runs Jeanne Cavelos Editorial Services, which provides editing, consulting, and critiquing services. Among her clients are major publishers and bestselling and award-winning authors.

Since she loves working with developing writers, Jeanne created and serves as director of Odyssey, an annual six-week summer workshop for writers of science fiction, fantasy, and horror held at Southern New Hampshire University in Manchester. Guest lecturers have included Harlan Ellison, Terry Brooks, Jane Yolen, George R. R. Martin, and Dan Simmons. Jeanne also teaches writing at Saint Anselm College.

You can visit Jeanne at her website at www.sff.net/people/jcavelos, or contact her at jcavelos@sff.net.